WHISKY BUSINESS

WHISKY BUSINESS

A Novel

ELLIOT FLETCHER

AVON

An Imprint of HarperCollins*Publishers*

WHISKY BUSINESS. Copyright © 2023 by Elliot Fletcher. All rights reserved. Printed in the United States of America. No part of this book may be used or reproduced in any manner whatsoever without written permission except in the case of brief quotations embodied in critical articles and reviews. For information, address HarperCollins Publishers, 195 Broadway, New York, NY 10007.

HarperCollins books may be purchased for educational, business, or sales promotional use. For information, please email the Special Markets Department at SPsales@harpercollins.com.

Originally published as *Whisky Business* in the USA in 2023 by Elliot Fletcher.

Designed by Diahann Sturge-Campbell

Library of Congress Cataloging-in-Publication Data has been applied for.

ISBN 978-0-06-338670-9

24 25 26 27 28 LBC 5 4 3 2 1

This book is dedicated to my anxiety.
Maybe one day we won't need each other.

Playlist

Caledonia – Dougie MacLean
Bad Blood – Taylor Swift
This Is Me Trying – Taylor Swift
Home – Edward Sharpe & The Magnetic Zeros
Beach Baby – Bon Iver
Invisible String – Taylor Swift
Sunlight – Hozier
Sparks – Coldplay
SNAP – Rosa Linn
Pretty Lips – Winehouse
Death By a Thousand Cuts – Taylor Swift
Mardy Bum – Arctic Monkeys
Like Real People Do – Hozier
Want Want – Maggie Rogers
I Wanna Be Yours – Arctic Monkeys
Cherry Wine – Hozier
Us – James Bay
Love Like This – Kodaline
Love Song – Lana Del Rey
Simply The Best – Bilianne
Oh Caroline – The 1975
Feel Me – Aeris Roves
Love Me Harder – Ariana Grande
Georgia – Vance Joy
Lavender Haze – Taylor Swift
Delilah – Aeris Roves
Perfect Places – Lorde

Belter – Gerry Cinnamon
Daylight – Taylor Swift
Sweet Nothing – Taylor Swift
Roots – Grace Davies
Something in the Orange – Zach Bryan
Feels Like – Gracie Abrams
I GUESS I'M IN LOVE – Clinton Kane
Calm – Vistas

AUTHOR'S NOTE

While *Whisky Business* is primarily a lighthearted read, it features content that might be triggering for some. These include: anxiety disorder, mention of online trolling with comments referencing weight and sexual acts, mention of a close family member death from cancer, mention of a previous controlling relationship, mention of family member with Alzheimer's, open door romance with multiple on-page sexual encounters.

WHISKY BUSINESS

1

APRIL

Caledonia – Dougie MacLean

Look forward, wee birdie. Obsession with the past is for failures. Winners keep their eye on the prize. My fingers tightened on the steering wheel as memories of my grandfather's favorite motto filtered through the cramped interior of my Mini Cooper.

As a self-indulgent seven-year-old whose singular joy in life was locating the next occasion that would put *me* center stage, I'd wholeheartedly agreed with him.

Looking back was for failures.

"The irony." I chuckled to myself now as I watched the minutes tick away slowly, my fingers drumming steadily on the dashboard. The elderly man who held every ounce of my attention, stooped as he was, raised a frail hand and urged my vehicle one car closer. Eager to take the cue, I pulled forward to the bobbing ramp at the stern of the ferry that made the twice-daily connection between the Isle of Skye and the Scottish mainland. *One car closer to freedom.*

The rented motorhome ahead of me—I knew it was rented because I'd spent the last forty minutes staring at a bumper sticker that read "Highland motorhomes: the adventure starts here!"—

pulled alongside him. The old man appeared, the sides of his too-big anorak whipping like the wings of a tiny bird caught in a storm. Still, he grinned toothily as he stamped their tickets and gestured to the obstructed mountainous island over his shoulder. With the rain came the mist, blocking out the shock of green with ghostly hands and rolling so low you only had to reach out to touch it.

I could practically read the words on his weathered lips; *Skye in Gaelic actually translates to mist, how appropriate!* His large knuckled hands twisted this way and that before he finally pulled a creased map from his pocket. Laminated, of course—a man who worked outside knew the challenges of Scottish weather like he knew his own face in the mirror.

Believe it or not, we'd had bright sunlight only fifteen minutes before.

Dudley, my wire-haired dachshund, gave an irritated whine from the backseat where I'd strapped his carrier. "Almost there, buddy. I mean it this time." His answering huff called me the liar I was proving to be. I could have wept as the motorhome's engine revved, pulling away. "*See*," I said, glancing at his little face in the mirror.

"Hullo, lass." The man's sunny voice greeted me the moment I lowered my window, pressing a hand to the roof of my car. "Ah, hope yer have a ticket or ye'll be swimmin' back tae the mainland."

I offered a tired little chuckle at the joke. I would bet all the money in my bank account (less than you'd think) he'd repeated it to every person he saw this week. Smiling best I could, I handed him my one-way ferry ticket, ignoring the rain soaking into my sleeve. He didn't take it. Instead, he peered into the back of my compact car, noting the stack of boxes and bin liners I'd hastily slung my clothes into. "What brings yer tae Skye?"

"Just visiting."

"Family, ay?"

"Something like that," I answered, purposely vague.

He looked delighted. "Anyone ah ken?"

"Probably not."

He tapped a finger to his lips, scanning me again from beneath his hood, entirely unperturbed by the raindrops cascading down his long nose. "A'm sure ah ken ye fae somewhere, lass."

That I couldn't deal with right now. "I doubt it." I extended the ticket further, rain soaking up to my elbow until he finally understood my meaning. Giving the ticket a discontented stamp, he motioned for me to drive on.

"Welcome tae Skye." His tone was decidedly less sunny.

Pulling away, I felt terrible. He was a talker and as a *fellow* talker, I understood the sting of that kind of brush-off. The man was *my people*. But it turned out, even the sunniest of personalities could be dimmed after a twelve-hour car journey from London. Throw in the white-knuckled driving of a human who'd forgotten what it was like to drive on the winding roads of the Scottish Highlands? I hadn't burnt the candle on both ends, I'd set the entire bloody thing alight.

The only thing I was fit for was food and a bed.

THE ENTRANCE TO SKYE WAS DELIVERED WITH VERY LITTLE fanfare. A narrow pier transcended the rocky Armadale Bay at the southern end of the island, shining prettily under the gray cloud cover. You could think of the island itself as resembling a hand with five stretched-out fingers, each finger a peninsula. We were in the thumb.

Despite the long journey, my Mini purred beneath me, completely at ease as I steered onto the shore-hugging lane that began to feel familiar. The road that would carry me fifteen minutes north to my childhood home was flanked along one side by half-bent trees. All that stood between my car and the expanse of reflective blue water on the other side was a low stone-built wall, giving way to the rugged mountain peaks of the mainland rising through clouds of fog.

The moment I passed the sign "Kinleith welcomes you," I hit my indicator and slowed. My eyes automatically scanned for the sharp bend so hidden among my grandfather's shrubbery, it had fooled even him on occasion, much to my grandmother's amusement. I could picture her chuckling from the passenger seat every time he was forced to swing the car around on the narrow country lane. So you could imagine my surprise at finding them not only cut back and neatly squared off, but a large wrought-iron gate sitting across the entrance.

"What the hell?" I murmured, coming to a stop. Kier had passed away almost three months ago. He was my last living relative unless you counted my mother, which I didn't. She was currently living her best untethered life in Thailand, or was it Bali now? Regardless, she was more like that friend from school who contacted you once a year to ask you to invest in their new wax melt company. And Kier . . . well, my grandfather wouldn't have spent money on something like this.

Turning in, I pulled the handbrake and clicked off my seat belt.

Dudley gave a pathetic yowl that said *if I don't eat in the next thirty seconds, death is imminent.*

"I fed you two hours ago, you little monster." A hastily scarfed-down meal by the side of the road as I'd attempted to pee behind a bush while simultaneously keeping my eyes peeled for anyone with a camera. I could already picture the headline: "Disgraced Starlet Damages Endangered Ecosystem Via Urination." The paranoia was second nature at this point.

I bet Julia Roberts never had to deal with this shit.

Beyond done, I didn't spare any thought to the rain. I jumped from the vehicle, hoping against all odds that whoever was last to visit the estate had thought to leave the gates unlocked. I gave a hard push and almost wept with exhausted joy when it swung wide.

The early May evening was uncommonly balmy, yet my teeth still chattered on the bumpy ride down the trail to the manor. I winced as I inched along the dirt road, every groove and pothole putting my city car's suspension under serious strain.

"You got it, baby, you got it," I purred, rubbing the dashboard lovingly. Soon enough, the track opened to a wide gravel drive-way; the ancient oak I'd broken my arm falling out of sat in its very center like nature's roundabout. Then there was the manor. The home of four generations of Murphys, the very same wind-torn saltire flag whipping from the slate roof's singular turret. Two stories built in Victorian-inspired style stood proud, its stone having faded to a light sand color over the years. The large lower-floor windows were almost entirely concealed by thick green ivy snaking around its structure like squeezing limbs.

I felt my mouth gape. In my years away I'd forgotten the true scale of the manor, its astronomical size eaten away by memories of cozy Christmases in the family room. Of the flapjack and lemon drizzle cake my grandmother, Elsie, baked every Sunday. It had felt normal then, my very own playground set on eight acres of land.

Perhaps it was the darkened windows, or the knowledge that not a single soul waited inside for my return that made it feel too big for one person. I pictured Kier rattling around those deserted rooms in the last days of his life and hated myself a little bit more. I should have been here. Should have known something was wrong.

Parking directly out front, I retrieved Dudley first before he could gnaw off one of his three remaining paws, transferring him from his pet carrier to his sling and settling his weight across my body. I could return for my bags once I had him settled.

"What do you think of your new home, buddy? It's very different from our flat in London, you'll have all this room to run around and we can walk down to the beach every morning." He gave my chin an excited lick, likely to collect any remnants of the sad sandwich I'd eaten on the ferry rather than in reaction to my words.

Scaling the steps to the front entrance, I gave the brass handle set on peeling paint a twist.

Locked. Well, that snookered that plan.

Stupid of me to think I'd find the front door unlocked—even if in life Kier had zero regard for home safety—but I'd left London in a wee bit of a rush. Tilting my head back, I measured the distance between the trellis and the second-story window with the broken latch and calculated the speed with which a human could fall fifty feet and walk away unscathed.

Dudley wiggled impatiently. "All right, all right, I'm thinking! No one can feed you if I'm dead. You'll be forced into a life in the wild, eating rats and rabbits too weak to outrun you."

Deciding against the second story, I skirted the exterior, ignoring the pebbled path that led to the old whisky distillery my great-grandfather had built almost seventy years ago. I circled around to the kitchen window at the back of the property, smiling when I spotted the ancient wood frame, for once relieved Kier hadn't seen the benefit in home improvement. Given the right amount of pressure, the pane should slide right up.

Climbing into the flower bed that at one time bore my grand-mother's favorite hydrangeas, I ignored the squelch of wet mud and the crime it was committing against my white sneakers and pushed. "Come on, *come on*—" Teeth gritted, I pushed harder, bending my knees and pressing my shoulder against the frame until I heard it groan. "Just open, you little bitch."

It popped with so much force I stumbled back, mud splattering up my bare thighs. "See," I said to Dudley, "easy peasy." Wiping my damp hands on my denim shorts, I stared into the dim kitchen that looked exactly as I remembered, all exposed bricks and beams—country-chic, as *House & Garden* would say. Except, this was actually just country and old. I swung my leg over the ledge as I called out to Dudley. "I've got skills you've never seen, buddy."

And that was how I tore the crack of my shorts breaking into my deceased grandfather's home.

I repeat: Julia Roberts never had to deal with this shit.

AFTER DROPPING THE FINAL BIN LINER FROM MY CAR AT THE foot of the stairs, I shed my soaked clothes for the first long T-shirt

I could find and proceeded to hang my damp lingerie along the radiator in the kitchen to dry. Keeping my eyes on the task of spreading out the delicate lace material, I balled up my favorite denim shorts that couldn't be saved and tossed them in the bin beneath the kitchen sink. I didn't dare glance at the empty sofas in the far end of what served as a kitchen and family room, where the ghosts of my family waited.

My grandmother, Elsie, knitting in her chair before the fire, so real I could almost smell the soot. I could hear her leaping to her feet, demanding Kier strip off his work overalls the moment he stepped through the door for dinner. Could see the grin Kier flashed at me that only grew more boyish as he aged, ruffling my tangled curls as he asked, "Good day at school, wee birdie?" Even my mother was there on the short stretches she cared to visit. Not cut out for the life of a young single mother, she'd spent the majority of my childhood working as a cruise ship entertainer. Back then I thought it was the most glamorous job I'd ever heard of and I'd badger her for stories until she buried her nose between the pages of a magazine. So much love and hurt had existed within these walls. All of it gone in the blink of an eye. My phone buzzed on the counter suddenly, drawing me from my hollow memories.

Guessing the caller, I didn't even look at the screen before answering. "You got my message," I said without preamble.

"April, please tell me this is a joke. One of those stupid pranks you like to play." Sydney was my roommate and one of the few friends I had in London. I could hear through the line that her voice was more nasally than usual, which I knew meant she was still wearing her anti-snore nose clip. As a fellow and *currently*

8

more successful actress, she was busy shooting her first feature film in Toronto.

"That was once and the pee cleaned right up!" I replied, for what had to be the hundredth time. The singular occasion in our eleven years of friendship I'd ever played a prank on her and she never let me forget it.

"I *hate* pranks."

"*I know.*" Boy, had I learned that the hard way. Our first week living together at the tender age of twenty, it'd felt like a rite of passage to throw my fellow wannabe-actress roomie a "welcome to the apartment" prank. Cling film on the toilet seat was classic and hilarious. Or so I'd thought.

"Well?" she demanded.

"*Well?*"

"*Well . . . please tell me* you haven't lost your mind and gone to Scotland!"

"Why would I tell you that when you already know I have? My message literally said 'gone to Scotland for a while, not sure when I'll be back.'"

"I was hoping your phone had been stolen . . . or you'd been kidnapped." I laughed, running my finger through a line of dust on the windowsill. Rain still poured, obstructing my view of the grassy bank and steep path that led down to the beach cove. "Have you been kidnapped? You hear about that sort of thing up there."

"In Scotland?"

"*Exactly.*"

I refrained from reminding her that I was, in fact, Scottish, even if my smoothed anglicized accent now suggested otherwise, and simply went with, "I think I'll be fine."

"Why are you doing this now, April? What about the job you had lined up?"

"Job? It was no better than a wet T-shirt contest. They wanted to let the male guests douse me with champagne before I served the drinks." Ever since my career had taken what you could call a bumpy side road, I'd accepted any job thrown at me. I'd done what felt like every reality show going: *Dancing with Celebrities*, *Celebrity Cook-Off* (twice), *Celebrities Go Dating*. I'd gone to PR events in ridiculous costumes and shoes that made my feet bleed, stood next to men who made my skin crawl with a smile on my face. I had lowered myself to the part of a money-hungry socialite. But something about the sight of that little white T-shirt had set me off. The words of the event planner had pretty much sealed the deal. *Darling, it's nothing they haven't seen before.*

It made me feel guilty about the early days when the jobs had come thick and fast, basically falling into my lap. By the age of twenty-six, I'd won a BAFTA for best supporting actress; a year later I had two Golden Globes to add to my collection. All that was left was an Oscar. I'd even taped a picture of one to my refrigerator, my eyes set firmly on the prize.

Eyes on the prize, wee birdie.

Like anything worth having in life, it took years to build my career and only seconds to break it, because six months later the notion of an Oscar was laughable when I couldn't even be certain I would work again.

"Oh, honey. Are you sure that Skye is a better alternative? You're on an island, for goodness' sake. Is there even a supermarket?"

Nope, but it had several convenience stores and we were in the time of food delivery. I would be absolutely fine. *Mostly*.

"Didn't Angela send the contract over to you? She said she would."

Angela of LDN Artists *had* contacted me and though she seemed to have a genuine, friendly nature, I'd yet to respond. "I don't know if I'm ready for that, I only got out of my old contract a few months ago, I need a bit of time to think." I switched her to speaker so I could rifle through the cupboards. Dudley might have been happily fed and snoozing with his legs in the air, but my stomach had begun to eat itself.

Sydney's voice echoed off the high ceiling. "But you've been vindicated, surely this is the time to get back out there."

It didn't feel like vindication, it felt like the darkest part of my life under a microscope while a group of middle-aged men who'd all seen my tits decided my fate. "Vindicated?" I snickered into the quiet. "Aaron might have lost his job, but we both know he got a huge payout for leaving quietly. He's going to be just fine, but I—" I'd lost years of what would otherwise have been an already fleeting career for a woman in the industry.

"That's why you need to get back to work."

"I'm not sure I want to get back to work." The truth of my words terrified me because I knew nothing else. I wasn't good at anything else. Add in the fact that I couldn't financially afford to keep this place if I didn't get back to work, and soon . . . my life was beyond a mess. I was the living embodiment of the meme of the guy walking in with pizza to find the entire apartment on fire.

But I couldn't say a word of that to Sydney because while we were friends, we weren't the sharing kind of friends, so I pushed a smile into my voice and said, "I'll think about it and read through the contract."

"Good. Are you sure you're going to be all right?"

"I'm sure." I looked around the kitchen, taking in the tattered deep-pine cabinets and the large six-seater dining table Kier had made himself as a wedding present to Elsie. I was in the shell of my childhood, blanketed beneath a layer of dust, but my next breath was the easiest I'd taken in years.

"What are you going to do?" she asked.

"I don't know." I bit a nail. "Whatever I want to do. Bake cookies and read all the neglected romance books on my e-reader. Go on walks. I could do yoga instead of circuit training . . . you know how much I hate burpees."

She laughed. "You'll be so bored you'll be crawling back to London by the morning."

The line went dead and the silence settled around me. "I guess we're about to find out."

2

APRIL
Bad Blood – Taylor Swift

W hat's the problem? The bed?" I could have sworn my dog looked put out. "The mattress is a little old but I brought our bedding from home, even that little blanket you like, see?" I held the scratchy green-and-purple tartan aloft—a memento of my childhood—for him to inspect and returned to setting up the bed. I hadn't been able to bring myself to step into my grandparents' old bedroom, despite it being three times the size, complete with an en suite. No, this would do for now.

I whipped off the dust sheet and flipped the mattress that was in surprisingly good condition. In fact, the entire room had weathered the years well. The pale pink-and-white striped wallpaper I'd picked out as a young teen because it was almost identical to Cher's bedroom in *Clueless* was curling slightly at the corners, and the floorboards creaked more than they used to. Other than that, it was like stepping into a time warp.

Once I'd smoothed the silky bottom sheet, I threw on my favorite jade-green throw pillows that looked extravagant in my

Instagram pics, when in fact, I'd picked them up at a bargain store. Looking at them now, in this place, I couldn't think of a better metaphor for my life.

I was just fitting the top sheet, my beige-knickered arse in the air as I battled to get the quilt right into the corners of the coverlet, when I heard it.

Pop. Slide. Grunt.

Pop.

Slide.

Grunt.

I knew that grunt, knew it intimately, because it was exactly the same grunt I made only hours earlier when I'd hoisted myself through the bloody kitchen window. It was the grunt of immediate regret.

Another rumble drifted up the staircase, low and definitely male. It was loud enough Dudley turned to the door, his tail beginning to flap in a semi-excited rhythm.

Thud. Feet on the ground.

That got me moving. I dove for Dudley, scooping the overfriendly terror up in my arms and covering his mouth before he gave us away. I didn't drive twelve hours to star in a lame B-grade horror movie that wouldn't even make it into cinemas. No, this shit would go straight to streaming. Or worse . . . DVD. *Oh, the metaphors were coming thick and fast tonight.*

Stumbling back a few steps, I clasped Dudley's tiny body to my chest as my mind churned over its options . . . *Calm down, nobody but Sydney knows you're here.* Shit. Nobody but Sydney knew I was here. *I'm a dead woman.*

I scoured the room for my phone while more noise sounded—

cupboards opening, pots and pans being pushed around—only to realize I'd left it on the bloody dining table. I had only minutes before they noticed it and ventured upstairs. I needed a plan, needed to go on the offensive. A surprise attack was always the most deadly . . . or something like that. I was five foot two, but I worked out every second Wednesday. I was scrappy, like a Chihuahua.

"You got this, you totally got this," I whispered assuredly to myself. Placing Dudley on the bed, I leveled him with the same "don't you dare move" look I used when he spotted a slow pigeon at the park. Then I rifled through my bags for anything that could double as a weapon. My only options turned out to be a can of spray deodorant or a pair of spiked-heel boots. The boots felt like an obvious choice for causing pain, but the deodorant . . . that could incapacitate him long enough for me to grab my phone and call for help.

Decision made, I removed the cap and crept out the door, my bare feet making easy work of the dated carpet. The stairs were a different ball game, there I let muscle memory take the lead, stepping this way and that over loose floorboards with all the efficiency of a teenage girl sneaking out after dark to drink on the beach with her friends.

Light from the kitchen streamed from the cracked doorway, the intruder's imposing silhouette flitting across the herringbone hardwood of the foyer. *So brazen.* I shook my head in disgust, clutching the can of deodorant tighter. What happened to cloak-and-dagger shit?

Sticking close to the wall, I let the continued commotion of his ransacking mask my footsteps as I tried to steady my heart rate. It was only when I reached the threshold and spotted the back of his messy brown head leaning over the kitchen island, drinking from Elsie's favorite mug, that I saw red. All fear fled my body. I didn't cower, didn't think, didn't breathe. Letting the bitter burn of justice fill my veins, I charged at him.

Three strides and I was on his gigantic back. He yelled out in surprise, immediately attempting to shake me off, but I was too quick, wrapping my legs around his waist as I screamed, arms circling a throat the size of a small tree trunk to lock me to him.

The intruder lurched forward and back, hip crashing into the work surface hard enough to upend a chopping board. Carrots flew like tiny missiles as a wickedly sharp knife crashed to the gray tile. I could admit the sight was strange, a criminal pausing to chop vegetables mid-crime, but I was in too deep, the bloodlust too real. Nothing existed but this.

Distantly, I was aware of a dog barking. Two dogs barking. Dudley and another, the second louder and lower in baritone. "What the hell is happening?" The mountain man sounded dazed, dinner plate-size hands coming up to break my hold. My grip began to waver. I had seconds at most before he overpowered me. "Who the hell are you?"

He sounded anxious. *Good.* "I'm vengeance, bitch," I hissed out between gritted teeth—*that line was completely improvised*—before lifting the can and pressing the plunger. A puff of coconut blossom misted the air, coating not just his face, but mine. It was wet and clawing, stinging my eyes, stealing its way down my throat. We yelled out in tandem and if I thought I stood a chance before, I certainly didn't now. I clung tighter as tears streamed from my eyes, but it was like riding a bucking bronco.

He clawed at his face, expletives flying through the air, and then we were moving. One of my hands slipped free as my back met the wall above the radiator. I fumbled for anything I could find, soft material meeting my fingers. I hoisted myself onto the surface, reaching around to stuff the material in his mouth. He shook me again, lurching forward. Two of the dining chairs became collateral damage in our scuffle, crashing to the ground as the barking grew impossibly louder.

I wanted to search for Dudley to ensure he was out of harm's way when this eventually came to a head, but the intruder stretched one of those bear paws back, grabbed me by the scruff of my shirt, and sent me flying through the air.

"Ouf." The sound puffed out of me like a cloud of dust. Not pained but surprised, as I bounced twice then sprawled flat on my back across the sofa. A shadow loomed over me, but all my bleary eyes could make out was a mass of hair and beard and plaid before hands pinned my shoulders down. I thrashed and the deodorant fell from my grip.

"Jesus, you bloody hellcat," he exclaimed, spitting the balled-up material from his mouth. "Explain. Right now!"

"Me explain?" I tried to claw at him, but he anticipated the move, hands slipping to my biceps and bracketing me to the cushions. How could he even see when my own eyes had been replaced by flaming fireballs? His hazy silhouette wiped at both eyes with his shirtsleeve and satisfaction almost won out over the pain. "I've already phoned the police and they're on their way. If you're smart, you'll get out of here before they arrive."

"You phoned the police, aye? Who'd you speak to?" He didn't

17

give me a chance to answer. "I know for a fact Tom turns his phone off after nine."

Damn this tiny island and its lack of crime!

Pushing all the authority I could muster into my voice, I stated calmly, "You, sir, are breaking and entering. Leave now and we can forget the whole thing."

His snort was incredulous. "Look, lass—" He broke off, twisting his face as though a veil had been lifted and we were now citizens of Opposite Land, where everything he thought to be correct was a cruel falsity. He released me and scrubbed his eyes again. *"April?"* He spoke my name with reluctant familiarity, not recognition. Which meant he *knew* me. Not as April Sinclair, but April Murphy. "What are you doing here?"

Hands finally free, I tugged the hem of my T-shirt to my eyes, wiping until I could see him clearly too.

Shock rooted me in place. Upside down and disgruntled beneath that messy hair and beard I'd mistaken for brown when it was actually a dark blond was Malcolm—Mal—Macabe.

Malcolm. Sweet relief poured through me.

It was unsurprising I hadn't recognized his voice, I could count on one hand the times I'd heard him speak during the summers he worked with Kier at the distillery. His face—well, I had no trouble recognizing that. The image above me blurred, shifting into the gangly teenager who'd teetered right on the cusp between awkward and beautiful. Too-large feet and restless hands that poked holes in the sleeves of his sweaters. Yet something about him had drawn me in enough to watch those hands become sure and steady when he slung barley off the back of a truck and loaded it into the warehouse. From ages fifteen to eighteen it was my favorite pastime.

Above me, his upside-down mouth moved and I realized he was speaking. "What are you doing here?"

Why does he keep asking me that?

"Umm . . . it's my house." Dudley chose that moment to hop up onto the sofa and settle into the crook of my arm. *And the award for the world's worst guard dog goes to . . .*

Malcolm's eyes flitted to Dudley and then to my sprawled position. Perhaps it was the way his blue-gray eyes dragged over me, because we both seemed to realize simultaneously what I was wearing . . . or rather, not wearing might have been a better description. My T-shirt was shucked up around my waist, leaving my full beige briefs on display. Swallowing, he backed up a step, cheeks burning a deep scarlet. *There*—that was the Malcolm I remembered. Instead of sitting, I stretched a leg out and watched his gaze track the movement.

I found I rather liked his eyes on me. I always had.

Jumping like he'd walked in on me changing, Mal righted the chairs we'd toppled and I finally noted the material dangling limply from his fingertips. My bra. The skimpy white lace one I'd left drying on the radiator. My mind hit replay on the last sixty seconds and a laugh tore from my chest. I'd just had a physical fight with Malcolm Macabe. I'd jumped him like a goddamned spider monkey and shoved my bra into his mouth. This was quickly taking the top spot as the strangest night of my life.

Pushing to sit, I wiped the tears from my cheeks and quickly found the source of the second barker: a gorgeous golden retriever now sitting at Malcolm's heel. Next to his very surly owner, they were night and day. The dog's entire body vibrated, his tail whipping jubilantly on the tile. Malcolm continued to glower, lips I knew from memory ridiculously full, half hidden by an impressive but neatly trimmed beard. His mouth was pressed in a firm line and made the surgery scar that had always stretched from his left nostril to the center of his top lip more pronounced. Time had faded it from a fleshy pink to white.

Noticing where my attention strayed, Mal looked down at his feet. *Fine*, I'd look at the dog instead. "Hey, gorgeous," I said, holding a hand out.

Malcolm issued a gruff "*Boy!*" but the dog was already moving, diving straight for the offered affection. Not one to be ignored, Dudley flopped on his back, pawing my arm until I stroked him with my free hand.

Malcolm watched the entire exchange through puffy, albeit wary eyes, as if my hand were a serpent about to choke the life from his beloved pet. Perhaps a fair assessment given the situation, so I went straight for the elephant in the room. "Look, I'm so sorry for jumping you and spraying you in the face . . . and the whole 'bitch' comment. If I'd known it was you I never would have—"

"—almost blinded me?"

I continued to stroke the dogs. "The deodorant is non-toxic, it never would have blinded you."

"I couldn't give a shit if it were bloody fairy dust."

I had to bite my lip against my brewing laugh. "The fate of our planet is everyone's responsibility, Malcolm."

"*April.*" His tone held a warning. If it weren't for the bra he still ignorantly clutched, I'd feel as though I was in the principal's office.

"Okay, fine, I'm sorry. Just let me explain . . . it's kind of funny really. I was upstairs in my bedroom when I heard you break in through the window. And like any woman faced with a predator—"

"Predator?" He looked seconds from blowing a blood vessel.

"—my mind instantly flew to the worst conclusion." I stood and the dogs danced excitedly at my feet. Just like teenaged Malcolm, he didn't meet my eyes and instead continued to stare at his boots.

"I didn't break in, I only came through the window because the safety latch was on."

"You mean the safety latch a lone woman might put on for, I don't know . . . safety?" I grinned brightly. It got zero reaction, *nada, zilch.* Not even a crack in his icy exterior. *Strange,* that smile usually worked on everyone. "Malcolm, I'm not blaming you. I clearly misread the situation and I'm sorry, so so sorry—I'm just trying to explain."

"How did you get in?" he cut in. Leaning back against the dining table, he folded his arms encased in dark blue plaid across his chest until the seams stretched. That unnoticed scrap of lace still right there. *Right. There.* I could swear to the goddess Meryl Streep I tried my best not to stare at it. "Tonight. How did you get in?" he asked again.

"Oh . . . the kitchen window." I gestured over my shoulder. "It's actually pretty strange now you think about it, we both used the exact same route to break in—wait, did you split your pants too?"

He merely raised a brow at that. "Wouldn't that make *you* the intruder?"

21

"Me?" I drew back. Why did this feel like a gotcha moment? "I grew up here, I'm Kier's granddaughter, that makes the manor mine."

"Granddaughter?" He scoffed darkly, the sound not at all aligning with the Malcolm I remembered. Apparently he didn't need to look at me to go for the jugular because he continued to stare at his boots as he spoke the words that flayed me right open. "Wouldn't a granddaughter stop playing dress-up for a few days to attend her grandfather's funeral?"

I knew my mouth hung open but I didn't have the faculties to close it. As a teenager, Malcolm was shy, painfully so, but never cruel. I hadn't expected a hug and an invitation to dinner—though I absolutely would have accepted—but perhaps a smile and a "hi April, nice to see you," or even a "let's catch up over coffee."

What on earth was going on? Perhaps we really were in Opposite Land. Or I'd hit my head during the scuffle and this was all an odd hallucination. "Malcolm—"

He strode toward me, bending just a fraction closer than appropriate, and gave his dog two soft pats on the rump followed by a muttered, "Home time, Boy." The dog gave Dudley an almost humanlike forlorn look but followed obediently. I watched the entire exchange in stunned silence.

Before he was out of sight, Malcolm tossed one final parting shot. A grenade really, disguised in gentle brogue. "Go back to London, princess. No one will be happy to see you back here."

I stared until I heard the front door close. Then I did the one thing I was good at . . . I acted. The quiver in my lips stretched into a smile, and a false brightness that had become so effortless melted into my voice as I said to Dudley, "Well . . . that was odd, but no matter, he probably had a really bad day. Tomorrow's going to be great, you'll see." I went about setting the kitchen to rights, crawling on my hands and knees until I'd retrieved every last carrot cube. Finally, when I ran out of reasons to stay downstairs, I trudged back up to my room that smelled too much of home and slipped into my freshly made bed, Dudley curled to my chest.

3

MAL
This Is Me Trying – Taylor Swift

Hmm, tae the right a bit a' think—no left, back tae the left . . . *left!*" I grunted under the weight, shifting the solid oak cabinet to the left a fraction of an inch. "The right again . . . *Perfect!* Aye, that's just perfect." Jessica Brown, proprietor of Brown's Coffee & Cakes, clapped her hands together and hummed in appreciation.

I'd shifted the heavier-than-it-looked oak cabinet all of a meter, from one side of the glass case that displayed said cakes to the other, because Jessica claimed her homemade jam could be seen better from the street at this angle. It made no difference in my mind, but Brown's was an institution around these parts, so when Jessica asked for help, you damn well offered if you wanted to remain a reputable customer. And . . . I didn't like the idea of her moving heavy items alone.

Wiping the evidence of the muggy morning from my brow and taking in the mess I'd unveiled, I glanced around the small café that had graced the village of Kinleith for over three decades. Where the cabinet had previously stood, the graying linoleum shone a bright white beneath a fine layer of dust balls, old till re-

24

ceipts, and what I would go to my death bed praying were choco-late chips. Better to get that cleaned away before food standards paid a surprise visit, I thought.

"Do you have a broom?" I asked her as she flitted behind the counter. Jessica appeared a decade younger than her seventy-six years and hadn't let the double hip replacement she'd undergone slow her down. She flicked the power back on, her blue rinse shin-ing under the overhead lights I'd switched over to LEDs just last month. It would save her a ton on electricity bills when the long winter hit.

"Yer a good egg, Mal," she said, handing over the small broom. Feeling the familiar burn in the tips of my ears, I dropped into a crouch, gathering up the mess as she continued to chatter.

"Speaking of bad eggs . . ." *Were we?* "How's that brother of yers doing?"

"You probably see Callum more than I do," I grunted. His sweet tooth was even bigger than mine.

"Fae nae more than a flying visit, he's always too busy tae chat."

I grunted again, binning the pan of dust and receipts that dated back to 2002 and sliding the tables and chairs into their usual spots.

This was why Jessica made the list of very few people I could stand to be around; she talked and talked without ever expecting a response. There wasn't the expectation of reciprocation that had me sweating and seeing black spots until I could make a beeline for the nearest exit. A well-placed grunt here, a nod there, and she'd recall to the rest of my meddling family all about the *amaz-ing* conversation we'd shared. This was all my necessary social-izing for the week right here.

"Did I tell ye my granddaughter always fancied him? Yer ken ma granddaughter, Maggie? 'Tis a shame she doesnae live closer, the girl had tae move aw the way tae Glasgow, all but shaved her heid an dyed it pink, she has." She tutted. "'Tis about time Callum settled down wi' a nice, local girl. Wi' a good job like his, it seems selfish not tae."

I refrained from saying that "a nice, local girl" would bore my brother to tears and diplomatically answered, "He's already married to his job."

She wagged a slightly crooked finger at me. "That boy will look up one day an realize he's old an ugly wi' nae hairline tae be seen an wish he'd found himself a wife."

I didn't disagree with that statement, mostly because I enjoyed the image of my charming big brother, who'd never stumbled a day in his life, losing that precious head of hair. I also couldn't help but notice she didn't inquire about *my* love life, as though at just thirty-two, I was already cursed to a lifetime of cooking far too much pasta for one person. The heat in my ears spread until I felt it engulf my entire face and my thumbs began the same old restless path, sweeping back and forth over the tips of my other digits. The jingling of the bell above the door announced the first customer of the day, providing the perfect cover for my exit.

"That's me, Jessica." I shouldered my bag and set down the bottle of whisky I dropped off every two weeks for her husband, Angus. As polite societal customs suggested, I nodded in the newcomer's general direction without pausing to put a name to the face and stepped onto the sun-soaked high street, freedom within my reach—

"Wait. Ye've forgotten yer payment."

My shoulders inched higher. "I told you last time, I don't need payment."

"Yer off yer heid, lad, now take it." She spun me with surprising strength, slapping a wedge of Victoria sponge cake into my empty palm. Jam and buttercream icing oozed between my fingers as a stray strawberry landed beside my boot. "Now, off wi' ye."

Straight in the hand, every time.

Bringing the cake to my lips, I cut right down the high street in the direction of the small village car park. The cobbled path sloped down toward the harbor where seagulls squawked and dove in the distance, gearing up for a busy day of stealing ice cream cones from unsuspecting holiday-makers. Recently hung bunting for the upcoming summer season whipped in the morning breeze like dozens of miniature kites. It wasn't even nine, yet the street was already teeming with movement. Locals greeted one another, wiping down windows and propping open doors to the array of small businesses along the half mile stretch. Sleepy-eyed tourists sought out breakfast and posed for pictures alongside the quaint buildings painted the multitude of colors that Kinleith had become famous for. *The rainbow walk,* as it was better known to many. The name was even starting to catch on with the residents.

Dropping my head and cutting around a group of giggling girls posing with matching peace signs before the bright-pink nail salon, I swallowed the final bite of cake, licking the icing from my sticky fingers as tension crawled along my neck. I hated this time of year, hated the crowds and the noise and the damage to our countryside that came with it. I understood the benefits of tourism for the local community, didn't mean I had to like it.

The second my old Land Rover came into view I pulled the keys from my pocket, pressure easing a fraction. Fast asleep, my golden retriever, Boy, took up the entire length of the back seat, exactly where I'd left him fifteen minutes earlier. "*Christ*," I swore, covering my nose and mouth as I settled behind the wheel. Despite all four cracked windows, he'd still managed to turn the small cab into a dutch oven. "We're going to have to reevaluate your diet, wee man." My dog rolled on his back and farted again in answer.

Backing out of the space, I started the short drive to the Sheep's Heid Pub, already reciting the words I would say to the owner, Ian, like a living script. *Last delivery of the day*, I reminded myself. One more stop and I could get back to the distillery—back to my cottage.

I had a routine that I stuck to religiously. Whisky deliveries once a week. Groceries twice. Takeout from Brown's every other afternoon. Small social interactions I forced because otherwise I'd barricade myself behind my cottage walls, never to be seen or heard from again.

It was Kier who'd enjoyed this part of the job, Kier who handled the product-selling and the socializing, while I did the grunt work. As he'd grown sicker, the responsibility had fallen to me more and more, and while our small circle of customers remained loyal, I couldn't shake the feeling that I was letting him down in some way. That every time I stuttered through a product delivery, or ignored a late payment I couldn't afford to ignore simply because I hated confrontation, I was failing.

I knew what people here thought of me. *The grump. The recluse.*

This village was both a blessing and a curse. Home, and yet I could never bring myself to feel quite at home in it.

Sure, I felt at home in my cottage with Boy, with Kier, and sometimes my siblings. But it didn't stop that rush of relief I felt when they left and the solitude I strived for surrounded me like a warm, non-judgmental blanket. Small communities stuck together, but they also had a penchant for gossip and judgment, should people not act in a way they found palatable.

It had never bothered me, until now.

I thought of my three siblings, my oldest brother Callum mainly, and the unfaltering ease with which he moved through life. He wanted to join the military? He joined the military. He wanted to go to University in Edinburgh? He went to University in Edinburgh. He wanted to move back to Skye and open his own veterinary practice? He returned to Skye and opened his own veterinary practice. He wanted to settle down with a nice, local girl? The only question left to ask was, which one?

A nice, local girl.

I didn't know why my mind immediately conjured up April.

April Sinclair back in Kinleith. I almost wouldn't have believed it if I hadn't driven past the mud-stained Mini Cooper parked out front of the manor this morning. I pictured her the night before, blurry, but that mass of red curls instantly recognizable. Bare limbs starfished on the old sofa after I'd tossed her like a sack of barley. The lacy article I'd hidden deep in my sock drawer. I shook my head, wincing at the memory.

April Sinclair was bad news.

Murphy, I reminded myself, hands curling around the steering wheel. April Murphy.

I never thought I'd see the day that she'd lower herself enough to return to the island, and if I had my way, she'd go right back to where she came from.

THE TIGHT BALL IN MY CHEST EASED ENTIRELY THE MOMENT I closed the door to the small workman's cottage attached to Kinleith Distillery.

Boy trotted straight to his bowl, gave a sniff at finding it empty, then collapsed into his oversize basket. From his usual spot beside the fireplace, he pitifully watched me heap oats into a bowl, add milk, and heat it in the microwave.

"You know the rules, wee man. I eat, then you do," I reminded him, setting the timer. I only had a handful of minutes to waste on eating if I planned to get the vat filled with barley before sundown and load the empty whisky casks. I still needed to replace the hinges to the Dunnage door—my tool kit had been sitting ready and untouched for at least a week. Now it was just me, the number of chores was mounting higher than there were minutes in the day. Callum came by to offer a hand when he could, but even that wasn't enough to keep me afloat. I needed another full-time employee but had no means to pay one. Right now, I was scraping by with part-timers and favors.

Pulling the steaming bowl from the microwave, I sat at the dining table that only just squeezed into the open-plan space, so long as I pushed it right up against the window. Boy gave another little moan I pretended not to hear.

I could clearly recall the night Callum had showed up at my door, a scraggly golden retriever in hand, announcing the pup needed a home. My "absolutely not" had fallen on deaf ears and he'd promptly thrust the dog into my arms and strolled right back to his car without a backward glance. I didn't have the room, the time, or the affection to give to a dog. Yet, here we were two years later, making it work.

The entire cottage was crossable in ten strides. The kitchenette only contained a compact fridge, sink, microwave, and hot plate, which was the reason I *usually* preferred to eat at the manor. In the center was a living area, television, two-seater sofa—though I never had guests—and the armchair I favored. The only things I refused to scale down were the king-size bed in the furthest corner and the rows of reclaimed-wood shelving that housed my film and book collection.

Small but perfect, and entirely mine.

It's not yours though, is it.

My hand went reflexively to the pile of papers on the table, to the letter I'd reread countless times in the last month, picking over the words I'd memorized at this point.

Reference to the last will and testament of Kier Angus Murphy.

Request denied by the beneficiary.

No legal standing.

Then there was the second letter, a response from the bank regarding my application for a business loan. Again, *denied*.

Denied.

Denied.

Denied.

I slammed my fist down, feeling no satisfaction when the heavy paper crumpled beneath the force. This place was mine, the cottage, the distillery. It *should* have been mine. For years I'd been in the process of purchasing Kinleith Distillery from Kier, making monthly installments with the promise of legal owner-ship transferring to me. Then he'd grown sick and all thoughts of legal documents and land titles had flown into the ether.

I wasn't a cold bastard; I missed my friend, the man who'd been more of a father to me than my own dad. But he was gone, and everything I'd worked toward had gone with him. And now, April *Murphy* had the cheek to show up here, smiling that princess smile, giggling over the amusing circumstances of our reunion when she had single-handedly benefited from my ruination.

No, she wasn't a *nice, local girl*. She may have been, at one point, but I'd witnessed the contempt in her eyes as she gazed around the manor last night, like it wasn't the prize she'd been prom-ised to inherit. To her, this life was small, *Kier* had been small. She'd been too busy with her fancy London life and her celebrity friends to see that Kier had busted his balls to keep the manor in good condition. To keep the distillery running while his health had begun to fail him. She couldn't be bothered to come back for his funeral, but was quick to return to cash in on something she hadn't earned.

I'd understood her absence in the beginning, when her career had rocketed out of the realm of understanding for mere mortals. Even the island had placed her on a pedestal; you couldn't walk down the street without hearing the name *April Sinclair* whis-pered with reverence. But those film roles dried up and as rumors circled in the press, the ridiculous reality shows began, and we all watched her claw at every opportunity to remain in the limelight.

I'd spoken to Kier once, encouraged him to reach out and offer her a place to stay for a while, knowing it wasn't my place. Maybe all she'd needed was an outstretched hand, and by default, they could take care of one another. She'd refused. Even when he'd grown sick, she'd refused.

I didn't understand. How could remaining on the fringes of an industry that had chewed you up and spit you out be a better alternative to here? Was she that addicted to the money and the fame?

Well, my home—the place I'd poured my sweat and blood into—would not be her meal ticket. April Murphy/Sinclair, whatever the hell she called herself these days, would have to take this place from my cold, dead hands.

4

APRIL
Home – Edward Sharpe & The Magnetic Zeros

A benefit of tossing and turning all night was rising early enough Wednesday morning to sip my morning coffee out on the bank, the scent of heather filling my nose, as the sun rose over the water. All the moment required was the hand-carved bench Kier had long ago promised he'd build for Elsie when he had a free day. He'd never had a free day.

Despite last night's rain, the day started sunny and dry so I'd taken Dudley on his first ever beach walk. I broke a sweat as I hauled his stocky little body down the steep, craggy path that zigzagged from the bank to the private cove. He'd returned exhausted and with sandy whiskers, slowing us both as we strolled back to the manor via the pebbled path leading past the old distillery.

The sheer size of the property grew more and more intimidating the longer I let myself take it all in. I owned all of this. I was *responsible* for all of this. The grass was short, and the bushes acting as a barrier between the manor and the distillery were neatly cut back. As the weeks of summer ticked away though, they would need maintaining.

Outdoors had always been Kier's domain, while the manor had been Elsie's. Never to be seen without a duster in hand, Elsie was a "dinner on the table at five, leave your dirty clothes by the door" kind of woman. Kier had been the fixer, the provider. I supposed it was the same for many older couples, coming from a time when traditional gender roles were so heavily structured. Had that resulted in Kier becoming a man who didn't really know how to take care of himself? Could the same be said for me?

As a child, when I wasn't reciting monologues in the mirror, I often found myself right alongside my grandmother. I could bake a mean lemon drizzle and thread a needle with my eyes closed, which was great—I loved all of those things. But outside that, I was completely out of my element. If something broke, I called a guy to fix it. Now, I wished I'd spent a little more of my childhood years out here in the dirt, learning from Kier how to be capable. I didn't want to *need* someone to fix my problems. Needing someone left room for manipulation, and that could never happen again.

After a few more minutes of walking, the stone distillery came into view. Almost as big as the manor with two stories, the whitewashed stone was almost blinding in the bright sunshine. *Kinleith Distillery* was depicted in large black letters facing the small gravel car park, the paint starting to flake and peel in places. A small workman's cottage jutted out to the left facing the sea, and I remembered the way it used to loom dark and unused on the property when I was younger. Around the back was a separate dunnage, its low ceiling and thick stone walls perfect for housing the whisky during its three-plus year maturation process.

See Kier, I did listen, I thought, shielding my eyes against the sun so I could get a good look at it. I tried the handle, wanting to look around the place for memories' sake, but it was locked. I tried again, pressing my ear to the door. I could have sworn I heard a dog bark. Dudley tilted his head as though listening too. Silence.

"The keys are probably at home," I said to him. "We'll come back another time."

Back at the manor, I showered, changed into my favorite baby-blue blazer with matching shorts, and dried out my hair. Then I sat at the breakfast bar, staring at my phone. I'd put off Angela's email long enough.

I'd met her on a handful of occasions through Sydney and she'd always come across kind, supportive, and professional. I didn't fear I'd be walking with my eyes closed into a situation I couldn't get myself out of with her. Yet, I knew I owed myself some time before making such a big decision. Figuring honesty was the best option, I chewed on my lip and wrote her back.

Angela,
Thank you so much for the offer of representation. Please believe I will give the contract serious consideration, but I have to be honest here, I need some time. My grandfather recently passed away and I've returned home for a while. I'm not sure for how long and I think I need this space to gain a bit of clarity. If you need to pass, I completely understand.
April Sinclair

There.

A weight lifted from my shoulders. Now I could start doing whatever the hell I wanted—once I figured out what that was. *Perhaps a trip into the village will help.* I'd barely stood from the table when her response pinged through.

April,
I get it! And we won't be passing, we want you aboard. Take as much time as you need. But how about this—I see any projects I think would be a good fit, I pass them your way?
Angela

Oh, she was good.

I didn't know a single actor who would pass on the perfect project. And for someone who'd been desperate to dig into a juicy character for years now, the offer of one would be too good to resist.

My hands flew over the screen.

Deal.
A

PLACING A PACKET OF SHORTBREAD INTO MY BASKET, I PAUSED at the shelf before reaching for another. *Screw it.* I reminded myself I was eating what I wanted now and threw in a large bag of cheese puffs and a six-pack of Irn-Bru along with a few cleaning supplies. Making one last pass around the small convenience store that sat just off Kinleith's main high street, I circled back to the till, pulling my bright pink heart-shaped sunglasses down over my eyes. It was total diva behavior and usually I'd roll my eyes at my own arrogance. Call it first-day nerves, or maybe Malcolm's words from last night really had gotten to me, but I wasn't ready to be recognized.

While I waited in line, I drew out my phone, opening up my favorite social media app to check the likes on a recent post. The picture was a close-up shot of my face, highlighting the minimalist makeup from a brand I'd been partnering with for the last year. Brand deals were my main source of income these days. I didn't love it, but it kept the money coming in and helped me stay relevant—whatever that meant. I had a lot of rules about the brands I promoted; I wouldn't promote any products I didn't love and use regularly. I refused to promote anything harmful—no fad-diet milkshakes or teas that made you shit your guts out. No fashion brands that mistreated their staff. No products tested on animals.

I kept the comments section open for fan engagement and, like always, my thumb hovered over the view icon. My turn at the checkout saved me from the den of vipers that would have likely sent me into a weeklong downward spiral, all because Johngreer901 from Vancouver said: *the only thing worse than your tiny tits are your movies.*

I shoved my phone back into my pocket and gave the pretty girl in her twenties behind the counter a small smile as I set my basket down.

"April?" The voice came from behind me. "April Sinclair, that's definitely you! Can I get an autograph!"

I stiffened, not even having time to check out the newcomer before feminine arms enveloped me, along with a scent I recognized.

"Juniper," I breathed out, returning the hug with a ferocity that rocked us from side to side.

Grasping my shoulders, she hauled me back to get a good look at me. "What the hell are you doing here? Why didn't you tell me you were coming?" One question flowed over another as I stood there, gazing into the face of one of my oldest friends in the world.

"It was kind of a last-minute decision and I only got in yesterday, I'm still getting settled." I nodded to the basket. "I guess I wasn't sure whether to . . . I didn't think—"

"You're staying at the manor? For how long? Please say at least a few weeks. Oh, we need to have dinner one night." Her blunt bob swayed as the words tumbled out so quickly, I feared her lungs might explode.

I clutched her wrist. "June, breathe."

"I'm sorry . . . I'm just so happy to see you."

I laughed, but her enthusiasm made me feel a tad guilty. I should have contacted her first. "I'm staying at least a few weeks, we have plenty of time."

She clapped her hands together. "Good, that's good. Oh—I just remembered, I'm meeting Heather for coffee." She checked the slim watch on her wrist. "I'm going to be late."

Heather. I smiled at the mention of the third member of our childhood friendship group. At school, we had jokingly nicknamed her May, so we could be April, May, and June. Kind of lame but also pretty cute. I hadn't spoken to either of them in years.

"You should come," she offered quickly, brows furrowing as she took in my basket filled with sugary snacks. "Unless you're having some kind of party?"

"No." I laughed, suddenly embarrassed. "All for me."

"Great, then you're free for coffee." She tugged me to the door.

"My shopping—"

June looked at the girl behind the counter who I noticed was staring at me with a slightly dazed expression. "Michaela, bag it up, will you. She'll be back in an hour or two." Michaela nodded but didn't take her eyes from me. *Shit*. So much for incognito. My name would be all around the village by nightfall.

The moment my tan loafers hit the sun-soaked cobbles, Juniper linked her arm through mine, knocking our shoulders together. At almost six feet tall, it was more her elbow to my shoulder. "Did you get even shorter?"

"Nope, I think that's all on your end." Her arm shifted, steering me around the corner and onto the high street. To my shock, we didn't find the tired, run-down street of my youth. What had once held little more than an outdated hairdresser, a DIY store, and a chemist had been entirely transformed. It was hard to believe I was in the same Kinleith and not between the pages of a children's book. "What on earth happened here?" I couldn't stop my head from swiveling. Everywhere I turned were bright colors and fantastical window displays. There was a book shop, an art gallery, a perfumery, even a pet store.

"Umm . . . tourists happened. Boatloads of them." I knew tourism had increased in Scotland in recent years, but seeing the change it could have on a community with your own eyes was awe-inspiring. "There was a point about two years back that the numbers grew so overwhelming, we struggled to service the mass of people visiting over the summer months . . . it was actually a little frightening. But the community adjusted, new businesses popped up, new B&Bs and campsites. The high street"—she gestured ahead of us—"became officially pedestrianized last summer to make it more pleasant for shoppers. The amount of tourists can still be a little intimidating," she admitted, her lips twisting. "Then I walk down here and witness firsthand how the island is thriving and it all feels worth it."

"It's amazing."

She spun, walking backward as she grinned, transforming her sharp features into something softer. "Keep that enthusiasm in mind when we get to Brown's, it hasn't changed a bit."

Brown's.

Nostalgia and a little bit of fear thrummed through me. Brown's was our hangout all through high school, mainly because it was the only place with a roof and copious amounts of cake that wasn't under the careful supervision of Juniper's and Heather's parents or my grandparents.

June led me beneath the familiar blue-and-white awning, eyes flicking to the tourists occupying the outdoor seating crammed onto the pathway. She ducked through the door and after a moment of hesitation, I followed. *People are going to see you eventually, may as well rip off the Band-Aid now.*

I hadn't even closed the door before two delighted shouts sounded. "I can't believe it's you." Heather Macabe drew me against her but I was immediately wrenched away.

"My turn. Out the way, ye dafties." Jessica Brown elbowed her way to the center of our little huddle, slipping off my sunglasses so she could cup my cheek. "Where have ye been, lass?" Never one to beat around the bush, I knew Jessica's question wasn't literal.

"I didn't know," I whispered, throat constricting as I held my tears at bay. "He didn't tell me what was going on."

"That man," she tutted, "always thinking he knew best."

"I should have been here."

She brushed a tear away with her thumb. "Aye. But ye here now, that's what matters." And as if she could see even my deepest worries, she whispered, "You'll do right by that place, I know ye will."

"Join us," Heather urged Jessica as the elderly woman handed over a huge teapot and three tea cups.

Jess waved her off and retreated to busy herself behind the counter, calling over her shoulder, "You three dinnae want an old lass cramping yer style."

I watched her with worry as she lifted a heavy tray of mugs from the washer. "Should she be doing that alone?"

June chuckled. "Try to stop her and you'll get a swat on your behind for the trouble."

Heather stirred a cube of sugar into her tea. "She only works three days a week now, her daughters handle the rest of the business."

I nodded, pouring out my own tea. It was wild how much this felt like old times, like I'd blinked and the last eleven years had flown by. Then I met their expectant eyes across the table. Perhaps not *exactly* like old times. *"What?"*

Heather waved a hand. "Oh, I don't know. How about the fact *April Sinclair* is sitting across the table from me and it feels bloody strange."

"Please don't call me that." I cringed.

As though our words had conjured this exact scenario, I caught the flash of a phone in a woman's hand a few tables down, camera pointed in my direction. I kept my focus on my friends and smiled through the small intrusion. If she was going to take a photo, lord let it be a good one.

"But you are *April Sinclair.*"

I shook my head. "Sinclair is just a stage name, you know that." Sinclair was Elsie's maiden name and at nineteen, I'd thought it sounded a lot more sophisticated than Murphy. "Legally I'm still April Murphy, and with you I'm just April."

"Still bloody strange though," she muttered.

It was an odd feeling to be so changed in the eyes of the people you'd grown up with, when to yourself, you were still the same girl who'd waitressed in this very café every Wednesday after school. I imagined it felt a lot like when Alice went to Wonderland and ate the cake that made her grow five times in size. Her fundamentals stayed the same but she was ultimately different, an oddity among the people who used to be her friends. It was why I'd stopped visiting. I hated the pointing and whispering, the way a walk through the village with Elsie would turn into a circus show where everyone wanted to weigh in on all the choices I'd ever made, like they had the right to an opinion.

Did it make me sound like a poor little famous girl? Probably. It was the life I chose. The life I wanted. But my feelings were still my own and they were as valid as anyone else's.

Still feeling their scrutiny, I plastered on a grin, searching for any change of subject. "Heather, your hair looks incredible, when did you change it?"

She smoothed a hand over the shoulder-length white-blond strands, her smile brittle. "About six months ago." She'd been naturally blessed with poker-straight chestnut locks that I'd never seen her cut above her waist. *This* was a dramatic change. June put a supportive hand on her shoulder as she blew out a breath. "Mike and I split almost a year ago."

"What? Why?" I looked to June, then back to Heather, waiting for one of them to laugh. They didn't.

Heather shrugged miserably. "I guess he didn't love our life—didn't love me enough. He moved to Australia. Software programmers are 'in demand' out there it seems."

I shook my head, taking a moment to process, to align this narrative with the teenage boy I'd known. Mike and Heather were high school sweethearts, he'd worshipped the ground she walked on. I remembered the day he left for university, the way he openly wept in front of all of his friends and promised to phone her everyday. He'd stuck to it too. And he'd left her.

Another thought dawned. "What about Ava and Emily?" Heather had twin daughters, they had to be at least six years old by now.

"He FaceTimes them once a week. He keeps asking me to let them spend Christmas over there . . . I haven't made a decision yet."

"And you don't need to," June cut in. "He's the one who left, he doesn't get to make demands. If he wants to see them he can get on a damn plane himself."

Heather nodded. "I know, that's what Mal keeps saying."

My neck prickled at the mention of Malcolm, Heather's older brother. Heather had three older brothers, Mal being the young-est male in the Macabe family. Callum was the eldest, followed by Alastair. Now, this was where things got a little complicated and a lot awkward because Alastair had at one time been engaged to Juniper (Island Life at its finest) when they'd both lived in Glasgow. That was, until six years ago, when June was forced to return to Skye after her father's sudden heart attack and remained to help her mother run their small B&B. Alastair had chosen—somewhat brutally—to remain in Glasgow. Not only had it left June heartbroken, it had inevitably caused a rift between my two friends when Heather couldn't completely disparage her brother.

I'd hated being so far away and somehow still caught in the middle. I'd raged for June, threatened to fly to Glasgow and relieve Alastair of his balls myself. But, deep down, a guilty little part of me had understood. Life on a remote island wasn't for everyone. Alastair's actions had been cruel, but wasn't it kinder to end it quickly than spend years building a life with someone, one foot always out the door?

Seeing June comfort Heather now, I had no doubt those old wounds were firmly behind them. "Heather, I'm so sorry for bringing it up, I had no idea."

"I should have told you. I'm just embarrassed, I guess." She planted her face in her hands and snickered. "I'm a thirty-year-old single mother working two jobs. It's not exactly the life I dreamed of."

June pointed her tea cup in Heather's direction. "You are killing it, mama."

I clinked my cup with June's. "Hear, hear. You are without a doubt the hottest single mother I've ever seen." I got my desired reaction when she giggled, tossing her blond hair dramatically.

"Okay, okay, we've circled the topic enough." June banged a manicured hand off the table. "It's your turn, April. What are you doing here and how long are you staying?"

I pretended to think, tapping a finger off my lips. "Umm . . . I have no idea and again, I have no idea."

At their quizzical expressions, I explained how I'd ended up here. How I'd discovered Kier's death from his lawyer who'd apparently been given strict instructions to only notify me after the fact. How I'd just packed up my car and driven here on a whim, not really understanding why, but knowing I needed to be *here*. And, largely, how I needed to decide what to do with the manor.

Ruminating over my growing list of concerns made me realize that while selling would break my heart, I wasn't sure I could afford to keep it.

"And amid all of this," I went on, dragging myself away from my darker thoughts, "my contract with my management company came to an end. I haven't signed with another agency yet, so I have some time, and this feels like the perfect place to spend it." I rushed through the bit about my career drama, hoping they would let me off the hook from going any deeper.

"Have you spoken to Mal?" Heather chirped.

I frowned. "Why would I talk to Malcolm?" Had he told her about last night?

"Because he runs the distillery, he lives in the workman's cottage . . ." She trailed off at my stunned expression. "Didn't you know?"

"I had no clue." At least that explained why he'd broken through the kitchen window last night. *Sort of.* "For how long?"

He'd worked at the distillery as a teen, but most of the local lads helped out to earn extra money during the summer months.

Heather squinted. "I don't know . . . years."

"Years?"

"Kier never mentioned it?" June asked.

I shook my head. *He didn't mention a lot of things.*

Heather sipped her tea. "No one knows that place better than Mal. If there's a way for you to save it, he'll find it. The distillery means so much to him."

"I walked past this morning and found it all locked up."

Heather chuckled. "Yeah, Mal does that, he doesn't like people just 'dropping by.' I'm sure he'll be relieved to see you."

"Doubtful." I snorted. "I ran into him last night and he was the opposite of happy, he all but told me to go back to London." *And stole my favorite bra.*

Heather's brows winged up. "He said that? It's not like Mal to be confrontational."

"Maybe it's my charm." I grinned, wiggling the arms of my sunglasses. They both giggled.

"Mal isn't happy to see anyone, you have to worm your way into that man's life until he doesn't know how to live without you. Just go and talk to him, knock until he realizes you're not going away. My big grump of a brother is actually a teddy bear underneath all that beard and plaid." She must have seen my doubt because she laughed again. "I'm dropping by to see him this afternoon, I'll soften him up for you."

"That might not be a bad idea." I pulled out my phone and said, "Give me his number just in case, he might respond better to a text message."

Heather rattled off his number and I saved it under *Gruffalo*. "When you see him, please don't mention my financial issues. I don't want him to worry unnecessarily about me selling, that's like . . . worst-case scenario. If I need his help it might be easier if he thinks I'm not conspiring against him."

I could tell that Heather didn't like the idea of lying to Mal, but after a flicker of hesitation, she agreed. "You're probably right."

5

MAL
Beach Baby – Bon Iver

Turning the lever with a grunt, I stood back, watching with satisfaction as fresh water from the stream spilled quickly from the copper pipes and filled the deep metal vat. The thing covered a large portion of the malting room's furthest wall and required the most amount of maintenance. With a metal spade, I stirred the golden grain into the liquid—a process called steeping that would significantly raise the barley's moisture content and ready it for germination.

The beginning was always my favorite part. The anticipation of a fresh batch. A new discovery. Every single cask of whisky had a personality, a fingerprint. No cask would taste exactly as another, no matter how closely the process was replicated. And the process was a lengthy one—the malting alone would take days to complete. Forty minutes to fill the vat with water. Steep for twelve hours. Drain. Air for fourteen hours. Repeat twice more before it could be manually transferred and laid out on the malting floor to germinate.

When I'd first joined Kinleith Distillery full-time, Kier had proposed the idea of switching to pre-processed barley. It would've been cost-effective, and we'd get to skip the lengthy germination procedure. But had we done that, the quality would have suffered . . . *in my opinion*. You got out what you put in, and sometimes going the extra mile and sticking to the traditional methods worked.

The vat wasn't even half full when Boy's ears pricked up, tail whipping like a helicopter propeller. He yowled and I quickly shushed him, creeping over to the head-high box window. *My* head height, at least, not the vertically challenged April Murphy's, because I'd used this very window to spy on her this morning when she'd rattled the door handle like she owned the place. Which she technically did.

Half of me expected to find her mass of silky red curls on the other side of the glass again. The other part of me that assumed she was already halfway back to London was unsurprised to find Callum grinning like a school boy, middle finger raised in my direction. I returned the gesture, but slid the bolt and cracked the door. Catching sight of one of his favorite humans, Boy lurched through the gap, paws meeting my brother's jean-covered thighs and delivering excited licks over both of his hands. Used to being covered in animal saliva on a daily basis, Callum didn't bat an eye. "Hey there, you furry terror." His hands smoothed over Boy's features, spreading around his eyes and checking his teeth in that clinical manner that came unconsciously to him. "How's my best boy doing? Taking care of this old grump?" He shot me a smirk. I lifted my middle finger again, then gave him my back to check the water level.

Callum came up beside me, gave his hands a quick wash in

the sink, and then dipped one into the steep, cupping a handful of grain and letting it flow through his fingers. "Should be a good malt," he observed appreciatively. "I would have helped but I had a full morning of appointments. Full day, in fact."

Giving it another stir, I said, "If you're so busy, what are you doing here?"

"*Ouch*, you're breaking my heart, brother."

I winced. "Sorry . . . there's just a lot going on right now."

He faced me, leaning a hip against the metal lip. "I'll come by this weekend and give you a hand."

"You don't need to do that." He already ran his own successful business, I didn't want him taking on my burdens too. "I have Ewan in tomorrow, it should help ease the load a little." The young lad helped out a few mornings a week, a little slow and far too chatty for my taste, but he meant well.

Callum clapped a hand on my shoulder. "I've got to stay in shape somehow if I have any chance of keeping up with you." I knew my brother was teasing. He was the only person who would dare tease me about my size these days. Almost a full head shorter than me, he was bulky but not as broad. He had that athletic build that women loved. Whereas I . . . I was so large I intimidated people. I felt the way women looked at me, occasionally admiringly, more often warily. It made me wish I could shrink inside myself.

Pulling a sandwich from his pocket, he perched on the edge of the vat and took a huge bite, observing me as he chewed. "Before I forget, Mum wants you at Saturday dinner this week."

There it is.

The corner of my mouth curled, pulling tight across the scar

51

down the center of my lip—the one left behind from multiple surgeries to repair the cleft palate I was born with. What many didn't know about a cleft palate was that often, there was more to it than the change to physical features. There were varying degrees of a cleft. Mine was severe, meaning the soft tissue in my mouth and throat didn't fuse in the womb, leading to issues feeding, swallowing, and later on, talking. Several surgeries and years of speech therapy later, only the small scar remained. But a childhood in and out of the hospital could leave other scars too, ones not so easily seen and understood.

Instinct had me twisting away from him. "I don't know if I can make it. I have too much—"

"It's lucky I'll be here to help out then," he said, effectively cutting me off. "So I'll tell her yes? Excellent." He clapped me on the back before I could utter another word of refusal.

Dammit. This was why my mother always sent Callum, he was impossible to refuse. He'd been the troublemaker growing up, a people person through and through, while I was content to stay in my room watching films or playing video games. Heather was slightly more reserved, like me, but still had a good group of friends to get her out of the house. Alastair—my only sibling who lived on the mainland—had been Callum's shadow, the two so alike and only a year apart in age, they were often mistaken for twins.

I loved my family, even if my dad and I rarely saw eye to eye on anything. I hated being in any sit-down dinner environment. It made me antsy. Made my skin itch. I *needed* to be on the move, hands hankering for a task to keep my mind steady. I also detested small talk, especially when the questions always turned to me.

"Are you seeing anyone?" Mum always asked, hope shining in her gray-blue eyes.

"How's work?" Dad would typically counter, searching for any reason to be proud of me. As a retired general practitioner and army sergeant, Jim Macabe expected big things from his children. Callum was a vet; not a doctor but close enough. Alastair had followed in the family line, working as a GP in Glasgow. Heather, a mother to twins, also got his old-fashioned seal of approval. And I . . . well, I let my eyes wander around the malting room. I worked at a run-down whisky distillery that I would never own, making less and less profit each year.

The differences were staggering.

Searching for any opportunity to change the subject, I asked Callum about his date from last weekend. He'd driven all the way to Inverness to meet the lass—a little extreme maybe, but the dating pool could be limited on an island with more livestock than people. He grinned boyishly around his sandwich. "I got home early Monday morning, we'll leave it at that."

A pang of envy shot through me like a bullet and for some bloody bizarre reason, April Murphy breathless and panting on the sofa came to mind again. I pushed the memory away at once. A person's mind went to strange places when they hadn't had sex in five years. Or was it six? Who was even counting at this point?

"So you're seeing her again?" I continued, voice harsher than it should have been.

He scoffed around his food. "Absolutely not. We had fun, not enough for another six-hour round trip, mind you."

"God forbid." I chuckled. "I suppose it's a good thing Jess has

53

a better offer for you. Though I can't be certain if the offer was for her granddaughter or herself."

"Jessica Brown might be the singular woman on this island I'd consider settling down with."

April's face flashed behind my lids again, this time laughing, letting Boy burrow into her hand. This was becoming a problem. *Even more reason to avoid her.*

LIKE ANY GOOD MEDDLESOME FAMILY, AS SOON AS MY brother left, my sister appeared. Blond hair swaying around her chin as she hopped down from her Land Rover. *What did a guy have to do to sulk in peace?* I could already feel a headache coming on.

Boy's tail wagged ferociously, pulling himself up onto his hind legs before she was even fully inside, as if he hadn't just spent fifteen minutes under my brother's attention. "How's my favorite nephew?" she cooed, squishing his cheeks together. "And my favorite brother, of course."

Yeah, she definitely wanted something. "Two Macabe siblings in one day, I'm starting to feel extra special. What's up?" I grunted.

Her small nose wrinkled. "I can't just drop by to see my brother?"

The guilt was instantaneous. "Of course you can, I'm sorry. I have a lot going on and Callum just dropped by to guilt-trip me into family dinner."

"*Ahh*, good old family guilt. If it helps, Emily is going through this phase of putting peas up her nose, maybe that will take the heat off you. Or I could dye my hair blue and remind Dad that I'm the screwup of the family."

I glowered. "You are not a screwup. And you know they love being grandparents." What I didn't say was our father would never be disappointed with Heather because he didn't expect as much from a daughter as he did a son. Sexist as hell, but that was just the way it was. Raising two beautiful girls while working two jobs, my sister was a fucking superhero. "And no rescue necessary. I am curious about the nose thing, though. Is it one pea per nostril, or as many as she can fit?"

She blew out an exhausted breath. "Who the hell knows, I'm just thankful the fascination seems to end with small vegetables. I don't have time for a trip to the emergency room."

She seemed stressed out. "Do you want tea?" I didn't drink tea or coffee, but I was sure some tea bags lurked in the back of a cupboard somewhere.

"No." Her car keys jingled in her hand. "I have to get the girls from school soon, I just wanted to check if it's still okay to pick them up on Friday? I have a shift at the pub."

"Of course. I collect them every Friday." Ever since her son of a bitch ex-husband up and deserted his family.

"*Right.*" She hesitated. "So . . . Guess who I had lunch with this afternoon?"

I frowned, thinking I'd missed part of the conversation. "Uhh . . . June? Juniper?"

"April Sinclair." At my flat expression, she hurried on. "Don't play dumb, I know you've seen her."

Oh, I'd seen her all right. *Shirt rucked. Legs bare. Lacy bra in my bedside drawer.* "Murphy," I choked. "Her last name is Murphy." I didn't know why that little detail bugged me so much.

"Whatever. We had lunch. Well, tea and cake technically."

"Why?"

"Because we're friends."

"When was the last time she spoke to you?"

She folded her arms defensively. "I don't know, the same time *I* spoke to *her*—three years ago maybe."

"So not that good of friends," I pointed out.

She ignored my snide comment. "You know what else? She looked really pretty too." She'd always been really pretty, every man on the planet was well aware of that fact. It was hardly news. "Of course, you already knew that," she continued.

Picking up my pace by the metal vat, I went back to stirring, shifting the grain into the water with more force than necessary. "Whatever you're trying to say, Heather, spit it out. You know I hate word games."

Her breath whistled. "She said you were like this."

My heart gave a painful thump. "She mentioned me?" My fingers flexed around the wood.

"Yep. She said you were mean to her." *Mean*. The world rolled around in my brain. "And you know what I said to her? I said, 'That's strange, my big, lovable brother can be a little gruff, but never mean.'"

"Get to the point," I gritted out, hating that I was only proving her right.

"I want to make sure you're all right."

"I'm fine. Just busy." *Too busy for this*, I almost snarled, only just swallowing the words.

She held up both her hands. "Fine. I'll get out of your hair."

"That's not what I meant—" I took a step toward her.

She halted at the door. "All I wanted to say is, I know you have a lot going on here, but try to go easy on April. She tried to hide it today, but she seemed really sad."

Sad. I filed the word away, right next to *mean*.

"She should be sad, her grandfather just died." I knew if I had any chance of convincing April to sell me the distillery, I needed to play nice. Normally I was good at playing nice. No one would call me friendly, but dammit, I could be agreeable. I'd made agreeable a bloody art form. April hadn't even been here for twenty-four hours and I already felt more agitated than I had in years.

"Exactly." She left me with that parting shot.

Stalking across the malting room, I yanked the lever off and hit the timer on the wall for twelve hours. With Boy at my side, we went straight to the dunnage, my body craving the punishing strain of shifting and hauling barrels.

Sad. The word struck me again and I slammed the door behind me, old hinges protesting under the force. I was in near darkness and the cool air pricked my skin. Even the scent of whisky, wood, and damp earth wasn't enough to calm me.

Whisky casks were piled three-high on wooden stilts. The new product was on rotation in the front and some as old as forty years sat maturing in the very back of the warehouse. Stalking down the row, I ran a palm over the roughened wood. "Sad," I grunted below my breath, gripping a single cask and rolling its weight a quarter-turn, all the while hearing April's brilliant laugh from the night before. I didn't think I'd seen her sad a day in her life.

I was fourteen years old the first time I truly took note of April.

Dragged by my mother to the yearly Christmas fair, I spent the entire evening crawling out of my skin. There were too many people, too much chatter. Christmas music blared and the heat from the hideous knitted sweater she'd forced us all to wear made me light-headed. When the concert began, I was relieved by the darkness. My mum performed with her church choir; a mixture of traditional hymns ending with an energetic rendition of "Rudolph, the Red-Nosed Reindeer" complete with a dance routine that had everyone around the town hall laughing. Just when I'd thought *finally, we can leave,* a twelve-year-old April took to the stage dressed in a long, old-fashioned nightdress, red curls barely contained in a thick braid down her back. I recognized her of course, Kinleith was a village of a few hundred people. But other than being my wee sister's friend, I'd never really registered her presence until she walked confidently out onto that stage as though in a daze. Sleepwalking, I realized. She was pretending to sleepwalk.

Confused murmurs passed through the audience. April paid them no mind and fell to her knees, scrubbing red-stained hands together and crying, "Out, damn spot! Out, I say!" The entire village—including me—had watched, utterly rapt, as she transformed into Lady Macbeth with blood on her hands. To this day, I had no idea if the performance was actually good. I remembered thinking it was bloody odd and a little out of place when she'd fallen to her knees and wept beside the cradle of baby Jesus, the Rudolph song still ringing in our ears. But I'd also been in awe. The thought of standing before those people—*talking* in front of them—left me in a cold sweat. But for April? Those few minutes she'd shone brighter than the sun, and I'd known even then that a person like her was too big for a place like this.

My thoughts went to Kier next, how suddenly frail he'd become toward the end, how he'd barely had enough energy to drag himself out of bed in the morning, let alone wash and dress himself. I remembered the way his lower lip trembled when he spoke of her, refusing to meet my eye when he admitted he wouldn't ask her to come home again because she had better things to do than take care of an old man like him.

So, no. April Murphy had no right to be sad.

6

APRIL

Invisible String – Taylor Swift

I got my first acting gig at nineteen years old. An advert for a frozen food company that never even made it to television. It was while leaving the small filming studio—which turned out to be nothing more than a taped-up green screen in a run-down London office block—that I bumped into Aaron Williams. He was a talent manager who, after seeing my audition, invited me for a meeting at his agency. When I thought back on that starry-eyed teenager, clutching Aaron Williams's business card to her chest the entire tube ride home like she'd won a golden ticket, I didn't feel anything. Not fury or regret. The man who'd started my career had ultimately been the one to end it, and it held a poetic kind of irony the sick part of me could appreciate.

I recalled the confidence I'd felt all those years ago as I approached the distillery for the second morning in a row. It was so early, the morning fog hadn't yet cleared the clifftop. Whirls of white cloud gave the land an ethereal atmosphere, like you could stumble upon a fairy sunbathing atop a lily pad.

Approaching the door, I prepared myself by envisioning I was on a red carpet wearing Vera Wang instead of my mud-stained sneakers. I knocked loudly and waited. When no answer came, I knocked again, knuckles rattling against the thick wood. I'd spotted what could only be Mal's Land Rover on my morning walk—I knew he was in there. This time, I would get more than two words in with Malcolm Macabe and charm him like I did everyone else.

With Dudley tucked against my chest in his sling, I balanced a thermos of coffee and lemon muffins I'd whipped up last night while bingeing episodes of *Grey's Anatomy* in one hand.

Some might say manipulation was afoot. I called it bringing out the big guns. If he didn't like my muffins, I had a dozen more of Elsie's recipes to get through; cherry scones, blueberry cheese-cake, coffee and walnut cake. I had nothing but time and endless bags of sugar.

A dog barked on the other side of the door followed by a hissed, "Quiet." Then silence.

Oh, hell no. My fist met the wood again, knocking in quick succession like an annoying little woodpecker. "Malcolm, I can hear you," I called, still knocking. "I can do this all day." My pounding fist sped until the wood gave way and I drew back just quick enough to avoid thumping him in the chest.

Malcolm appeared harried, hair flattened on one side and rumpled on the other, like he'd rolled straight out of bed. I also begrudgingly noted that he looked sort of beautiful in the morning light. Or he would, if it weren't for the tight scowl scoring deep lines across his forehead. I was certain his mouth was also

61

twisted in displeasure, but it was hidden beneath the thick beard I wanted to graze my fingers across. He wore more plaid; today's was faded red with a frayed hem, sleeves pushed up past his elbows and a white T-shirt beneath, already spattered with black marks. I wondered if his clothes always looked this way, worn and dirtied from hard work. I wasn't usually a rough-and-tumble, plaid-and-denim kind of girl, but Malcolm wore it like a second skin. It made me conscious of the straight-leg trousers and high-neck blouse I wore.

Ignoring his obvious annoyance, I thrust the plate of muffins at him and flashed my most award-winning smile. "Why, good morning, Malcolm. Muffin?"

He didn't even look at it. "I'm allergic to dairy." At his heel, his golden retriever attempted to burrow through the minuscule gap between him and the door. Mal batted him back with a soft hand.

"Then I think Heather might be trying to kill you, because she said they're your favorite."

"Seems to be the theme of the week," he said and his gaze lowered, taking in Dudley strapped across my chest. "What the hell is that thing?"

I assumed he didn't mean the dog, so I answered, "A dog sling."

I could have sworn he muttered *ridiculous* beneath his breath. Then louder, "Does the wee guy not have legs?" Sarcasm. Definite sarcasm.

"He has a strict sleep schedule and doesn't fully wake up until eleven," I joked. He rolled his eyes like it was the stupidest thing he'd ever heard. That was fine, if he needed me to play the ditzy little actress with her dog in a bag, I'd do just that. Wiggling the plate, I smiled again, showing my entire top row of teeth. "Are you going to take a muffin?"

"I already ate."

"Oh . . . well, can I come in?" I started to peer around the door and his hand came up, gripping the frame.

"No."

"Why?"

He sighed. "I'm busy."

"Perhaps I can help, I wore my most comfortable flats."

His gaze cut down my body, taking in my clothing. The assessment didn't feel positive or negative, more affirming. "No." He started to close the door but I caught it with my foot.

"What if I promise not to get in the way?" I lifted the thermos. "I brought coffee."

He paused, considering, and . . . pushed the door wide. *Ding, ding, ding. Ladies and gentlemen, we have a winner.*

He stepped back, giving me room to pass, and when the door closed, he shifted back further still, thumbs rubbing over the tips of his long fingers. He seemed nervous.

My smile was bemused as I unloaded the muffins and coffee on the windowsill and released Dudley from his sling. As soon as his paws touched the ground, he and the golden retriever bounded at one another, an array of yips filling the air as they jumped and tumbled. My insides felt like melted marshmallows as I watched.

"That dog only has three legs," Mal said from behind me.

I whirled to face him, my hands clutched beneath my chin, pulling out my best Scarlett O'Hara. "Oh my stars, how did I not notice?" My smooth southern drawl echoed in the stark space.

Mal shook his head, bending to sink a hand into the giant vat of water we hovered beside, the single piece of equipment in the long room.

"Oh, come on! That one was hilarious."

"I think we have differing definitions of hilarious."

I stuck my tongue out at his back. When he continued to ignore me, fiddling with various dials on the wall, I took that to mean he wasn't kicking me out anytime soon. I poured out the coffee, offering him a tin mug that he accepted with a swipe and set beside his feet. "What's your dog's name?" I asked, my focus straying back to the dogs who'd melted in a fur-filled heap on the floor.

"Boy," he clipped.

That made sense. "When I heard you call him that I assumed it was a nickname . . . why did you name him 'Boy'?"

I could tell by the hunch in his back that my questions agitated him. "I didn't plan on keeping him, so I called him 'Boy' and it stuck."

"Not keeping him?" My attention snapped to the gorgeous dog again. "How could anyone not want him?"

"Like I said, I'm busy. I don't have time for distractions."

That was definitely a pointed comment. I could take a hint. Easing away, I used the distance to observe what I knew was the malting floor. It looked exactly as I remembered. Darkly paved, with several supporting beams down the center. Small hatched windows lining either side of the structure, offering an uninterrupted view of the craggy coastline that gave way to rolling blue waves. Hooks hung beside the door holding instruments of various sizes—I couldn't name the purpose for half of them. I was running a finger over the prongs of a rake when he surprised me.

"If you're here to persuade me to let you sell this place out from under me, a cup of coffee and a muffin isn't going to cut it. That is the plan, right?" He still had his back to me, stirring the barley in the vat as water started to rush in.

How did he know? As though he'd heard my unspoken question, he snickered, and it was a sad replica of a laugh. "Your eyes have been flashing with pound signs since you got here, princess."

Princess. He spat it like an insult.

"I'd planned at least a week's worth of muffins, actually." I sniffed. "How about a carrot cake? Would that work?"

"When has a carrot cake ever convinced anyone to do anything?"

"You haven't tasted mine," I shot back, and I could have sworn his ears flushed. I sidled closer, tracing a finger along the lip of the basin. The liquid inside turned a light brown as water mixed with the barley. "This looks pretty new."

He tensed, flicking me a look over his elbow. "Aye, I replaced it two summers ago."

"You did, or Kier did?"

He knew what I was asking. "*I did.*" The syllables were like a clash of metal. He looked disgusted. "You seriously plan to sell this place for parts, like a broken-down car?"

"I don't want to." Could he honestly think I was so heartless I would sell off Kier's legacy without a thought?

He faced me full-on, eyes gunmetal gray as his temper rose. "Then don't. Sell it to me."

"To you?" Hope sparked like a struck match. "You have the funds?"

His chin dipped, boots scuffing across the floor. If I knew him well enough, I'd say he was embarrassed. "Not quite. Kier and I had an agreement, I was giving him a portion of my wage every month with the understanding that ownership would transfer to me. He knew you'd never move back permanently."

That hope sank so suddenly, my knees almost buckled alongside it. *Kier, what did you do?*

"You were buying the distillery from Kier?" I needed to hear it again. Needed to clarify the depth of the shitstorm Kier had dropped me in.

"Yes."

I licked my dry lips. "How much did you pay?"

His head tilted. "Close to twenty thousand."

"Twenty thousand!" *Kier had taken twenty thousand from him.* I stumbled back a step, catching myself on the side of the vat. *Twenty thousand pounds.* That couldn't be right. Deep down though, I knew it was.

How did I begin to explain to this man who'd been loyal to my grandfather for so many years that Kier never had any intention of selling him the distillery because I already owned it? That I'd purchased the manor and all the land that it stood on to bail Kier out of his gambling debt, back when I'd been comfortable and foolish enough to think the big paychecks wouldn't come with an expiration date.

"That's not—I can't—" I couldn't get the words out.

Malcolm's jaw clenched and those eyes became chips of ice. "You mean you don't want to."

I could have laughed at the irony. I wanted nothing more than to sell the distillery to him. It would solve everything. But he had no means to buy it. Hands on my hips, I retreated to the window, downing my now cool coffee in a single gulp as I raced through my options. This had to be salvageable. I refused to be the grim reaper for both of us.

Malcolm was right, the distillery should belong to him. Now I knew he'd given all that money to Kier in good faith, there was no way I could find a new buyer.

I glanced around again, an idea starting to take form. Whisky was big right now, and tourists from all over the world were flocking to Scotland, Juniper had said so herself. I might not be able to sell to him now, but one day in the future, once we became profitable, maybe I could.

"Okay, just hear me out. I might have a solution."

He crossed his arms and boy, were they impressive. "And what's that?"

"Together, we get this place running." I flung out a hand. "You clearly know what you're doing, and I—"

"It's already running," he snipped.

I mirrored his posture, folding my arms until we were like boxers in a ring, sizing one another up. "And what was your turnover last month?"

"What do you know about turnover, princess?"

I let the nickname roll right over me. "I know this place can't be making a lot, Kier's lawyer told me Kinleith Distillery had ceased trading," I said, gesturing to the crate of empty bottles beside the door. "You don't even have a label on the bottle!"

"It doesn't need a label."

"How will anyone who isn't a local know what they're drinking?"

He was silent for so long I thought he wasn't going to answer. "We don't need tourists."

"Oh, Jesus." Pressing the heels of my hands into my eyeballs, I prayed for strength I no longer possessed. "It's like the dark ages, you need me more than I thought. Do you even have a website?"

"*Why* would we need a website?"

Well, that answered that. My laugh was just this side of crazed. "If you want me to sell to you, we need to actually make an income—"

"There is no *we*."

I pushed as much steel into my voice as I could muster. "We work together, those are my conditions. Take it or leave it."

Just when I thought his scowl couldn't cut the lines of his harsh features any deeper, he proved me wrong. "Don't pretend like you're giving me a choice."

That was the closest to a "yes" I was ever going to get. "Wonderful." I clapped my hands together, drawing the attention of the dogs who'd taken to snuggling together in a patch of sun, Dudley playing the part of the little spoon. "This is going to be so much fun."

From his side of the room, Malcolm observed me like one might examine a foreign body beneath a microscope. Like he didn't know how he'd come to be in this situation and couldn't fathom a way out of it. "Why do you care so much?" he finally asked. I knew the answer mattered to him.

I settled on the easiest explanation. The truth, but not quite. "It's Kier's legacy . . . this place meant more to him than anything."

"Not anything," Malcolm replied. And for the first time, he looked directly at me. He gave me no time to prepare myself as he stripped me bare, simultaneously seeing too much and not enough.

Like a default setting, I fell back on that smile that set everyone else at ease and started for the door. "I'll see you tomorrow . . . partner. Come on, Dudley." He gave Boy one final lick and followed me out the door.

7

MAL

Sunlight – Hozier

I wished I could say I'd dressed in the first shirt my hands had found, instead of changing three times this morning. I wished I could say I'd had a full night's sleep, not the tossing and turning I did until even Boy had grown agitated. I wished I could say I wasn't staring at the door right now.

But if I said any of those things, I'd be a damn liar.

Knee-deep in the vat, I relished the sound of metal cutting through grain, shoulders rolling as I transferred spades of chitted barley, sprouted and ready for germination, to a wheelbarrow.

Ewan had come in a few hours early this morning. Laying the grain was one of the few days a month when an extra pair of hands became so essential I allowed myself to pay him overtime.

I didn't even pretend to listen as he jabbered on about some hiking trip he'd planned next weekend. "—we only have the two days, so won't complete the full ninety-six miles, but I reckon we'll get at least to Rannoch Moor—"

"That's great, how about you start spreading."

Untouched by the bite in my words, he gave a little two-fingered salute, finally lifting the rake he'd spent the majority of the morning leaning against. "Sure thing, bossman."

I hopped over the lip, boots crunching on stray kernels as I wheeled the heavy barrel to the furthest corner and tipped the grain straight into a mound on the malting floor. Ewan got right to work, probably sensing I was pulled tighter than a rubber band. Even Boy had sunk down quietly beside the door, chewing dutifully on an old toy he usually wouldn't spare a glance.

I repeated the process again, sweating as I put my back into it. I knew April hadn't been serious about helping out. This job was tough . . . dirty. The princess would never lower herself to this kind of manual labor. But she could have had the decency to let me know instead of wasting my time. *I'm relieved really*, I told myself, grunting as grain hit the floor at Ewan's feet again, raining down quicker than he could rake it. A woman like April had no business hanging around here. She was too sunny, smiled too much, laughed too freely. I supposed that was easy when everything went your way.

I'd loaded my fourth barrel when a commotion at the door jerked me to a stop. Boy's tail wagged, nose snuffling through the small gap along the bottom. "No, Boy," I whispered. He looked back at me over his shoulder, features flat in an expression of "oh I'm definitely gonna."

"Don't you fucking dare," I warned, grasping for any shred of authority I had left.

He ignored me. Head tipped back and front paws beating at the wood, he howled a siren call that reverberated off the walls. Ewan dropped his rake with a clatter, hands shielding both his ears. "Bleeding hell, who's out there?" He made a move to check.

"You stay here," I said too quickly. "Keep working . . . I'll only be a minute." Refusing to be left behind too, Boy barged around me, almost taking my legs out as the door cracked and he bounded onto the gravel. "Who isn't trying to kill me this week?" I muttered, righting myself on the threshold.

His elated hops quickly slowed when his new best friends were nowhere to be seen. Then his ears pricked and he raced off toward the office, tail whipping at the closed door. "There's no one in there, Boy!" I called, trailing after him. "The door's locked." His answering whine said otherwise.

Realization was a cold splash of water. *No, she wouldn't.*

Of course she would. And when I peered through the small hatch window, there she was, April *bloody* Murphy, sitting at Kier's desk chair, rifling through every single drawer of his ancient desk as though they belonged to her. I groped for my keys, flinging the door wide. She didn't even glance up as it crashed against the brick.

Boy dove ahead of me, greeting Dudley with an excited whine. "How?" Ire practically oozed from my lips.

Her small hands clasped the arms of the chair as she spun to face me, like she sat on a throne rather than an office chair with shit lumbar support. "The window," she stated. *No way.* The window was more than four feet off the ground, she could only be five herself. "It's a lot lower on the outside," she continued, reading exactly where my thoughts had gone.

"Because the entire lower floor is laid below ground level to aid temperature control."

"The more you know, I guess." Her head tipped as she leant back. The shorts had made a comeback, tiny little navy ones that offered a full view of strong calves and smooth pale thighs as she kicked one leg over the other. On her feet were open-toed sandals, tiny square toenails painted the same baby pink as her fingernails.

I looked away, taking in the mess on the desktop. "You sure have a thing for breaking and entering through windows."

"Did you miss the part where we discussed how the distillery belongs to me?" I detected no malice in her voice, just harsh facts sugarcoated in her candy floss tone.

"You could have asked for the key."

A deep red brow winged up, making her freckles dance across the bridge of her nose and cheekbones. Her nose was small, as straight as an arrow, ending in a delicate elfin tip. No hint of the slightly aquiline nose she'd been born with remained. "Would you have given it to me?"

Yes, if it meant you didn't risk hurting yourself. I'm not a total bastard. What I actually said was, "Poking your nose around wasn't part of our agreement."

"But working together was."

"You call clandestine explorations 'working together'?" Her full pink lips tipped at the corners, revealing a dangerous, beguiling little grin. I filed it away for future examination.

"Clandestine," she repeated, swishing the swivel chair in a full circle. "I like that word." Heat crept up my neck. "I like the way you look when you say it."

I lurched. Too slow to cover the reaction her words spurred. She had to be joking, attempting to throw me off-balance. I held my ground, speaking to the wall above her head. "You can't flirt your way out of this."

Her soft laugh touched each corner of the room. "But it's so much fun."

"Debatable."

Something rustled. "How about breakfast?"

I smelled something mouthwateringly sweet, cinnamon and sugar. Nope. I wasn't falling for that again. I'd eaten the entire plate of lemon muffins she left behind yesterday, and the little witch knew it too. Bypassing the offer completely, I nodded to the door. "Come on, then."

"Come on what?"

Maybe I was a bastard, because something danced inside my chest at her confusion. "We have work to do."

"I am working—"

I tutted sadly, starting up the steps. "It's all hands on deck today, I'm afraid." As expected, she didn't follow. I waited outside the door and called back, "We're wasting time, princess."

She appeared a second later, looking wonderfully disgruntled. "What does all hands on deck mean, exactly?"

I smirked, even though it pulled at my scar and made the result crooked. "It means, prepare to get those pretty little hands dirty."

She snorted, the thick braid that contained her curls whipping over her shoulder. "I'm not dressed for manual labor."

No. She wasn't. "Probably should have thought about that."

Her eyes flicked down nervously, square little teeth biting into her bottom lip. I sighed. "Wait right there."

I glared down at Boy as he followed me to the dunnage, his tail flicking happily. "Little traitor. Don't think I didn't see you lick her hand." If anything, his tail wagged more. "Oh yeah? You think she's pretty? Well . . . no chicken for dinner. Just plain old dry biscuits, you're going to hate it."

We both knew the threat held no real weight.

I FOUND APRIL EXACTLY WHERE I LEFT HER, STARING DOWN AT her phone with a little crease between her brows. "Everything all right?" I didn't know why I asked. I didn't want any details about her life.

If she was surprised, she didn't show it. "Everything's great. Just a text from my friend Sydney." She slipped the phone into her back pocket.

Sydney. Was that a man's name or a woman's? *Doesn't matter*, I reminded myself. The distillery was the only thing that mattered, and I would play this little game with her for as long as it took before she grew bored and went back to London or Beverly Hills or wherever else.

Shaking out the overalls I'd retrieved from the dunnage, I held them out. "For your clothes," I said.

"Oh." Her fingers curled around the gray material. "Thank you." She seemed genuinely touched by the gesture.

I shifted on my feet. She shouldn't be, they were huge and stank of mildew. "They'll get the job done."

She nodded and set an expensive-looking purse on the stones, then lifted a leg, fiddling with the complicated looking strap around her ankle. *Jesus, we'll be here all day.* Before I could think better of it, I whipped the material from her hand and lowered to my knees, spreading the fabric wide. "Leg."

"What?" Her question sounded dazed but my cheeks burned too fiercely to look at her.

"Leg," I said again, clearing my throat. "Put your damn leg in the hole, princess." She placed one hand on my shoulder for balance. Her foot slid through the material, delicate bone and tendon brushing against my thumb. I squeezed the fabric. Moved to the next leg. She had freckles there too. Tan little starbursts on each of her toes. I could have let go then, but I eased the material slowly up her legs until my hand brushed her inner thigh. We both jerked and I released the fabric. She didn't catch it in time and it pooled around her feet again. She scrambled for it, ripping it up her legs as though she were naked. I didn't help this time. I didn't move from my knees either.

What the hell was happening? I could barely breathe.

She'd closed half the snaps by the time I climbed to my feet. I still didn't trust myself to speak, just turned and headed back to the malting room, trusting her to follow. A huge part of me hoped she didn't.

8

APRIL
Sparks – Coldplay

Y ou've been gone ages," a voice complained as Malcolm marched ahead, ducking his head in order to make it through the low door. Peering over his shoulder, I was surprised to find a gangly boy in his early twenties—hair as red and curly as my own—dripping with sweat while clutching a rake like a lifeline.

"Had something to sort," Malcolm's deep baritone replied, giving me chills. *That voice.* When I ignored the words that came with it, that voice *did* things to me. Delicious things. He should narrate the smutty audiobooks I loved to listen to. It would be like having a sexier James McAvoy whisper in your ear. And James McAvoy was exceedingly hot.

Then his meaning registered. Was I the *something* here?

The young lad was clearly thinking the same thing, because his eyes shot to me and screwed. When I smiled, he blinked. "You're . . . you're April Sinclair."

My expression faltered and I knew Malcolm caught it. Hating feeling caught out, I pushed as much cheer into my voice as I could muster and held my hand out. "The one and only." *Christ.* Even my eyes wanted to roll. "I usually smell better than this, I promise." My free hand picked at the gray overalls that swamped my frame.

He took my offered hand, squeezing my fingers as he pumped it enthusiastically. "I know . . . I mean, you look like you'd smell wonderful." His cheeks turned cherry red. "I mean . . ."

I laughed, I couldn't help it. "I know what you mean." I looked back to Malcolm but he was already halfway into the large vat, spade in hand, pretending we didn't exist.

"I'm sorry," I said to the boy. "Our surly overlord neglected to tell me your name."

"Ewan . . . Ewan Davies," he replied eagerly.

"Nice to meet you, Ewan." I meant it, his features were kind. Oversize in a way that made him look younger than he likely was.

"Now the pleasantries are over, how about some work gets done? It's why I pay you after all," Malcolm grouched, not even looking up from his shoveling.

Beside me, Ewan jolted and threw me an apologetic glance. "Right. Sorry, boss."

And I—I just stood there. I wasn't going to let this grumbly giant intimidate me in my own establishment. I knew it was bold to come in after twelve years away and swing my metaphorical dick around, but it was literally the single piece of leverage I had. "You're going to pay me?" I said, turning to him fully.

He paused, taking a moment to fold his hands atop the spade's large handle. Fine dots of sweat covered his nose and sharp cheekbones. "I can't pay you."

I pouted in a way I knew would irritate him. "What if I need to buy a new handbag?"

Gray eyes flicked to my lips. The look didn't feel critical this time. "I'm certain you can find a lonely islander to buy one for you. If the rumors are correct, you love a sugar daddy."

I held back my flinch. The rumors were *not* correct. "Been reading up on me, boss?"

I'd suspected the second the nickname left Ewan's lips moments ago that Malcolm hated it. The flexing of his jaw confirmed it. That, or I'd hit a little too close to the mark with my accusation. His gaze fell. "Don't ask stupid questions, princess. Just get to work."

My hands went to my hips. "It's a little hard if I don't know what I'm doing."

"Ewan," he snapped, and the boy practically fell over his feet in his haste to help me.

"Here, grab a rake off the wall." He pointed to the rack of equipment. "You'll probably want to start with a small one." Once I'd selected a small rake with a smooth wooden handle, he motioned for me to follow him. "Bossman is pouring the chitted barley, that's the hardest bit. It's our job to rake it into parallel lines. When it's warm like this you want to rake it thin, aim between eight and twelve centimeters deep."

I observed the work Ewan had already completed, a neat line of golden grain. "How hard can it be?" I could have sworn I heard a snort from the other side of the room.

Ignoring him, I threw myself in.

AS IT TURNED OUT, IT WAS PRETTY FREAKING HARD.

After the fourth grunt of "rake in *straight* lines, princess," I was ready to throw myself on his back and finish the job I'd started in the kitchen three nights ago.

I was sweaty. A knot the size of Glasgow had lodged its way

between my shoulder blades and I had a splinter that stung every time I gripped the damn rake. We weren't even halfway finished.

Other than a fine sheen across his forehead that only served to make him look more appealing—objectively, y'know, if you were into grumbling Gruffalos, which I most certainly was not—Malcolm looked exactly as he had two hours ago. It made me seethe inside.

At least Ewan was in as bad a shape as I was. He paused every five minutes or so to complain that "it never gets any easier" to whoever was willing to listen. I was two complaints away from shrieking "shut your damn mouth, Ewan," but instead, I settled for biting my lip and keeping my head down. Ewan seemed like a crier.

I'd felt Malcolm's eyes on me only a handful of times and pretended not to notice. I knew what he was doing . . . working me to the bone, assuming I'd throw in the towel. Didn't he know a woman in the public eye had to develop the skin of a shark? I couldn't count the number of times I'd been told I had a "face for the stage." Or offered a higher salary if I lost ten pounds before shooting started. I'd had directors scream in my face. Costars come on to me while their wives waited in their trailer. Millions of people had seen me naked on screen and made judgments on my body—there was a chance that list included *him*. If he wanted me to quit, he was going to have to try a lot harder.

"Why are we doing this again?" I asked, resting the instrument of torture against the wall so I could re-braid my sweaty hair.

Ewan, seemingly eager to show off his knowledge, jumped in. "We are trying to trick the barley into germinating. That's why it's important you rake it evenly, or the germination won't be even."

80

Smart. "Do you ever wonder who figures this stuff out, like who was just sitting at home and went 'I wonder what happens if I soak this barley in water for three days then lay it out on the floor'?"

It was Mal who surprised me by answering, "The Scandinavians. Early evidence shows they were the first to discover malted barley to brew beer."

"Why am I not surprised you know that?" His eyes met mine, uncertainty turning them cold. And despite the torture I'd endured this morning at his request, I needed him to know I wasn't teasing him. "It's cool. It's important to know the history of things, especially if it's something important to you."

Instead of softening like I'd hoped, he turned away as though I hadn't spoken. I tried my best not to let it get to me. I knew it wasn't entirely personal. As a teen, Malcolm had always been quiet, if not a wee bit kinder. So I did what I did best; I picked up that infernal rake and I talked.

Starting on the fresh pile Malcolm had just emptied out for me, I said, "This reminds me of a film I did once—" Ewan halted working, all ears. "A period drama about a young woman found walking the woods of a country estate with no memories."

"My mum loves that movie," Ewan said at once, then instantly flushed again. Bless him and his pale skin. I appeared entirely naked in one scene—well, except for an extremely itchy merkin glued to my vagina. The scene he was most definitely recalling this very moment.

"*Anyway* . . . there was an intricate scene out in the fields where we had to cut wheat with scythes. The original plan was to use body doubles for the bulk of the physical labor, and me being a

81

complete novice insisted on doing all of it myself. The first day, at least. Any creative integrity faded real fast when I woke up the next morning and couldn't use my arms." I chuckled. "And when the film finally premiered, I watched that scene a hundred times trying to pick myself out from the body double, you couldn't even tell!"

Ewan launched into a series of follow-up questions. *Was your costar nice?* Yes. *Is being an actor as glamorous as it seems?* No. *Have you stolen anything from a set?* Yes.

I didn't mind the questions, it was human nature to be fascinated by fame. People loved getting a peek behind the curtain.

Malcolm, on the other hand, could only take so much. I'd barely even started recounting the time I'd accidentally kissed George Clooney backstage at the Oscars when he interrupted, dropping the wheelbarrow with a loud crack. "If you two aren't even going to pretend to work, at least use this time for your lunch break."

Ewan and I glanced sheepishly at one another as Mal stalked to a bag propped beside the door and pulled out a wrapped sandwich. Malcolm ate like he did everything else: with focus and ferocity. It's like he was racing himself to eat it quicker than he had the day before.

"How long do we get?" I whispered to Ewan.

"Thirty minutes, though the boss only takes about five."

Thirty whole minutes. "Use them wisely," I replied, going to my own bag and pulling out my water bottle.

Ewan followed, retrieving his own packed lunch. "He's usually not this grumpy, I wonder what's gotten into him."

Hmm . . . I wonder. I wasn't sure if I should be flattered that

I apparently had such a lasting effect on his mood. Taking another pull of water, I ran the back of my hand over my sweaty forehead and went to check on Dudley. Tired from playing, he and Boy had long since found a sunny patch to doze away the morning. I filled his little travel bowl with water, watching with heart eyes as they took turns to drink.

"I think they might be in love," I said to Malcolm.

"They're dogs," he replied after a beat.

"Well, I think it's cute." I stroked them both, ruffling their sun-soaked cheeks. "Boy doesn't have any allergies, does he?" Another huff I assumed meant no, so I handed them both a treat. *He thinks I'm ridiculous.*

Suddenly needing some air, I decided to take the remainder of my break out on the bank. Lying among the purple heather with both dogs at my feet, I nibbled on homemade granola bars, reading one of my favorite bodice rippers that I'd never dare let Malcolm see, *The Duke's Promise.* It was bliss.

I probably should have used the time to dig the splinter from my finger, because by the time I returned to work, it was starting to throb.

Tiredness made Ewan and me a lot more subdued in the afternoon and we had the entire floor covered within a couple of hours, every inch of white concrete hidden beneath a blanket of gold that smelled like breakfast cereal. The scent reminded me of Kier. I would breathe it in every time he hugged me, pressing my nose into his strong chest.

Settling my rake against the wall to shake out my achy hands, I watched Malcolm run the back of a broom over the grain, evening out the spots we'd apparently laid too thick. "What happens next?" I rubbed at my fingers, wincing when my thumb passed over the splinter.

"We lay it out for six days, turning the grain once a day to ensure the germination is—What? What's wrong?"

"Huh?" My head shot up. He was scowling at me. "Oh." I waved my injured hand. "It's nothing, just a splinter. I have some tweezers up at the manor, I'll take care of it—"

But he'd already swiped up my hand, tugging me closer to get a better look. The top of his head was level with my face and I got a whiff of his fresh shampoo. "You should have said something earlier."

"It's fine, it barely even hurts anymore—ahh!" A thick finger probed the wound's tiny entrance.

"Come. Ewan, you can take off." Hand shifting to encircle my wrist, Malcolm tugged me after him and I barely had a chance to wave goodbye to Ewan before we were into the pleasant afternoon sun. Neither of us spoke as we rounded the building, stopping beside a door I now knew led to his home. "Wait here."

I didn't, of course. Both of the dogs and I trailed him into his very tiny but charming home. There was stuff everywhere, but it didn't feel cluttered. Compact kitchen that gave way to a cozy sitting area, complete with a log burner I could picture Boy curled up before. Giant television that seemed to be a staple in any bachelor's home. I spared a glance to the humongous bed in the furthest point of the room, only long enough to see the dark navy sheets were neatly made. I hastily turned my attention then to the wood shelving taking up almost an entire wall, stuffed full of books and DVDs. I didn't know people still collected DVDs. Only

Malcolm's beleaguered sigh stopped me from inspecting every one of them.

Rummaging through a drawer, he nodded to a chair at the small dining table. "You might as well sit as you already invited yourself in."

"This is a really cute space," I said, perching on the rickety chair.

Grunt.

"How long have you lived here?"

"Long enough."

"Long enough for what?"

"Just—long enough." He slammed the drawer shut, a small first aid kit in his hand. "Put your hand on the table." I complied, biting my lip to hold back a laugh. I might've been the one with the splinter but he was like a bear with a thorn in his paw. Malcolm took the chair opposite. So narrow was the table, his knees knocked against mine. Unzipping the bag, he took out several small items, an alcohol wipe and a Band-Aid. "If you hurt yourself, you need to say something right away. When you work with your body, you have to take care of it. It's your most important tool."

Too distracted by the feel of his leg against mine, it took me a moment to notice the pair of wickedly sharp tweezers. Any fun I'd been having shriveled up and died at the sight of them.

My fingers curled in on themselves and I started to rise. "You know . . . I can totally take care of this myself. You probably have better things to do."

I didn't get very far. His hot flesh caught mine and my arse hit the seat. "Of course I'm going to take care of it, April. Now stop being a baby."

I wasn't sure if it was the fact he'd called me April and not "princess," or his insinuation that I was scared that made me relent. But when he cupped my palm in his much bigger one, bent in close and raised those tweezers, I looked away. They dug in with a sharp pinch. "Ahh—"

"You're fine."

I tugged instinctively and he held me tighter. "Ouch! That stings—"

"It wouldn't sting if you stopped wriggling—"

"Do you have press so hard—"

"Keep still."

"—ahhh!"

"Got it!" He held the huge splinter caught between the prongs triumphantly. "See, it's tiny, nothing to worry about."

"Nothing to worry about? You nearly removed my entire finger!"

I caught the barest hint of a crooked smirk on those full lips. "Please, enough of the drama, princess."

He peeled open the alcohol wipe and slathered it across my skin, causing another shout of protest. He actually laughed that time. *Laughed.* Well, it wasn't a laugh, more of a loud exhale, like an angry rhino. But I was taking it. A win was a bloody win. He peeled open a Band-Aid and wrapped it around my injured finger.

"There. You'll live to see another day." He smoothed it down one final time and set about packing away the first aid kit when I finally got a look at the bandage. It was a baby-pink princess Band-Aid. And I could not resist.

"Who knew you were such a big Disney fan?"

His cheeks turned pink and his fingers stilled. "I look after my nieces once a week."

"Right."

"I do! Every Friday afternoon."

With what I knew was a shit-eating grin, I gave his shoulder a pat. "Thanks for taking care of me."

"Making sure you don't lose a finger from your own carelessness isn't taking care of you." The frown was back in full force.

I stood. "Same time tomorrow?"

I waited for his answer. Just when I thought he wouldn't reply, he said, "Aye. And stop flirting with Ewan, it's not fair on the lad."

"What?" A laugh tore its way from my throat.

He folded his arms on the tabletop. "He doesn't understand you actors, he might think it means something." *You actors?* What the hell did that mean?

Deciding I didn't care to find out, I flashed him my flirtiest grin, brushing a finger down the grain of the wood only a hairbreadth from his hand. "When I'm flirting, *boss*, you'll know about it." I held his gaze until he swallowed. "Now . . . if you'll excuse me, I think I'll go and take a very long bubble bath."

9

APRIL
SNAP – Rosa Linn

How's it going at the distillery?" Heather asked the moment I settled with my coffee at Brown's the following weekend. I'd been touched when she had texted to invite me. I hadn't at all expected to be brought back into the fold quite so quickly after years away. It reminded me of what I'd always loved about this little community . . . they opened their arms to one another.

I shrugged, looking between June and Heather at their equally eager faces. "I've been hanging around all week—helping out." *When Malcolm lets me.*

"Yeah, Mal mentioned something about that, but I meant with Mal. Specifically."

"Oh, you know, he hates me." Any improvements I'd foolishly assumed we'd made that first day were quickly lost. If anything, he'd grown even surlier, grunting any time Ewan or I so much as spoke. It was even worse on the days Ewan didn't work. Under Malcolm's silent, stoic supervision, I'd turned the barley twice a day and painted dates on casks in the dunnage. All along, I sent sneaking looks at him rotating casks using a small forklift, a process that helped reduce the amount of liquid lost through evaporation, or so he'd told me when I asked. When he caught me watching, he'd told me, like a scolding father, that I wasn't (under any circumstance) to use, touch, or sit on the forklift . . . which of course in my brain translated to "April, you must use the forklift."

Lastly, Malcolm had taught me about the fermentation process. While mashing the barley, yeast was added to a sugary liquid called wort—yes, every part of this process sounded revolting—then transferred into a large container called a washback—*disgusting*—to ferment. After about fifty hours, when the top began to look a bit like porridge—again, *disgusting*—it was ready to be distilled.

The demonstration had taken thirty minutes with him pulling out little vials of liquid displaying the variations of alcohol content and showing me the shining copper still that he cleaned religiously every morning, whether or not it was used. He'd gotten me to sniff the wort, explaining how a trained nose would be able to properly pick out the level of fermentation. I'd quickly realized the only time Mal enjoyed talking was when he was talking about whisky, and though I'd only retained about 90 percent of the information, he was a wonderful teacher. He spoke slowly and thoroughly. When I asked questions, he didn't scorn them but answered thoughtfully. I was becoming so addicted to asking questions I made little notes during the evening of things to ask the next day. Pathetic, but I'd long ago accepted my insatiable need to be liked.

Oh, and outside of the distillery, there was the time he'd caught me climbing back up the steep path after a morning walk on the beach, Dudley's damp body tucked into his sling. *"You really shouldn't go down there, you'll hurt yourself on the rocks,"* he'd barked at me.

"He said that?" Heather asked.

"Okay . . . so it wasn't exactly a put-down, but it was more about the way he said it, how he looked at me."

"How did he look at you?"

"Like he couldn't believe he'd stopped to talk to someone who's so clearly an imbecile." And after I finished relaying the exact depth of his scowl—a seven on the Malcolm's Scowls chart I was putting together—June and Heather looked at each other.

Then June gave me a sympathetic smile while Heather clapped her hands together. "This is amazing," she crowed, laughing.

I looked to Juniper, certain I must have missed something. June just shook her head. "Ohhh no. I know what you're thinking, Heather. April just got here, you can't start that crap."

"Start what?" I asked.

"She's trying to set the two of you up."

I laughed so loudly I knew I was drawing attention. A real, rasping laugh that tore from the pits of my stomach. Until Heather said, "I'm not trying to set them up—I don't need to, my idiot big brother is clearly into you."

I pressed my cheeks into my hands, staring at her. "What's really scary is that I can't tell if you're joking."

"It's obvious."

"How?"

"My brother hardly talks to anyone, even his family."

I met June's eye again. She looked as dumbfounded as I surely did. "And?"

"And—" She dragged the word out. "He talks to you, you said so yourself. He wouldn't have warned you to be careful if he didn't care," she finished pointedly.

She may as well have been speaking Wookie for all the sense it made in my head. "I'm pretty sure he was avoiding the hassle of phoning an ambulance if I fell to my death. He's tolerating me. A fact he's made pretty obvious."

She was already shaking her head. "No. I'm telling you, this is just Mal's way. If he didn't like you, you'd be pretty much invisible to him."

"You make it sound so complimentary," I deadpanned, making June snort into her coffee, before I went on. "Heather, I am well past the age of deluding myself into believing if a boy pulls your pigtails on the playground, it means he likes you. If a guy's into you, he shows interest. Not that I even want him to be interested—or anyone for that matter. I'm only here for a few months, remember?"

"Okay, okay." She held her hands up. "I'll let it go. I don't agree, but I'll let it go."

I released a breath. "Thank you."

"How's the B&B going?" I asked June.

Her lips pulled down. "It's fine. Busy as always . . . it's great, but me and Mum can't agree on anything right now. I think we're making enough money to redo the bathrooms so we don't have to call a plumber out once a week and discount rooms, but Mum's so tight she doesn't want to spend a penny on anything that isn't *necessary.*"

Heather and I winced. "Working plumbing seems pretty necessary."

"I love the job, more than I ever thought I would when I first came back, but sometimes I wish it were all mine, so I could make all the decisions without her breathing down my neck because it isn't how she would do it. Does that make me awful?"

"As someone who has a very complicated history with their mum, absolutely not. Mothers get to us like no one else can." Or in my case—my mother's *absence* had molded me into the woman I was. As an actress and singer on a cruise ship, she'd traveled to every corner of the globe. When I was a child, I'd thought the world began and ended with her. I would stand out on the bank for hours, staring at the water and imagining her sailing back to me. Once it became clear that wasn't going to happen, another craving took form. If she liked to travel . . . well, I'd travel even further. She was an actress, I'd become a better one.

"Don't forget the cat," Heather cut in, drawing me from my thoughts.

"Cat?" I questioned.

"Oh, I'm fostering a cat for Kelly, the veterinary nurse. They're looking for a permanent home for her, but I've been watching her for a few weeks and my mum is now allergic to cats apparently."

I thought back. "Didn't you have a cat as a kid?"

"Yep."

I huffed a laugh. There were times I wished I had a better relationship with my mum, but this wasn't one of them. We'd formed a tentative relationship over the years, something more like friendship than mother and daughter. I no longer felt that wrench of resentment in my gut every time I thought of her. That's as good as it was going to get.

As we finished our coffee, the topic moved on to Heather's job at the Sheep's Heid Pub in the village and she recalled a rude customer she'd served the night before. "He said any reputable pub would serve Jameson's and so I told him, 'That's Irish whisky, pal. You're not in Ireland.' I don't think he liked that." She snorted at the memory. "I managed to sell him Kier's whisky eventually. Well, Mal's now, I suppose."

I brightened. "That's amazing. You sell a lot of it at the pub?"

She shrugged. "Some. Mainly to locals." That meant no.

A worried wrinkle marred her brow that reminded me so much of her brother. "How is it all going? I worry about Mal and I know Callum does too. He's sunk so much of himself into that place and he was the only person keeping it running for so long, I don't know what he'd do without it."

Guilt. Anger. Worry. They all rolled together, all of it aimed at Kier. "If this all works out, we won't have to find out. Let me show you what I've been working on." I pulled my phone from my bag, opening up my emails first to show them the new label I'd had a designer friend create for the bottle. I'd wanted to keep it traditional, so it was a simple white label with "Kinleith Old Scottish Whisky" in gold writing, and the outline of the Isle of Skye below.

"That looks incredible," June said.

"Have you showed Mal?" Heather asked.

I shook my head. "It only came through a few hours ago." I wouldn't admit I was nervous to show him. I didn't want him to think I was trying to take over his business. "We've been working on a website too." I loaded it next, handing it over so they could flip through the site I was really damn proud of. "I'm setting up a social media page, but I need to nail down our ideal content, so I'm still in the researching phase."

"You've been working really hard on this." Heather handed my phone back.

"I care about it." I shrugged. It had become about more than Kier's legacy or keeping my family's home. I wanted Malcolm to succeed too, because even if he was a total grump, he deserved this. "A designer friend of mine owed me a favor, he did most of the work on the website and label. I've also been thinking of something else . . . I want your opinion before I take it to Mal."

"Sounds ominous," June quipped.

I stuck my tongue out. "Remember the old tasting room?"

"Vaguely." Heather tipped her head. "Your grandparents used to throw parties there."

I nodded. "It's not in use anymore, it's filled with broken casks and equipment. But I was thinking, if I cleared it all out we could throw a little launch party for the new whisky label." I wiggled my fingers in excitement.

"It's a great idea," June said

"But?" There'd definitely been a *but* there.

"Mal's going to hate it," Heather finished.

"Oh, he's definitely going to hate it," June agreed.

Probably.

"If it saves the distillery, he's going to be thanking me." On his knees, preferably.

No. Nope. Not going there.

"ARE YOU HEADED STRAIGHT BACK TO THE MANOR?" HEATHER asked as we stepped out onto the street.

It was breezy today, so I pulled my black blazer with tiny embroidered daisies over my tank top, fastening all the buttons.

"In a bit, I have to stop at the pet store."

"Treats for Dudley?" June asked.

"Yes, but I also want to pick something up for my little fox family."

They shared twin looks of bemusement. "Fox family?"

"Yep, it's the strangest thing. Every morning, I've been having my morning coffee out on the bank, then three days ago a little family of foxes showed up, five scraggly little things. I panicked at first thinking they wanted to eat Dudley, so I gave them a few of his treats to distract them while we got away. Now they come back every day at the same time . . . it's pretty cute actually."

Heather laughed, throwing June a knowing little look.

Juniper just rolled her eyes. "Damn city folk, you're going to catch rabies."

"I don't think that's a thing anymore."

She pulled her car keys from her bag. "Don't come running to me when you're foaming at the mouth."

Blowing kisses over their shoulders, they both walked in the direction of the car park outside the town hall. I headed for the little pet shop further along the high street I'd yet to visit. Perhaps I would pick something up for Dudley and Boy. When had I started thinking of the two of them as a double act? They were becoming adorably attached to one another. I thought it was adorable, at least. I could tell from the way Malcolm frowned every time his dog wagged his tail in my direction he didn't like it, as though he were colluding with the enemy.

Pet Palace was painted a sunny, lemon yellow. Flower boxes with bright petunias and geraniums sat beneath windows that framed the propped-open door. The inside was tiny, with only enough room for a small counter that held an old-fashioned till and rows of shelves stacked with food, toys, and treats.

"Oh—hello, handsome," I said, spotting the cat. A ginger tabby lounged in a bed the shape of a crown, confirming I was, in fact, among royalty.

I reached down to pet him when a voice rang out, "I wouldn't do that if I were you." I snatched my hand back so fast I almost fell on my arse. A high, lovely giggle followed the warning. "He looks more charming than he is, I'm afraid."

The cat's whiskers twitched in what I could have sworn was disappointment. "Better than looking less charming than you are, I suppose," I replied, finally straightening to get a look at the owner of the melodic Australian accent.

The curvy brunette was already gaping at me. "You're April Sinclair." Oh. If any famous person ever said they got used to random people recognizing them, they were lying. She must have read my uncertainty. "No, no—I'm not, like, a crazy fan." She grimaced, ringing her hands together. "I know that's exactly what a crazy fan would say—and I am a fan—but what I meant was the whole village has been buzzing with gossip about you being here and—" She closed her eyes and shook her head. When she opened them again, she gave me a sweet if slightly timid smile. "Let me start again. Hi, you must be April, I'm Jasmine."

She held her hand out and I took it with a laugh. This entire situation was bizarre but also not the weirdest greeting of my life. "Nice to meet you, Jasmine. I've been wanting to come into your shop all week, you have some lovely things."

She continued to stare at me and I cleared my throat. She startled, hands flapping at her face. "Sorry, I'm doing it again. I've never met a celebrity before, I don't really know what to say."

I laughed again. Despite the weirdness, I liked her. "I promise we're just as boring as every other person on the planet. I know . . . how about you pretend I'm just one of your regular customers, what would you say to me then?"

She looked a little horrified at the idea of role play, but nodded and swallowed. "Morning, April. What can I do for you?"

She'd never be an actress, but it got the job done. "Weird question, do you have anything suitable for foxes?"

"Foxes?" she repeated, and I wondered what kind of reaction I was about to get.

I explained my situation with the small fox family I'd inherited. She didn't look surprised or confused, she just grinned and said, "Wait there, I have just the thing," and raced into the backroom in a flurry. I had a sneaking suspicion that Jasmine and I would become great friends.

10

MAL
Pretty Lips – Winehouse

Later, I would wonder how exactly I'd found myself in this situation. Today was not that day. I didn't have room for it.

It was almost two weeks since April's arrival and I'd become so in tune to her comings and goings. I knew she walked her dog around seven on weekdays before she came down to the distillery, and around nine on weekends. I'd also deduced from the lingering cobwebs of sleep still clinging to her posture that her morning walks were the first thing she did after rolling out of bed. So I'd foolishly—*foolishly*—assumed it was safe to begin using the kitchen in the manor again, so long as I was quiet.

Two days in a row now, I'd left the manor feeling like my head was on back to front. On Sunday morning, instead of approaching the back entrance to find the kitchen dark and empty as I expected, I found April. Standing on the top step outside the wide open kitchen doors that faced the bank, she sipped her coffee with her eyes closed.

I could have left, she hadn't seen me approach. I took one step of retreat, then caught sight of what she was wearing. Dwarfing her short frame was a cumbersome floral dressing gown made from a shiny blue material. And on her feet, a pair of slouchy knit socks. It was a monstrosity. A million miles from those colorful little jackets and shorts she insisted on wearing every day. I was certain Granny Macabe was buried in something similar.

Opening her eyes, she startled at the sight of me. "Malcolm." Her cheeks turned the same pink as her lips and she straightened, running a hand over the neck of the gown, clearly embarrassed to be caught looking anything less than perfect. It was the first time I'd ever seen her embarrassed about anything. "What are you doing here?"

I didn't respond. Couldn't have, even if I'd wanted to. The smattering of freckles across the bridge of her nose shone in the slow expanse of morning. Pinks, oranges, and reds setting her ablaze, far more stunning than the view she gazed at. It shouldn't have been sexy. What she wore categorically should *not* have been sexy. But—*hell*—it was. The way it cinched at her waist then split around her bare thigh as she shifted from foot to foot.

I'd done a good job up to this point of not being attracted to her. I mean, I'd always been attracted to her, but in a safe, *hypothetical* way. A "never gonna happen" kind of way. Looking at April now, I remembered all too easily why she was my first crush. My only crush, really.

As a teen, I'd catch her staring at me while I worked summers at the distillery; my clothes would become too tight, my face feeling like it might melt under her attention. But I knew with certainty it never meant anything on her end, even when she'd join me for lunch on the bank. We wouldn't talk. She would read one of her romance books and I'd pretend to read whatever I'd dug out of the village library that week.

April was lively, exuberant. If she liked someone, she didn't stop talking to them. She didn't act that way with me. I didn't even let myself imagine it. A boy who could barely look his own siblings in the eye would never attract a girl like April Murphy.

She must have caught where my eyes had strayed because she cinched the knot on her dressing gown more tightly. "I'm sorry, Malcolm, I usually save my more scandalous attire for my overnight guests." *Did she have overnight guests?*

"What are you doing here?" she asked again. Not rudely, but surprised—as though I'd drawn an invisible *Do Not Cross* boundary line down the middle of the estate.

I straightened, focusing on the wine-red coils at her temples. "The cottage doesn't have a proper kitchen . . . Kier always let me use the manor's. If it's a problem—"

"No. Of course not." She stepped aside to let me pass her on the stairs. Not far enough because I caught the hint of vanilla in her coffee.

I went about my business, cooking the eggs I'd brought with me on the stove as the dogs lingered at my heel, hoping I dropped scraps. It would have been polite to offer her breakfast, but I couldn't push the words past my lips. As I was plating up my food, she spoke over her shoulder without turning from the horizon. "It's so pretty here in the morning, so peaceful. I'd forgotten."

"What's a view compared to endless beauty salons and nightlife, right? You must be desperate to return to London." I'd spoken without thinking, but knew there was truth to it. Skye wouldn't satisfy her for long. It's why she'd left in the first place after all.

"Why do you always do that?" It was the most heat I'd ever heard in her voice.

"Do what?"

She looked at me. "Twist every word out of my mouth until it becomes an insult." I left without eating my eggs. Set the plate down and strolled right by her without a word. *Real fucking mature.*

That was yesterday, and when she didn't show up at her usual time of nine o'clock today, I paced around the dunnage like a bull in a cage before eventually deciding to wander up to the manor for a drink—and maybe to check on her. I called Boy now, moving quickly. She liked to walk down to the cove from the path at the bank; it was steep with lots of rocks jutting from the grass. She might have hurt herself. My thoughts spiraled on the walk over, ready to face all manner of situations. *Blood and broken limbs. The manor sitting empty because she'd taken my words from yesterday to heart and left without a word.* I practically took the kitchen door off its hinges, stumbling over myself to get inside.

And there she was, in the very center of the family space wearing some stretchy little trousers, her heart-shaped arse in the air. *Yoga.* She was late because of yoga. I didn't even notice my sister until I stumbled to a stop and banged my knee hard on the kitchen island. She panted out a laugh. "Okay there, brother? You're looking a little peaked."

I knew my face was flaming, knew I looked like an absolute idiot. So I barked, "You're late."

April dropped onto her knees, rubbing at her face and neck

with a small towel. "You said there was no point in me being there on mornings you clean out the dunnage because I get in the way." I had said that.

"Right." *Dammit.* "Well, I'm bottling this afternoon if you want to help."

"Really?" Her features practically lit up.

She always looked this way, like a semi-pulsing live wire lived beneath her skin. Every job I set her she completed with enthusiasm—even the horrible ones. She asked insightful questions and never seemed bored at the technical details that would have others checking out. I couldn't decide if it was fake, she was an award-winning actress after all. Her excitement always felt a little too much for me to handle because deep down, I craved it. I wanted it to be real.

"I can't remember the last time I tasted Kier's whisky," she said, then laughed, her eyes glistening pools of jade as she turned to Heather. "Actually, I can! Do you remember Andrew Taylor's beach party?"

Heather part groaned, part laughed and they fell into conversation about the night I recalled well. I remembered finding them stumbling along Cairnwell Lane after Heather phoned, interrupting the two thousand-piece puzzle I was close to finishing, begging me to pick them up and not tell Dad. Heather was vomiting behind a post box by the time I got there, April diligently attempting to hold her hair back. They'd been drunk and giggly the entire drive to the manor, and I'd deduced somewhere along the way that April had snuck a bottle of Kier's whisky to take to the party.

Hopping to her feet now, April efficiently rolled her mat away. "I'll be down in fifteen, I need a quick shower." And . . . that image would be forever lodged in my mind.

"I thought you always bottled every other Friday?" Heather asked as soon as we were alone.

I shifted, occupying myself by taking a dirty mug from the table to the sink and rinsing it out. "Jacob couldn't work this Friday," I lied quickly, incriminating Jacob, our master distiller. "And if April is serious about learning the business, it's important she understands every stage of the process."

Her arms folded on the island opposite me, rolling her lips between her teeth and smiling in that way she knew irritated me, like she had a secret she couldn't wait to share and it was going to bring the whole damn house down around her. "So it wouldn't be because April's doing an admin day on Friday but you knew she was excited about seeing that part for herself?"

That was exactly it. "Nope. As I said, Jacob had to switch out his day."

Her lips pressed together again and I felt like cling film, I was that transparent. "That's fine, keep your secrets, brother."

AS SOON AS I UNCORKED THE CASK, APRIL SQUEAKED, LEANING in for a closer look. "How long has this one been maturing?"

"Almost four years."

She'd changed before she got here, swapping out the yoga leggings that made my eyes cross for another one of her little suits. This one was pale pink, a color that should have clashed with her hair but didn't. I'd thanked the current cold snap when she strolled in wearing trousers instead of her usual tiny shorts until she'd turned to take in the space and I saw the way they molded to her arse.

"I thought it only had to be three years?" She looked up at me and I made a point of staring just above her eyes. I didn't know what had gotten into me, it was like that bloody *granny* dressing gown had sapped all of my good sense.

"Three years is the minimum legal requirement, but the longer you let it mature, the smoother the whisky becomes. We have casks that are almost forty years old."

"Forty years? I don't have that level of patience."

"Whisky is all about patience. Now—" I forced us back on track. She had a way of distracting me without even trying. "Each barrel will lose a percentage of liquid as it matures, that's what we call the angel's share—"

"Angel's share. That's adorable."

"It's not supposed to be adorable it's . . . never mind, once the cask is open, it's emptied in the trough." I hit the big green button with my foot and the conveyor belt shifted, all four barrels rolling at once, emptying into the deep trough below.

"You mix several casks together?"

The fact she'd even noticed blew my mind. When we hired new workers, passion was always the most important part of an application. The hours were long and the work hard. In a small community, passion wasn't always available and you were forced to hire the only capable pair of hands. April had the passion and I wasn't even certain she was aware of it. I'd accused her of being a princess, and if she was on a mission to prove just how wrong I'd been, she was succeeding with flying colors.

"Most whiskies, even a single malt, are blended. It allows us to achieve a higher level of consistency."

"Right." She nibbled her lower lip, storing away that information. "Then what happens?"

I pointed to the pipes running from the trough. "These pipe it to the storage and blending tanks."

"So once you've mixed it, how do you ensure it tastes the same every time?"

"That would be my job, lass." Jacob's heavy tread echoed off the steps as he ducked through the door, already pulling his arms from his worn corduroy jacket.

April startled, clearly not expecting the newcomer. Then she caught sight of him. "I remember you."

"Aye, that's good, otherwise you'd have broken this old codger's heart." In two steps he caught April up in his arms and pressed a smacking kiss to her cheek.

She drew back, flashing him that megawatt smile I was only used to seeing in photos. "How have you been, Jacob?"

"Good, lass. Real good. Not as good as you, I expect."

Her cheeks turned a pretty shade of pink, though I noticed she didn't confirm or deny. Instinct flared, that one that told me April wasn't quite as content as she wanted the world to believe. Perhaps she wasn't as adept at hiding it as she thought she was. Perhaps I noticed because it was the same look reflected back at me in the mirror every morning. Or perhaps I noticed because, deny it as I might, I noticed every little thing about her.

"Started without me, did you?" Jacob said with a good nature I couldn't return.

"I need to show April the bottling process."

If he thought it odd, he didn't comment—the blending plant was his domain, after all. "Right, right," he said, and swept April under his wing. She followed, completely at ease. It was the perfect opportunity to make an escape. To clear April's perfume from my nostrils and get my head on straight. I had a to-do list as long as my left arm, every item calling for my attention.

But for whatever reason, I stayed, like this moment held importance. Shifting, I reclined against the wall, my eyes bound to April's face as Jacob cupped her shoulders, encouraging her to peer inside the blending tank. The instinct to step in, to remove his hands from her, was as sharp as it was absurd. I was not jealous of Jacob, the very thought was ridiculous, the man was pushing seventy and happily married for almost fifty years. But when he whispered something between demonstrating the standard checks for the characteristics of our chosen flavors and aromas, she giggled, and that zap flared through my gut again. *Hell.* I scrubbed a hand along my lower jaw, the rough bristle a reminder I needed to trim the damn thing. *Add it to the list.*

What must I look like to her? I wondered, giving into my weakness to study her while I knew she was distracted. I traced the tight spiraling curls that brushed her neck, sneaking loose from the tie that bound the rest of her impressive mane. That hair had featured in my dream last night. Memories flooded me, those curls spread across my pillow, tickling my thighs as she rode me. When I imagined her, she was always on top.

Not memories, I scolded myself. Those things had never happened. Never would happen.

I caught her looking at me sometimes, at my face and hands when we worked side by side, not that she tried to hide it. I'd known women to admire me, felt their heated gazes on rare occasions. Heard their whispered words on even rarer ones, when loneliness drew me to a stranger's bed.

To April, I was an enigma to be understood. While she . . . well, I couldn't call her a temptation, because no scenario existed where a woman like her would invite me to her bed.

She was a distraction. An obsession.

Perhaps I should have taken Jasmine up on her offer when I gave her a ride home last month. She was a beautiful woman. Fun and inherently kind. *Which is exactly why you said no*, I reminded myself. I couldn't stir up that kind of discomfort with a person I genuinely liked, a person I was certain to see around the village for the foreseeable future.

I wasn't built for a relationship, didn't have the emotional capacity to invite another into my life. Not because I couldn't see myself opening up, no. I knew I could, with the right person. But I also knew I couldn't offer the words to keep them there. Women wanted declarations, they deserved comfort, reassurance, gentility. None of those I knew how to express.

I rubbed at my tired eyes, dropping my fists immediately when April's laugh thrummed through me again. I didn't want to miss a second of it.

She appeared enraptured as the brilliant amber liquid poured into a dozen glass bottles. Jacob showed her how to complete a sensory inspection, holding a bottle beneath a white light that made every perfect angle of her face glow as she helped him inspect for defects or floating particles. She pulled a pack of labels from her bag, handing them to Jacob so he could smooth them precisely over the glass. And when he placed the finished product in her hands, she looked at me and beamed. The smile was full and unrestrained.

Click.

It was like the flash of a camera behind my eyelids, my mind immortalizing every detail of that moment. I could swear my heart fucking stopped. And when it restarted, that next thump in my chest had her name on it.

I needed to watch her taste it.

I needed it like I needed my next breath.

11

APRIL

Death By a Thousand Cuts – Taylor Swift

Can you believe it?" Sidling up to Malcolm, I held the glass bottle aloft with all the pride of a new parent showing off their firstborn. Perhaps I would send some unsolicited pictures of it to every person I knew. *We get it, Julie, you had a baby. No one thinks that little alien is cute but you.*

Just kidding. Sort of.

"I mean . . . I didn't really do anything, it was all Jacob. But I don't think he could have gotten through it without my emotional support."

Malcolm said nothing—not unusual for him—but he didn't scowl either. I dropped a hand to his arm. "Hey, is everything okay?"

He looked at my hand for a long moment. "Fine. Everything's fine." Then he stepped back, shrugging off my touch. He was acting weird, no less gruff than usual, but there was a definite edginess that hadn't been there an hour ago. It settled around him like a thick fog. He shook loose of it, taking the bottle from me and holding it up to the light for his own inspection. "Nothing quite like holding the finished product in your hand, is there?"

"No," I replied with unleashed wonder. Until this moment, I'd never truly understood Kier and Mal's dedication to the job. As a kid, all I'd known were Kier's long days, unpredictable hours, and the toll it took on his body. They had machines and methods in place that made the job easier nowadays, but the work was still grueling. Never in my life had I been as dog-tired as these past weeks. Three a.m. wake-up calls and twelve-hour days on a blistering cold film set had nothing on this.

When I'd pushed the cork into the bottle, the smoky scent of peat and sweet caramel lingering in my nose, I'd had to hold back tears. It was the smell of home.

Kier and Mal and Jacob . . . they'd shared this labor of love. And in three years' time, someone would hold my hard work in their hand. Call me an overly emotional female, I wouldn't deny it. I also wouldn't deny that it fed the part of my soul I'd only ever found in front of a camera lens. Every emotion must have been written across my face because Mal's fierce countenance softened a fraction. An indistinguishable change to someone who didn't have a playbook of his every scowl.

"Come." He gestured to the door. As I followed, he called back to Jacob, "You good here?"

Jacob chuckled. "Aye, lad. I've only worked here forty-eight years, I think I'll manage."

Ignoring his sarcasm, Malcolm gave Jacob a wave and pushed the door open, stepping back for me to duck beneath his arm. The crack was only slight and as I stepped through, it brought my back flush with his chest in a move that felt purposeful. My shoulder grazed hard muscle and I felt his body lock tight, tension rippling from his skin through to mine.

I stumbled onto the top step, almost tripping as my legs failed me. He caught me, hands locking tightly around the tops of my shoulders. "You okay?"

I nodded, not trusting myself to speak.

What the hell was happening?

Two days ago he couldn't stand the sight of me, and now—now I was still certain he couldn't stand the sight of me, but something had also changed. There was a current . . . a *pressure* that hadn't been there before. Was it me? It didn't feel like me. I flirted and teased, but I'd always done those things. Which could only mean . . . the change was him.

The tread of his boots chased my light feet on the stairs. I hugged the bottle to my chest, feeling the weight of his stare as we stepped outside, crunching over gravel that carried us between the dunnage and the main building.

I expected him to lead us into the dunnage. There was a cask delivery due this afternoon and I knew he needed to clear the space before the shipment arrived, so I was surprised when he followed the path up that would lead us to his cottage. Without the protection of the building from the elements, the wind whipped around the open clifftop, tossing my hair and raising goose bumps along my arms as I drew them tighter around me. Mal glanced down at the movement and frowned, picking up his pace. Unlocking the cottage door with the single brass key he carried, he nodded for me to go ahead. "On you go, before you freeze to death."

Freeze to death. The wind chill made it feel colder but it couldn't have been less than twelve degrees Celsius; on the low side but still acceptable for May in Scotland.

I didn't know what to make of this Malcolm. How to act. It was like trying to dance to your favorite song and being unable to catch the beat. Unsure of the reason for our visit, I lingered in the designated dining area, glancing around the cozy cottage I'd only been in once before. It felt a little bigger without Boy's wild presence. Malcolm had left him up at the manor to keep Dudley company for the day. It was vital the mixing lab remained sterile, which meant no furry friends.

While he quietly closed the door, I set the bottle of whisky on the table where an unfinished puzzle caught my eye. I rounded the table to get a better look from the front. It was advanced, likely two thousand pieces. From what he'd already put together, I could see the finished result would make up dozens of bricks, all in varying shades of the same color. "Is this Lego?" I asked, running a finger across the finished top corner.

"Aye," he clipped.

I looked at him sidelong, quick enough to catch the high color on his cheeks. "That's really cool. I loved doing puzzles in my trailer while I ran lines. Nothing as difficult as this though."

Shucking out of his thick navy sweater, it became hard to decide if I wanted to watch his biceps strain beneath his white T-shirt or his face as it flitted from flushed to uncertain, before settling on what I would call his Wary Scowl. The wary scowl only came into play when he didn't know what to say next. So I let my eyes fall back to the puzzle and picked up a dark green piece, searching for its home. I knew he was watching me.

What had started as brief glances was beginning to feel like a game now, both of us watching while the other wasn't looking. Each time, we tiptoed a little closer to the line. I didn't know what waited on the other side of it, if anything.

And I was desperate to know.

"Do you mind?" I asked before slotting it into place. I would never play with a man's puzzle without asking permission first.

"Touch anything you like." It was like all the air was sucked from the room. I heard him stutter. My hand froze over the puzzle, the piece still clutched between my fingers. If I looked at him now, I knew I'd find his face flaming red. So I spared him, cleared my throat, and slotted the piece home with clammy fingers.

Giving me a wide berth, he burst into motion, making his way to the solitary high cupboard in the kitchenette and pulling down two tumblers. "You said earlier you hadn't tasted Kier's whisky in a long time, I thought you might like to try it now."

Oh. "Open the bottle you mean? It seems a shame to drink it so soon."

"So soon? Princess, it's been sitting in the dunnage for four years. And it's just a wee nip."

I supposed, when he put it like that. I handed the bottle over, making certain not to let any part of my skin touch his. He seemed to be doing the same. The room felt like a pressure cooker, certain to blow.

"What do you think of the label?" I asked, moving us onto safer ground.

His eyes flicked down like he'd just noticed it. "Aye . . . it's bonny." I'd hoped for a little more reaction, but let it slide. This was all a big change for him.

He uncorked the bottle with quick, sure movements, pouring

two fingers of amber liquid into each tumbler. He held one out for me to take and our fingers grazed this time, his thick calloused digits folding over my freckled ones as he curled the glass into my hand.

"I don't have any ice," he said.

"That's fine." Bringing the whisky to my face, I took a long inhale. Sweet, spicy, and just a little bitter. His eyes were the brush of petals across my lips while I sipped.

"Hold it on your tongue," he instructed, muscles in his arms bunching where they folded over his chest. I did as I was told, letting it pool in my mouth. A heat that didn't belong to the whisky hurtled through me. He hadn't drunk any of his yet, waiting—watching—for my reaction. "Good girl . . . now swallow." His voice was like water rushing over rocks as his eyes trailed down my throat, following the burn of the liquor.

I held in my cough, my entire body burning. "Well . . . it's nicer than I remember."

"Aye." He cleared his throat and sipped his own. "I suppose it improves with age."

I clutched the tumbler tighter, speaking the words that had been on my mind since I watched him uncork the casks. "It's so weird . . . drinking something that Kier had a hand in making. It makes me feel closer to him, like a part of him is still alive somehow. It also makes me want to cry like a bloody baby. Does that make sense? It probably sounds silly to you."

"It doesn't sound silly at all." He licked his lips. "Kier would have been proud of you today."

The tension simmered. It wasn't often I felt uncomfortable, but right now, I was stretched too thin. My thoughts raced too quickly to grasp a single one. I knew he was waiting for me to say something, but I had no idea what my next line was supposed to be. What part I was even playing. I faltered back a step, spinning to face the shelves I'd been desperate to explore the first time. Now they were nothing more than a distraction.

"Have you read all of these?" There had to be over a hundred books here, all non-fiction from what I could tell. It was like a small library.

"Of course." His tone suggested it was a stupid question. He confirmed it by saying, "Why would I buy a book and not read it?"

"You've clearly never heard of a TBR, friend." He seemed content to let me browse, so I edged closer, brushing the tip of my finger over a spine that read *Sapiens: A Brief History of Humankind*, and settled on one simply named *Space*.

"TBR, it means To Be Read," I continued, pulling *Anatomy: A Human Science* from the shelf and flipping the cover. "I've discovered that buying books and reading books are two completely different things." I turned back to him, holding the book aloft. "What's the coolest thing you've learnt from this?"

As quick as a gnat, he answered. "We're about one centimeter taller in the morning than the evening. During the day, the soft cartilage between our joints and the vertebrae in our spines compress, making us smaller."

I didn't know what I'd expected . . . something more profound perhaps. The surprise made me laugh, and I continued flipping through the pages. "That doesn't seem fair, some of us need all the height advantage we can get."

He made a *hmm* sound at my joke and I returned to scouring the shelves. If he was allowing me to snoop, you could be damn sure I'd take advantage of it. I loved being nosy. Not in a gossipy way, but a childhood-stories, dusty-photo-albums kind of way. Other than the books and a photo of him and Kier with their arms wrapped around one another's shoulders, Mal had nothing remotely personal lying around. It was like an Airbnb with no guests.

"I'm sorry," I said, shifting a few steps to the DVDs.

"Why?"

"You tense every time I touch something."

"I like things neat."

"I know." I made a show of using only my eyeballs when perusing his film collection. The man sure had eclectic taste. There were classics, foreign titles, sci-fi, straight-to-DVD titles, even a few romcoms. For some reason, Malcolm struck me as a three-hour war film kind of guy.

"I haven't seen this one yet." I pointed to *The Sixth Sense* just to fill the silence. Then I froze on one titled *Indigo Ridge*. I was in that movie—my very first feature film. It hadn't been a big role, more of a blink-and-miss situation. *Had he known I was in that movie when he bought it?* I began to pull the DVD from the shelf and, forgetting it was alcohol in my glass, I took a massive gulp. Malcolm's fingers caught it before I had it free and slid it back into its spot, startling me so completely I swallowed the entire mouthful.

My insides caught alight.

Holy crap.

Curling in on myself, I hacked with immediate regret. Coughing over and over until Malcolm had to steady me, plucking the tumbler from my fingers.

"You're supposed to sip it."

"A bit late for that," I wheezed. "*Shit*, I think it's in my lungs."

"You're all right."

He carried my glass to the sink, added a few drops of water and returned as I was wiping tears from my cheeks. "That should be better."

"I thought whisky was supposed to be drunk neat."

He swirled his glass. "It can be enjoyed that way, but it started as nothing more than a ploy to sell more bottles. Kier had a great highball recipe you should try if you fancy something a wee bit sweeter."

You can touch anything you want. Hold it on your tongue. Good girl . . . now swallow. If you fancy something a wee bit sweeter. He had to be kidding with this.

I swallowed, doing my best to ignore the rocking sensation in my stomach. "I'd love that."

He shrugged. "It's just a recipe."

Perhaps. It felt more like a peace offering. Deciding that was the perfect lead-in, I said, "That would actually fit in perfectly with something I wanted to talk to you about."

His brows winged up and he settled back against the table.

Assuming this was the only encouragement I would get, I forged ahead. "I popped into the old tasting room the other day—"

"No."

I barked a surprised laugh. "You haven't even let me finish."

"Don't need to, the answer's no." He straightened like we were done.

We weren't done, not by a mile. "Answer to what? I didn't even ask a question."

He gave me his best glower. "You want to open that room up and parade tourists through my home, just like you want to post us all over your silly wee websites. I won't let you make a mockery of us."

I was stunned silent. All I could get out was a breathy, "Make a mockery of you?" *Silly wee websites?* What year was he living in?

"You think I don't know what you do for your day job." The way he air quoted the word job made me want to snap his damn fingers off. "We're not selling false eyelashes, or throwing booze-filled orgies—this is a serious business."

I laughed but the sound was angry and twisted. It was all I could do, I needed something to alleviate the pressure in my head or I'd explode and take the entire island out. "You're kidding me, right? Kier built that tasting room himself, he held events all the time when I was a girl."

He slammed the tumbler down on the table and the entire thing shook. "Yeah, until he realized they made barely any profit."

"It's vital we get the brand name out there, we won't succeed without that."

"*We* have a loyal customer base right on our doorstep. People here know Kier . . . knew Kier," he corrected himself quickly. "They respected him."

I swallowed hard, hating the words I was about to say. "A loyal customer base who are buying less and less of your product every month because tourists only want to drink name-brand liquor they've actually heard of."

His mouth flattened and his stance widened. If I'd expected him to shout, I was wrong. Instead, he looked me dead in the eye and clipped, "I'm doing the best I can."

"I know that." I pressed my hands to my chest. "Let me help you, that's all I'm trying to do."

"We are not some little hobby for you to amuse yourself with for a few weeks before you find something better to move on to," he said. "I don't need *your* brand of help."

Men often had that way of dismissing me, like I was too stupid, too vapid to bring anything of worth to the table. Reducing me to nothing more than a pretty arm piece. Having Malcolm pull the same tired shit left me seething. I pushed it down and raised my chin, holding my nerve. "I disagree."

"What makes you such an expert all of a sudden? I thought you were an actress? I don't need you to come in here and tell me how to run my business."

This is going nowhere. If we continued, all we'd do was talk in circles and insult one another. Choosing to be the adult here, I stared him down and said as plainly as I could, "I wanted to talk to you as a *courtesy*, to keep you involved. Don't forget that I don't need your permission."

He almost smiled and it was the most cutting expression I'd seen from him yet. "Does it give you a little thrill every time you get to remind me of that?" His eyes were storm clouds, boring straight into mine. It was as unnerving as it was electrifying, probably because it didn't happen often. When he looked at you, he *looked*. I felt like he could see right beneath my skin, to every insecurity I tried so hard to hide from the world.

I didn't reply, incapable of forming one. I was so angry I wanted to smash things. So before I let myself go for his damn Lego puzzle, I snatched the bottle of whisky from the table—he could swivel if he thought I'd leave it for him to drink—and marched right out the door, almost crashing into a man on the threshold.

I hurried past, barely registering Callum's amused chuckle. Perhaps he was laughing at the irony too, because the corner I'd stupidly thought Malcolm and I had turned ended up being a cliff edge.

12

MAL

Mardy Bum – Arctic Monkeys

Well . . . that went well." Callum smirked from his slackened spot on my threshold, attention on April traversing the path back up to the manor with furious, jerking strides. His chin began to dip down her body, expression fading from humored to something closer to admiring.

I gave him a hard shove. "Shut up. What are you doing here?"

We both watched her disappear through the gap in the hedge growth, and it was only then that he ducked inside, shaking his head. "Oh, I don't think so . . . you are not asking the questions here." Set on ignoring him, I began clearing away the half-empty whisky glasses. "Silence, is it? You have nothing to say to me?" His tone bordered on accusing.

"What the hell are you on about?" When Callum was in a mood like this, it was better to let him get it out of his system. I emptied my glass down the drain even though it was a shame to waste perfectly good whisky, but I was in no mood to drink it now. When I had April's in my hand, I noted the small outline of her lips on the rim and pressed my thumb to it. A perfect replica.

For a moment back there, I thought she might have let me kiss her. Would they have been hot and pillow-soft? Or sweetly painful, like the sting of a viper?

"I just interrupted an argument between you and April Sinclair. She's obviously staying at the manor." Callum ticked off his fingers. "How is this the first I'm hearing about it?"

Murphy. "Why would I tell you?" I let the still full glass thud to the counter.

His finger pointed at my chest. "Traitor."

"Even I know the entire village is gossiping about her return, Mr. Pillar of the Community."

He glowered, though it was no match for mine. Plus, the laughter lines around his eyes betrayed him. "I heard the rumors, I just didn't believe them."

"Well . . . believe it. And enjoy it while it lasts, I doubt she'll be here for long." The words made something in my chest tighten, thumbs passing over the tips of my fingers until it eased.

"Because you scared her off."

"If only that were possible," I sniped, the sentiment feeling a little less true than it had days before.

"What's she doing here?"

"I don't know—" I threw my hands out. Why was he so bloody interested? "Lording over her newly acquired land? What's it to you, anyway? You're like a damn housewife when it comes to gossip."

He laughed, flashing all of his teeth. "Any man is going to be curious when a woman like that moves in down the road." Something sharp settled in my gut. "So . . ." he pushed. "What's the story?"

My gaze snagged on the puzzle I'd spent countless hours on the night before. My first emotion when she'd spotted it was acute humiliation. Not many single men in their thirties spent their evenings building puzzles with their dog. I knew Callum certainly didn't. And then, with that sunshine way of hers, she'd flipped the feeling on its head and a vision of the two of us on a lazy Sunday came to the forefront. The fireplace crackling, April in my lap, dressed in nothing but one of my T-shirts as we slotted puzzle pieces into place.

Never gonna happen.

"There isn't one. She's here to cash in on her inheritance, so bored she's making social media pages for the distillery and threatening to host tasting events." The "can you believe the nerve" behind my words was heavily implied.

"I think it's a good idea."

I scrubbed a hand down my face. "Of course you do." I was starting to get a headache.

"Exposure is vital for the success of any business."

My head shot up. "How long were you listening at the door? That's almost word for word what she said."

"Because we're right."

Annoyed with her as I was, I didn't like the way Callum established them as a team. "I hate pomp and posing, it feels cheap."

With an expression I read as you poor, naive fool, he retrieved his phone from his pocket. "Perhaps if you got an actual phone instead of that piece-of-shit brick I'm certain you found in a time capsule, you might already know this."

"It's an iPhone."

"And at least ten years old." He swiped across his screen.

"It does everything I need it to do," I said.

"Here, take a look through this." He handed me the phone where the first account he'd opened was that of a whisky distillery on the isle of Islay. Arty images of whisky casks and raw ingredients. The black-and-white shots were beautiful and tasteful, and didn't just showcase their product but also felt like a love letter to the land.

Then a few more taps and all I could see was April. My hand trembled around the device. "This is her account?"

He nodded. "Look through the posts."

I needed no instruction. "You follow her?"

"Yes. So do twelve million other people." Twelve million. That was over double the population of Scotland.

There were so many pictures, I didn't know where to look. Every one of them her, but not as I'd expected. Images of her and Dudley, laughing into the camera. At a charity event, so unbelievably beautiful as she smiled with some man's arm around her. I didn't even look at him.

I paused on a short video of her doing her makeup, holding the product up to the camera so I could see it. It didn't feel cheap. She was selling, of course, yet it felt genuine. My hand tightened around the phone. I'd made it sound like she was selling herself.

"She has a platform," Callum spoke over the video playing on a loop. "Like it or not, when she talks, people listen. You'd be an idiot not to take what she's offering."

No. I'm an idiot if I don't apologize.

"And the tastings?" I voiced my final concern.

He buffed his hand along his bristled jaw, silver starting to glisten among the light brown. "I still think it's a great idea. Why don't you try talking it through with her, set some parameters that will make you feel more comfortable."

I nodded. "Aye, I'll think about it." We lapsed into silence. The level of exposure that came with an online presence felt scary. Inviting people into my home, the single place I found solace? That was truly terrifying. But Callum was right. If April's ideas saved the distillery, along with Jacob's and Ewan's jobs, I had to take the risk.

"Are we going to get the dunnage cleared?" he asked eventually.

Right. I had a delivery coming. "You don't need to help." I said, repeating the old party line.

He only clapped me on the shoulder and headed for the door. "And yet here I am, rearranging appointments because that's what families do."

"I appreciate it."

"Where's Boy?" he noted, once the dim light of the dunnage folded around us.

"I left him up at the manor . . ." I trailed off. If I wanted my dog back, I would need to face her sooner or later.

Reading my face, Callum chucked. "Perhaps later is better if you want to hold on to your balls."

THE SUN WAS BEGINNING TO SET, YET I REMAINED ON MY hands and knees, scrubbing the malt floor with a fixated vigor. A task I usually reserved for Ewan because it was too simple to get wrong, but here we were. Sinking the scrub brush into the water, I lashed it back against the cement with more force than necessary, focusing on nothing but the scrape of the bristles.

After Callum helped me store the fresh casks, we'd both been sweaty and panting. Callum had a satisfied smile on his face, the one he always wore after an afternoon of backbreaking work. He'd left to go back to his large home on the other side of the village to shower and spend his evening scrolling through his dating app, adding to his copious number of matches. I'd skipped dinner, begun fixing the dunnage door before realizing I didn't have the correctly sized bracket, and scrubbed the windows in my cottage. When that hadn't proven enough, I moved on to the malt floor.

It was odd without Boy here, and I felt my eyes continually flicking to the corner he usually occupied. This was the longest stretch of time in four years I'd spent without him, other than his overnight stay at the vet last summer when he'd caught a stomach bug. I was certain the little traitor was in his element, playing with Dudley and basking in April's tender affection. Something that felt a hell of a lot like longing scored down my chest.

I needed to get my shit together and apologize. It was the only thing that would stop this unsteady feeling pounding through me. It felt like trying to balance on the bow of a ship. I knew I'd hurt her earlier. April, who was magnificent at letting people see exactly what she allowed them to, had slipped. It was only a moment, a mere fraction of a second, but I'd seen behind the glass. She'd looked insecure and small for the first time ever and I realized I'd put her on an untouchable pedestal. I was as guilty as every other person who dehumanized a celebrity, believing they didn't feel the same insecurities as the rest of us.

I scrubbed harder, feeling my knuckles start to split on the wood.

I knew if I hadn't been so keyed up about her being in my space, seeing my lonely little life, I wouldn't have reacted so strongly. It wasn't an excuse—hell, who knew, maybe it was. She'd been touching my things and asking questions no one had ever asked me. I'd been desperate for her to keep going while needing her to stop. It was a mindfuck.

I breathed in tandem with the motion. In, scrub. Out, scrub.

How does that make you feel, lad? I heard Kier's voice in my head. The question he'd always asked when he knew my feelings were becoming too much.

Irritated, I silently answered.

Why are you feeling it?

Because I can't speak to a beautiful woman without acting like an arse.

How do you deal with it positively?

Clean until I work up the nerve to retrieve my dog and apologize.

I didn't need Kier's voice to know it was the opposite of positive. I threw the brush back in the bucket, watching beads of water spray across the room. The thought of apologizing made me feel hot and itchy. I wasn't good at it.

Sighing, I scrubbed a wet hand down my face. I could go to her and admit everything was changing fast around here and that change unsettled me. Promise I would try to loosen the reins a little without admitting that she brought these intense feelings out of me. I could be honest without being transparent.

Hurrying back to the cottage, I took the notebook I kept beside my bed to record my intrusive thoughts when they kept me awake at night, and noted down everything I needed to say. Rereading until the words solidified in my brain. When I passed the rows of shelves, I grabbed a DVD without thinking, tucking it into the pocket of my jacket as I flew back out the door.

Waves crashing on my left, I navigated my way easily in the dark, boots sliding over juts in the undergrowth. I could walk this path drunk and blindfolded if necessary. Perhaps I should install some solar lights so April didn't trip and hurt herself. As soon as I passed through the hedge, light illuminated the lower floor of the manor. I followed it like a sailor would a lighthouse through perilous water.

I was headed for the kitchen entrance at the back of the house when I spotted her, one foot propping open the door to the out-building. That spectacular round arse in the air, fully visible from where I stood, as she attempted to lift a wicker basket filled with logs into her arms.

That got me moving. Cutting from the path to the grassy bank, my long strides ate up the distance in seconds. "What are you doing?" I called before reaching her side.

She startled but didn't halt. "Starting a fire, this is where the logs are kept."

I knew that was where the logs were stored, I'd split every piece of wood myself. I watched her struggle a moment, almost bent in half as she attempted to drag the basket over the lip of the door. "You've overloaded the basket," I pointed out.

"Yes. I can see that," she sniped back, and I felt a warm flicker of amusement unfurl.

She released the door and I caught it, stepping in closer while she pulled the top four logs off the stack, tossing them back into the pile. She still grunted under its weight, but she got it off the ground. "You're going to hurt yourself."

She turned, a fine sheen of sweat glistening across her forehead, hair a riot of curls. "What? You're not going to offer to carry it for me?"

Oh yeah, definitely still pissed at me. Like an angry little kitten.

I attempted to mold my features, going for lightly chastised, when all I really wanted to do was laugh. I came over here dreading what was to come, and within two minutes in her presence, I felt the rope unraveling itself from my chest. "Why would I do that when you're perfectly capable of carrying it yourself," I said, when in truth, I was dying to snatch it from her grasp. I didn't know much about women, but instinct warned me April was a woman who hated being made to feel incapable.

Still straining under its weight, she squinted at me. The right answer, I realized, but I gave it too easily. She wanted to argue. Pushing my expression into the most neutral position possible, I stared steadily back at her. Not tonight, princess. I'm here to make it up to you.

After a beat, she pushed past me and I trailed her to the door, my eyes once again falling to her behind in the soft gray shorts she'd changed into. Knowing I was a bossy, moody son of a bitch didn't mean I fell into controlling, alpha-male bullshit. She wanted to carry the heavy basket, she could carry the damn basket.

Taking the steps ahead of me, she balanced the load on a raised knee, attempting to reach for the door handle with one hand. Logs clacked against the rim, rolling precariously. Perhaps I wasn't as evolved as I thought, because that's where I drew the line. Okay, new plan, she can do what she wants, doesn't mean I'm going to stand back and watch her injure herself out of pure stubbornness. Darting around her, I grasped the door handle before she could. "Glare all you want, princess, I can take it."

She only looked at me, moss-ringed eyes tracing over every one of my features until she reached my scar. I squirmed. She breezed by like I hadn't spoken.

What did that mean? Did she want me to follow? For a brief second, I considered calling Heather to ask her advice, nixing it just as quickly. An adult male asking his wee sister for female advice would carry me over a line I wasn't yet desperate enough to cross.

Inside the kitchen, Boy greeted me with an excited yowl, a sound more cat than dog as he dove from his spot on the sofa to press into my hands. I gave his chin a good scratch, a part of me relaxing with him back at my side.

Like any good double act, Dudley followed, dancing around my feet as though I hadn't ignored his presence for weeks. Rearing back determinedly on his hind legs, his singular front paw scooped at the air. I admired his determination, making it the only reason I bent down to give his wiry chest a scratch. When he licked the back of my hand, I didn't stop him, but I did frown at April's back where she unloaded logs into the wood box beside the fireplace. "I don't let Boy onto the furniture," I said.

She snorted. "He looked pretty at home up there for a dog 'not allowed' on the furniture."

Of course he did, the wee shit doesn't listen to a thing I say.

"Like any animal doing something it shouldn't," I pointed out, not sure why I was pushing it.

She kept unloading the logs, slim fingers stacking them three high. "You should loosen up a little, Malcolm. Animals chafe under strict rules, they are always going to break them."

She would say that. A "little hellion," Kier used to call her, always sneaking out of the manor at night, drinking when she shouldn't. She pushed at any rule placed upon her. "Some people thrive within barriers," I grunted out.

"Or do they simply feel more comfortable within the confines? Surviving and thriving is not the same thing."

We were no longer talking about animals. Bloody hell, this was not why I came here. "Thanks for the free therapy, I'll be sure to point the dozens of failed therapists I've visited in your direction."

She didn't even flinch, not at the heat in my voice or the admission that I was—have been—in therapy. I wasn't ashamed of it exactly, ashamed it didn't work was closer to the truth, but I didn't like people knowing my business. No one but my mother knew about the therapy, and that was only because she'd set up every appointment.

"You're doing that wrong," I finally snapped, sick of the silence and tired of watching her pile the logs in the grate that way. "You're never going to get it to light."

"I googled it, it seems—"

"You googled how to light a fire?" I shook my head, striding closer to kneel beside her. "Didn't Kier teach you anything?"

"Apparently not," she snarled right back at me, thrusting a log against my chest. I ignored the sensation of her little fist burning through my layers of clothes, and how I felt it in every molecule of my body. I had to be bloody starving for human contact if something as small as that could make my heart pound.

I pressed her hand back. "Do it yourself, I'll teach you." She paused at the offer and I knew she was about to turn it down. "Come on, princess," I taunted, letting the words hum. "Do you want to come running to me every time it gets cold? You're in Scotland now, there's a lot of chilly nights in your future." I kind of loved that idea, April windblown at my door, begging me to help her. I set the thought aside for later and focused on her little scowl. She was doing that a lot tonight.

"I didn't come running."

"You would have in about thirty minutes when the bloody thing didn't light."

"No, I wouldn't."

No, she wouldn't have, she'd have suffered in silence. That knowledge didn't sit well.

"I'm teaching you. No arguments." I focused back on the barren fireplace. "Remove the logs." She complied without argument. "Now, you want to start with a little paper, there should be some old newspapers in that box." I nodded to the small wooden chest between the log burner and the television stand. "Get some of the kindling, those are the smaller pieces of wood, and the matches."

She returned with all the items in her freckled hands, settling slightly closer to me than before. Our thighs brushed, her bare skin hot against the denim covering mine. I cleared my throat.

"Right . . . newspaper first, you don't need much, just something to catch alight. Next, add three or four bits of kindling around it . . . keep a bit of space between them . . . perfect." I nodded. "Now add two decent-size logs, the drier the better."

Tongue between her lips, she settled the logs, then shifted them, following my instructions to the letter. I almost told her it didn't need to be perfect, people had made fires from a lot less, but I couldn't bring myself to ruin it for her.

"Like that?" she asked uncertainly and I had to clear my throat again.

"Aye . . . that's perfect." Perfect. Perfect. Perfect. Learn another word, pal. I grabbed the box of fire lighters, peeled a white square from the packet, and held it out to her. "You could light it just like that, but it's a lot easier with one of these."

"Is that not cheating or something?"

"Cheating who?"

She shrugged. "I don't know . . . every chest-beating male in the world."

I chuckled, the sound more like a breathy gust of air. "Why make it harder than it needs to be?"

Seeming to agree, she accepted it and followed my instructions to push it to the center of the stack. Then she struck a match, laughing happily when the paper set ablaze, followed by the kindling. I stared at her, eyes memorizing skin that glowed a sunset orange, her hair a burnt scarlet.

Click.

Shit.

"I did that myself," she said eventually.

133

"Yes you did."

She turned to me, her features soft and warm, a coin flip from the way she'd looked at me five minutes earlier. "Thank you."

Dammit, I hadn't even apologized yet. Shifting away, I clamored to my feet and perched on the edge of the sofa. The dogs instantly swarmed me, but I let my hands fall between my open knees, looking as near to her eyes as I dared. I made it to the small freckle on the bow of her top lip. "I'm sorry for my behavior . . . earlier, I mean. I'm not . . . well, you see . . ." I straightened and swallowed, wishing like hell I'd pulled my scribbled notes from my pocket before beginning this shit show. "I'm not good at this." I was suddenly glad not to be looking at her because that was a bare-minimum, one-star, do-not-recommend apology.

"Not good at apologizing?"

My eyes fell further, taking in the comfy, oversize T-shirt she'd paired with her shorts. Gone was well put together April, this was relaxed April. Sunday morning in bed April. I scrubbed at my beard. "I'm not good at any of it."

She made a hmm sound, before: "Accepted."

"What?"

"Your apology, I accept it."

"Just like that?" I asked incredulously.

She shrugged. "You meant it, didn't you?"

"Yes."

"Then I accept."

Could it really be that simple?

Like she'd read my silent question, she laughed. "Mal, let me give you some advice. Women aren't as complicated as men like to make out. We don't need you to walk across hot coals when all we're looking for is a sincere apology. That's always the part that gets missed out."

I nodded, fully taking the words on board. "Whatever you want to do regarding social media, you have my blessing. Not that you need it," I added. "And the tasting, I'd like you to go ahead with it as long as you would be okay with me setting some boundaries. I know the land belongs to you, but it's been my home for a long time and I—" I broke off, unsure how to word my anxious thoughts.

"Whatever you need," she agreed immediately. "We'll keep it small, set boundaries for where guests can explore. You won't even need to be there if you don't want to." I nodded my thanks, breathing slightly steadier now. "Now that's out of the way," she said cheerily. "I was thinking you should try being my friend again, start up the old book club."

"We were never in a book club."

"Sure we were, I gave you my copy of *Twilight* that summer, remember?"

How could I forget? She'd shown up one day carrying a plain black book with only a pair of hands holding an apple on the cover. It stood out from the covers her books usually bore; scantily clad males tearing the petticoats off their lovers.

She'd obviously caught me sneaking glances because she held it out to me as soon as she turned the last page. Struck stupid, I'd accepted, reading it cover to cover in a single night. Even at seventeen, the premise had seemed ridiculous. A teenage girl dating a hundred-year-old vampire addicted to the scent of her blood?

But something about it had clearly enraptured April because the following day, she'd shown up with the sequel. Then the third and fourth.

I read the entire series that summer, hoping to learn her secrets. Then school started up and things returned to normal. By the time the next summer rolled around, April was a year older, adventurous and restless. Hanging out with her friends rather than at the distillery. And the rest was history. Until now.

"I'm a great friend," she urged as though she were trying to convince me.

"I'm not."

"I think Heather would disagree."

I cringed. "Does a sibling even count?"

"I wouldn't know." She smiled sweetly. "But I'd say yes, sharing blood doesn't guarantee a person's presence in your life. If she's there, it's because she wants to be."

Bloody hell. The sentiment was like a vise grip around my heart. What the hell was she doing to me? Throwing out these emotional bombs I was in no way prepared to dodge. Tears sprung suddenly in my eyes and I blinked them away, propelling to my feet before I could start weeping. Only then did I remember the DVD I'd shoved into my pocket. It felt completely lame now but I'd brought it as an olive branch of sorts.

Pulling it from my jacket, I set it on the arm of the chair. "For you to borrow," I rushed out, already turning on my heel. "Goodnight. Let's go, Boy." There was no chance she missed the wet emotion in my throat. I didn't even stop to see if Boy followed, just opened the kitchen door and bounded down the steps. My feet slowed when I reached the hedge row, a boundary line of sorts, and my breath rushed back into me. Boy's wet nose pressed into my hand and I looked down at him. Only his eyes were visible in the moonlight, but I felt the steady beat of his tail on my thigh. Always so happy to see me.

"How much did I embarrass myself back there?" I asked him.

His silence said it all.

I'D JUST SLID BENEATH THE BED COVERS, A PAINED GROAN falling from my lips, and reached to turn my phone off like I did every night, when it buzzed in my hand.

Unknown number: So he was dead the entire time?

Mal: Who is this?

Unknown number: Bruce Willis, obviously. Try to keep up.

An olive branch. I'd extended one and she offered one right back.

Mal: How did you get this number?

Unknown number: Is that really what you're focusing on right now?

Unknown number: I feel like my entire life has been a lie.

Unknown number: How have I got this far in life without seeing a single spoiler?

Mal: You seriously haven't seen The Sixth Sense before?

Mal: 'I see dead people.' It's one of the most well-known movie quotes ever.

Unknown number: All right, Critics' Choice, I've been kind of busy.

I paused, fingers hovering over the screen. I should leave it there. This way pain lies, a sensible voice whispered.

Mal: So . . . did you enjoy it?

The moment I sent the text, I closed the conversation, locking the screen. A few exchanged texts didn't make us friends.

I put the phone back on the side table, but I didn't turn it off.

13

MAL
Like Real People Do – Hozier

April and I were becoming friends. I thought.

The only other person I'd ever called a friend was a recently deceased seventy-five-year-old. I clearly wasn't an expert, but as I reread the text message on my phone screen, it definitely felt that way.

Unknown number: Can you send me the highball recipe you recommended?

I paused my raking, setting the instrument against the wall to glance at her. Sitting at one of my rickety dining room chairs, her laptop balanced across her thighs, she sipped her coffee and went back to typing. The cup she'd poured for me was rapidly cooling on the lip of the steeper. I still couldn't bring myself to admit I hated the taste.

April had worked in here the previous day too, only yesterday, she'd stood awkwardly by the windowsill, balancing her computer on the painted brick with one hand while she typed with the other. Continuing work on the website—or so she'd told me—I was still too anxious to ask for more details. It didn't slip my notice that she'd chosen to work here, with me, despite the less-than-ideal surroundings. Preempting she'd do the same today, I'd arrived early, dragging one of the chairs in after me. If she insisted on working here, there was no sense in her being uncomfortable, I reasoned with myself. *Just part of being a good boss.*

My early arrival allowed plenty of time for overthinking. By the time she appeared, I'd grown edgy and tired from turning possible opening lines over in my head. *Good morning. Did you sleep well? I thought you might need somewhere more comfortable to work. Did you dream of me like I dreamed of you?*

Well . . . not that last one, but any of the first three would have been acceptable. Not exactly award-winning conversation skills, but they would have sufficed. Only, when the time came, I didn't say any of those things. When she thanked me for the chair, I ducked my head and ignored her, ears burning too fiercely not to give me away. From my periphery, I noticed her shiver, hands chafing against her bare arms. Even during summer, it was cold here in the morning. I made a mental note to dig out a blanket tonight. *Idiot.*

I shook the thought loose, focusing on my phone screen instead.

Mal: Why are you texting when we're in the same room?
Unknown number: Because you respond better to me in text.

Did I? I resisted the urge to turn and determine if she was serious or teasing.

Unknown number: Highball?

Mal: Kier kept it classic. Whisky, ginger beer, lemon.

Unknown number: Sounds easy enough.

Mal: Thought you didn't like whisky?

Unknown number: I said that when?

Mal: Your dry heaving was enough of a statement.

Unknown number: Funny.

Unknown number: I know you tried to kill me on purpose.

Mal: *I* tried to kill *you*? You have a short memory, princess.

"It was one time! Let it go already," she shouted aloud and I couldn't contain my grin.

Unknown number: The recipe isn't for me. I was thinking I could post some cocktail recipes on social media, something for people to try at home.

I started to write that I knew a few more recipes she could use when my phone pinged again.

Unknown number: It's also something we could offer in person, like a cocktail-making class.

Unknown number: I'd keep it small like we discussed . . .

Unknown number: And only if the tasting goes well . . . otherwise we can forget it.

I could tell by the way the messages pinged too quickly for me to read that she was nervous about bringing this to me. I felt like a prick. I felt like an even bigger prick when I knew I couldn't agree. It was a good idea. A great fucking idea, but . . .

Mal: Don't you think we should focus on one thing at a time?

Unknown number: You're right! I'm sorry, I'm excited and getting ahead of myself.

Mal: I'm happy you are so excited about this place. Kier would be proud of you.

Three dots appeared on her end, then disappeared. I wanted so badly to turn and read her expression, but she was correct about the text message thing, I felt more confident conversing with her that way, so I did.

Mal: Have you set a date for the tasting?

Unknown number: Two weeks on Friday

Unknown number: I'm making an invite as we speak. Heather secured access to the online village bulletin board so I can post it there.

Mal: That's a thing?

Unknown number: Apparently so. And harder to get into than the Oscars.

Mal: If there's anything I can do to help, let me know.

Unknown number: Well . . .

She paused.

Mal: What, princess?

Unknown number: I was hoping we could open one of the forty-nine-year-old casks to sell on the night. Give it an exclusive label and set it at a higher price.

Unknown number: It would be a great way to honor Kier's work.
Mal: By making a profit?
Unknown number: Exactly!

Those casks were special, could I really just open one up like that? I glanced back to find her eyes already on me, petite features a painting of quiet hope, braced for disappointment. She bit her lip and I knew I was bloody done for.

The distillery and everything in it belonged to her, we both knew it. Yet she'd come to me with this idea, and if I said no, I knew she'd respect that decision. I pocketed my phone and got back to work, unwilling to see the delight on her face as I grunted, "I'll get to work on it tomorrow."

April being April let out an ear-piercing squeal, so high-pitched both of the dogs jumped to attention. Her arms circled my waist, barely meeting in the middle, and it was my turn to start. Her soft curves molded against my back and all I could think was how sweaty I must be. *Could she feel it? Did I smell?* "You're the best, grumps." She spoke the words between my shoulder blades and the skin on every part of my body pebbled. "Thank you, thank you . . . I won't let either of you down."

Click.

SITTING IN MY FAVORITE ARMCHAIR, A FORGOTTEN BOOK spread across my lap, I stared down at the photo on my phone screen with a vast amount of confusion. It was a blurry photo of two drawings, both of two stick figures drawn by a hasty hand. In the first, they were laying top and tail in a wiggly lined rectangle. In the second, they spooned one another.

I waited. Knowing April, she undoubtedly had more to say. Not even thirty seconds later my phone pinged and my heart leapt with it. Over the past few days I'd begun to associate the sound with April. Every time, my heart reacted the same. I was Pavlov's dog, salivating to the sound of a bell.

Princess: He could totally have fit on the door.

I scrolled back up to the drawings, studying them until it clicked. My head fell back, body shaking with peals of laughter. My vocal cords strained from misuse and Boy popped his head up in his basket, clearly confused by the hacking sound coming from his owner.

Mal: Titanic?
Princess: What else?
Princess: This is daylight robbery! I've been robbed, Mal. Robbed of a happy ending!
Princess: JACK COULD HAVE FIT ON THE DAMN DOOR!!!!

Still smiling, I typed back.

Mal: You'll get over it.
Princess: No I won't, I'm bereft.
Mal: You've seriously never seen this film?
Princess: As a kid, sure.
Mal: Were you upset then?
Princess: Elsie used to turn it off before the end. Now I know why.

I laughed even harder.

Mal: Damn! Elsie did not set you up for adulthood.

Princess: Now I'm wondering what other films I'm remembering wrong.

Mal: Forrest Gump?

Mal: Bridge to Terabithia?

Princess: That cute film about the two kids who create a magical land?

Mal: DON'T WATCH IT!!!

Princess: Why? How does it end?

Mal: They all live happily ever after.

Princess: LIAR! I'm googling . . .

I waited, grinning down at the screen. It didn't even take a minute.

Princess: NO! This is the worst day of my life.

Mal: Sorry to be the bearer of bad news.

Princess: No you aren't, you love finally getting me back for choking you with my bra.

Princess: I'd still like that back, by the way!

My eyes flicked to my bedside drawer where I'd hidden the lacy garment. She'd have to find it first.

We were approaching dangerous ground. She must have sensed it too because my phone went dark in my hand.

And then . . . *ping*.

Thump, thump, thump.

Princess: It's just as well about Jack. He probably would have pushed Rose overboard eventually anyway.

Mal: Elaborate, princess.

I swore it was like she spoke another language sometimes.

Princess: What are you texting me on? A satellite phone?

Princess: It's a joke, because Leo only dates women in their twenties. Gross, but sadly true.

Princess: Don't you pay attention to current events?

Mal: Are we counting celebrity gossip among current events? I thought you more than anyone would hate gossip.

Three dots appeared and then disappeared.

Appeared and then disappeared.

My hand tightened around the phone, suddenly realizing how that sounded. Maybe I'd taken it too far—

Princess: Touché.

Fuck. I exhaled heavily, fingers flying over the screen, wishing I could brush away that last comment.

Mal: The issue isn't if they could both fit but whether the door could stay afloat. It was lack of buoyancy that killed him.

Princess: Well, shit.

Princess: At least Rose got to keep that big-ass diamond.

Mal: The true moral of the story I think.

Princess: HA!

Thump, thump, thump.

Princess: I almost worked with Leo once.
Mal: Continue . . .
Princess: About six years ago, but neither of our schedules matched and they ended up recasting my part. I think the project got shelved eventually.

It was easy to forget sometimes how big April's world was. Mine stopped where the final stone of this island met the water. But April . . . ? She could have anything she wanted.

My heart thumped for a different reason.

I forced myself to reply.

Mal: Sounds like it would have been a big deal.
Princess: Probably . . .
Princess: And he obviously would have fallen madly in love with me. I could be sipping cocktails on a beach somewhere right now instead of freezing my butt off in Scotland.
Mal: Do you have enough wood for the fire?
Princess: More than enough, daddy. I was making a point.

I reread the message a dozen times, blood singing, other parts of me straining.

She was joking. She had to be.

Mal: I thought he only dated women in their twenties? You'd be right where you are now, princess.
Princess: I HATE YOU!

And then, like she knew exactly what it had done to me . . .

Princess: Night, daddy.

I was tempted to reply, to say something flirty. *I wasn't flirty.* So I stuffed the phone beneath the closest cushion, scrubbing a hand over my face. When I'd calmed myself enough to head to bed, I pushed to my feet and found Boy staring at me. "What are you looking at?"

His head tilted and I could have sworn his eyes said "get a hold of yourself, man."

That dog saw too much.

I headed to my small bathroom, undressing as I went, and climbed straight into the shower. Setting the temperature to cold, I ducked beneath the shock of water, pressing both hands to the tile so I wouldn't be tempted to reach down and squeeze my straining cock. Jerking off would feel too much like giving in, and I needed to focus all of my energy on getting over these feelings. It didn't help when our text conversations were occurring more frequently. I never started the conversations, but I always engaged. And as the days passed, they'd taken on a more flirtatious tone. On her end, because like I said, I did not know how to flirt.

Last night she texted and asked me to play a game where we both had to send the last photo we'd taken on our phone at the same time. I thought it was a little strange, but played along. The moment hers loaded on my ancient phone, I realized my mistake. It was a photo of her and Dudley down at the bay, Dudley's whiskers wet and sand-coated. She wore dark sunglasses, her curls blowing in the breeze as she smiled brilliantly into the camera. The photo wasn't revealing, cutting off just below her shoulders. But it showed enough for me to see the wings of her collarbone and emerald-green bikini top. The color against her creamy skin was enough to make me dizzy.

And then the horror set in.

She'd sent a stunning selfie. And I'd sent . . . *oh god*. I'd sent a half-blurry shot of the wooden washback, seventy-two hours into the fermentation process.

Twenty-four hours later, the memory still made me ill.

If she texted tomorrow, I wouldn't respond.

• • •

Princess: What are you doing?

Mal: Watching Sleepless in Seattle.

Princess: REALLY??

Princess: I love that film.

Mal: I kind of guessed when you demanded I watch it ten times this week.

Princess: "I knew it the very first time I touched her. It was like coming home . . . only to no home I'd ever known."

Princess: "I was just taking her hand to help her out of a car and I knew . . . it was like magic."

Princess: I'm weeping!

Mal: Are you going to recite the entire bloody movie?

Princess: Maybe . . .

Mal: I'll stop watching.

Princess: ☹

THAT GOT THE BAREST SMIRK FROM ME.

I was grumpy tonight, and I discovered the reason the minute Tom Hanks opened his damn mouth. His irritating, too charming mouth. No wonder April loved this movie so much, it was what women wanted, romance and tooth-rottlingly sweet monologues. A man who could make a woman fall in love over a damn radio show.

For the first time that week, I ended the conversation first.

14

APRIL
Want Want – Maggie Rogers

Y ou still haven't signed the contract?" Syd's voice was a high peal down the line.

Sweat pooling beneath my arms, I clutched the phone tighter to my ear, squeezing Dudley's stocky body to my slick chest with my free hand. I traversed the steep path down to the bay with slow steps. Even my knees were sweating. The chill from the previous week had scorched away thanks to the tail end of a heatwave blowing in from southern Europe and it was hot. *Really hot.* I didn't mean to be so predictably British about it, but it might be too hot.

Perspiration mingling with the scent of sun cream I'd slathered on before leaving the manor, I felt a million miles from the April Sinclair persona I was used to slipping on every morning. I hadn't felt like her for weeks now, if I was being honest with myself.

"I told you, I need to take some time. I said the same thing to Angela and she understood." I panted, flicking out the toe of my sandal to dislodge the tiny pebbles that had snuck into the sole.

"Time for what?"

"I don't know, grieve my grandfather perhaps?" I replied sardonically.

"He died months ago and you weren't even that close." I winced. Sydney had this way of saying exactly what she was thinking without pausing to consider whether anyone else wanted to hear it. I usually found it refreshing. "I'm sorry," she said right away. "That sounded awful. I shouldn't have said it like that."

"Then what should you have said?" I didn't try to hold back the bite in my voice. It was close to a million degrees in my bedroom last night and I'd slept maybe an hour. I was cranky as hell.

"That your grandfather wouldn't want you throwing away your career for the sake of misplaced guilt."

Was that what I was doing? Throwing away my career?

My career had been smashed to pieces by someone I thought I could trust, and I'd spent years trying to cobble it back from the rubble. The idea that I no longer cared incensed me. It was possible to care *too much*. Caring too much had consumed every part of me. I was just starting to get those pieces of myself back.

I paused at a divot in the path facing the water and sat down on a boulder pushing up from the overgrowth. Tall grass parted under my weight, long-stemmed thistles with their purple bulbed heads reaching out to brush my bare arms. My eyes fell closed against the sun's warmth, flashes of yellow through translucent eyelids. "This isn't guilt—it might have started that way, but I'm happy here, Syd, I feel like I can breathe properly for the first time in years."

It was funny, for months after I moved to London, I would stroll down to Oxford Street or Trafalgar Square and stare in wonder at the city lights, at the people rushing about their busy lives. *This is living*, I'd think, *everyone has a purpose, a place to be*. Now I felt that here, as I never had as a child. It held a different kind of buzz, less thrilling but more . . . right. Like a river converging to bring me to this place at this precise moment.

"So . . . you're never coming home?"

"Of course I'm coming home, I can't stay here forever." For the first time, the declaration held less weight. "Angela said she would—" Movement in the water caught my eye, a dark head rising beneath the waves and dipping down again. Strong, tanned arms cut through the current like a knife through butter. And there on the shore was Boy, dozing in the shade of a rock beside a pile of dark fabric. My eyes cut back to Mal, the cerulean water just clear enough to make out his solid form beneath. *Holy shit.*

"She said she would . . . ?" Sydney prompted down the line.

Right. "Sorry—" I blinked. "The line is bad. Angela said she'd send any scripts of interest my way."

"Has she sent any?"

"Not yet."

"She will, she's a fantastic agent."

"I know, I trust you." As though attached by an invisible thread, my eyes sought Mal out again. With impressive speed, he swam as far as the rocky outcrop where the waves foamed and spat with ferocity, turned beneath the water, and cut back before repeating. "Look, Syd, I have to go, but I'll call you tomorrow, yeah? I want to hear all about the movie."

She snorted. "Of course you do, love. Perhaps luring you back with dazzling set stories will be my new tactic." I laughed too, thinking that might be the only one to work because it was the one thing about my old life I missed. The feeling of a new script and the first tingle of excitement at the table read. Costume fittings, long hours in a makeup chair. The inevitable wrap party and the emotion that came with creating something you cared about. *That* I missed.

Hanging up, I climbed to my feet, dusting off the bottom of my short pink summer dress. The slope became easier from here on out, a soft incline where dry earth gave way to sand and flat pebbles perfect for skimming. I set Dudley on his feet and he gave a wobbly prance, adjusting his uneven weight to the terrain. The waves were louder down here but Boy still heard him, climbing to his feet and trotting in our direction.

I bent, running my hand down his damp fur, suddenly feeling awkward. I wasn't confident enough to swim very far out, but I'd worn my bikini beneath my dress, planning to take a quick dip to cool off. With Mal here, I didn't know how to proceed. I walked further onto the beach, feet sinking until soft sand covered my skin. Thanks to the curvature of the rocks, no breeze flowed down here, and the air was humid and sticky. Sweat pooled on the back of my neck and between my breasts.

I didn't know if Mal had seen our arrival or simply finished with his swim, but suddenly he was there, strolling from the water like Daniel Craig as James Bond. I knew I was staring. I also knew my mouth was open.

It was the same as most bodies, muscle and skin, a smatter of chest hair and two nipples. But on Mal . . . I'd always known he was big. Wide-shouldered with biceps that unintentionally strained the fabric of every shirt he wore. But this . . . well, it bordered on ridiculous. Water sluiced down his chest in rivulets, glistening beads getting caught in the small clefts between muscles not gained from hours in the gym but by rugged, physical work. He wasn't even wearing swim shorts, simply tight black boxers that clung to *everything*.

I didn't know if it was his continual blushing or that his shoulders often curved in on themselves as though apologizing for taking up too much space in the world, but either way, I hadn't ever pictured him like this. I had imagined him. *Often*. Only it was more sexy-country-farmer than rippling Adonis.

I had to look away, I *had* to, before I begged him to throw me over his shoulder. The whimpering noise I was making must have warned him he was currently starring in his very own strip tease, because he looked right at me, eyes widening with surprise.

I whirled, and took off running. The sand made the soles of my shoes slippery, and as soon as I hit a large flat stone, my feet flew out from under me. I landed hard, smacking my elbow. "I'm sorry," I called over my shoulder. "I didn't mean to . . ." Pain flared up my arm and I clutched it to my chest. I was panting. Stuttering. I never stuttered. The heat must have melted my brain. "I mean . . . I should have announced myself."

He was at my side in a heartbeat. "Are you all right?"

I couldn't look at him. "Yes, I'm fine." I shook my arm out and hissed. "Ouch, *shit*. No—" Seizing my shoulders in his hot grip, he lifted me to face him, taking my forearm into his calloused hands. I looked down at it purely so I wouldn't look at his chest again, and noticed the skin was red and inflamed. Heat was rolling off of him in waves. I could smell him, sweat and salt and sea mixed with something citrusy. As if hypnotized, I swayed into him and he steadied me again.

I couldn't be this close to him right now. I extracted myself, moving my arm tentatively for him to see. "It's fine."

At the action, he seemed to become aware that he was nearly naked. His cheeks and ears flooded crimson and he fumbled for his pile of clothes, forcing wet legs into dark blue jeans and drawing green plaid over his top half, unevenly fastening the buttons. As beautiful as his body might be, it was that missed button hole that made me want to throw myself at him and lay kisses over every speck of exposed skin.

Clearly Mal wasn't feeling whatever insane pheromones I currently drowned in, because he assessed my arm again with a frown, his scar turning a stark white. "It looks like it might bruise, we need to get some ice on it."

I needed to end this interaction. "I will."

He came a step closer and I edged one back. "Did you come to swim?"

I looked longingly at the swell of water. "I planned to, but I might just skip it now."

"I can wait and walk you back up, the movement might be good for your elbow."

Any other time, the idea of stripping off my dress and slipping into the water while Mal watched might get me hot. But right now, I was so aware of how disheveled I must appear. My hair in a frizzy pineapple atop my head, sweat sticking to my temples and rolling down the nape of my neck. "I think I'll just head back, it's a bit warm down here for Dudley anyway." The excited splash of Dudley's feet in the shallow waves called me a liar and I felt bad for cutting the boys' play short.

Of course Malcolm didn't call me out, just tucked his feet into his boots, scooped up Dudley with one hand and curled the other around my non-injured elbow, letting Boy guide us back up the bank. I didn't need him to steady me, it actually made it more difficult with both of us squeezing onto the narrow path. But I kept my mouth shut, basking in the thrilling heat of his touch while I fought to keep my breathing steady as the incline began to take its toll.

Minutes later, when he tried to follow me up the grassy bank to the manor, I flat-out refused.

"It needs to be taken care of." He looked pissed.

"I can handle it," I insisted.

"Do you know where the ice is kept?"

I chuckled. "I'm sure I can figure it out." He opened his mouth to argue again. "What I really need is a long cold shower, so unless you plan to help with that, I won't need you."

His mouth froze mid-word, the rest of his body following. The warm breeze tousled his damp hair—the only part of him that moved. And then he glared at me and the spell broke. "I think you'll manage." Only, his tone didn't sound quite as disinterested.

"Are you sure?" I called to his retreating back. "What if I can't hold my loofah?"

His grumbling reply was lost in the wind, the middle finger he held up was not.

I giggled all the way back to the manor.

AFTER MY SHOWER I ATE MY LUNCH OUT ON THE BANK, LIStening to the sea and cries of gulls. Too hot for anything else, I nibbled on crackers and grapes straight from the fridge. In the open doorway, Dudley was cooking himself in the sun while lying on a towel I'd soaked in cold water. That dog was a juxtaposition I would never begin to understand.

I was still cursing what an idiot I'd been this morning when I heard the familiar yipping of my little foxes. Relief eased through me. It was a few days since I'd seen them and I worried about them in this heat. Emma appeared first—the white patch of fur around one eye made her the most distinguishable—followed by Geri and Victoria. Mel B wasn't far behind, and limping right at the back of the pack was Mel C. She had always been the most nervous around me—even when I offered her food, she sniffed at my outstretched hand awhile before begrudgingly taking a bite.

This was more than nerves.

I crouched as they approached, tossing treats out until only Mel C remained. "What happened, sweet girl?" Blood stained her white paw. Something had attacked her.

I reached for my phone, calling Heather without a second thought.

"Hey," she answered breathlessly. "Everything okay?"

"Yeah, your brother is a vet right?" I worried my lip, still looking at the blood oozing from the wound. She had to be in a lot of pain.

"Callum? Aye, his practice is on the high street but he doesn't open on Saturdays."

"Would he make a house call? I'll pay him extra."

Her voice dropped. "Is Dudley sick?"

"He's fine. It's . . . something else," I quickly reassured her. Not sure how she would react if I told her I wanted a visit for my pet fox.

"Right . . . I'll give him a call, see if he can drop around."

"You're the best."

Mel C was still letting me stroke her head from where she curled up at my hip when a text came through.

Heather: He can drop by in an hour x

"EVENING, LASS." CALLUM MACABE'S RUMBLING BROGUE WAS almost as devilish as the grin he flashed from the foot of the stoop. The move was obviously practiced and yet I couldn't deny its effectiveness when my immediate response was to reach up and smooth my hair back.

Oh, I bet the ladies just love him.

My fingers locked around the heavy wood of the front door, my feet rooted to the spot as I took him in. I'd forgotten how alike the male Macabe siblings looked. Heather was such a tiny little thing, with the same delicate features as her mother. Not at all like her brothers. They shared the same statuesque build and shoulders that could block out the sun. Full heads of hair that could go from blond to brown in an instant, though Callum's was beginning to streak with silver. Sharp noses and high cheekbones. It was only the eyes that set them apart. Where Mal's were an icy blue that reminded me of turbulent storm clouds on a January morning, Callum's were the azure blue of the water in the bay. It would be all too easy to fall right into them. And yet . . .

I blinked. Stepping back to give him room. "Good to see you again, Callum."

Small lines appeared around his mouth, the sign of a man who laughed freely and often. "Likewise. Heather said over the phone you needed a vet?"

"Thanks for coming on such short notice." I pressed back against the door, propping it open for him to walk through.

"No thanks necessary. I'd be lying if I said I wasn't hoping to bump into you." He winked in my direction, adjusting what looked like a medical bag on his shoulder. "I was beginning to think Mal had locked you away in his cottage."

The words were playful and, like every idiot to come before me, a smile slipped free. I hid it, giving him my back as I led him to the kitchen and family room.

He followed. "Heather said you were a wee bit evasive on the phone. Is there really an injured animal or were you just eager to see me again?"

I snorted, glancing back over my shoulder. "Eager enough to fake a medical emergency?"

He shrugged, unperturbed by my incredulity. "It wouldn't be the first time."

I stopped and turned, disbelief evident in my tone. "Women make fake appointments to spend time with you?"

That grin flashed again. "All the time."

I folded my arms, eyeing him shrewdly. He had to be lying. "What excuses do they make?"

"The usual . . . limping dog, stomach issues that turn out to be flatulence. I prefer the more exciting ones. I saw a goldfish once that refused to eat, and even a wild hare another lassie caught in her garden."

My brow flattened. "Why would they do that?"

He bent closer, like he was sharing a secret. "Because I'm a catch."

I snorted and he laughed, enjoying my obvious disbelief.

"I hope you billed her for time-wasting."

"She bought me dinner and we called it even."

"You went to dinner with her?" He only winked again and I pointed to the offending organ. "I think you have a problem with your eye, you should get that looked at."

He shifted closer. "And I'm beginning to think you called me here under false pretences."

Dammit. "This way."

He was silent as he followed me through the kitchen, but I sensed him looking around like Heather had when she came over for yoga. The manor was a big part of Mal's life and it suddenly occurred to me his siblings may not have been privy to this part of it. When we got to the back door, I watched his attention flick from Dudley, still bathing in the low sun, to Mel C.

"A fox?"

"Yep." If I thought there'd be further questioning, I was wrong. He dropped his bag by his feet and knelt, going into one of the side pockets and pulling out a stethoscope he hooked around his neck, all playfulness disappearing.

"What's wrong with him?"

"Her," I corrected and his attention moved back to me. "It's her front right paw, it's all bloody and has bite marks. Something attacked her."

He moved in slowly so as not to startle her. Mel C blinked her dark eyes open, watching him warily. He held out a hand for her

161

to sniff and after a pause she leant in, sniffing all of his extended digits before moving on to his palm and wrist. "That's a good girl," he encouraged, bringing the other hand around to pet her little head. I had to blink back tears. This skittish little baby was letting him touch her, pet her. How easily that trust could be betrayed in the wrong hands.

Keeping her head still, he pulled a small pen light from his bag, blinking it in both of her eyes and ears. "When did you first notice the injury?"

"This afternoon. I saw her two days ago and she was fine."

The stethoscope came next, easing it below her outstretched paws to her chest, and I watched his lips move as he counted. "That's a good girl," he cajoled again when she blinked at the cool metal. "Her eyes look clear and bright, so I'm not worried about an infection." He withdrew the stethoscope to run a hand down her back, gently lifting her tail to check her behind. Only then did he pull on a pair of latex gloves and assess her bloody paw. The blood had started to dry, turning her coarse white fur rust brown. As soon as he touched it, she yowled and withdrew.

I moved on instinct, dropping to my knees so our elbows brushed. I gave her head a comforting stroke. "Come on, Mel C, as soon as it's over you can have an extra treat." The look she returned said only three treats would do. "Deal," I muttered. "Manipulative little fox."

"Mel C?" Callum's voice broke our battle of wills.

"Yeah, like the Spice Girls. There's five foxes in total."

His lips twitched. "Big fan, are you?"

"Aren't we all?"

He considered, then said, "Fair enough." Pushing to his feet, he snapped off the gloves and stuffed them into a pocket. "Do you want the good news first or the bad news?"

My heart clenched. "Good news."

"The paw will be just fine. I'm going to give you a few days' worth of antibiotics as a precaution to stave off any infection."

My breath was short. "And the bad?"

His grin was back. So like Mal, yet not at all. "He's going to need a name change."

My head whipped back to Mel C. "He?"

"Yep."

"Well, damn." I snickered. "You'll always be a Spice Girl to me, Mel."

Callum's next laugh was rasping.

SIPPING MY MILKY COFFEE ON THE LOWEST PORCH STEP, I watched Mel C and his friends scamper off toward the line of hedges, smiling happily to myself at the renewed pep in his step.

Callum had managed to get an antibiotic in him yesterday before I threw his smirking arse out the door. Nicely, of course. Playboy or not, he'd done me a huge favor and hadn't charged me a penny, no dinner necessary. Not that he hadn't offered.

This morning's events were far more entertaining. Mel C had eyed every offering of food shrewdly, managing to spit the small white pill out no matter what treat I concealed it inside. Peanut butter was the eventual winner and Dudley had ducked beneath the kitchen table the moment the jar appeared. With peanut butter usually came claw clipping.

Mel C had eaten that shit up, his rough little tongue licking my finger clean.

I was just finishing off the dregs of my coffee when Boy came bounding into view. "Hey, handsome." He sniffed the hand I held out to him before fleeing to the kitchen to seek out Dudley.

His owner appeared moments later, hair a damp dark brown from his morning shower, a carton of eggs tucked beneath his arm. My eyes dragged over him, taking in the usual jeans and fitted navy T-shirt he wore. No man had a right to look that good in jeans and a T-shirt, especially a man who I knew put very little effort into his appearance. "Morning." He stopped a few feet away, unable or uncaring to hide the way his eyes swept over me in return.

I pressed my bare legs together and stood. When his eyes moved with me, they sharpened on my pajamas. Tight shorts in a soft pink that ended at the top of my thighs and a slightly cropped strappy top that matched. They weren't London skimpy, but they were sleepy-island-village skimpy. And judging by the way Mal's entire body drew to a stop, he agreed. His expression changed in an instant, from calm to panicked, along with something I couldn't quite read, as if the situation had evolved into something he was not equipped to deal with.

I glanced down. *Shit.* My nipples were saluting him good morning. I started to draw my arms up and then stopped. It was a million degrees outside and they were just nipples, what were a couple of nipples between friends? I'd seen his yesterday, after all— *and you can't stop thinking about them.* Still, the point was valid. I backed up into the house, refusing to cover myself and draw more attention to them.

"Good morning," I finally said back, bare toes pressing into the cool tile. I held my empty mug aloft. "Coffee?"

"What?" He shook his head like a wet dog. "Oh . . . aye." He followed, his booted steps slow and measured as if treading on cracking ice. I filled both our mugs, leaving his black as he seemed to prefer, and we fell into preparing our breakfast, keeping to separate sides of the island. Breakfast was usually a quiet affair, but this felt different—a pressing tension saturated the already humid air. I felt his sidelong glances while I chopped a banana, throat moving as he worked himself up to say something, then backing out at the last moment.

The difference between *this* and yesterday afternoon with Callum suddenly felt stark. A rush of guilt trailed the thought. I'd enjoyed Callum's attention, his flirting. It meant nothing, but it felt like I'd wronged Mal somehow. Which was stupid, since there was nothing between Mal and me.

I settled in at the bar with my bowl of yogurt and fruit. Content to wait Mal's silence out, my attention drifted to the idiots rolling around on the rug. I worried about Dudley with bigger dogs at the park sometimes. Not only was he a lot smaller, but his three legs also meant he didn't have the best balance and couldn't take the level of roughhousing other dogs could. But Boy seemed to know exactly when to draw back. *Ugh, their little hearts will break when we head back to London.*

"I noticed my brother's car here last night."

"Huh?" I snapped from my thoughts.

He was staring down into the pan as he stirred the sizzling eggs, throat working. "My brother. His car was here last night." It wasn't exactly a question.

I couldn't help teasing him, nodding around the piece of banana I popped in my mouth. "Late-night orgy, you should have come along."

The wooden spoon clattered and in true Mal fashion, he looked as though he might pop a vein. "Are you . . ." He gulped. "Are you messing with me?"

I shifted on my stool, crossing one leg over the other so they landed beside his hip. His eyes found them. "Why would I be messing with you? *It's just stuff us actors do.*"

"April." My name was a command I obeyed. Embarrassingly quickly.

"Jeez, all right. I'm messing with you. Heather called him to arrange a house call."

"A house call?"

I continued on with my breakfast, scraping the last of the yogurt from the bowl. "Yes, a vet appointment for my fox."

"A vet appointment for your fox," he repeated.

I peered around the room like I was looking for something. "Is it just me or do you hear an echo?"

His entire expression shuttered. *"April."*

"My real name twice in one morning, what a treat," I drolled, giving him a wide berth as I circled around to the sink.

He turned with me, tracking my movements. "Cut the crap, you know exactly how that sounded. What was he really doing here?"

Biting my lip, I gave him my back while I rinsed out the bowl. "Perhaps you should ask him."

He didn't pause. "I already have."

Well, shit. I tried to imagine it, Malcolm calling Callum—going to his house even—demanding to know why he'd been here. My hand clenched around the soapy sponge. "You sound jealous, grumps." I wiped the bowl out again just to give my shaking hands something to do.

166

"I'm not . . . that's not why I . . ." His voice was hoarse. "I wanted to make sure everything was all right."

"And what did Callum tell you?" He was closer now, if I stepped back we would be touching.

"Something I wouldn't repeat to a lady." I started to laugh but it cut off in a rough exhale when I felt him. The barest slide of his wide chest, blazing heat beneath thin cotton, tickling my shoulders. His breath stirred the hairs at the nape of my neck which, at his height, could only be possible if he was staring down at me. Both of my hands had sunk beneath the suds, any pretence of cleaning gone. My eyes fell shut and my head rolled back, landing snuggly between the muscles of his chest. *We fit. We fit just right.*

He groaned. Not aloud, but I felt the rumble of it in his chest. That tortured sound echoed in one ear, his racing heart in the other. My own beat even faster and I felt like it might explode through my chest if I didn't find a way to slow it. *"Princess,"* he pleaded.

It took a second to remember how to speak, to make sure the next words from my lips weren't a command for him to fuck me on the kitchen counter. "I told you . . . he came to check my fox. Mel C." His chin must have dipped because I felt the scrape of bristles snagging in my curls. Barely a touch, yet it was more—so much more—than I'd ever felt with anyone else. My eyes rolled. Instead of panting like I needed, I stopped breathing all together. At any moment he would realize what he was doing and draw away.

"Since when do you have a fox?"

How did he sound amused when I . . . I couldn't even think straight. "Since . . . since . . ."

"Princess."

"Fuck." Like it had an express pass to my vagina, the pet name that had annoyed me only last week made the skin between my thighs slicken.

He chuckled like he knew what it was doing to me, the first true laugh I'd ever heard from him. It was sweet and smoky like whisky.

"What the hell is happening?" The voice that came from my lips no longer belonged to me. I felt his chin move again, dipping until his jaw brushed my ear. Hands clamping down on the counter either side of me, caging my body in. I might have whimpered, there was no way of knowing.

"You were telling me about your fox," he prodded.

My fox. *Why did that sound so dirty?* "Right . . . Mel C . . ."

"Mel C. Is that her name?" His voice rumbled against my skin and my head tilted, completely on instinct. I was no longer in control of this ride.

"*His* name."

His nose met my skin, dragging from the curve of my jaw down to the strap of my top, goose bumps trailing in its wake. He inhaled and it was his turn to groan. "What happened to your fox, princess?"

"His paw, something bit him." My hands left the water to grip the basin, barely noting the water dripping down the front of my body.

"So you called my brother?"

"I called *Heather.*"

"To call my brother?" The commanding tone was back and the answer tore from me.

"Yes."

It seemed to wake him up. I felt the briefest brush of hips, the

168

hardness concealed beneath the fly of his jeans, then he retreated and my back arched, following him to the very last second. Air flowed between us, still sticky and oppressive but less consuming. I started to turn but he placed a hand on my shoulder. "I need to get to work," he said without further explanation.

What was *work*? "Right . . . of course." I clutched the counter tighter. It was the only thing holding me up.

He retreated, urging Boy out ahead of him. "Princess?" he said. I think I uttered a reply. "Stop feeding the foxes before one of them bites you."

15

MAL

I Wanna Be Yours – Arctic Monkeys

Princess: Do you mind if I come by and switch the DVD out today?

Her text stared back at me as it had for the past thirty minutes. It sat right below the unanswered text message from the day before.

Princess: I'm popping into the pet store over lunch, Jasmine put some treats aside for Dudley and the foxes. Want anything for Boy?

It was two days, a full forty-eight hours since the incident in the kitchen.

Incident being a chickenshit term for being overcome by jealousy that April called out a vet to help an injured animal, because that vet happened to be my attractive, happy-go-lucky brother. Let me spell it out one more time for all parties involved. I got jealous

170

because she called out my brother, the village veterinarian—big underline there—to help a wounded animal. I sounded like an insane person. And I couldn't even be quietly jealous. It was so damn obvious, she'd stated it out loud.

"You sound jealous, grumps." I cringed every time I thought of it.

If that weren't embarrassing enough, I'd pushed her up against the counter and ground my rock-hard cock against her. Not even the memory of her sweet arse cheeks cupping me through my trousers was enough to wipe away the burn of humiliation. It was like a bridge troll dry-humping Snow White.

And yet here she is texting you, a traitorous little voice whispered. *She responded to you in the kitchen.* No way would I have pressed my cock against her if she hadn't. Unless I'd misread the signals. Misread her breathy moans. It wasn't like I had a lot of experience reading women. *Shit.*

My mind churned, thoughts pinging from one impossible scenario to the next. Anxiety crept across my chest and tightened like shadowy vines. With trembling hands, I read her text again. The only way around this was to act normal, act like nothing happened. And if she slapped me and demanded an apology next time we were face-to-face, well, I'd muster the courage to stammer through it and then move to New Zealand.

What the hell would I do in New Zealand? Did they even have whisky? *Of course they do. Focus.*

Mal: What happened to your plans for tonight?

I'd overheard her talking on the phone to Juniper outside the dunnage yesterday morning, they were going to the Sheep's Heid.

Great job not being creepy.

A single blue tick appeared, then a second. She'd read it. For the next thirty seconds, I gripped that phone like it was the final plank of a sinking ship. Three dots appeared and my breath caught.

Princess: June's new rescue isn't fitting in well, she has to skip.

No idea what that meant. I didn't really care.

Princess: I'm thinking The Texas Chainsaw Massacre.
Mal: You said The Sixth Sense scared you.
Princess: I said it was creepy.
Mal: If you found that creepy, I don't think you can handle Texas Chainsaw Massacre.
Princess: MAL!!!
Princess: It's just a movie, I'll be fine.

16

APRIL
Cherry Wine – Hozier

I'd made a big mistake.

Huge. Bloody. Mistake.

The chainsaw whirred again. I jumped, smothering a throw cushion over my eyes, as poor Pam's on-screen cries seeped into the dark room. *People actually watch this for fun?* I tried to block it out, to slow my breathing until the scene was over. Pam screamed again and I'd officially had it. Every ounce of feminism fled my body as I dived across the bed and grabbed my phone to call for male reinforcement.

April: Mal!!

My hands shook.

April: Mal, help me.
April: SOS!!!

Mere seconds passed before the phone rang in my hand.

"Are you okay?" He sounded breathless.

"No." My voice was an embarrassing squeak. "I need you."

"I'm on my way, princess. What happened?"

"The movie! It was a mistake, you were right."

"The movie—" He broke off and then his voice became clearer. "*Jesus*, April, I thought you were hurt! Turn the movie off."

"I can't!" I cried, fully aware I sounded like a baby but too scared to care. I made the mistake of looking at the screen again and Pam, poor, sweet naive Pam, was being impaled on a meat hook.

"Why not?"

"Because I need to see the end . . . Does it have a happy ending?"

"Of course it doesn't! It's about a psycho family of cannibals."

"They're cannibals?" My voice went impossibly higher.

"Turn it off!" The command was deafening. Dudley poked his little head up from the mound of blankets.

"I can't. I'll be terrified forever if I don't see the ending."

He sighed and it was a relief to hear it, Mal being frustrated with me felt normal. "Shit . . . fine. Don't move. I'll be there soon."

"Thank you, Mal. Thank you, thank you, thank you." The line went dead and I squeezed my eyes shut, prepared to wait.

I didn't have to wait long. Not even a minute later I heard his tread on the stairs, the creaky third step that caught everyone out.

Following the sound on the television, or maybe just dog instinct, Boy's nose appeared first. Snuffling his way through the door, he padded quickly across the floor and hopped straight onto the end of the bed like he'd done it a thousand times, settling beside Dudley who flipped onto his back to get closer.

His owner, however, stopped on the landing, toeing the threshold that led to my room. My breath stalled. It felt like days since I'd properly seen him. Working on the website and social media kept me busy. I'd also begun the ordeal of clearing the tasting room for the event next week. So when he lingered, I ate up the sight of him.

I suddenly wondered if he'd ever been in here over the years, if he'd been curious enough about me to snoop. The way his eyes darted over the dated wallpaper and movie posters, I knew that wasn't the case. His attention finally drifted to the bed. To me. "This movie has you so terrified you had to call me, yet you didn't lock the back door."

Not what I was expecting. "I remembered but I was too scared to go down and lock it."

"Dammit, April, lock the damn door." The words were as labored as his breathing. Cheeks flushed. Hair tousled and slightly damp. Had he run here?

Yes. Instinct gave me the answer I knew he'd deny to the back teeth. I let the knowledge settle with a secret smile. Mal was beginning to care for me. And him grumbling about locking the door was the only way he knew to show it. "I will," I answered him, settling further beneath the covers. "Thank you for coming." He grunted, eyes chasing my hands as they rearranged the bedsheets. "Are you going to come in?" I asked.

"I don't know." The words were rough, and suddenly, I was back in the kitchen two days ago, the imprint of his cock against my lower back.

The memory was cut criminally short by a piercing scream from the television. I flinched, shoving the throw pillows back over my eyes. "No, no, no . . . what is wrong with these people? Just get in the car and leave! Why do they always go back?"

He huffed again, closer this time. I heard the sound of his boots being removed, then the bed dipped dramatically to one side as his big body settled. He didn't touch me, but the skin along the right side of my body tingled and I held my breath as the sheets rustled. "I thought you were being dramatic," he said.

I squished further into my cushion shield until all the light from the room winked out. "I've never been more scared in my entire life."

"So just a little dramatic then?"

"Please . . ." I groaned. The sound muffled. "I need you to not be enjoying this. Can you do that?"

"You think I enjoy seeing you scared?" The bed dipped again and I felt him shift closer. My temporary temptation was stronger than my fear because I turned my face a fraction to see him. Above the covers, Mal reclined back against the pillows, looking soft and content. He gazed back at me, eyes storm-cloud gray in the low light. "I'm not smug, I promise. Just wondering why the hell you're still watching it."

"I told you," I whispered. "I need to see the end so I know it's over."

"There's like five sequels."

Curling into a ball, I buried my face into the pillow again. "Why would you tell me that?" He laughed, the second I'd heard and the second I'd missed with my own eyes. "I hate you."

"Me? I tried to warn you!"

"Warn me harder next time! Say 'April, if you watch this movie you will shit your pants'!"

"Have you?"

"No!"

His next laugh was throaty and I lifted my head fully, determined to watch. One hand pressed against his chest and his head tipped back, compressing the pillow as he smiled, eyes closed. A moment of pure release. Watching him felt intimate. Would watching him orgasm feel this gratifying?

The thought alone was enough to make my body tighten. My thighs squeezed together as my nipples shrank into tight buds, scraping against my thin top. There was something really wrong with me because sounds from the movie filtered through my lusty haze, something hard beating against flesh with a sickening squelch. I flinched back behind my makeshift cover. "What's happening now?"

"You don't want to know."

"Yes, I do. What I'm imagining is probably so much worse."

"Then look at the screen."

"*Mal!*" He didn't get it.

"All right, all right . . . Jerry is being beaten to death with a hammer."

I blew a long, steadying breath through my nose. "Why would anyone make this—No. Better question. Why would anyone *enjoy* this?"

"Bad time to tell you it's based on a true story?"

I shook. I was literally shaking. "There is never a good time to tell anyone that. Ever."

He snickered again. This time I was too scared to enjoy it. Too quick for me to process, his thick arm curled around my waist and drew me into his side, his clean fragrance with a hint of citrus enveloping every one of my senses. I stiffened, zero idea how to proceed in this situation. I didn't want him to feel uncomfortable, didn't want him to feel that because he was here in my bed, he owed me anything more than friendly comfort. Mal clearly had more control of his faculties than me, because his hand shifted to my bare shoulder, exerting gentle pressure until I relaxed into the crook of his arm. His chest bobbed rapidly beneath my cheek, revealing he wasn't as unaffected as he appeared. I opened my eyes to watch it.

Up. Down.

Up. Down.

Up. Down.

With his free hand, he searched behind him until he found the thick blanket hooked over the headboard and settled it over both of us. "Better?"

I grinned stupidly behind the cushion. "Yes."

"Good," he grumbled, back to growly Mal in an instant. But I swore when I felt a hand smooth down the back of my hair, it was shaking. I tucked myself closer.

After a minute of silence, I asked, "What's happening now?"

"Sally's being chased back to the gas station."

"Why's she going there?"

I felt his huff all the way to my toes. "Because everyone in a horror movie is an idiot."

"Mal?"

"Yes?"

"Am I irritating you?"

He sighed. "No."

"You sure?"

"Yes!" I grinned again, glad for my concealed expression. Despite the circumstances, I was enjoying this far too much. The close proximity. The grumbly rumble in his chest. It was a soothing balm to every jangled nerve.

"Mal?"

"*What?*"

"Why do you own this movie?"

His chest rose and held. "I don't know."

"Do you watch it once a week?"

"No."

"Have you killed? Are you likely to kill again?"

"That's it—" He started to rise and I flung my arms around his waist, clinging to him.

"I'm sorry . . . I'll be quiet. I promise. Please stay."

His body solidified for a heartbeat, before he lowered himself back against the headboard. This time, he didn't fully relax—it felt more like a pretence of relaxation, an imitation of what he thought his body should be doing. I kept my arm tight around his waist, and my cheek slid to the hard plane of his stomach. He didn't point it out. Neither did I.

As we settled into the remainder of the movie, his hand curled over my shoulder, so low, his fingers tickled back and forth over my drumming pulse. I didn't point it out. Neither did he.

SOONER THAN I WOULD HAVE LIKED, THE CREDITS BEGAN TO roll, plunging my bedroom into near darkness. I hadn't watched a single minute of the second half of the movie and at some point—likely irritated by my body continually flinching against his—Mal lowered the volume on the television and started whispering commentary here and there. I suspected he was purposely missing out some of the more gruesome parts, and at times straight-up bullshitting, because just before the end, he'd said, "Leatherface is dead. Sally and Franklin got away." That didn't exactly add up if there were five sequels in existence.

As the names trailed across the screen, I felt the precise second he became aware of the close press of our bodies. I was half in his lap by that point. His left leg had found its way beneath the sheets and my right leg was curled around it, bare toes pressed to his jean-covered calf. The rough drag of his fingertips across my collarbone ceased and he cleared his throat. He was going to leave. I scrambled for any way to keep him just a little longer.

"What was it like here when it was just you and Kier?" The question came out in a rush, one I'd wanted to ask but wasn't certain he would answer.

He hesitated. "You mean . . . toward the end?"

"Yes," I whispered.

He didn't speak. The silence so drawn-out, I feared he never would again. Then: "It was sad at times . . . most of the time. Peaceful in others."

"Peaceful?" I couldn't imagine how.

"He accepted his fate early on . . . never fought it when he discovered the chemo hadn't worked. Those final few weeks were spent eating the food he liked, watching the films he loved . . .

yours mostly. He was on strong medication so was never in much pain."

That did little to ease me. "And when it wasn't peaceful?"

"Horrific." His voice cracked down the middle.

And the pain . . . the pain I'd carried in my heart all these months stretched until it encompassed my entire chest. I felt like I couldn't breathe around it. I held him tighter. "I'm so sorry."

His face pressed into my hair. "Where were you, April?" I'd asked my question and this was his, the one he'd held in all these weeks. "You never came back. Why?"

Tears pricked my eyes. "Because I didn't know." I thought the truth might feel like a weight off my chest, but it felt like an excuse.

"He didn't tell you?" His tone was a palette of surprise and skepticism.

"No."

His heart began to thunder beneath my cheek. "He told me he did. I asked him point-blank, and he replied, 'She said she's too busy.'"

Oh, Kier. Something sharp lodged itself in my throat. "I swear I didn't—"

"I know." His reassurance was instantaneous. "Now that I actually think about it, that's exactly the type of shit Kier would pull. Fuck." His eyes squeezed shut. "The things I said, I'm so sorry—"

He didn't get what I was trying to say. I pushed to sit, but we remained tangled. The palm of my left hand pressed flat against his chest, directly above his heart. "I *should* have known. I phoned him two weeks before he died and he sounded off. When I asked,

181

he fed me some bullshit about having a cold. I should have pressed harder."

"There was no way you could have known if he didn't want you to."

"I could have visited more." He didn't respond because he had no reassurances to offer me. I should have visited more and we both knew it.

I could tell Mal about the money, the reason for our estrangement, but all it would do was hurt him. And with Kier gone, all the gambling and the debt no longer angered me as it once had. When I thought of it now, all I felt was sorrow. He must have been suffocating beneath the weight of all his worries without a single person to turn to. More tears gathered. As if Mal sensed them, the light on the bedside table flicked on and he came into view. A lavender glow from the lampshade painted half of his face, making the line of his cheekbone cut like a knife above his trimmed beard. Reclined beneath me, he looked cozy and rumpled among my sheets. I wanted to tie his hands to the metal frame and keep him there forever. If he were in my bed every night, I knew I wouldn't wake each morning with the same empty ache in my chest. He would dispel every lonely thought from my brain, the way he'd kept the monsters at bay tonight.

He watched me too. Eyes tracing over my cheeks to my lips and down the slope of my neck. What did he see when he looked at me? April Sinclair, failed film star? April Murphy, failed granddaughter? Those tears fell slowly, like the first drops of rain before a downpour. A warning to take cover. My eyes closed, not wanting to witness the moment he climbed from my bed and left. Mal didn't deal in emotions, especially the messy kind.

That's why the touch on my cheek was such a shock, I almost drew back. He pushed up on his elbow, his hand so large it almost encompassed the entire left side of my face. Work-worn fingers dipped into the hair at my temple while this thumb swept a line from my jaw up to the corner of my eye, catching a single tear. The drag of his calluses made me shiver. He must have mistaken it for the beginnings of a sob because he shuffled even closer, bending the knee my leg was hooked over, half dragging me into his lap. He was so tall, that even with my extra height, his lips sat at my hairline. I felt the tickle of his next words through the coiled strands. "If he'd asked you to be here, would you have returned?"

"Of course." I didn't even have to think about it.

That hand slid to my jaw, thumb landing at the corner of my lips as he tilted my head back to look at him. His eyes bore into mine and my next breath went absolutely nowhere. He'd never looked at me like that before. So fully, like he wanted me to know I had all of his attention. "Don't blame yourself. Don't place his choice on your shoulders. We may not understand it, but it was the way he wanted it."

The way he wanted it.

"What if he didn't want me here because he didn't want me in his life?" *What if he never really loved me . . . like my mother didn't?*

He mulled over his answer.

That was one of my favorite things about him. He didn't talk to *talk*, didn't say the first thing that came to mind like most men I knew. If you asked him a question, he thought it through, gave it the time it deserved. You might not like the answer you received, but you'd know it was the truth.

"He loved you," he finally said, hitting the proverbial nail square on the head. "He was so proud of you."

"Really? He said that?"

"The ten episodes of that bloody dancing show he forced me to watch spoke for itself."

Kier had watched it? *Mal* had watched it? I tried to picture the two of them in the family room, whisky in hand as they settled in for a Saturday night of sequins and ballroom dancing.

I smiled and his attention slid to it, throat working on a swallow. "What are you smiling at?"

"Trying to picture you dancing along to show tunes."

"I don't dance." No. I imagined he didn't.

His gaze fell to my lips again, then back to my eyes. It was like watching a loaded spring, wound tight and then releasing again and again. On the next bounce, I caught his cheek. His fingers still gripped my chin and our hands overlapped. His breath stuttered, chest expanding and brushing mine in a caress that made me whimper. It was so long since I'd touched someone this way. Since someone had touched me. "Mal," I whispered, praying that single syllable could convey everything I was incapable of asking for.

I felt the change in him before it even happened. His features morphed into something more determined. Tension transferring from his shoulders and down his arms to tug me closer. I all but fell against his chest, arms circling his neck, breasts molding to the solid mass as my legs spread to straddle him. One of his legs remained bent, his socked foot planted firmly on the mattress. That had me sitting directly in the V of his lap and I felt . . . I felt everything. The rock-hard length he made no move to disguise pressed along the seam between my thighs. My lip caught at the sensation, teeth biting as I strived to hold back my reaction, my gut screaming at me not to rush this because his eyes weren't on me anymore, they were pinched shut. His cheeks and ears painted fire red. His entire body trembled.

"Mal . . ." I whispered. "Mal, is this okay?" His nod was jerky. Eyes screwed tighter.

I should move, I decided. I started to retreat but he caught me, drawing even closer this time. The entire length of our bodies lined up and he dropped his forehead to mine, blanketing my lips with harsh pants. "Don't move, princess . . . Please don't move."

"I won't." My fingers slid down his neck and across his shoulders, rubbing in tight circles. And when his eyes flitted open and met mine, only then did I move.

I drew closer until our mouths were a hairbreadth away and paused, ready to pull back at the slightest sign he might not want this.

He licked his lips and I closed the distance, finding myself surprised at how soft they were. I didn't press, just held there, letting him decide what happened next. His answering groan was deep and masculine, his body softening beneath mine like chocolate melting on a stove, warm and sweet and delicious. It was the tamest first kiss of my life. The only one to ever make my eyes prick and my nose sting. After a long moment, I pulled back until only our lips brushed. "Was that all right?" I sounded like I'd been running.

The slam of his lips was his only answer, the tempo changing so quickly it took me a moment to catch up. His mouth slid over mine, hands tracking up my back, shaking, clenching and stroking, until they tangled in my hair, both fists tugging my head back to receive his onslaught.

I followed his lead, lips parting eagerly at the first brush of tongue. It flicked mine in a sensual slide into my mouth. I rose on my knees to take more of him.

I'd expected hesitancy. I'd expected more sweetness. He'd pulled a one-eighty on me and now I was partaking in the *dirtiest* kiss of my entire life. It was wet and a little messy. I could tell he was unpracticed, but what he lacked in skill he made up for in sheer enthusiasm. Mal kissed me like both our lives depended on it.

He had me on my back in a heartbeat. Hands gripping my waist, he flipped me until I was splayed out across the width of the bed. When he pressed his weight against me, I couldn't recall if our lips had actually separated.

My legs spread open and I dragged him closer, desperate to feel his weight. He answered with a hard, slow grind that made me cry into his mouth. Then he was saying my name. *April. Princess . . . I need . . . fuck . . . I can't breathe when I'm near you.*

I needed our clothes gone. I needed him on me—in me. I was ready to beg for just that. One second his tongue was in my mouth, fingers starting to dip beneath the band of my shorts, the next he was on his knees above me. Only then did I hear the shrill ring of my phone. It felt like moving through mud, attempting to recall if the last thirty seconds had even happened. The sight of Mal kneeling between my indecently spread thighs confirmed that it had.

The phone stopped ringing and our harsh pants filled the room. Neither of us moved. His gaze was far off, staring right through me, and something in my chest crumpled a little. "Mal . . ." I started to apologize and broke off. I didn't want to be sorry.

The sound of my voice seemed to unlock him and he launched from the bed. His foot caught on one of his stray boots and he stumbled, almost falling. I shot up, hands reaching as if I could steady the trembling giant. But he was already moving, snatching up his boots, not even pausing to put them on.

Boy's head popped up from the foot of the bed where both dogs were still sleepily tucked together as if they hadn't just bared witness to this earth-shattering event. Mal stayed him with a hand and he flopped back down atop the blanket. I watched as he halted at the door with his back to me. "I should . . . I've got to go." His rasp echoed off the high ceiling so I got to hear the shut down twice.

Yeah . . . I think I got that part. I didn't speak the words aloud; for the first time in my life I was stunned into silence.

"I'll leave Boy with you tonight . . . to watch over you, I mean," he said before fleeing. Forget the third step, I heard every unbridled landing of feet on the staircase. Normally so sure-footed, he crashed and cursed and stumbled. My ears followed him through the kitchen and out the back door until the silence settled.

I flopped back onto the pillow. "What the hell just happened?"

The clean scent of him washed over me and I yanked the pillow from behind me, tossing it across the room. As if in league with his owner, Boy flipped onto his back and farted, slow and so high-pitched Dudley woke with a start, then buried his face beneath his paw. "Some guard dogs you two are."

17

MAL
Us – James Bay

Mum's going to call you," Callum grunted, his spade slicing through the mound of wet peat and dropping it into the open kiln.

He'd arrived early today. The morning light had still been hazy when I dragged my bleary-eyed arse out of bed to greet him. If he'd been surprised to find me indisposed, he didn't show it, declaring only that he had no appointments for the day and wanted to be put to work. I didn't believe him. He was one of only a handful of vets on the entire island that didn't specialize in livestock—he was busy. I'd dropped by the surgery on a number of occasions and the phone always rang off the hook. I wasn't one to look a gift horse in the mouth when I could use the distraction, though, so I kept my suspicions to myself.

In silence, we worked quickly, Callum familiar with the methods. He worked the wet while I worked the dry, loading it simultaneously into the kiln. This process would flavor and then dry the grain stored in the room above us, giving the whisky its unique smoky taste.

Even as we worked efficiently, a part of me still longed for April's sunshine presence. The single time she'd helped with the drying, she'd voiced such random questions.

"What would happen if I got locked in there with the grain?"

"You would die, princess," I'd answered incredulously. It was pretty bloody obvious. At its warmest, the drying room reached around eight degrees Celsius.

"Yes. But how?"

She'd been genuinely curious, knowing my interest in anatomy perhaps. So I answered to the best of my ability. She'd only smirked and said, *"So cool."*

Little freak. There could be none of that now.

I shoveled harder as the realization clanged through me, sweating as I broke the already small chunks of dry peat into even smaller pieces. The heat from the fire roared, only stoking the tangle of emotions that coursed through me every time I remembered what happened last night. What I'd done.

April had started it, sort of. It was more like a mutual starting . . . but I definitely finished it. I was the first to initiate contact, pulling her against me in the bed because I'd been absolutely desperate to touch her in some small way. And seeing her so scared—comforting her had felt good. *So fucking right.*

Then *she* kissed *me.*

I still couldn't make sense of it in my mind and I'd dissected it from every angle, replaying the moment so many times I could re-enact the entire encounter from memory alone. The only reasoning I could come up with: she was upset about Kier and wanted comfort. And I'd shot it all to hell by pouncing on her like a dying man in the desert.

I *was* in the desert—a sexual desert, if you will. My dry spell was so long it had become my natural climate rather than a lengthy summer. Yet I'd acclimated. Women had come on to me in the past, Jasmine only months ago. I'd said no. Lack of sex was not the issue here. *April* was the issue. Wanting her beyond reason was the issue. And I'd proven now that I could no longer be trusted alone with her.

I hadn't gone up to the manor this morning. Hadn't retrieved Boy. He'd wandered his way in an hour ago and I knew it was from her encouragement. Callum questioned it while bending to give him a pat, and I answered honestly that he'd stayed at the manor the night before, too messed up to even consider lying. Thankfully, I had enough sense not to mention that I'd dry humped the world-famous actress who lived there, already coming in my pants by the time I pulled back. I alone would be privy to that level of shame.

"Couldn't drag yourself away, huh?" For a moment, I thought Callum was talking to me, then he gave Boy's cheeks a ruffle and continued. "Can't say I blame you." A growl scorched up my throat like dragon fire and I only just managed to staunch it. Of course he was interested in April. Even my dog was besotted with her. Was it the copious amount of peanut butter treats she kept in her pockets or the green eyes that drew him in? Either way, we had dangerously similar tastes.

I felt Callum's attention and paused, wiping sweat from my forehead. "I said, Mum's going to call you today." He grabbed his metal water bottle and drank deeply. He offered it to me and I took it.

"Why?" I wiped my mouth with the back of my hand, tasting peat on my lips.

"Why do you think?" He didn't give me a chance to answer. "Lunch on Saturday, you haven't been for over a month."

For good reason, I didn't say. "I've been busy," I muttered.

"Too busy to show Mum you're not dead? When was the last time you even called?" I winced. I loved my mother fiercely, but with my mum always came my dad. "I'm not trying to guilt you," he said, reading my expression in that way I hated.

"Oh, really?" When did I become so transparent? The answer was sitting a hundred yards away, lovingly restoring the tasting room ahead of the event next week.

"I'm just stating a fact." He dropped his shovel again and turned to me, slicking his sweat-soaked hair back. "Just come to lunch and you'll be good for at least another month."

I hated when he made it sound as though spending time with my family was a chore, because it was the truth. Sometimes it did feel that way. I wanted to say it wasn't personal, that after an hour with *any* large group of people I felt as though I needed to sleep for a week. But I didn't know how, so I only said, "Fine."

He nodded once. "Good. You should call her first, she'll appreciate that."

Christ. I pulled my phone from my pocket, waving it aloft before I dialed. He gave a small smile of approval and nodded to the door. She answered on the third ring. "Is that my elusive wee boy?"

Guilt slammed through me. "Hey, Mum. Sorry—"

"None of that." She'd never once made me apologize for my quirks. "Callum told you about lunch on Saturday."

Told me, like I didn't know it happened every bloody week. She

192

was giving me an out I didn't deserve. "Aye." My throat worked. "I'll be there."

"Good, that's good, Mal. Your dad and I can't wait to see you."

Your dad and I. I stared into the flames, listening to the crackle as she told me all about the new art commission she was working on. I barely heard a word of it. Knowing I hated talking on the phone, she didn't keep me long, promising to catch up properly in a few days. As soon as I hung up, the murmur of voices drifted from outside.

Ewan wasn't working until later this afternoon. They could only belong to two people. Any notion of avoiding April fled and I ducked out into the muggy air before I could pause to think about what I was doing. What I would even say.

Standing close together, my brother and April laughed conspiratorially. That flirtatious smirk of his lips while he watched her head tip back, revealing the length of her regal neck.

I marched over to them, gravel spitting from under my boots. "What are you doing out here?"

"Just taking a small break," she explained as Callum continued the conversation they were having.

"Of course I can, lass. It's no bother."

"Of course you can what?" I knew I was being a high-handed arse, but I couldn't seem to stop.

April answered. "Your brother kindly offered to install some shelves in the tasting room for me."

"Shelves?" She hadn't mentioned any shelves.

"I ordered some last week to hold the bottles behind the bar, they were just delivered."

Callum's hand found my shoulder, squeezing tightly. "And I said I would be happy to help, so long as my brother doesn't mind loaning out his tools." He winked at April and she laughed, rolling her eyes.

It was that tiny—probably unconscious—reaction that solidified it for me. I never should have kissed her. What chance would I stand with my brother so obviously interested? So I nodded, my next words tasting like ash in my mouth. "Of course . . . you should definitely help her."

April wore dark sunglasses, but I felt her stare like a brand, hotter than the kiln I'd spent the last thirty minutes working beside. "Perhaps you could teach me," she finally said to Callum. "I'd like to learn how to do it myself." The night I taught her to build a fire flashed through my mind, followed by every moment we'd spent together in the distillery. What else could I teach her if she allowed me? When it came to her, I had the strongest urge to coddle and take care like I never had before, while simultaneously wanting to push and see how much she could take.

"You got it, lass, give me thirty minutes to finish up here."

She flashed him that little Hollywood smile and we both watched her walk away. "You two still aren't getting along," Callum stated once she was out of sight.

I forced my features into something neutral. "Everything's fine; we don't spend enough time together for it to matter."

He scratched his jaw, watching me closely. "So you aren't interested in her?"

The confirmation *he* was punched through my stomach like an iron fist. "No."

He grinned and it was so easy, so charming. I'd never hated it more. "Then you won't mind if I shoot my shot? It's not often we have a woman like that on the island." His fist thumped off my biceps and I stared down at the place it struck. "Man, she was so hot in that movie . . . what was it called? You know, the apocalypse film where she seeks revenge on that entire town of men who murdered her sister . . ." He snapped his fingers together.

"The Only Girl in Town," I supplied.

"Yes, that one! She kicked butt in that movie." He didn't seem aware of the tension creeping into my body. We hadn't fought physically since I was ten years old and caught him stealing my comic books, but right then, I wanted to pummel him into the ground. Callum might be a serial dater, but he was always respectful. Was it April's celebrity status that made him think he could say what he wanted?

I drew to my full height. Fists clenching. "Shut up, man. She's still Kier's granddaughter." It was a shitty shut-down. Sexist to tie respecting her to respecting Kier, but I didn't know how else to shut him up without bringing more questions to my door.

So when his brow flicked up questioningly, I did what any adult would do, I flipped him the bird and stormed away.

"DON'T SET IT LIKE THAT, LOVE. YOU KNOW YOUR DAD LIKES HIS cutlery on the left." My hands paused over the table setting before rearranging until all the cutlery sat on the left-hand side. I'd been in my parents' quaint cottage on the opposite side of Kinleith for only thirty minutes and I was already itching to leave. I hadn't even seen my dad yet.

Once the table was laid, I went about setting the pink apology tulips I'd purchased on the way over in a vase and added water.

Callum was out in the back garden clearing leaves from the gutter because Dad could no longer safely climb the ladder, so it was just me and Mum. I shut off the tap, carrying the vase to the table. I set the stems in the center beside the fresh Greek salad and sliced bread. "Where is Dad anyway?"

"Out in the greenhouse. He's been spending a lot more time there since he retired." He'd been retired from the village GP surgery for almost six years, yet Mum still spoke about it like it was last week. "It's mellowed him out some, I think it's all that fresh air," she continued brightly, her impeccably styled hair swaying as she followed me around the table. *Always attempting to build a bridge between us*, I thought. If it hadn't happened in the first thirty-two years of my life, I couldn't imagine it happening now.

Crossing back to the small but neatly organized kitchen, she returned with a jug of lemonade, another place setting, and an extra set of cutlery. Shifting the others down, she squeezed it on the end of the table."Why are you setting an extra?" I asked, counting again to make sure I hadn't missed one. Mum and Dad at either end. Callum and me on the left. Heather, Ava, and Emily on the right.

"Oh, didn't she say? Heather's bringing a friend. You must remember Kier's granddaughter, she moved away to be a singer."

"An actress." My heart thumped. "April's an actress, Mum."

"That's the one." She beamed and slight crinkles creased the corners of her eyes, the only sign of her sixty-five years. "Always such a lovely girl." Before I could even process the knowledge April would be joining us, a car honked outside and the twins dashed in seconds later, hugging my mum before wrapping their tiny arms around my legs. They were in their matching phase.

Matching twin braids, matching pink summer dresses, they even had matching gaps where their front two teeth had fallen out last week.

"Uncle Mal, Uncle Mal . . . we had a visit from the tooth fairy!" They bounced up and down on their toes.

"You did, aye?" I dropped to my haunches. "And what's the going rate for a tooth nowadays?"

"One million pounds!" Ava cried, opening the tiny little handbag strapped to her wrist and holding it out for my inspection, dozens of copper coins jangled around in the bottom.

I must have mumbled something to my niece, I wasn't sure, because she took off running and suddenly, my eyes transfixed on April. Pretty as a picture in my childhood home, a bouquet of white flowers clutched to her chest. She wore a short lemon-yellow summer dress that hugged her perfect curves, hair half tied back, her face clear of makeup and glowing. Mum rushed over to greet her and I didn't catch a word of the exchange. I knew the afternoon would become a blur from there.

Callum came in through the side door next, kissing every newcomer on the cheek. When he reached April, he squeezed her waist, lingering longer than strictly polite. I studied their entire exchange. We were sitting down at the table when my dad entered, but I hardly noticed because April sat directly across from me, leaving me hypnotized by the way her mouth closed around a floret of broccoli. The way her throat rippled when she sipped her lemonade. I was being too obvious, barely speaking a word to anyone. Barely removing my gaze from her.

It wasn't until April looked right at me that it registered someone had said my name. My dad. "Are you deaf as well now,

Malcolm?" April flinched, turning white as a sheet. She looked confused.

I cleared my throat and forced my eyes to the man at the head of the table. Not quite as big as his sons, though his presence still loomed largest in this house. Perhaps it was the old army sergeant in him. "No, Dad. Sorry, I didn't hear you," I said at the same time Callum spoke his name with warning.

"I said, have you got yourself a proper job yet?"

"Jim—" My mother's tone was sad but didn't do enough to intervene. My mind scrambled, chest growing tight, and beneath the table my fingers twisted together.

"Maybe if Kier gave you a day off now and again you could start exploring other options." My father rattled on like she hadn't spoken, never lifting his eyes from his plate. I sensed April tense as I did. "We're always needing help at the surgery. It wouldn't be a doctor's salary, mind you, but it's respectable work. I'll put a word in for you at work on Monday."

"Work?" Heather cut in, looking baffled as she poured herself another glass of lemonade. "You haven't worked at the surgery for years now."

"He means volunteering," Mum cut in quickly, smiling brightly. "He helps at the drop-in center once a month."

"And Kier—" Callum flicked a look at April. "You know about Kier, Dad."

Dad's cutlery slammed against the plate. Everyone looked at him. Even the twins' hushed chatter came to a halt. "Don't back-chat me at my own table, *boy*." Dad spoke to Callum in a tone I hadn't heard him use for years. His eyes were glazed over, like he was looking right through him.

Callum muttered something beneath his breath and started to respond, but it was April's sweet voice that sliced through the tension. "That's such a lovely painting, Iris." She nodded to the massive canvas hanging at my back. "Is it one of yours?"

My mother preened and before anyone could stop her, she said, "Yes, hen, it's my vulva."

April choked on her lemonade, eyes watering. Heather and Callum snickered and I almost dove across the table to give her the Heimlich.

"Sorry." April giggled, wiping at her tears. "That's not at all what I expected you to say."

"What's a bulva?" Emily piped up from the other end of the table. Callum snickered again.

"You know what a vulva is," my mother began to explain. When my dad threw her a warning look, she simply waved him away. "The female body is a magical thing, it's important we appreciate it."

"Hear, hear," Callum cheered, lifting his glass aloft.

"Iris," Dad warned again. So different were my parents, I wondered for the millionth time how a free-loving hippy visiting Skye on an artist's residency had settled down with a grumpy ex-soldier turned general practitioner.

My mum pointed over her shoulder. "That vagina brought four children into the world."

"Very true." April giggled again. It was so lovely, the rope around my chest loosened just a little. When I imagined her doing it just for me, it eased a little more.

My mum stirred her pasta. "April, you have a beautiful body. I'd love to paint you."

It was my turn to choke. My knee smacked off the table hard enough to rattle every dish. April flushed prettily and actually looked as though she was considering it. *Holy fuck.*

"Can I think about it?" she finally settled on.

"Of course." My mother scooped more pasta into her mouth as if she were arranging a dental cleaning. I was sweating. Heather cursed, attempting to dislodge peas from Emily's nose. Callum hid his grin behind his glass and my dad . . . he didn't even glance up from his plate.

18

APRIL
Love Like This – Kodaline

Are you really going to let my mother paint you?"

I snorted, bringing the tart lemonade back to my lips. "Of course not." I was all for women being open with their bodies—I myself had been naked before a camera more times than I could count—but there were some intimacies I couldn't bring myself to share. I ran a finger around the sweating rim of my glass, catching the beads of condensation. Heather and I sat beneath an umbrella in her parents' back garden, scented lavender bushes at our back. I took a moment to enjoy the sound of bees buzzing between the stems amid lengthy bursts of delighted squeals as the twins soaked each other with water guns.

Callum was the one to start the game, and I'd done my very best not to stare behind my sunglasses as his white T-shirt soaked against the impressive lines of his chest. I mean, I *might* have looked just a little out of pure, innocent curiosity. Who knew a village vet was required to be in such good shape? He was beautiful to look at but did nothing to stir any real heat in my chest.

Even in the shade, the day was sweltering, but I enjoyed the heady thrum of it. This way, I could blame the rising tension in my body on the lingering heat wave and not the way Mal had watched me every moment since I'd stepped across the threshold like a sexy, pissed-off hawk. What I couldn't understand was why? At first, I convinced myself it was all in my head. I had no other way of explaining why he'd been avoiding me since The Kiss. Why he'd dismissed me so thoroughly the morning Callum attached the new shelves in the tasting room. I couldn't make sense of it. Even before, during lunch, I saw Heather and Iris exchange knowing smiles and knew they'd noticed it too.

I shouldn't have come. I also couldn't bring myself to leave. I'd been lonely this week without him and Boy, and just the thought of going back to the manor alone tonight, with nothing but my phone and social media apps for company, made something in my gut twist sharply.

Stretching out across the soft blanket, I lengthened my legs until my bare toes touched the grass. "Do you want to go for a drink at the pub tonight?" I asked Heather. It's what I would do if I were in London. Accept an invite to any event sent my way, drink and dance until the hole in my chest temporarily stitched itself closed.

"Wish I could, but I picked up an extra shift, the girls are sleeping here tonight." I hated that my friend was scrambling for any shifts she could get her hands on. There had to be something better out there for her, something with steady hours and good pay that didn't drag her away from time with her girls. "You should still come down though, invite June and I might be able to sneak in a drink with you guys if it's quiet."

"That's a good idea." I reached for my bag as a shadow fell over me.

"What's a good idea?" Mal's boots might have been touching my toes, but it was his sister he addressed.

She shielded her eyes from the sun, smiling up at him. "April coming to the pub tonight."

His expression flattened so quickly I couldn't read it. It drove me crazy. "It can get a little rowdy on Saturday nights."

Heather laughed. "We're talking about Sheep's Heid, not a strip club."

"Skye has one of those?" I said, feigning interest. Mal didn't even pause to spare me a glance and instead chimed in with a pointed remark aimed my way.

"The island is buzzing with tourists right now." Tourists who might recognize me, is what he meant.

I didn't love the idea, but I was feeling just enough self-pity in that moment not to care. "Then it's a good thing I love meeting new people," I snapped back.

If I thought the sun was hot, it had nothing on Mal's glare. *Good.* A flutter built in my chest, the same one I felt when I stepped in front of a camera. I looked directly at him as I slid my phone from my bag and pulled up June's number. "I'll tell her nine p.m.," I said to Heather. We all knew it was for Mal's benefit. He didn't utter a word to stop me as I sent off the text and got an immediate thumbs-up.

"Perfect." Heather pushed to stand, shoving her feet into her sandals. "I have to head out, I need a shower before my shift starts. I'll see you later." She rose onto her toes and kissed her brother's cheek. I could have sworn she whispered, "Play nice," before she strolled over to say goodbye to the girls.

And then it was just me and him.

I half expected him to say more about the pub, try to convince me not to go, but he just looked down at me stretched out on the blanket, in that intense way I'd come to attribute as his. I normally enjoyed being on the opposite end of that stare so I could say something snarky or flirty to make him blush. But I knew what he was waiting for. "About the other night—"

"Don't," he cut in, holding out a trembling hand like he might ward me off. But I needed to say this, needed an answer to the worries that'd been circling my mind like a clogged drain from the second he stumbled from my bed.

I pushed to my knees, an accidental move that made it look as if I were begging. His nostrils flared and I knew he also made the connection. "I'm sorry if I went too far . . . did something that you weren't comfortable with."

His eyes bulged, looking horrified for a beat before he leashed it again. It almost scared me sometimes how well this man could hide his emotions. "You didn't do *anything* that I didn't want you to do." He spelled it out very clearly—*He'd wanted me.* "But it still shouldn't have happened."

I was about to demand he tell me why, not understanding the big deal of two consenting adults enjoying one another, when Ava darted over. She dove onto the blanket, spreading her hands and feet out like a starfish as beads of water soaked me and her uncle.

"I'm so tired," she droned like an eighty-year-old. Her cheeks were flushed cherry red from running.

Laughing, I flopped down beside her so we were shoulder to shoulder. "I think that means it's time for more ice cream."

Her little brown eyes flew open and slid right to Malcolm, the true authority figure here. "Ice cream? Can I, Uncle Mal?"

He smiled softly. "Grandma only has mint choc chip left, you hate mint choc chip."

Her hands scrunched. "No, I don't!"

He tapped a long finger off his lip. "I remember you saying all little girls hate mint choc chip ice cream and Uncle Mal should get to eat it all."

"No!" she bellowed again, but she giggled as he hoisted her wet little body over his shoulder.

In a single heartbeat, Emily appeared too, equally wet as her dark curls stuck to her cheeks. Bouncing on her toes, she chanted, "Ice cream, ice cream." Something in my lower abdomen did a strange little flip as I watched them. I'd never seen this carefree side of Mal before. He was laughing, face entirely open. There was no hesitation, no cogs turning in his mind as he decided what to say. A million miles from the intense, unsure man his father had cut down at the dining table.

I didn't know how any of them could stand it.

Jim Macabe had always been gruff. As a girl, I'd been a little nervous around him, preferring to play at the manor or the inn with June's parents. Observing Mal practically wither under his harsh words, I'd wanted to scream at him. I could tell Callum felt the same, and I didn't know how he'd held back.

Emily twirled on the spot, making her skirts swish as she held her hands out for Mal to look at. "Look at my nails, Uncle Mal. April painted them for me."

Setting Ava down, he stared at her little hands. "They're beautiful, but I thought blue was your favorite color."

She flashed the bright pink tips again. "It was, but now I want to look like a princess, like April."

Princess. The word carried a weight neither child could understand. A tremor rocked through Mal, his hands fisting until they were bone white. Focusing on the girls, he nodded back to the house. "Grandma will get you ice cream if you hurry."

I waited until they were out of sight before speaking again, very quietly as though he were a startled doe. "What happened the other night meant something to me. If I want you and you want me, I don't see a problem."

"April." My name was a snarl. So dismissive it transported me back to our earliest interactions. "You need to leave it alone. I can't . . . I don't want you—" His entire body was taut. Sweat beading his brow. "Not anymore." *Not anymore.* I flinched involuntarily, shifting back on the blanket. Mal winced and air whistled through his lips. "That came out wrong. What I'm trying to say is—" I didn't care what he was trying to say. I knew what he was doing. Panicking and lashing out. Drawing a line in the sand and planting himself firmly on the other side of it. It wasn't new behavior for him, but this time I was tired of it.

Pushing to my feet, I squared up to him until my raised chin brushed his chest. "I'm a big girl, Malcolm, I don't need you to let me down gently. If all you wanted was a hookup, you should have said so."

"April—"

Refusing to let him see how much his words hurt, I skirted around him, heading for the house. My smile was bright as I offered my goodbyes, accepting sticky-fingered hugs from the girls and promising to have an answer about the painting for Iris. When Callum offered me a ride home, I might have been too enthusiastic in my acceptance. I told myself not to look back at him, but as I snatched up my purse and followed Callum out the front door, Mal's regretful stare was the last thing I saw.

"YOU ARE EVEN HOTTER IN PERSON, HOW IS THAT POSSIBLE?" the American beside me drawled. A lock of blond hair dipped across his forehead, obscuring bright, slightly bloodshot eyes. He planted an arm on the tabletop of the small booth in the Sheep's Heid, crowding me against the bench until I began to feel a little claustrophobic.

The pub was traditionally Scottish, all dark wood and upholstery in a faded tartan color. The ceiling was low and lined with thick beams, prompting many of its taller patrons to duck their heads every time they stood, or risk crashing into one of the glass light shades.

As evening drew in, the temperature had dropped some. That hadn't stopped everyone and their dog coming down to cool off with a cold beer. Heather was so busy I'd barely glimpsed her small head darting behind the four-deep crowd surrounding the bar. People spilled out into the beer garden and down onto the docks, and my head buzzed as conversations became louder and more animated with every drink consumed. Perhaps we should have sat outside instead.

Or perhaps I should have turned down the offer of a fifth drink. I'd already reached my usual three-drink limit when the two American tourists approached Juniper and me. I knew the second I locked eyes with the Captain America lookalike he recognized me. His blue eyes had flared wide and there'd been just the slightest hitch in his step. When he opened his mouth and I heard his gorgeous southern lilt, I no longer cared. It wasn't going to lead anywhere, but if he wanted to spend his evening flirting with an ex–movie star so he'd have a good story to tell his friends once his travel year came to a close, I'd happily lap up the attention.

Earlier, in line for the loo, I'd made the mistake of checking my social media page after seeing I'd been tagged in a picture. It was of me and June coming out of Brown's the week before. I wore cutoff shorts and a white tank top, dark sunglasses covering the top half of my face. Thankfully, they'd had the decency to blur Juniper's face out.

If it was curiosity that made me click on the picture, it was pure masochism that made me read the comments.

mydogisbetterthanyours: Definitely pregnant.

smith169: She's such a bad actress, I literally can't stand her.

ned6simpson: At least her tits are bigger now. She'd probably let me cum on them, dirty slut.

onlyurmum: I wish she'd fuck off already.

There were a few nice comments in there too, but my eyes only sought out the bad. I clicked on ned6simpson's profile, unsurprised to see photos of his wife and children staring back at me. His bio read: "Family, God, Football: in that order." I'd been half tempted to send a screenshot of his comment to his poor wife but flicked out of the app before I could act on that vicious little urge.

That, coupled with my hellish encounter with Mal that afternoon, had me off-kilter and self-conscious. A dangerous combination. Captain America's whispered compliments had soothed me for a little while, but I was beginning to feel drunk and sad. I was also craving roughened brogue instead of southern drawl, which probably meant I needed to drink more.

Nestling closer to him, I swiped the pint of Guinness from between his hands and brought it to my lips. He chuckled, watching me. "I like a woman who can drink," he said, the interest in his tone impossible to miss. I tried to latch on to that feeling, pressing the glass back into his grip and not retreating when it brought us closer.

"Is that so? What else do you like in a woman?" His grin deepened, tongue flicking out to moisten his lips. I was distantly aware of a gasped "holy shit" from his friend, and June cursing beneath her breath. I didn't think the two of them were hitting it off and I was probably a bad friend for not checking.

I paid them no mind, dropping my hand to his wrist to play with the corded leather bracelets he wore. He cupped my cheek, winding a curl around his finger. "Red hair."

"Lucky me. What else?" I leant closer. I was almost in his lap by this point, letting his free hand explore my thigh, fingers flirting under the edge of the short summer dress I still wore.

His thumb brushed roughly over my lower lip. "Fuck-me lips like these—are you going to let me fuck your mouth tonight, April?"

June cursed louder and I was distantly aware of her rising to her feet. But it wasn't her voice that had me snapping back.

"I think that's enough." Something smacked hard off the table. "Aye, I'm talking to you. Put your hands where I can fucking see them." Roughened brogue. Mal. Looking angrier than I'd ever seen him.

Wyatt—I was certain his name was Wyatt. Or was it Brody?— leapt to his feet, jolting the table. Guinness spilled across the surface, dripping into my shoe. Testosterone snapped between the men like a live wire. He started in Mal's direction.

"I wouldn't. This won't end well for you," Mal warned, a dark glint in his eyes.

"Steve. It's not worth it, man," his friend said, catching him by the shoulder and holding him back.

"Steve!" I cried out, snapping my fingers in his direction. "*Steve*, like Captain America." Everyone but Steve turned to me.

June just shook her head. "Sweet lord, get me out of here."

Steve, perhaps finally noting the height difference between him and the fuming Scot, gave me a final longing look and groaned. Digging into his pocket, he drew out a square card and laid it flat on the table. I didn't know people still carried business cards. "I'm here another week. Call me."

He had balls, I had to admit it, because Mal glared down at that business card like Steve had whipped his dick out. With one final scowl at Mal, the two men stalked out of sight.

"Finally." June scrambled from the booth, pushing Mal aside. "Out of my way, I'm about to piss myself. I'll meet you outside."

The crowd parted easily for her because every head was already turned in our direction. I barely noticed them, too busy staring up at the scowling giant. He planted his fist on the table, sweeping the business card to the floor. When he crowded me like this, I felt breathless, the furthest thing from claustrophobic. I was still mad at him, but I couldn't quite reach that feeling now.

"Home time, princess," he whispered. His voice swept over me like a warm blanket as he held out a hand. Later, I would blame the alcohol, because I didn't hesitate to take it.

19

MAL
Love Song – Lana Del Rey

June appeared the moment I propped April against the door to her Mini Cooper. Just in time too, because I was beginning to feel like a creep, ushering a drunk woman out into the night while she belted out a Whitney Houston tune she didn't have the lung capacity to carry.

Even as I held the majority of her weight, her head began to loll against my palm. She was absolutely plastered. How had this happened?

"I don't know what happened." June answered my silent question, eyes bright from alcohol but alert. "She seemed fine when we got here—quiet, but fine. Then she read something on her phone and suddenly she was on a mission to make every wrong choice."

All of those *wrong choices* raked through me, firing up the urge to hunt down Steve and plant my fist in his face. My entire body still shook from the encounter.

The prick had known exactly what he was doing.

"June!" April cried, stumbling toward her friend and squishing her cheeks together. "You are so beautiful. I wish I looked like you." Her legs lasted all of two seconds. My arms snapped around her waist before she could stumble, settling her weight back against my chest to keep her steady.

June laughed, the sound not entirely amused. "At least she's a happy drunk."

"Aye, there is that," I agreed, tipping my head to the small bag slung across April's body. "I'll drive, you grab her keys out." Going into a woman's bag definitely felt like one of those *do-not-cross* lines. Juniper fished them out and had the passenger-side door open in seconds, helping me wrestle a wiggling April into the front seat. "Do you think she's going to vomit?" I worried aloud, retreating to let June buckle her in.

She drew back, shrugging her slim shoulders. "At least it's her car."

Not exactly my concern, but I chuckled because it felt like the correct response. As I slid behind the steering wheel, my knees immediately compressing against the dashboard, I realized this was probably the first time I'd ever said more than two words to Juniper Ross. Weird when you considered she'd been engaged to my brother. Weirder still when I was able to navigate my way to her small family inn without any direction. Village living, I supposed.

It wasn't until she started unbuckling her seat belt in the back that I considered she might have wanted to go home with April. I halted her exit, clearing my throat. "I can . . . I can take you back to the manor if you'd feel more comfortable." One eyebrow, dark as a crow's wing, flicked up. *Shit.* "What I meant to say was . . . she's . . . safe with me, June. I would never—"

Her hand grasped my arm and squeezed. I'd always found Juniper intimidating. She could be sharp in a way a lot of women didn't allow themselves to be. She didn't pretend to be someone she wasn't to make herself more palatable. I admired her while simultaneously having zero idea how to act around her. I knew she wasn't a fan of my family, leading to Callum snidely nicknaming her the harpy a few years back. She didn't seem so bad and obviously cared about April and Heather. "I know she is. Any other man, and I wouldn't even contemplate it. You're the good Macabe brother, Mal." Tipping forward, she planted a smacking kiss onto a sleeping April's cheek. "Take care of our girl." I idled until the hall light to the B&B flicked on and then turned down the lane.

Our girl. Was I that obvious? *Yes.* I'd practically claimed her tonight. Nearly punched a guy in front of the entire village. I would have done it too. I wanted to do it. Wanted to prove my devotion with bloody knuckles. I wasn't sure what that made me. For the first time, I didn't really care to analyze it. As I turned left onto Castle Street, I let my gaze wander over her soft features flashing beneath the intermittent street lights.

"Why are you staring at me?"

I startled at her voice. Her eyes were still closed.

"I'm not," I lied. I felt like I'd spent half my life trying not to look at her, and since that kiss, I couldn't stop. A single moment of weakness and I was ensnared. She was the opposite of Medusa; instead of turning me to stone, looking at her woke me up, made me feel unsettled and so fucking settled at the same time.

"Why were you at the pub?"

"I ... uh ... well, you see ..." I decided it was better not to lie. "I wanted to make sure you were all right. I didn't plan on interfering until—well, you heard what he said."

"You mean the part where he said he wanted to fuck my mouth?" *Jesus.* My hands gripped the steering wheel as I sputtered. "Did it ever occur to you that I might enjoy him saying those things to me?"

"No," I barked, something viscous seeping into my veins. "It didn't."

"Were you jealous?" She didn't leave me time to answer. "You have no right to be jealous." Her voice still held the slightest slur. A part of me hoped she wouldn't remember a moment of this in the morning because I couldn't hold back what came next.

"You're right. Doesn't change the fact I'm so jealous I can practically taste it, princess." The way she'd looked at me in my parents' garden—the hopeful openness of her features slamming shut—cut at me now, like barbed vines creeping across my chest. I wasn't thinking as the words had flown from my mouth, only wanting it to be over. For her to stop looking at me like I was worth something. As soon as she'd fled, I wanted to stuff the words back down my throat.

She was silent for so long I thought she'd fallen back to sleep. "You're confusing," she said wearily.

I laughed. A single, sharp burst of air. "Welcome to my brain."

THE CAR HAD BARELY COME TO A STOP WHEN SHE UNBUCKLED and slipped from the vehicle. Her steps were more sure-footed now, but I still raced to meet her, ready to catch her if she stumbled

215

on the uneven gravel as she skirted the outside of the manor. She bypassed the kitchen door and I knew at once where she was headed. "You should probably get inside, it's not safe out here in the dark."

She ignored me and clambered up the slight hill to the bank. Her feet slid on the dewy grass and I pulled her to a stop before she could get any closer to the steep drop. You couldn't see the water below, but it made its presence known, crashing against the rock face in a comforting hush. She must have decided this spot was as good as any because she sank to the ground, lying straight on her back, hair and skirt pooling around her in the mossy earth, just as it had in my parents' garden before I ruined everything.

Head tipped back, she shielded her eyes as though staring into bright sunlight. "This was our spot, do you remember?" Of course I did. "I used to come out here every day hoping to see you. It was the best part of my day." Her confession shocked me enough that I lowered to my knees beside her. That was not at all how I remembered it. I recalled my panic every time I tried to speak to her. My worry that perhaps she pitied me, saw me as nothing more than Heather's friendless big brother.

"It's so pretty here," she said, the wonder in her voice leaking out into the silence. I laid back to take in the view as she did, tucking my hands behind my head. The stars hung so low they made up a glistening blanket, woven with a hundred points of light and hues of midnight blue, streaked with flecks of the deepest purple. You could see the northern lights from here on occasion, but we were well past the season for it. "I'd forgotten what it's like to be able to see the stars so clearly. I think I eventually stopped looking up at all." She sounded so desolate, my heart cracked right down the middle.

Before I could reply, she rubbed at her bare arms, brushing away the sudden chill blowing up from the water. I fumbled with my sweater, stripping down until I wore only a white T-shirt. I didn't dare touch her, so I draped it over her upper body, memorizing how she looked cocooned beneath my clothes. She was more beautiful than every star in the sky.

Click.

"We should put a bench out here," she said. "Elsie used to love watching the stars, she'd lay out here for hours, pointing out constellations or making up names for ones she didn't know. Kier promised every summer he'd build one for her."

I ached to reach for her. "If you want a bench, you can have a bench, princess." Her head flopped to the side and we stared at each other. What was it about her face, the curve of her lower lip, that had me borderline obsessed? Did other people not have lips? I couldn't remember.

It wasn't until I saw the solitary tear track across her temple that I realized she was crying, the second time she'd cried before me, and I knew this time I was partially to blame. I closed the gap, brushing it away with my thumb. "What's wrong? Is it that guy from the pub? Did he—" She shook her head, still crying. "Stop crying," I demanded, voice harsher now like it might shock her tear ducts dry. "Please stop—"

"I had a nose job when I was twenty," she whispered quietly, like a shameful confession, and I was stunned into silence. Of all the things in the world, I didn't expect her to say that. "I was twenty and my manager convinced me it was necessary if I wanted to be considered for leading roles." She raised a shaking hand to run a finger down the length of her slim nose, between her brows all the way to the fine elfin point. "What I hate the most is that he was right. Talent means nothing if you don't look the *right* way."

My hatred was like a hydra, growing multiple heads. One for me, one for him, one for Steve, and one for anyone else who had ever left that stain of shame in her eyes. I cupped her cheek until we faced each other, imploring her to hear my words. "It's your body, princess, you can do whatever the hell you like with it. Screw what anyone else thinks."

"I don't like it—I *hate* it. I don't look like my grandmother anymore."

"Yes, you do. You have her green eyes." I swiped my thumb beneath one, catching more tears. "You have her brilliant hair that never faded with age. Her smile." She sniffled, the tip of her nose turning pink. "Please, princess, yell at me, hate me for how I acted this afternoon, for how I've judged you, but please stop crying . . . I can't bear it." Without thinking, I swooped down to press a butterfly kiss to the tip. "You're stunning. With this nose . . . your old nose, Pinocchio's nose . . . you would still take my breath away."

The stars were reflected in her watery eyes, making her look ethereal and otherworldly. "I don't blame you. I know what people see when they look at me."

"What do people see?"

"A failure who's only good for one thing." I wanted to argue, but I needed to hear what she had to say. "Shallow. Vapid. A stupid bimbo with small tits and a pretty face."

"You are not shallow, or vapid, or stupid," I snarled.

"Oh yeah? Would a smart person sign a contract with a man who'd hold their career hostage when they refused to sleep with him?"

"What?" Her words were like a thunder strike. I pushed up onto my elbow, almost too stunned to speak. But I needed to be certain of what she was confessing to me. I wasn't sure she'd even meant to. When I tucked her hair behind her ear my hands were trembling. "April . . . what you're saying . . . that's a crime." It wasn't nerves that made me stutter, but fury.

"I know." Her voice was so small. Then, in the space of a heartbeat, she changed. Anguish melted from her features until they held . . . *something else.* I couldn't pinpoint the exact emotion, but I knew it wasn't real. She bit her lip, inching an increment closer. "Do you know the best part about being an actress?" Her small finger met the center of my chest. "I can be anyone you want." Lower and lower it brushed, down the planes of my abs, and I knew I needed to stop her. That knowledge didn't hold back the shudder her touch brought forth. "Who do you want me to be, Mal? I can be fun and sultry, sweet and shy, anything you want." She began drawing circles, brushing ever closer to my belt buckle, but all I could see were the tears still drying on her cheeks.

I caught her hand. "I only want you to be you."

She shook her head, hair sliding against my skin. "What if I don't know who that is?" Then she slumped back against my arm, asleep, as though that final confession took everything from her. I caught the back of her head in my palm, mind racing as I attempted to process everything she just told me.

I swallowed back bile as my stomach lurched, feeling so off-kilter it took me two attempts to pull her into my arms. My entire body swayed unsteadily, but still I walked to the manor, clutching her in a protective embrace. Maybe if I held her tight enough, I could erase anything bad that'd ever happened to her, stop anything bad from ever happening again.

I hardly remembered my journey through the lower level and up the stairs. Or setting her onto her unmade bed beside Boy and Dudley. When I started to tuck her in, she stirred again, awake enough to go to the small bathroom beside her bedroom and change into clothes I pulled from the cabinet. A pair of fleecy pajamas too thick for the summer evening, but I couldn't stand the thought of her being cold.

She laughed to herself as she brushed her teeth, opening and closing her mouth to show me how the buzz of her electric toothbrush sounded like T. rex. *Does she even remember what she said to me outside?* She half removed her makeup, leaving dark smudges beneath her eyes. Following her into the bathroom, I urged her to sit on the closed toilet lid while I grabbed a damp flannel, wiping the remainder away until her skin was pink and slightly puffy. Then, I untangled the jeweled clips from the back of her hair, brushing through the knotted curls with a comb I found on the vanity. I felt her observing me, a bemused little smile on her lips. As soon as I set aside the comb, she shifted closer so she was in the circle of my arms, her forehead a hairbreadth from my lips. I knew what she wanted, but I drew back, unwilling to take even this slightest thing when I didn't trust she was in the right mind to mean it.

I finally wrangled her into her bed, tucking the sheets up to her chin, but still her whispered words filled the room. "I'm so cold, Mal."

"I'll grab another blanket—" I started to withdraw but she clutched my T-shirt in her small fist, speaking as though she didn't even hear me.

"I want someone to keep me warm . . . I want . . . I want to be important to someone." Her voice broke in the middle. "I want someone to text me every day and ask me what I want for dinner so I can reply 'no idea.' I want someone to wonder where I am . . . I want someone to *see* me." I'd hurt her. I saw that fully now. My cold shoulder and accusations. I'd been a bastard to her since the moment she'd returned. At my parents' house, at work . . . throwing out mixed signals in an effort to protect myself. Failing to see that she needed protecting too.

It amazed me that I held the power to hurt her. All of these weeks, I'd seen myself as a blip on her radar. A single star in an endless sky. A glare on the windshield you put on sunglasses to block out. When to me . . . she was becoming the whole sun.

When her breathing turned even, I allowed myself to brush her hair back, whispering into the shadows, "I've wondered where you were my entire life, princess." Then I leant against the headboard on the empty half of the bed. If she woke up, I didn't want her to be alone.

It was there I noticed the copy of *Twilight* on her bedside table, the front cover so bent and tattered I knew it was the one she'd loaned me all those years before. She must have dug it out at some point. Taking it in my hands, I flipped the cover, heart stalling at the title page. At my name scrawled over and over again in a teenaged cursive, dotted with little pink hearts. I ran my thumb over those tiny annotations like I could draw the ink directly into my veins.

I looked at her face again, and made a decision. *Screw it*. I was going for it.

20

APRIL

Simply The Best – Bilianne

Staring at my reflection in the bathroom mirror, it was easy to convince myself I hadn't done anything embarrassing the night before. My skin looked pale and sallow but makeup free. I couldn't have been *that* drunk if I'd managed to wash my face and put myself to bed.

I'd woken mercifully alone, Dudley tucked into the crook of my arm. Precisely how it should have been.

What awaited me in the kitchen revealed just how wrong I was.

Mal, a tea towel hooked over one shoulder, gazing up from the pan on the burner and giving me what might have been the sweetest smile to ever exist. A single dimple popped in the apple of his cheek. Damp dark blond hair dipped across his forehead. A lethal combination that stunned me into silence as he set a steaming cup of coffee on the breakfast bar, followed by a plate of chocolate muffins. "Perfect timing." He smiled again and seemed to hold my gaze with a purpose I didn't understand. Then, as though he'd forgotten a significant part of whatever the hell this was, tripped his way around the counter, almost knocking over one of the stools while yanking out the other. "Please sit."

That's when I knew I'd fallen down the rabbit hole. Mal didn't smile like that—not for me. I hovered on the threshold, not daring to take a step in either direction should I disturb this dream I'd tumbled into. I knew I was being awkward as hell because his smile became uncertain and he fumbled with the coffee, nudging it in my direction with a heavy hand that made it splash over the rim. "Dammit!" He whipped the tea towel from his shoulder, mopping up the spillage as his cheeks flushed heavy crimson. "I used the vanilla syrup you like . . . I hope I made it right."

Those words got my feet moving. I slid onto the stool, taking in the spread of food while sipping the overly sweet coffee. A small vase of daisies sat beside a bowl of chopped fruit—my usual breakfast—and the plate of chocolate muffins. "Jess said they're your favorite," he explained. When I glanced up, that sweet smile was still fixed to his features, but the corners were beginning to quake.

The memory hit me like a wave. The American—*Steve*—plying me with alcohol. Flirting with him until Mal intervened. I barely stifled the urge to bury my face in my hands. I was a thirty-year-old woman, how did I get myself into such a mess?

I saw the breakfast for what it was then . . . an apology for upsetting me at his parents' house. *I don't want his pity.* I started to slide from the stool, lifting my coffee in acknowledgment. "Thanks for this—"

"You haven't eaten yet."

"I'm not really hungry," I lied, self-preservation kick-starting my fight-or-flight mode. It wasn't a good idea for me to spend time around Mal anymore. He was attracted to me, wanted me in a physical sense, but he didn't want *me*. Not really.

For a second I could have sworn he looked hurt, but his tone remained indifferent. "No bother, I'll put it in the fridge in case you get hungry later." He began packing the food away in that methodical way of his, turning off the burner under his egg pan, placing my favorite muffins that contained a pocket of melted chocolate in the middle back into the white bakery box. My stomach rumbled and I snapped, snagging the last one from the plate before he could take it.

"I might be a little hungry," I said, breaking off the top and putting it into my mouth.

"Fair enough." He hid a smirk behind a glass of orange juice he sipped as we watched one another from our separate sides of the island.

"You're not drinking coffee," was the only thing I could think to say.

"No . . ." He winced and his shoulder curled. "I actually should tell you . . . I can't stand coffee."

The truth ticked through me. "Why lie? Why let me bring you coffee every morning?"

He rubbed his palm over his bristled jaw, an action I'd seen him make when he was anxious. "I wouldn't call it a lie, exactly. More like a misunderstanding that got out of hand."

"You could have corrected me at any point."

"I could have"—he nodded jerkily and swallowed—"but I was

too busy soaking up any scraps of yourself you were willing to offer. Even if it was just a brush of our fingers around the thermos you handed me every morning."

That was in the 0.1 percent of sentences I'd have ever predicted would leave his mouth. I let my mug thunk to the counter, really allowing myself to look at him. He still looked nervous, but I'd missed the hopeful energy swirling about him. The buzz that preceded something spectacular.

"You were an arse to me yesterday, Mal. Why?" I demanded.

He didn't hesitate. "Because I've been trying to pretend I feel nothing for you. Because lashing out felt easier than admitting I've been pining away for you like every other person on the planet." His shoulders inched higher with every word that raced from him, but his voice didn't waver once. I could feel my heart beating in the back of my throat, a racking pulse that reminded me of drinking too-sweet wine. "I'm so sorry. Yesterday in the garden, you were saying everything I've dreamed of hearing from you, and it shook me. It's like I was outside myself and I couldn't breathe. I needed it over. Then you ran and I hated myself. It's not a good excuse," he continued. "But I hope you'll let me make amends."

Amends. I let the word sink in. "How do you plan to do that?"

He started around the breakfast bar, still holding the bakery box, and halted half a step away. He was so imposing when we were this close, a gentle giant who held the power to wound me with only his words. "However you want . . . however you'll allow. I'll do anything, princess, just name it."

Ah. "You mean like sex?"

He coughed so hard it sounded like he was choking. "*Jesus,*

April . . . no! I mean . . . aye, that's what I want, it's all I can think about half the damn time, but—"

"What about the other half?"

His gray eyes flicked over my face with a softness I wasn't accustomed to. "Your texts. How you make me laugh in ways no one else can. The way you treat Dudley and Boy like they're your actual children. The cluster of five freckles across your clavicle." His voice pitched low and he inched closer, nodding to the covered spot between my throat and shoulder. It burned through my thick pajama top. "The fact you feed a pack of wild foxes and haven't contracted a deadly disease yet. The smile you wear only when you watch the sun rise over the water. That damn green bikini I need to see with my own eyes. Even that disgusting dressing gown." Those eyes fell shut and when they opened again, they smoldered. My mouth dried. "So, aye, princess, I want your body, but that's only a fraction of what I want from you."

I felt a number of things in that moment. Surprise and elation. Relief and longing. A simmering heat low in my gut as his words took root. And yet, and yet, and yet . . . every word out of his mouth was perfect, but my hurt from yesterday solidified that this had extended past two adults enjoying one another. Now my longing dueled with a sharp edge of fear. I wrung my hands together, time stretching as he awaited my response. "Mal . . ." His name was an exhale. He straightened, bracing himself for rejection, and I stared at his throat so I wouldn't have to see it. "Can I maybe get a bit of time to think about this?" A part of me railed inside, fists banging against my chest like an angsty teenager, screaming, *no, no, no.*

His throat bobbed thickly. "Of . . . of course, take as much time as you need." I nodded and kept my eyes averted as he stepped closer. His head descended until it almost brushed my ear, his crooked smile in my eye line. "Just so you know," he whispered. "I don't consider *time* and *space* to be mutually exclusive, so expect to see me around."

And then the bastard left with my muffins.

21

MAL
Oh Caroline – The 1975

I considered myself to be a man of few emotions. Anxiety, obviously. Annoyance, rarely, usually just around my father. Was hunger an emotion? It felt like one. What I'd *never* been was so easily frustrated, especially when it came to the opposite sex. That was on me, I guessed, when I'd never found myself in a situation where a woman had a reason to avoid me, and if I had, I certainly hadn't noticed.

As it happened, turnabout *was* fair game because I'd been avoiding April for weeks and now that I wanted to spend every single second in her sunshine presence, she was avoiding me.

Had she found it this irritating? Probably not.

Work was my only distraction. Jacob and I had pulled some extra hours to get enough product ready for the tasting. He'd been excited to open the forty-seven-year-old sherry casks, reminiscing on the exact day they'd been sealed, while I swore I could feel Kier breathing down my neck with every drop I poured.

But it wasn't enough to completely clear April from my thoughts. I wasn't only frustrated, I was impatient. She continually skipped breakfast and avoided the distillery. Yesterday, I'd sought her out as she was coming out of the tasting room, only for her to duck behind a hedge the second I spoke her name. She played it off, claiming she'd dropped an earring. When I offered to help her find it, she said perhaps she wasn't wearing earrings after all and hurried away.

I didn't know what to do with that. Leave her alone, or keep trying? If Callum wasn't interested in her also, I might have broken down and asked his advice—but he was and I hadn't.

Which is why it had come to this.

I ran my hand over my tie again, straightening it into the hollow of my throat. I checked my appearance again in the small bathroom mirror, smoothing the heavy twill of the purple, green, and gray kilt I rarely wore. "How do I look?" I called to Boy. He lounged in his basket beside the unlit fire, chin resting on the wicker edge. He looked up and cocked his head. "That bad?" I asked aloud. His huff seemed to say "you're taking fashion advice from a dog, you tell me."

"Fair enough." My clammy hands pushed a tuft of hair that wouldn't sit right back into place. *Better to get it over with,* I convinced myself. April's face came to mind, how hard she'd been working, how much this evening meant to her. I turned for the door with a touch more determination. "Don't wait up."

"YOU CAME." APRIL'S TONE WAS SO INCREDULOUS, THE STATEMENT sounded like an accusation.

She was cloistered over at the small bar with Heather, laying out a number of pristine glass tumblers onto trays. The small tasting room that had been no more than a dumping ground for over a decade looked incredible. A band was setting up instruments beside the door. Garlands of ferns inlaid with heather and deep purple thistles hung from the beams. Round tables clung to the corners of the square space adorned with white linen tablecloths and pillar candles. A long grazing table I knew Juniper had a hand in creating was already set out, stretched across the furthest wall. Brie and handmade bread sat beside salty pretzels and dark chocolate. Grapes and figs, crackers and sweet chutneys. Everything designed to pair well with our whisky.

That wasn't what took my breath away.

April leaned over the bar, hands a flurry of activity and . . . she was stunning. Her calf-length dress was a light blue, giving her skin a pearlescent glow. A full skirt swished out from her hips like a bell. The bodice made a neat heart, revealing the tops of smooth breasts. Delicate little straps tied together in tantalizing bows I was desperate to tug on. My feet carried me closer as if detached from my body. *"Princess . . ."* If there was an end to the sentence, I didn't reach it.

She turned to me more fully, flicking a long, loose curl over her shoulder. The top half was clipped away from her face with gold jeweled combs. Delicate little pearls sat in her ears. "You're here," she stated again. That was when I noticed her taking me in the same way I did her—starting at my kilt and moving slowly up my body. By the time her eyes met mine, a light flush had spread over her chest. It was subtle, but enough to give me hope.

"Of course I'm here. Did you think I would miss it?" She was halted from answering when Ewan ambled through the door, smartly dressed in dark trousers and a white shirt, his red mop of hair neatly combed back from his face. He, along with Heather, would be serving drinks tonight.

"Hey, April," he called, giving her a wave. "Where do you want me? I'm ready to be put to work."

"You're a lifesaver, Ewan." She hurried over to him, heels clacking, skirts accentuating the sway of her hips. A throat cleared over my shoulder but my eyes clung to April.

"*Hello, Heather,* it's so nice to see you too. Thank you so much for spending your Friday night saving my distillery out of the goodness of your heart," my sister drawled sarcastically.

"You're being paid to be here," I shot back over my shoulder, still watching April as she led Ewan around the room, indicating for him to begin filling the water jugs.

A wad of napkins bounced off the side of my head and I finally looked at her, giving her a playful grin. "Can I do anything to help?" She did a double take, staring at me in surprise. "What?"

"Nothing." She shrugged and tipped packets of cubed ice into a metallic cooler before unscrewing a bottle of whisky, pouring two fingers in each glass. She was dressed similarly to Ewan, short blond strands pinned back, a thin black tie neatly fastened around her neck. "You just seem different, that's all." Her eyes flicked over my shoulder and I knew she was pinpointing April as the reason.

"Just trying to be supportive."

"I wonder why that is."

Shyness crept back in. I might have been ready to win April over, but I didn't feel ready to discuss my feelings with anyone but her yet. I straightened, arms crossing over my chest. "Do you need my help or not?"

"I think I've got it covered."

"Then I'll be over there." Stealing one of the tumblers of whisky she'd just poured, I nodded to the darkest corner and slunk away.

22

APRIL

Feel Me – Aeris Roves

Another forty-seven?" Heather asked, slightly wide-eyed as she pulled another of the extremely pricey aged blends from the shelf behind her. "That's the fifth bottle you've sold in an hour."

"I know!" My arms landed on the bar top, my toes doing an excited little dance in my shoes. "I have no idea what's happening." When I asked Mal to open one of the old casks, I'd known it was a risk. The payoff was turning out better than I'd anticipated. I ran the back of my hand over my forehead. The night was sticky and while we'd pushed the large double doors wide open to catch even the slightest breeze coming off the water, it was still sweltering in here.

Heather laughed above the energetic thrum of the folk band, pushing her own sweat-slicked hair behind her ear. She slid the bottle of whisky into one of the expensive-looking wooden boxes she'd helped me source at the last minute and handed it to me over the bar. "What's happening is you're the best sales woman I've ever seen in my life. Old Murray couldn't have pressed his cash into your hand any faster if he'd tried."

"He's sweet," I argued, gulping down the glass of water she handed me. I hadn't stopped talking for even a minute. Almost half the village had shown up, everyone eager to say hello and congratulate me on the event and tell me how proud Kier would be. Many asked for photos and I signed a few autographs; it felt strange but I'd happily complied. I'd smile for a thousand photos if it helped get Kinleith Whisky on the map.

"Sweet?" She laughed even louder, setting out fresh glasses on a tray and adding a few ice cubes. "We are talking about the same Gordon Murray, right? The old man didn't lift his eyes from your chest once."

Squealing, I covered my chest with both of my hands. "Don't tell me that, I still have to go back over there." Not that there was much to see. The baby-blue dress didn't offer a whole lot of cleavage as this was a family-friendly event, after all. I was also massively overdressed. Most of the men had opted to dress in clan colors—purple, brown, and green with a touch of gray—needing little excuse to hark back to their roots. The women, though, had dressed far more casually in floaty summer dresses. Mine was formal, appearing both sweet and expensive with tiny floral details stitched into the full skirt. A trick I'd learnt early on in my career: it was always an advantage to have all eyes in the room on you. And I wanted all eyes on me tonight. Fashion had a way of attracting attention like nothing else.

"Better you than me," she said, handing the tray to Ewan, who bustled off with an enthusiastic smile. "I'm sure if you need any help, one of my brothers would be more than happy to step in." Her barb was said with humor and her teeth flashed, like she'd peeked into my brain.

My fingers fluttered with the soft tulle of my skirt as I fought to keep my eyes from straying.

Amazed he'd even shown at all, Mal was still here and sitting in the corner, looking as unapproachable as ever. Few people had spoken to him other than his siblings and mum, who had popped down briefly to show her support. He'd had a short and seemingly friendly exchange with Jasmine, the pretty pet store owner I had lunch with last week, and gone right back to sipping whisky from a glass that never appeared to empty.

I'd been trying all evening to ignore him and focus on the event, but like we were tied with an unbreakable cord, my attention kept drifting back to that corner. Even with the scowl he wore, he looked mouthwatering in his kilt and suit jacket. I wanted to burrow my hands beneath the jacket to his chest and press my nose against his neck. The temptation only worsened when I caught the way *he* was looking at *me*, with a longing so acute it made my bodice feel too tight and my hands tremble. So, like a coward, I pretended not to notice him. It was childish, but his sudden one-eighty had me on edge.

I asked him for time and he was giving it to me. He hadn't pushed me for an answer or brought up our conversation in the manor kitchen almost a week ago. It would be petty of me to drag this on any longer out of spite. He'd apologized for his harsh words, which I now had to either accept or draw a line in the sand and move past these feelings. The second option didn't seem like a choice at all; my attraction hadn't lessened—we wanted each other. It wasn't going away.

Heather had joked about her brother Callum too, yet other than the single dance he'd dragged me into the moment he arrived, he'd long since abandoned me to work the room in that boyish way of his. He'd snuck in a few kisses on the cheek here and there, which I'd playfully batted away. We both knew there was nothing more in it. I was talking zero chemistry between us. Not even a crackle. He'd danced with Jessica Brown three times, perhaps he was interested in her. Glancing over my shoulder now, I spotted Callum beside the food table, pulling a handful of grapes off the stems and popping them into his mouth. He said something to Juniper that had him grinning, and her scowling and flipping her middle finger. *Weird.* If anything, Callum's smile only grew at her reaction. He stepped closer and she drew back, bumping into the man behind her. Apparently her grudge extended to all the Macabe men.

I snapped out of my thoughts and tried to remember what Heather had said. *Right, her brothers.* "I don't know what you're talking about," I finally answered her.

"Please." She snorted and I stuck my tongue out as I backed away.

"DID I SAY THANK YOU?" I SAID LOUDLY TO JUNIPER ABOVE THE pound of music, pausing my rounds to inhale the plate of food she'd hidden for me behind the bar. She and her mum had taken care of the catering, charging me only for the cost of ingredients.

Juniper looked beautiful and sophisticated in a tight black dress that hinted at the gothic fashion she'd favored as a teenager. She waved my words away, black nails glinting. "Only like a hundred times."

"Well, thank you another hundred. I couldn't have pulled all this off without you. You and Heather have been life savers these

237

past few weeks and your mum looks like she's having a good time." I nodded to Fiona—an exact replica of what I imagined June would look like in thirty years—laughing with a group of women I recognized from the village.

June sounded strained but her eyes softened as they landed on her mum. "I think getting her away from the B&B for a few hours is a good reminder that there's more to life than those seven rooms."

"Perhaps she needs to go on one of those singles' holidays," I joked. "She could meet a man."

"That's not a bad plan, perhaps I'll join her."

I smirked. "Dry spell?"

Her eyes flicked across the crowd. "Something like that."

"You should try online dating."

"On an island?" June laughed loudly and from across the room I saw Callum glance in our direction. "No, thanks, last time it matched me with my cousin Brody."

That reminded me. "Hey." I snapped a bread stick between my teeth, crunching slowly. "What did Callum Macabe say to you before?"

She waved a hand dismissively, but tension rippled through her willowy frame. "Nothing worth repeating."

"Really? It didn't look like nothing. You looked pissed off."

She rolled a shoulder but held herself stiffly. "Just his usual charming self. I feel like I'm the only person who can see straight through all the pomp and bluster. Alastair was just the same."

Of course he made her think of Alastair. Out of all the Macabe siblings, Alastair was probably the one I knew least about. June had

238

always had a crush on him growing up and I remembered him being handsome and studious, his attractive smiles coming easily. He was very similar to Callum in that way, they even looked quite similar, now I thought about it. Both wiry and more *classically* handsome than Mal. Nowhere near as rugged. I couldn't picture either of them flipping a fifty-kilo cask of whisky single-handedly.

The next song began, a slower tempo number as the band began to wind down their set. I lowered my voice as I started to say to June, "Hey, if you ever want to—" Movement in my periphery cut me off and all the oxygen was sucked from the room. All of *mine* at least, because I was the only one who seemed to notice Mal cutting across the dance floor, determination etched into his features. I allowed myself to look at him and he gazed right back, heading straight for me.

June must have noticed too because she paused, a grape pressed to her lips. "I wondered how long it would take him."

I had no time to wonder what that meant. He drew closer, eyes rolling from the tips of my hair down to my feet. I knew I was doing the same. He'd removed his jacket and his white dress shirt cut an impressive line across his chest. His shirtsleeves were rolled up to his elbows and I studied the flex of muscle and thick veins. What was it about forearms that made them the epitome of the female gaze? Someone with half a brain cell left would have to answer, because Mal was going to ask me to dance. I could hardly believe it, but the evidence was plain as day when he cleared his throat and started to extend his hand.

A feeling of intense rightness had me reaching back. There was no choice, only the knowledge that my hand belonged in his. Not fate but something more unexplainable—inevitable, like the laws of gravity. But the hand I found was smoother, wrong somehow. The eyes I now looked into were clear blue rather than storm gray. Callum grinned down at me. "Time for another dance, lass." Then he swept me onto the floor. My body locked in protest, searching for Mal over my shoulder, just in time to see his head disappear out the side door.

23

MAL
Love Me Harder – Ariana Grande

I was drinking alone in the dark and my cock was hard, what a pathetic combination. I could barely taste the liquid on my tongue, but I opened my mouth for another large pull. I never allowed myself to overindulge in whisky, hating the point where I could no longer experience the intricate flavors and it became just another drink, like guzzling cheap beer at a house party.

But right then, I needed to stop thinking.

Needed to stop thinking of April in that blue dress that made her look like the princess I always accused her of being. So perfect. I knew she didn't wear the dress to torture me, but the end result was the same. I'd barely taken my eyes off her the entire night and I wasn't the only one.

I swallowed back the remainder of the glass, sinking down onto the cask I intended to claim for the rest of the evening. I'd been headed back to my cottage, when I found myself in the dunnage instead, in this cool, dark corner perfect for drowning sorrows. Even the loud groaning of the dunnage door being pushed open wasn't enough to drag me from my wallowing. It was probably Ewan collecting more crates of whisky because April was selling bottles faster than I could keep track.

I reminded myself never to doubt her again. It was all I'd been doing for weeks, even while becoming her friend. I was an arsehole. No wonder she wanted nothing to do with me. What did she really even need me here for?

I poured another drink with shaking hands. I was spiraling, letting old doubts creep in. When the first clack of heels reached my ears, I *knew* it was her.

From my hidden corner, I observed April slide the door closed behind her and move deeper into the stalls, her hair a fiery flash between the barrels. She paused at the end of my row, reaching into the stack of crates for a bottle. Another forty-seven. When she straightened, she startled, a hand flying to her chest. "Shit . . . Mal! You scared the crap out of me."

I didn't trust myself to speak, so I sipped from my fresh drink and watched her step closer, placing the bottle on the nearest shelf. She worried her pink lip between her teeth. "Is everything okay, Malcolm?"

Malcolm. Is that where we were? "Why wouldn't it be? I have good whisky . . . and it looks like you just sold another very expensive bottle."

She brightened. "I know, can you believe it? That's ten tonight."

I could believe it, but I said nothing again and we fell into silence. Unlike every other silence between us, this one felt awkward. I was used to feeling out of place. Used to feeling like the one to blame when uncomfortable moments arose. But never with her; she always had a quip or a joke that made me feel less like a bumbling idiot. Like I wasn't constantly searching for the right thing to say or the right way to act and coming up empty.

"Why are you hiding in here?" Her voice wavered through the shadow and I knew she regretted asking the question. She knew why. I'd been a breath away from asking her to dance. Everyone in that room knew it, except my brother apparently. How quickly I'd been humbled.

I didn't dance. Not as a hard rule, but mostly because I had a suspicion I wouldn't be very good at it. I wanted to dance with her, though. Watching her all night, I'd become obsessed with the idea of holding her so close in front of everyone. It had taken two full drinks and a pep talk from Heather to gather the confidence to ask. Would she have said yes if my brother hadn't swept her away? The question was driving me insane.

"My brother is a good dancer." The statement fell from my lips before I could stop it.

She showed no reaction. "Yes, he's definitely . . . enthusiastic." *Enthusiastic*. Why did it feel like there was an insult in there somewhere? "You didn't answer my question. Why are you hiding?"

I lifted my glass to her. "I'm not hiding, I'm drinking."

It wasn't an offer but she pulled the glass from my hand and brought it to her own lips, taking a small sip and licking the excess with her tongue. "Kier liked to drink alone too, when my grandmother drove him to distraction." She took another small step, close enough for me to smell her perfume, something light and floral. "Is someone driving you to distraction, Mal?"

Christ. Goose bumps broke out across my skin. Perhaps it was the gentle buzz in my veins making me brave, perhaps it was her.

I plucked the glass from her fingers with one hand and circled her waist with the other, tugging her into me. She came all too willingly between my bent legs, the plumes of her skirt spreading over my lap like sea foam. I could barely see her in the darkness, bolstering me further. "When we kissed in your room . . . I said it shouldn't have happened. What I wanted to say, what I should have said, is that you undo me in a way that scares me. That's why I ran."

Sitting on the cask, I was only a few inches taller, so I felt the puff of her hot breath on my neck. Unable to fully make out her features, I lowered my mouth to hers slowly, every tiny particle of my body screaming out for me to do it faster, claim her quicker before she changed her mind, but I let my intent show. There would be no misinterpretation this time. And then she was kissing me back.

Our lips pressed and we both exhaled, sharp but sure. Her lips were as soft as I remembered, and I dragged mine over them twice more. I knew the scruff of my beard must scratch, a fact we both seemed to appreciate, because she dragged me closer. Deepening the kiss, she pulled and sipped from my lips, her tongue dancing and flicking over mine. My hands bunched at the back of her dress, fists gripping the fabric, but I held taut, letting her run this show. This would not be like last time when I'd behaved like a depraved idiot. Plundering her mouth so hard, so roughly, there was no way she could have possibly enjoyed it. I started to slow the kiss, to set a steady pace. Trying to stay calm. But her nails dug into my arm and she drew back just far enough to say, "Please don't start being polite now."

I cupped her face. "I'm trying to be gentle."

"And if I prefer you rough?"

Fuck. This couldn't be real . . . it just couldn't. A fresh wave of lust hit me so hard it was almost blinding. Then, I was the one being devoured. The force of the kiss stunned me. If it weren't for the cask beneath my legs I would have landed on my backside as she threw her weight against me. Both of her hands clutched at my face, short nails dragging through my beard and into the hair at my temples. I groaned, crushing and lifting her against my chest, feeling the drag from her bodice through my shirt. My left hand began frantically searching through the layers of her skirt until I found the smooth expanse of her thigh and tugged it around my hip.

Then, we were turning—I was turning—pressing her back and over the cask. Her back bowed and I arched over her, the only way to keep our lips connected. We were half wild, scrambling at one another as I lifted her and sat her on the barrel. Her dress plumed around her, far too pretty for a desperate act like this in a dark, earthy warehouse. The knowledge only spurred me on. I wanted it to get dirty, I wanted tears in the bodice and stains on the hem. I wanted to bring my princess down to my level.

She went easily, falling back on her elbows and spreading her thighs for me. *For me.* Her head fell all the way back and she opened her mouth wider for my tongue. I clutched her face in my hands, slowing it down, savoring the feel of her between my palms. She tasted of everything good, whisky and sunshine and Christmas morning. It was a kiss that fogged windshields, the sticky heat penetrating the thick stone walls, driving us higher.

Her hands were at my kilt, shucking the material up and over

245

her skirt. At the first graze of her finger on my thigh I grunted, squeezing my eyes shut and dropping my forehead to her shoulder. "Wait, wait, wait . . ."

Her breath was ragged. "Is something wrong?"

"No, no—never. I just . . . I need to touch you first. I can't think of anything else." It pained me to stop her, the thought of her small hand around my cock was enough to blow a blood vessel. I took both of her hands from beneath my kilt and pressed them to the sides of the cask, drawing back just enough to catch her eye and communicate that she keep them there. She bit her lip but nodded.

I began at her chin—that proud little point had captivated me since I was fourteen years old. I kissed it, licked it. Her lips dipped for my mouth but I was already moving, trailing my tongue down her neck, tasting what I'd only ever scented. I grunted again, the only sound I was capable of when my lips found the swells of her breasts. I dipped my nose between them, into the heart of her bodice, smelling perfume there too. "Did you wear this dress to torture me, April?" I didn't need to look up to feel her nod. I licked the curve of one, from the center to the tormenting little bow hanging over her shoulder, leaving a wet trail behind. I placed a bite on the other, holding her still as she jerked and shuddered. "Too rough?"

"No."

Good. I did it again, licking, biting, pulling her bodice down with my teeth, but I didn't expose her. Not here. Not when anyone could walk in and see her. I trailed kisses down her body, and the beads of her dress scraped and caught through my beard, the bite of pain the only thing keeping me sane. As I fell to my knees, her words from the car blew through my mind. *Did it ever occur to you that I enjoyed him saying those things to me?*

I circled her ankle, letting her shoe drop from her toes, and pressed a kiss there. "Are you going to let me fuck you with my mouth tonight?" The words poured out of me, unbidden, but when she moaned, I pressed my smile into her skin so hard I hoped I left an imprint. "Come on, princess, don't hold out on me now. I need to hear your words."

She squirmed on the cask. *"Prick."* I laughed, trying to recall if I'd ever had so much fun doing this. It was always a mix of nerves and panic, overshadowed by blind need.

"That's a start." I pressed a kiss higher, flicking my tongue against her smooth calf. "More." I needed to hear that prim little voice telling me what to do, just like she did in my dreams.

She laughed breathily. "I hate you." But then her hands were at the sides of her skirts, trying to pull them higher. I knocked them aside.

"More, April," I urged, dipping my head beneath her skirts to kiss the inside of her knee.

"When men are between my legs, I like it better when they get to the point." Her voice was only just clear enough for me to hear. Her legs tightened around my head as if to punctuate her point. I wanted to see us from her view. Me, stained-kneed and wild, head shifting beneath pretty tulle. An erotic image I needed immortalized in her mind.

"Princess, do you want my mouth on you? Tell me now."

"Yes." I felt her fall back further, and from my position, I could see the lengths of her hair almost touching the floor on the other side of the cask. *Fuck.* "Yes . . . that's what I want."

"Good girl." I hummed the words into her skin and pushed higher, the very center of her calling to me like a homing beacon. My nose brushed lace and my tongue followed, swiping along the crease between her thigh and underwear. *Shit.* She was beginning to drip down her leg. I lapped it up, half savage as she trembled. "Hips up, princess." My fingers curled around her underwear and tugged the moment she complied, drawing them down and off her feet, knocking her second shoe loose. I drew up from beneath her skirt, eyes locking on hers as I tucked the pretty white lace into my jacket pocket. Her nostrils were flared and she bit her lip. "You're amassing quite a collection," she said. I knew her pretty skin would be flushed.

I no longer had it in me to joke in return. I pushed back beneath her skirts, no delaying this time as I licked her slowly . . . if there was a heaven, this was it. I could happily die here, on my knees between April's legs. A single taste was all I got before I heard it—muffled voices, a low timber almost identical to mine, and the creak of the dunnage door. A dark, vicious part of me wanted to continue, to let him see. April was pliant in my arms, she would have let me continue none the wiser.

I scrambled to my feet, tucking her skirts back into place. "Mal," she gasped, disappointment echoing in her tone. *You and me both, princess.*

I pressed my finger to her lips, cocking my head to the door. Her eyes flared, hearing it. She didn't look panicked . . . shocked, perhaps. A voice in my head warned me this was not a good way to be caught. I started to draw her from the cask before remembering her lack of shoes. Lifting her instead, I pressed her flush to my chest as I carried her through the stalls to the furthest wall. Her hot little breaths met my neck as she clung to me, all ten fingers pressing into my shoulder, thighs circling my waist.

There were no windows this far back, no light. She shivered at the cooler temperature and I clutched her tighter, not able to stop the kiss I pressed to her lips. I should have given her my jacket. When she returned the kiss with startling force, hope bloomed through me. We'd been interrupted and she still *wanted* me. She hadn't seen sense. We reached the back of the room and I pressed her into the wall, my cheek to hers. We were breathing so loudly I almost couldn't make out my brother's words. "You're certain she came this way?"

"Yes, she came to collect another forty-seven." Heather. *Hell*, it was a real family affair.

"*Mal . . .*" April's near-silent plea eclipsed everything else. She squirmed in my arms, hips pressing and seeking against mine. I knew what she needed.

"Can you keep quiet?" I husked. *Bloody hell. What was I saying?*

She bit her lip, nodding frantically. My hand came to cover her mouth and her answering moan was powerful, her head falling back against the wall. I was doing this. This was happening. My hand fumbled beneath her skirts until I found her center. She was hot, bare, soaked. I stroked once with a single finger and she bucked in my arms, her nails digging into my shoulders. I stroked her again, slower, pausing to make a circle over her clit. Her eyes flew wide and her lips opened around my palm covering her mouth, teeth sinking into my skin with a sharp pinch that nearly buckled my knees. "That's it . . . bite me. I want you to leave a mark." I panted, pushing into her then, one finger and then two, setting a steady rhythm. "Fuck, baby, you're perfect. Feel how well you take my fingers. I need to watch you take my cock next." Our eyes were locked, foreheads almost touching.

A few more passes was all it took before she was tightening around my fingers. She was the one about to come but I was the one out of my mind. Talking. Saying things I'd never usually say. I didn't even know if I was being quiet . . . didn't care. Her hips rolled, trying to take more of me. Mine rolled back, the rock-hard length beneath my kilt hitting her thigh. I heard Callum's heavy tread angle down a stall close to us. Was I being loud on purpose? Was my hand loosening over her mouth? I had no idea.

Needing to taste her again, my mouth dove into the crook of her neck, laving at her pounding pulse until her head shot back. Her release was silent, long and searingly hot as she convulsed in my arms. I came in my boxers seconds later with a low groan, cock still pressed against her. Then we stared at each other, chests rattling. The entire exchange couldn't have been more than a minute, but I felt utterly changed.

"Here it is." Heather's high voice cut through the fog, followed by the clank of crates moving. "Perhaps she went up to the house to check on Dudley. Do you think I should look for her?"

I turned just enough to catch sight of them. Heather held a few bottles in her arms facing the door. But Callum, he was looking at the ground—at April's shoes. His head snapped up, staring right at me. Not *at me*, the corner I'd tucked us into was too dark. And yet, I pressed closer to April, my free arm caging around her in a bid to cover as much of her as possible.

"I'm sure she'll be back," Callum eventually said, steering

Heather down the aisle and out the door. It clacked closed, and I released April's mouth but kept her hiked against the wall. Neither of us said a word. It was too dark to fully make out her expression, so when she pressed lightly against my chest, I set her down at once. Her bare feet met the grubby earth and I was about to lift her again when she stumbled back, her expression slackening with horror.

"Princess," I murmured, reaching for her. But she was already hurrying toward the cask, gathering up her shoes.

"I'm sorry . . . I shouldn't have . . . I'm sorry I made you do that with them there."

Was she serious? "You didn't *make* me do anything. I was fully onboard with every single second of that." I opened my mouth to admit that I felt more alive in those five minutes than I had in my entire life, but I shoved the words down deep before I terrified her.

She nodded jerkily and I could tell she wanted to say more, but her glance flicked back in the direction of the party. "I should get back. I can't believe I left for this long, tonight is too important."

This is important. "We should talk about this." Was she upset because Callum might have seen us? Or at the way I spoke to her?

"We will, I want to. I'm so sorry to ask this . . . but can we do it later?" She turned for the door, smoothing her skirt and tangled curls, clutching up the strewn bottle of forty-seven at the last moment.

I followed. "When later?" I demanded.

"After the tasting is done." She rose onto her toes, pressing a hasty kiss to the corner of my lip.

The kiss eased my panic slightly, but the tinge of worry was too sharp to ignore. "Come by the cottage . . . if you want to."

"It might be late."

"That's fine." I wouldn't be sleeping anyway.

Then she pushed through the door, her fiery trail of hair the last part of her to disappear from view.

24

APRIL
Georgia – Vance Joy

Stepping back into the tasting room, I caught sight of Heather's hand waving over heads, beckoning me over. I plastered a smile on my face, holding the bottle of forty-seven aloft like an explanation as I wound in her direction. The tasting room was a lot emptier than when I left, the band had finished their set and were lazily packing away instruments while picking over the last of the food. "Sorry—" I started to say, then noticed Callum at her side, with what I could only describe as a shit-eating smirk on his face. I'd abandoned him the moment our dance ended to go in search of Mal, never thinking he might follow. There was no way he could have seen us. Could he have?

"There you are. I was beginning to think you'd gotten a better offer," he said smoothly as I neared. His hand extended to me, palm up. I stared at it. I wasn't sure what he was asking but I knew I couldn't take it.

"You have something on the back of your dress," Heather said, a little divot of genuine confusion appearing between her brows.

"Oh." I startled, twisting my skirts around. Not just something, black grease-like smudges stained the entire back of the fine material. *Shit.* "I must have brushed up against something in the dunnage." My voice was high as I scrambled to smooth the marks away.

"Something dirty for sure," Callum agreed. My fingers froze. He knew—the bastard definitely knew. I stepped on his toes on my way to the bar. He only laughed loudly and followed, Heather right on his heels. "I haven't seen Mal for a while either."

"*Hmm?*" I opted for confusion. If he wasn't going to come right out and say it, neither would I. "Oh, I think he left, it's not really his scene." I wished I were there with him, but I needed to get tonight finished. I was the host, I couldn't just disappear and expect no one to notice—plus I'd meant it when I said tonight was too important.

Placing the forty-seven in a box engraved with the Kinleith Distillery seal, I passed it off to Heather, who disappeared to deliver it to the customer. Callum and I watched her leave in silence, but my toes tapped impatiently against the floor. Would it be too rude to start ushering people out the door? Callum started collecting empty glasses and stacking them on a tray and I couldn't take it any longer. "Please don't clean up."

An eyebrow winged up, his fingers halting. "Why wouldn't I help?"

Because I suspect you have feelings for someone you can't have, but just in case I'm wrong— "I don't want to lead you on." I spoke the last part aloud.

Before I could blink, he dropped to one knee, clutching at his chest. For one second of blind panic, I lurched forward to catch him but his head flew back, more shouting than singing, when he

254

belted out, *"Shot through the heart, and you're to blame, you give love a bad name!"*

I knew stragglers were watching us curiously, but I laughed anyway. "I'm sorry," I said, offering him a hand. I knew then with much relief the apology wasn't necessary, he had no interest in me, which meant—

He leapt to his feet, towering over me once again as he pressed a smacking kiss to my cheek and said, "Just so you know, Mal can't sing as well as me." He winked and went right back to cleaning up.

MAYBE I SHOULD HAVE TEXTED FIRST, I THOUGHT, CHAFING MY hands against my arms as I stood on Mal's stoop. Though it was after one a.m., a soft light emanated out the small hatch window along with the low buzz of the television. He was definitely awake. Dudley whined impatiently at my feet. "Don't look at me like that," I said to him. "I just . . . need a second." He stomped his single front foot. Glowering at my dog, I knocked softly. He didn't answer. "He's probably busy . . . we should come back another time." I could have sworn Dudley's next whine was filled with judgment.

Swallowing, I faced the door down like it was an enemy. Earlier in the dunnage was the hottest experience of my entire life and I'd come harder than I ever had—ever. But part of me worried he would regret it. *He didn't seem like he regretted it*, a voice whispered. With that in mind, I took matters into my own hands and tried the door handle—of course it was open—and stepped inside. Regardless of what came next, we needed to discuss it like adults to—

255

I stopped short at the threshold like I'd run headlong into a wall. It took my brain several heartbeats to catch up to what my eyes were seeing. My face, far larger than anyone should be forced to see their own face, on his widescreen television. *A Stranger at the Gates.* I immediately recognized it from the image of a younger me dressed in nothing but a sheer white nightdress, hair unbound around my shoulders.

My character, Lyra, crept down the servants' staircase of the large country estate in which she worked as a governess to the viscount's young ward. Unlike present me, Lyra strode into the viscount's study with purpose, slight shoulders pushed back. Lord Devon didn't look up, but his hand stilled over his correspondence, grip tightening around his pen. "Miss Stewart, the hour grows late."

"It does." Her voice—*my voice*—echoed smokily.

He straightened in his chair, posture imposing as he finally looked at her. "You should not be here." Devon spoke the words but it was Mal's voice I heard in my head.

"Because you do not want me here?" Lyra sidled closer and Devon shot to his feet, moving behind his chair and gripping the back of it, as though the barrier might stem the oncoming tide between them. It had been raging ever since he found her out in the woods weeks before, soaking wet, injured, and without her memories. Lyra stepped up to the desk, her hand tracing over the various pots of ink and paper, stroking the pen he'd just held. Lord Devon's breath rattled as did Malcolm's. My attention snapped to him sprawled on the sofa, watching him watch *me* on the screen.

Bolstered by the sight, I crept closer. He hadn't noticed me yet. Dudley took my slight motion as an invitation and barreled around my legs, his short claws clacking on the hardwood as he rushed straight to Boy's basket. Mal jumped to his feet, head whipping around exactly like Lord Devon's just had. His eyes were wide with panic, flicking between me and the screen and then back again. "April . . . I wasn't . . . I didn't . . ." He fumbled for the remote on the sofa, only succeeding in turning up the volume until my breathy voice was all that could be heard in the room. "*Fuck!*" His hands were trembling, cheeks blazing the deepest scarlet. "When I saw the tasting room all locked up, I didn't think you were coming. And then the film randomly started on the television . . . I wasn't watching you, *I swear.*"

His words made me wilt with disappointment. But his clear embarrassment could only mean one thing . . . he *knew* what came next. He'd watched this movie before. I waited for my own embarrassment to rise, along with the usual fears that came with strangers watching and analyzing my body, but none came. If anything, it had the opposite effect. I *liked* the idea of Mal watching me. Admiring me. I stepped closer, watching his too-large fingers jab at the control buttons. "You weren't watching me?"

"*Of course not* . . . I was flicking through the channels. It was already on." As if in a trance, we both watched as Lyra drew nearer; they were arguing now. Devon ordered her back to bed and circled the desk to keep his distance, furious in his adamance that he didn't want her.

The remote control clattered to the floor. The back snapped free and the batteries careened beneath the sofa. Malcolm dove after it, dropping to his hands and knees, scrambling to reach them. "Wait," I urged, circling the sofa to stand on the rug.

"I'm sorry." He didn't pause his frantic search. "Not just for this, but earlier too. I should never have taken it that far or spoken to you that way."

"How did you speak to me?"

He tensed, refusing to look at me. "You know exactly how I spoke to you and it wasn't appropriate." *I thought it was perfectly appropriate.*

"And if I don't want you to be sorry?" I didn't know if it was my words or the rasp in my throat, but he paused, falling back on his heels.

"You don't?"

"No."

"You . . ." He licked his dry lips. "You liked it?"

"Yes."

His swallow was visible. So was his ever rising color, spreading to his ears and down his neck, making him glow beneath the low light. "Then why did you race off?"

"For the reasons I said. I needed tonight to be a success. But also . . ." I paused, searching for courage. I'd never let a man make me feel nervous before, I had no intention of starting now. "I thought *you* might regret it and given the circumstances, running away felt safer in the moment."

He jerked in my direction, still on his knees. "I could never." He shook his head. "I'm desperate for you, April, haven't you realized yet?"

This man. This sexy, shy, dichotomy of a man. How I wanted him. "I'm starting to," I said. "How about this . . . What if instead of constantly questioning one another's actions, we try giving each other the benefit of the doubt?"

He looked at me. *Stared*. Like I wore silk instead of cotton. Like I was the most beautiful thing he'd ever seen. "I think I can agree to that." I barely heard the words over my thundering heart.

The television caught my attention, I watched my hands as they pushed Devon back into his stately desk chair. He fell easily. *Willingly*. Without stopping to think, I grasped Mal's arm, tugging until he rose to full height. For his size, he was pliant to my touch, allowing me to steer him to the armchair and push him down in the exact same manner as my film counterpart. He landed with a soft thud, gray eyes drawing up my body to settle on my face. We stared at one another, a million words passing with just a single look. I reached for him, my thumb spreading over his cheekbone and down the length of his clipped beard. He swallowed beneath the touch, shifting in the chair until his thighs spread beneath the kilt he still wore. His fingers curled into fists.

"Hands where I can see them," Lyra and I said at the same time. Mal's eyes flared, understanding and something else in their depths. On screen, Lord Devon cursed beneath his breath, but my eyes were only for Mal as I awaited his decision. When his hands moved, fingers bracing over the arms of the chair, I knew it was instruction to continue.

Lyra and I moved to the center of our respective rooms. I was a beat behind, but I caught up quickly when she began the lengthy process of undoing the dozen tiny buttons of her night dress. I removed my T-shirt first, my hands sure on the overwashed cotton . . . watching Mal watch me. And he *watched*. He looked starved. The fabric fell in a pile at my feet and he adjusted his position, eyes trying and failing to hold my gaze. His fingers cut deep grooves into the armchair and a notable bulge pressed beneath the moss green of his kilt.

"Is this how you imagined me?" we asked in unison. I pressed my thumbs beneath the waistband of my shorts, letting them fall too. I wore nothing beneath. I came here for this exact purpose.

"Yes," both men responded, the same raw baritone to their voices. I knew Mal wasn't playing a part. His eyes were on my breasts and between my legs with a slightly dazed expression, as though this was the first time he'd ever seen a woman bare to him. I wasn't certain he even registered the scene still playing. I let my fingers brush my thighs, then slid them higher, over the curvature of my hips and across my soft stomach. Slowly turning on the spot so he could see me from every angle. Only when he groaned did I stalk closer, with him tracking each sway of my hips.

"I've thought of you too, my lord," I whispered along with Lyra, stopping so close I could feel the wiry brush of his leg hair against my shins. "In the dead of night when only the devil listens." Slickness was pooling between my thighs, so wet I was certain he must see it because his tongue poked from between his lips. I spun and lowered myself into his lap, spreading my thighs so they split over his legs, my naked body draping over his much larger, fully clothed one.

"*Jesus* . . . fuck, princess." His entire body jerked, hands breaking their hold on the arms as if to touch me, then snapping back before making contact.

I lay my head back on his shoulder, angling myself so he could see the entire length of my body. He followed the movement, inhaling my hair, tracing my ear with his lips, then pressing into the curve of my neck. "I know it's wrong," I rasped a fraction of a second behind Lyra. "I hope for mercy from this torture every day, but the moment the sun goes down—" I broke off, biting my lip as my hands began to roam across my chest, catching my nipple without pausing. My hips started to roll and I felt him then, hot and hard as granite against the small of my back.

"What . . . what do you think about?" he panted.

"Your hands." I picked one up as we veered off script. Holding it in mine, I allowed only the tip of his finger to trace my collarbone, the single touch enough to make me shudder. Next, I grazed it down the center of my chest to cup my breast, his hand burning beneath mine. "First, you touch me here." His curse was far more violent than his touch. He squeezed me gently as though I were infinitely precious, rough thumb rolling over my beaded nipple while his hips rolled against my arse. I was soaked, dripping onto the weave of his kilt. Something about being entirely naked and in control while he was fully dressed made it all the more erotic.

"Where do I touch you next, princess? I know it doesn't end here." The heady quality to his voice made me squirm, back arching impossibly as I continued our journey down my body. Our fingers grazed the inside of my thigh, sliding through the wetness coating my skin. "Yes," he hissed, trailing his finger through it, spreading it further down my thigh then back up to my folds. "Who are you wet for, me or Devon?"

My head rocked back on his shoulder and I cried, "You, Mal . . . only you."

Hands still joined, our index fingers dipped inside, one of his, one of mine, sliding easily to the first knuckle. It took me a moment to get used to the delicious fullness; his fingers so large, I couldn't even comprehend how big his cock must be. He groaned at the first touch, hips thrusting harder as his other arm circled my waist, holding me tight to him as I began to ride our fingers. "Look at you," he groaned, head tipping over my shoulder to watch. I looked down, seeing our fingers disappearing inside me. "Look at how perfect you are. Look how we fit together." He tugged me even tighter to him. "Feel how hard you make me, only you, princess. Only ever you."

Oh god.

My movements picked up pace, hips snapping until there was no discernible rhythm. He husked dirty words into my ear, nipping and laving at the lobe until I was out of control. Until I was crying out, gasping and shaking as the short but powerful orgasm rocketed through me. His shirt was sticking to my skin, our sweat turning our bodies slick.

I was still coming when he lifted me, raising one of my legs until I sat facing him in his lap, thighs cradling his hips. The television was long forgotten as Devon and Lyra began to devour one another as hungrily as we did. Mal gathered my hair in his fist, pulling my head back and licking my neck as I continued to ride him, grinding against his covered erection. My hands tore at his shirt, struggling to remove it. His joined in, wild in their intent as he tugged, buttons popping free and hitting the floor like tiny pebbles. Once his chest was bare, my hands roamed, kissing his mouth while I stroked his nipples until he swore, brushing through the patch of light brown hair as he lifted my hips and dragged his kilt up, fumbling to free himself.

The first graze of his cock at my entrance made me groan. "Condom?" I rasped into his open mouth.

He froze, clutching my hips like I might float away. "I don't have any. *Fuck.* I haven't . . . I haven't in years."

Years? This man was glorious. How the hell could that be possible?

"I'm on birth control," were the words that left me immediately.

His expression slackened. "I'm clean. The times I've had sex . . . it's never been without a condom."

He didn't ask in return, trusting me fully. I said, "Me too," anyway. The words were permission and we dove for one another again, our lips a graceless battle of teeth and tongue. He tucked his kilt out of the way as I rose onto my knees and, with his guidance, sunk slowly onto his length.

"Oh, fuck!" He bucked. "Wait, *baby* . . . please wait." My giant threw his head back, eyes squeezing shut while his thumbs brushed back and forth over my nipples, attempting to regain control of himself. The problem was, I didn't want his control. I wanted him desperate and grunting. I wanted him lost in me.

Keeping my hips as still as possible, I licked up the length of his neck and bit at his ear lobe. "Are you ready yet, my lord?"

He laughed and it resembled a dying animal. "A thousand lifetimes wouldn't have prepared me for you." Humming at his sweet words, I moved my hips in the tiniest circle. His groan was deafening but he allowed it. My next undulation was bigger, sliding the length of him almost to the tip and back in.

"*So good,*" I said, pressing the words into his skin.

Rough hands stroked up my spine and beneath my arms, cupping my breasts, strumming my nipples as my movements sped.

He let me set the pace, touching and watching as I rode him. *April.* My name was a prayer, seeping from his lips like water rushing over rocks. "That's it, baby . . . just like that, just like that." His hips were lifting from the cushion in a sensual slide that left me reeling. "Is this how you finally kill me?"

"Perhaps." My grin felt wicked.

"Good. Ride me until my heart explodes." So I did. My head tipped and my thighs burning, I didn't stop. Recalling his lust-filled plea from the dunnage, I removed his hands from my breasts, bringing one thumb to my lips and sinking it between my teeth, while I pressed the other over my clit. I bit down as I tumbled over the edge, eyes on his as I rode every wave of it. He watched me through glazed eyes and gritted teeth, groaning as he held off his own orgasm as though desperate to memorize mine. When I started coming down, I bit him again, the fleshy part of his palm that time. He exploded, crushing me to his chest while he spilled into me over and over again. *April, April, April.* He cried out, eyes finally falling shut, bliss lightening his entire face.

My name sounded like an ode. It felt like a promise.

25

MAL
Lavender Haze – Taylor Swift

What the hell just happened?

One minute I was sulking alone in my cottage, mindlessly flicking through the television channels in an attempt to stem the reminders of what a moron I'd been earlier. For anything that would keep me from going up to the manor and acting like a moron all over again. Then her face was on my screen like a cruel taunt. The film I knew by heart. The film I'd driven all the way to Inverness to watch on the day of its release years before.

I told myself it wasn't right to watch it now with her so close, but still I'd settled onto the sofa and raised the volume until it felt like she was in the room with me. And then she was, like I was Pygmalion, creating the perfect woman from clay and water.

My humiliation was so fierce I thought I might die from it, but somehow—*somehow*—she turned the most embarrassing moment of my life into the one all future happiness would be measured against. I knew with absolute certainty the single image I would carry to my death bed would be April, writhing in my lap as though it were the most erotic thing to ever happen to *her*, while I'd barely been able to string a coherent thought together.

Even with the musky scent of sex and the sweet perfume of her hair filling the air, her soft curves pressed to my chest, I wasn't entirely convinced *it had really just happened*. She started to stir, peeling her sweat-slicked skin from mine. I resisted the vital urge to hold her tighter.

Green eyes flitted over my chest, then my face. She had the slightest blush to her cheeks and for the first time, I didn't feel embarrassed about the heat in my own. "Do you want me to go?" she croaked after a beat.

Never.

I'd made my desire for privacy pretty obvious over the weeks, but my need for her was stronger. Having her here felt *right*. "No." I shook my head, letting my fingers dip into the curve of her waist and over the silky skin of her lower stomach. I'd seen her on screen countless times—I knew she had a beautiful body. Seeing her in the flesh, having my hands be the ones allowed to caress and stroke and bring her pleasure, almost overwhelmed me. She was so stunning, I didn't know it was possible for a person to be put together so perfectly.

My fingers stroked higher, over the tips of the breasts I'd been too distracted to take in entirely before. I took their weight in my palms and she sat back on my thighs, head tilting until her fiery hair tickled my skin. "Good." She hummed in pleasure. "I think it would tear Dudley's heart out if we left now." In sync, we turned to look at our dogs curled up together in the basket beside the unlit fire. So bloody adorable. "I think they might like each other more than we do."

"I don't think that's possible." Her eyes came back to mine, the flush on her cheeks even brighter now. I wanted to lick it. I wanted to worship at her feet. And I would. But first— "Come on." I stood and lifted her smoothly. She squealed happily, clinging to my shoulders as I carried her the few steps to my bed and set her in the center. She instantly reclined on her elbows, completely unabashed in her own nakedness, and watched me with amused curiosity as I collected her stray clothes. I supposed most people wouldn't be shy if they looked like her.

Depressing the mattress with my knee, I held the T-shirt up, waiting for her to poke her head through. She complied easily but offered no help as I threaded her arms through the sleeves. I hated covering her, but it was a little chilly here and I couldn't concentrate when she had no clothes on. There wasn't a single other thought in my head.

Once I had her dressed, I pulled the sheets back and managed to grunt, "In." Hardly my most charming moment, but I was quickly losing control of my vocal cords at the thought of having her in my bed all night. It was going to take every ounce of discipline I possessed to keep my hands to myself, but I'd do it. I would let her sleep undisturbed if it meant I had to tie my hands to the bed posts.

Sinking beneath my sheets, she laughed and tugged the corner to her face. "They smell clean."

I frowned. "What were you expecting?"

"A single pillow and crusty sheets." She made herself comfortable against my pillow on the side where I usually slept. I was already anticipating it smelling like her. "I should have known you aren't like most men."

That felt like a compliment. I forced myself not to analyze her words from every angle as I crossed the room to turn out the light and switch off the television. Then, second-guessing myself, I quickly made a fire small enough to burn for an hour or two, just long enough to get her warm. By the time I made it back to my bed, she'd removed her shirt again and was sitting up against my headboard. Sheets pooled around her waist and wearing only an innocent smile that didn't suit the devilish glint in her eyes, she said, "Watching you made me hot." Slowly, she reached up to remove the clips that held the heavy top half of her hair. My head was light, the laugh that left my lips hoarse. "I'm surprised you didn't make me light it."

Any notion about letting her sleep fled and I dug beneath the cover to free her foot, pressing a kiss to the arch. "No lessons tonight, I want to take care of you." My eyes were hypnotized by the sight of her nipples hardening again in the cool night air. Her head fell back against the headboard, small fingers drifting over her pale stomach. I knew I wasn't what anyone would describe as a loquacious man, but with April, I managed to say the right thing without even trying. It made me want to tell her every single thought in my head. Climbing onto the bed, I unbuckled my kilt with practiced fingers, my thoughts only on what had been interrupted in the dunnage. "Do you want to be taken care of, princess?"

"Yes." My hands tugged at the bedsheets and she lifted her hips free.

"Legs open as wide as you can this time. I'm not getting interrupted again." She complied immediately, a tiny whimper catching in her throat.

Anticipation made my blood pound and I pressed flat against the bed, the pain exquisitely sweet as my cock compressed between my body and the mattress. Meeting her eyes over the swells of her body, I placed a gentle, wet kiss to either thigh, loving the tremors in her legs when she hooked them over my shoulders. Her toes grazed the length of my back in her attempt to drag me nearer. "Patience," I murmured the word into her skin.

"It's been *weeks*, Mal, I've been bloody patient."

I laughed, letting the breathy sensation touch her wet folds. She bucked, cursing wildly. I'd only ever done *this* once before in my life, and I was too anxious to do anything but hope that my partner enjoyed herself. I felt no nerves with April, though, and to hear she was as tormented as me all of these weeks bolstered me enough that when I finally pressed my tongue to her, I held her eyes, letting her moan ripple through me.

I pulled back enough to whisper, "I want to buy you flowers and take you on a date, would you like that?"

I licked her again, longer this time, drawing a soft lap of her clit.

Her answer was a mewling *yes*.

"And make you breakfast. Do you like pancakes, princess?" I lapped at her opening now, sinking my tongue between her folds until I felt her clench around it. Fuck. My hips bucked reflexively into the bed, right there with her.

"Yes, *yes!*"

She dragged me closer with strong thighs and my hands curled around her hips, lifting her to my mouth. "Good girl, *fuck*, you taste incredible." I laved at my lips, languishing in the musky, feminine taste of her.

"Mal! Mal, please don't stop." Her hands dove into my hair, pulling until my scalp prickled.

"After breakfast, I want to draw you a bath. I won't fit, but I'll squeeze in with you. Do you want that?" She didn't answer so I eased away from her center to nibble at her soft thigh. She whimpered my name and her hips wriggled, seeking my mouth. "Answer the question, April."

"Yes! Yes, that's what I want. That's all I want!" I wasn't sure she even knew what she was agreeing to, but I groaned all the same.

"I want to hold your hand," I confessed. Her cries grew and I was just as lost as she was, thrusting against the bed, mindless as words poured from me. "I want you to teach me to dance, will you do that?"

"Yes, anything!"

I dove back in like a man possessed, biting and licking and lapping until I knew she was close. Just before she peaked, I flipped onto my back, dragging her with me so her thighs pressed either side of my ears. A fantasy I'd held for years finally coming to fruition. She squealed, clinging onto the headboard to right herself. "On my face, princess." The hundreds of times I'd imagined this scenario raced through my mind like an erotic flip book. I'd dreamed it, coming in my hand before I was fully awake.

Those stunning eyes widened with understanding. "I've . . . I've never—"

"Good. Neither have I."

She bit her lip and I knew she was considering it. She was so wet, it coated her thighs and the lower half on my face. I needed more. "*Now*, April."

"What if you can't breathe?"

I smirked. "I'll be able to breathe."

"But what if you *can't*?"

I curled my hand around her thigh, the tips of my fingers pressing into the magnificent swell of her arse. "I'll squeeze twice." I demonstrated, knowing the precaution was unnecessary, needing her on my mouth faster.

Still she hesitated. "What if I kill you immediately?"

I couldn't contain my laugh this time. Holding her still between my hands, I lifted my head and gave her a long, slick lick, groaning when I pulled back. "Princess, if the last thing I taste in this world is your pretty little pussy, I'll die a happy man."

"God." Her head snapped back and she lowered instantly. I caught her delicious weight in my hands, holding her eyes as I parted her and pulled her clit into my mouth. Her hips snapped in tantalizing little thrusts, her desire running in rivulets down my chin and onto my throat. I caught as much as I could, drinking her down, an addict to the taste of her. "I'm so close." I knew she was, I could feel it in every tense line of her body. I kept doing exactly the same motion, flicking her clit with the flat of my tongue, terrified that if I changed it up she'd lose her high. My hips were thrusting into nothing, come beading at the tip and trickling down my length. I was desperate to reach down and palm myself, but I held off, needing to be inside her when I came.

When her orgasm hit, her mouth dropped open in a silent

scream, her entire body arching. Her hands reached back to clutch my thighs, nails digging into muscle. I kept on nibbling, licking, until she slumped forward and begged me to stop.

"Holy shit." She repeated the curse over and over again. "What the hell was that?" If I had an answer, I wouldn't have been able to speak it. Her desire might have been quenched, but mine was a volcano fit to burst.

With rough hands I dragged her down my body, kissing her with the same ferocity I licked her pussy. "I need to fuck you, can I do that?" Instead of answering, she pulled me back up the bed, trying to flip onto her back. I stopped her, telling her, "I need you on top again." She didn't question me, only reached between her legs for my throbbing cock, rubbing it between her folds in a motion that had us both cursing, teasing me over and over again before pushing the tip of me inside, then repeating it all over again. "Now," I commanded, eyes crossing at the pained pleasure. She only shook her head and continued her onslaught.

"Have you ever played just the tip, Mal?" My shaking head rustled against the sheets. "Good. You tortured me, now it's my turn."

She slipped me from her, pressing my length against her hot center, and leant back until only the very tip of me dipped in and out. My gaze fell to where we joined, mesmerized by the sight. "Enough," I begged eventually. She kept going and I caught her around the ribs, dragging her face down to mine for a savage kiss. "If you don't fuck me right now, I'm going to come all over those pretty tits."

Her laugh was serrated like the edge of a knife. "That's not the threat you think it is."

Any reply I might have given was lost when she sunk down on me, squeezing around my cock like a glove. *"Baby . . . that's so good."* I gasped the words over and over, my hips lifting to reach hers. Sweat pooled on my chest, our shared desire dripping into my lap, causing every drag to echo obscenely. It pushed me higher, even the sounds of our fucking turning me on. When she reached behind her to cup my balls, my eyes almost rolled back. And when we reached our release together, her cries were soft and feminine where mine were like the howls of a wolf. I refused to look away from her face even once, committing every second to the vaults of my memory.

REACHING FOR HER FELT AUTOMATIC WHEN I SLIPPED BACK beneath the covers. She came just as enthusiastically, snuggling beneath my arm and pressing her soft body down the length of mine. *Calm down*, I warned my body at the feel of those curves. I could fuck her forever and that wasn't an exaggeration. Her breathy moans alone would be enough sustenance to survive for weeks. At the same time, I hated the idea she might think that was all I wanted from her, so I willed all thoughts away from my aching, half-mast cock—though she must have been able to feel it against her thigh—and pressed a kiss to her sweaty forehead.

"So . . ." She stroked a hand up my chest, brushing over my nipple and through my chest hair to the other. "You're a bit of a dirty talker, Mal." It was like someone lit a match inside me. My skin scorched and I wanted to dive beneath the sheets. At the time, it had felt right, but now . . . *what if it was too much?* I must have started to withdraw because her leg clamped around my hips. "I'm not trying to embarrass you. I liked it." She pressed closer, a hand sinking dangerously close to the hardness concealed by the thin cover. "I liked it *a lot*. It was just a little . . . unexpected."

Holding her thigh, I shifted onto my side so our eyes were level. We shared the same pillow, her tangled curls spread across the white linen, an image plucked straight from my fantasies. *Click.* Another memory for the vault. "It was unexpected for me too, that's the first time I've ever been like that," I admitted with some hesitation.

"Really?" Her squinted expression called bullshit.

"Yes. I can count my sexual experiences on one hand, and this . . . this felt different to every time before." The confession felt like a power trade.

Her eyes widened. "On one hand? Are we including the thumb?"

"All the words that just left my mouth and that's what you're focusing on?"

She laughed wickedly and I kissed her, needing to feel it on my lips. "I'm just surprised," she said when I pulled back. "You're really good at it . . . unfairly good, actually."

Click.

"I read a lot."

"*Hmmm,* lucky me. Nerds always do it better." She flung herself over my chest, a hand delving beneath the covers until she held my cock in her silken grip. I groaned long and low, head burrowing against the pillow. "So, how many are we talking, exactly?" She held her other hand up, fingers and thumb spread wide.

I knew what she was asking so I shook my head in answer. She gave me a slow pump and my mouth dropped open at the sensation. Then she lowered her thumb and I shook my head again. Another pump and she lowered her index finger. That time I nodded.

Three. Three women, including her.

She kept stroking me slowly. "How is that possible?"

"It shouldn't . . ." Her thumb circled the head. I could barely talk. "It shouldn't come as a surprise . . . that a borderline reclusive whisky distiller doesn't see . . . see a lot of action."

"It does actually. Skye is brimming with hot, young tourists who'd give anything to trade places with me." I heard how genuine her words were and I couldn't help wondering how her vision of me differed from my own. When she looked at me, I felt capable, dependable. When she touched me, I felt desired. Women had *desired* me in the past and her comment about tourists wasn't too far off the mark. Callum joked that he saw more action in one busy summer season on Skye than all the years he lived in Edinburgh.

"It might make me selfish," she continued, the speed of her strokes picking up. "But I'm glad the number is so few." *The number doesn't matter, it could be zero or a hundred, there's only you now.* Somehow, I held the words in, dragging her back across my body instead with a swiftness that had her giggling.

Her hands landed on my chest. "On top again?" She sounded surprised.

"Yes," I gritted through my teeth, already lining myself up. "Is that all right?"

She answered by dragging my all too willing mouth down to her breast.

ONCE WE WERE SPENT, WE SLEPT.

April took up two thirds of the bed and wrapped my sheets around herself like a cocoon, which was fine, because I kept waking to drag her closer.

It was the best night's sleep of my life.

26

APRIL
Delilah – Aeris Roves

My vagina is broken. That was my first thought as I woke.

The weight of the small dog at my feet felt familiar, but everything else—the masculine scent clinging to the sheets, the slightly too-soft pillow, the burning between my legs—brought each delicious moment of the night before racing back. My eyes shot open. Mal's cottage was so still I knew I was alone. The clock on the wall ticked, Dudley and Boy breathing in easy tandem. *Why didn't he wake me?* Then I reminded myself of our promise to give one another the benefit of the doubt.

Before I could worry further, there was a faint crinkle of paper from the pillow beside me. A note rested atop one of his folded plaid shirts. I sat, giving Boy's soft coat a stroke as I read Mal's messy scrawl. *If you wake before I'm back, go to the kitchen x*

The kiss at the bottom was a little smudged, like he wrote it without thinking and tried to wipe it away. I knew my smile bordered on deranged as I pulled the shirt over my naked body and raced to the kitchenette as though it were Christmas morning.

Three cooked pancakes waited on a plate beside another note that read, *Heat me*. A bag of ground coffee and various bowls were spread over the counter, covered with foil. When I peeled each back, I found chopped fruit, nuts, and a small container of maple syrup. *How early must he have gotten up to prepare all of this?* I wasn't even hungry, yet I heated the pancakes thoroughly, tears pricking my eyes, then ate every morsel beside a vase of daisies I was positive hadn't been there the night before.

When I took my plate to the sink, another note awaited me, balanced on top of the copper taps. *Bathroom*. Real tears formed as I took in the unlit candles lining the tub, along with a jar of bath salts. I removed the lid and inhaled. Lavender mixed with something sweet. Mal didn't strike me as a lavender kind of guy.

Get in. At least thirty minutes. The note at the bottom of the empty claw foot tub read. I laughed, hearing the clipped demand in my head. Last night, even when sweet and tender and forfeiting all control, there was an air of authority to Mal's tone. It gave me goose bumps just thinking about it. Sweet Mal was undeniably sexy. But *bossy* Mal? That side I was desperate to play with too.

I sunk into the hot water with a groan, letting the healing salts soothe my strained muscles. He wasn't here, and yet he still found a way to take care of me. I'd been in year-long relationships where I never found that level of comfort in my partner. Laying my head against the lip of the tub, I let myself imagine for the first time what it would be like to truly belong to Malcolm Macabe. For him to belong to me. Every day would be like this, because if Mal held another's heart, he would treat it as he did everything that mattered to him—with thought, purpose, and rigid determination. There would be no half measures.

For just a moment, soaking in his bathtub, in his cottage that contained the few possessions he held dear, I imagined that woman could be me.

I EVENTUALLY FOUND MAL IN THE DISTILLERY, BENT OVER THE washback, reading numbers from a small dial. It was muggy here thanks to the heated yeast, and his hair stuck to his temples. "How's it looking?" I asked. He startled, smacking his head hard off the wooden washback lid. "*Shit.* I'm sorry. I thought you heard me." I raced to his side. Instead of addressing me, he dropped to a crouch, greeting Boy and then Dudley who licked his hands with enthusiasm. When he finally turned those storm cloud eyes on me, I found him blushing. "Good morning," I tried again.

Still crouching at my feet, he cleared his throat, eyes roving over what little I wore, still clad in only his plaid shirt and a pair of comfy socks I stole from his bedside drawer. On my search I also discovered the location of the bra he'd been holding hostage along with lacy underwear he'd taken from me the night before. I returned them to their hiding spot with no small amount of glee. "Morning." His voice was a rough caress.

I brushed my thumb over the soft length of bristle above his lip. "I hope you left this shirt out for me because you aren't getting it back."

His hand circled my calf, smoothing up my leg to cup behind my knee. "I did. It looks a lot better on me than it does on you." I felt my brows arch. "I mean . . ." He shook his head dazedly. "It looks a lot better on *you* than it does on me."

I couldn't help but laugh, something about his nerves putting me at ease. Cupping the back of his head with both hands, I drew

279

him from a crouch and up to his knees. His jaw just reached my breasts this way and I saw the exact moment we both realized. His cheeks were still aflame but he licked his lips. "I was thinking"—my voice shook slightly with something that absolutely *wasn't* nerves—"I could make you dinner tonight, to thank you for breakfast."

"You don't need to thank me for breakfast."

I clutched his head more tightly, exasperation in my tone. "I'm trying to ask you on a date, Mal!"

Realization dawned and his eyes became wide circles. "Oh . . . *Yes!*" His nod was a perfect impersonation of a bobblehead. "Yes, I'd like that."

"Good." I laughed again, something I was doing a lot of lately, and wrapped my arms around his shoulders to kiss him in what was only supposed to be a quick peck. Instead, it quickly spiraled until he sat on his heels and I was in his lap, grinding myself along the front of his jeans. His hand crept up my shirt, and he growled into my mouth at finding me bare, before gripping both arse cheeks and drawing me tight against him. The entire thing was obscene and ridiculous considering we'd had sex three times only hours ago and my vagina felt like it had been through a cheese grater. But I was impossibly wet, and moaning. And if he wanted to fuck me right here on the cement floor, I was fully on board with that happening.

"Mal?"

We both recognized the voice and I instantly began to draw back. But Mal—he kissed me harder, forcefully bending my body back until I arched over his lap. He was doing it on purpose, wanting Callum to see us. The notion *should* have pissed me off, yet it only turned me on further. My moan filled his mouth, nails digging into his neck. He pulled back just far enough to husk out, "I'm so fucking gone for you, do you even realize?"

"Brother, have you—*oh*—"

Eyes on me the entire time, Mal gave me another slow open-mouthed kiss, then stood, lifting me with him. I wanted to scream at Callum to go away so Mal could finish what he'd been saying. *Gone for me? Did that mean . . .*

"Good morning," Callum said. And when I spared him a glance I found him with his arms crossed over his chest, a smirk directed at his brother. "Though it looks like some of us are having a better morning than others." I huffed a chuckle and Callum's bright eyes pinged to me, tsking. "April, you're looking very disheveled . . . definitely not how I left you."

Mal's snarl was so vicious, Boy let out a low whine. Then he maneuvered me behind him, blocking my bare legs from Callum's view. The borrowed shirt covered me from wrist to mid thigh, offering a lot more coverage than the clothes I usually wore. It didn't seem like the right time to point that out.

Callum raised both his hands placatingly, backing up before Mal could say a word. "I just came to collect my music system. I'll come back later. I can see I caught you at a . . . *rough* time." He snickered at his own joke and I had to bite my lip to keep from laughing too.

"Very funny . . . get the hell out of here," Mal snarled in return.

"Already gone." When the door closed behind him, a weird silence settled.

Mal turned back to me, taking both of my hands and rubbing his thumbs over my knuckles. "Do you still want me to come to dinner?"

The question surprised me. *"Of course."*

He looked relieved and that thumb went to the collar of my shirt next, dragging down the line of buttons. "Can I bring anything?"

"Just yourself."

He looked confused again and hesitated, ready to say more, but at the last moment he tugged me against him to place a sweet kiss on my cheek. My heart squeezed at the action, startled at the depth of my feelings for him. If he were anyone else, I would say I had sex-tinted glasses on, but I knew it was more than that. This man had his tongue inside me not even ten hours ago, and it was all I could do not to tear off my clothes and spread myself across the workstation like an offering. No one had *ever* gotten me this hot before.

Rising onto my toes, I pressed my own kiss to his bristled chin and then against his ear where I whispered, "And for dessert . . . I was thinking I could put on a tiny silk nightdress. I have the perfect one in mind."

His throat worked around a swallow, fingers digging into my hips. "I don't want you in silk. Wear those little pajamas—you know the ones. I haven't been able to stop thinking about them."

This man.

"I think I can do that," I said, and before I could give in to the urge to kiss him again, I drew back, rounded Dudley up, and left, forcing myself not to look back.

I'D JUST SET TWO WINEGLASSES ON THE DINING TABLE WHEN Heather's face appeared at the kitchen door, her grin bright as she waved through the glass. "It's hot as balls out there." She bustled through the door the moment I opened it, heading straight for the fridge before registering the pasta sauce slowly cooking on the stove. "Oh, did I come at a bad time?"

"Not at all."

Fridge forgotten, she cut back to the rarely used dining table, running a finger over the various sets of cutlery set out atop my grandmother's favorite table cloth, still stiff from the starch. I may have gone a touch overboard. "What's all this?"

I shifted, hands squeezing behind my back. "I, uh, I have a date. At least, I think it's a date."

"With Callum?" She frowned, taking in the food preparation again.

"No." For the first time I considered the fact that my friend might have a problem with this. She'd pushed me toward Mal in the beginning, but the joke she made about Callum at the tasting may have left her thinking I was playing one brother off against the other. "It's Malcolm."

"Malcolm? My *brother* Malcolm?"

"Yes." My tone couldn't be more tentative.

"Yes!" The swift clapping of her hands made me jump. "I knew it! I bloody knew it!"

"Knew what?"

"You and Mal! You've always had a crush on him, it was so bloody obvious. My brother can be harder to read, but I guessed right away . . . there's something about the way he watches you when he thinks no one's looking."

My hands stilled on the pink peony flower arrangement. "How does he look at me?"

"Like . . . you're a *revelation*." I swallowed thickly. "Like you're a puzzle he has no idea how to solve but wants to try anyway."

I didn't know what to say. "I'm not that complicated," I whispered eventually, carrying the vase to the table.

"No," she agreed with a sad sort of smile. "But to Mal you are. My brother is the best man I know. Don't tell Callum or Alastair that, but it's the truth. He's smart, kind, and loyal. He gives without taking. He has the biggest heart, but outside of his family and Kier, he's never given it to anyone because deep down I think he's afraid it won't be accepted, like he doesn't deserve to be happy." She let out a soft cry, wiping tears from her cheeks, and I went to her, wanting to cry too because everything she said was true. I hugged her and she hugged me back. "What I'm trying to say is— please don't hurt him."

"I would never hurt him. *Never*." I shook my head vehemently. "I know you suspected I had some interest in Callum, but there was nothing. From either of us."

She pulled back, waving a hand. "Oh, I know that. Callum isn't attracted to you at all."

"Um . . . *ouch*?" I knew I'd said it first, but having Heather confirm it so bluntly still stung my pride a little.

"I didn't mean it like that! We've been scheming to get you and Mal together for weeks."

"What?" I gaped at her. I'd guessed that morning Callum had purposely been attempting to make Mal jealous, but Heather too? "You're serious?"

"Yep. Now—" She clapped her hands like a drill sergeant. "Everything needs to be perfect. Is that what you're wearing?"

We both glanced down at the loose shorts and tank top I wore. "What's wrong with this?"

"Mal won't care, but it's a little sloppy."

I laughed. *Where the hell was my sweet friend?* "Babe, please don't become a matchmaker, it goes to your head."

"Just call me Cilla Black." Then she broke into a god-awful rendition of "Surprise, Surprise."

"You're thinking of *Blind Date*," I said.

She threw me a glare. "We really don't have time to waste. You get dressed, I'll sort this mess out."

"Aye, aye, captain."

"DOES HE PREFER WHITE OR RED?" I HELD UP THE TWO BOTTLES of wine I'd picked up from the village store. The selection had been pretty limited.

Heather nodded to the red. "It's the only alcohol he drinks outside of whisky."

I stored that nugget of information away. "You think I should have grabbed some whisky from the bar?" I chewed my lip, wondering if I had time to dash down and grab one.

She threw me a bemused grin over the pasta sauce she'd taken charge of. "You're nervous about this."

"I'm not nervous." I blew out a breath, clutching the back of the breakfast stool. *"All right,* I'm nervous, yes. I've never really done the dating thing, all my exes I met through work and we sort of fell into relationships. And Mal is . . ." *Special.* I couldn't say it aloud.

She smirked again and plucked the wine from my hand, poured out a healthy glass and pushed it back to me. I gulped half of it down, barely tasting it, then pressed out the creases from my skirt. It was a warm evening so I'd changed into a silky, calf-length skirt in jade green that clung to my hips and a white tank top with a high neck and wide straps that showed a strip of navel below the hem. It felt summery and playful but not too sexy.

Last night had been an unreal encounter I wanted to repeat immediately, but I wanted Mal to feel comfortable despite the promise we'd parted on. Heather's words flashed through my mind again.

How does he look at me?

Like . . . you're a revelation.

That made me want to curl up on his chest like a cat and never leave. It was madness to be having thoughts like this after only one night together.

It must be the five orgasms, not counting the one in the dunnage. My mind instantly nixed the thought. It wasn't the orgasms—it was Mal. I loved that he taught me to do things for myself instead of taking charge and doing it *for* me because he knew I was capable. The way he looked at me and saw everything, even the parts I tried so hard to hide. I'd even grown to like the way he grunted whenever I said something ridiculous. *Crap.*

"The pasta just needs a couple more minutes." Heather's voice shook me from my daze.

"Thank you, you've been a life saver." I rounded the island to take over but the doorbell rang. The front door. We both look at each other.

"It can't be Mal, he would have used the back," she pointed out.

Right. "Back in a sec." I cut down the hall into the foyer, tucking the length of my hair behind my ears. Whoever it was, I hoped I could get rid of them quickly. It took me a second to unjar the lock, stiff from disuse, and when I finally drew it back I froze. Mal. He'd trimmed his beard to a fine layer of scruff, hair brushed and styled away from his face. Loose flower stems starting to crumple in his fist.

"I'm early." He caught my surprise and stepped back.

I had to peel my tongue from the roof of my mouth. "You didn't have to knock."

"I didn't want to just come—" He cut off, eyes dragging down my body and up again. His breath puffed out of him like a cloud of smoke. "You look so pretty." The flowers crumpled further.

"So do you." He really did. He wore a perfectly ironed white dress shirt open at the collar and tucked into black trousers that showed off his trim waist. If my compliment registered, he gave no acknowledgment. I pushed the door wider and it took him a moment to move, trailing me to the kitchen without a word, Boy at his heel like always.

Mal froze in the doorway when he spotted his sister. "Don't mind me, brother, I was just leaving."

"Heather kept an eye on the food so I could change," I explained.

He still didn't speak, but I watched his cheeks tint pink as his eyes met hers. I turned to Heather, but her features were carefully blank. When I coughed pointedly, she threw up her hands. "Right, right. I'm leaving."

I squeezed her hand as she passed. "Thanks for the help."

"Anytime." Tucking her bag over her shoulder, she threw back, "Have fun, kids. I left some condoms on the counter—"

"Bye, Heather!" Malcolm beat me to the punch, his face fit to burst by the time the door swung shut.

"I'm sorry—"

"I'm sorry, that was—" We spoke over each other, then fell silent.

I tipped my head back, looking into his handsome face. "I'm sorry about that, I planned to get rid of her before you got here. I promise I didn't say a word about last night."

"I . . . I wouldn't mind if you did."

"Oh." He didn't mind them knowing about us. That knowledge beat around my chest.

"I'm sorry that my siblings have the most annoying habit of turning up at the wrong moment. We aren't all that close, I swear."

I laughed. "I actually like how close you guys are, I always wanted a sibling growing up." The timer on the oven dinged and I raced around the island, turning down the burner before it boiled over. "Sorry . . . just a second. I hope pasta is all right, I know it's kind of a safe option but I forgot to ask what you liked."

"It's perfect." I paused what I was doing to look at him and we both smiled. It was sickeningly cute, but I felt so happy I didn't even care.

I nodded to the table, dishing pasta onto the plates. "Please sit. I opened a bottle of red wine but I have water or juice if you prefer."

He glanced at the table first, spotting the vase of peonies I set out earlier, then to his hand, seeming to remember the half-squished flowers he held. His shoulders drooped and he spun back to me. "I'm sorry I'm making such a mess of this."

Dinner forgotten, I circled back to him and took the flowers from his grip before he could do any more damage. They were the same white daisies from his cottage that morning. I could tell from the cut of the stems they'd been handpicked. "They're beautiful," I said. An old boyfriend sent me a wall of pink roses once, like an entire six-foot wall. Actually, his *assistant* sent them to me. Matt had called the following day to inform me how expensive they'd been. I'd take these crumpled daisies over a wall of roses every damn time.

"I promised I'd take it slow tonight," was the only warning I gave before I surged to my tiptoes and planted my lips on his. His hands caught my shoulders like it was their only purpose in the world and then his lips opened beneath mine. The perfect first-date kiss. It started sweet, open lips without tongue. And then his hand wrapped around my neck, thumb pressing my chin up, and it deepened. *Oh*, how it deepened. He sipped from my lips like it had been weeks not hours, backing me up to the island, half lifting me when the timer dinged again. I laughed, drawing back. He looked drunk. "Perhaps we should have gone to a restaurant," I joked.

"Probably." He released me long enough to place the flowers in a jug. I finished dishing up the pasta, adding the tomato sauce while he poured the wine, pausing over my glass and waiting for me to nod before topping it off. "This smells amazing," he said when I placed the dish before him.

"Elsie taught me to cook. It helped keep her close when I moved away, even more so after she died."

He nodded, twirling pasta on his fork. "I remember. She always used to make cherry chocolate cake on a Saturday and bring it down to the distillery. Best day of the week."

"I'd forgotten about that! I'll have to dig out her old recipe books, I'm sure it's in there somewhere."

He groaned around his mouthful, which I assumed was at the thought of my grandmother's cake rather than the pasta. "Don't let Jess know. Elsie made that cake for an Easter bake sale one time. It was so popular, Jess didn't talk to anyone who bought it for a week."

289

I shook my head, laughing around a mouthful. "How did I forget about their rivalry?"

He grinned, setting his fork down and reaching for his wine. "No idea, it was legendary. Every Christmas fair they tried to out-bake one another, the birth of baby Jesus all but forgotten in the face of the village bake contest. The corner store used to order in more chocolate just for them."

My smile felt huge. "I've missed that. London can be so full-on sometimes, it makes you forget the little things."

His eyes met mine then flitted away. "Do you like London?"

I shrugged. "Most of the time. I like that I can get a pint of chocolate brownie ice cream delivered to my door at three a.m. and hear twenty different languages in a single tube ride." I swirled my pasta, feeling his attention. "I don't like that I can't see the stars from my window or hear the sea as I fall asleep. I don't like how little I actually know the people I call friends." The truth of it clogged my throat. I'd spoken only to Sydney and only a handful of times in the weeks I'd been here. Had anyone else even noticed my absence? I didn't realize how alone I'd been until I came here. "And you? You never wanted to go somewhere else?"

He didn't even think about it. "Never."

"I envy that. If I could wish for anything, it would be contentment." I knew I was revealing too much but I couldn't seem to stop. "I always have this little voice in my head whispering I need to do more, achieve more, and if I can do that, then I'll have succeeded."

He chewed slowly and swallowed. "You don't think you're successful?"

"Some days yes, some no." I had a split second to decide how honest I wanted to be. In the end, I figured it was better to lay it all out there. "Sometimes it feels like I'm constantly playing a part, an actress that never gets to hear the word *cut*. So I keep trying to say the right thing and do the right thing, and the scene keeps on rolling." He'd fallen so silent I cringed. "I'm not making any sense . . ."

"You are." He'd grown still, jaw slightly ajar as though he were seeing me for the very first time. "I think everyone has that voice that says they aren't enough. Some people just hear it louder than others. *You* are a success, whatever the hell that even means." His hand crossed the table to grasp mine. "Kier watched that dance show every single week with tears in his eyes. There wasn't a single moment he wasn't proud of you." When he reached the end, his voice was thick. I recalled his nervousness as he approached me at the whisky tasting. His head between my thighs, grunting how he wanted me to teach him to dance.

I picked up my glass, swirling the contents. "You thought it was shallow," I stated.

He sighed. "I didn't. I *thought* you were using it as an excuse not to come home. Now I'm aware Kier didn't even tell you he was sick, I know better."

His words sunk in my stomach, turning the food bitter. I needed to tell him the truth, about Kier's debt and the distillery. Then I thought of the single photograph on the shelf in his cottage. Him and Kier in the distillery, Kier's arm around his shoulder. I couldn't do that to him, couldn't tarnish what they had. Not when business was finally on an upward curve. I'd looked over the numbers from last night, and they were promising. If I could get us out of this mess, he would never have to know.

WHEN BOTH OF OUR PLATES WERE SCRAPED CLEAN, HE ROSE to collect them.

"I invited you, remember?" I said, pulling myself up to stand.

"Sit down, princess." He topped off my drink, brushing a hand over the back of my neck as he passed. "You cooked, I'll clean."

Leaning back in my chair, I sipped my wine, enjoying the sight of him in the kitchen as he rolled the sleeves of his shirt past his elbows. The muscles in his forearms flexed and released as he rinsed the dishes and set them on the draining board. He was the hottest man I'd ever set eyes on, there was no contest. My stomach clenched, the promise I'd made that morning to take it slow filtering through my mind. Though, he'd also ground his erection into me against the kitchen island not an hour before, so that promise was pretty much moot. My legs shook as I stood. "I think I'm going to change into something more comfortable before dessert."

He looked me over again, as though sad to see the skirt go. "More wine?"

"Please, just a little, though." I'd already had two glasses. I raced up the stairs, pulling the pajamas from my top drawer with two hands—the ones he requested and I washed especially. I brushed my hair and applied a small spray of perfume. Then, I was racing back down, excitement thrumming through me.

He had his back to me, head half in the fridge, putting away the leftovers. He must have heard my footsteps because he asked, "What did you plan for dessert?"

"Me," I replied in a voice not my own. His entire body locked, like I'd pressed the pause button on the entire room, followed by double speed, because he spun so fast jars rattled in the fridge door. His eyes devoured me. *Holy shit.* "Is this what you wanted?"

He nodded, shaking himself from his stupor and clipped, "Come here." I moved dutifully and when I got close enough, he ran his shaking index finger beneath the wide strap, barely grazing my skin until he reached the small cluster of freckles. "How are you even real? I spent the entire day convincing myself that last night was some kind of stress-related out-of-body experience."

"Are you stressed?"

"Yes . . . No." He came closer, the tips of his shoes skimming my bare toes. "I've never felt more at ease in my entire life while at the same time, I should probably get my blood pressure checked by a medical professional."

My laugh was pure delight. "I think there's one of Kier's old monitors lying around if you want to get a reading. I don't want you giving out on me, old man."

He ignored my jab, dropping his head to run his nose up the column of my throat. My eyes were starting to roll back when I stopped him with a hand to his chest. His hold loosened at once. "I was thinking about something you said last night."

"Last night?" His jaw twitched. "If I said something . . . If I went too far . . ."

"You didn't." I curled my arms through his, locking our bodies together. "I want you to push every one of my boundaries, Mal, just to see how far they stretch." His hands clenched against my hips. "But first—" I eased away, picking up my phone on the kitchen counter, already hooked up to the speaker, and pressed play on the slow song I'd picked out just for this. "You said you wanted to dance with me."

I took my time returning, letting him decide how it played out from here. He stalked my every step, mesmerized by the sway of my hips as I easily caught the sensual beat. He backed up a fraction. "I've never danced before . . . I don't know how."

"Yes you do." I held out my hands and he clutched them like a lifeline. "There's no rules to dancing, only what feels right." He let me drag him to the rug before the fireplace, his expression that of a man fit to walk the plank. I wanted to laugh and cry at the same time. How had no one begged this wonderful man to dance with them?

He held himself stock-still as I started to sway. Hands squeezing tight to mine, I moved them in time with my hips, slow and steady until he started to loosen, watching my body, enraptured by its every dip and roll. The song picked up speed, a male voice crooning through the speakers about his love Dahlia, and Mal began to move with me. It was jolting and awkward as he lurched from foot to foot. Surprising, given the smooth roll of his hips against mine last night. This man *knew* how to move. I grinned widely when he counted beneath his breath, so nervous his feet stumbled. His features were taut. Eyebrows two violent slashes across his forehead. To others, he might look angry. Now I recognized it as the expression he wore when he felt something strongly.

The chorus hit again and I spun in the circle of his arms, giving him my back and pressing the round of my behind into his lap. A hand snapped to my hips, clutching fiercely, while the other pressed down on my stomach. His lips went to my neck and I felt them curl into the smallest smile. The song ended and started from the top. We kept dancing, our bodies pressed so tightly there wasn't a scrap of my skin on which I couldn't feel him. On the third rotation, I glanced back at him over my shoulder. We both breathed heavily and there was definite wood tucked against my lower back. "Remind me again how you have no dancing ability?"

My question went unanswered as he was too busy spinning me around and backing me up against the dining table. Lifting me onto the surface, he picked up my forgotten glass of wine and brought it to my lips for me to sip before drinking deeply himself. Red still stained his lips when his mouth descended to my chest, sucking my peaked nipple right through the fabric. I gasped, dropping back onto my elbows. "Is this all right?" he rasped. I think I said yes. If not, the way my legs squeezed around his hips was answer enough. His lips moved to my other breast, leaving a stain of red behind. "Do you want to know what I did that night? The day I came to the house and saw you in these little shorts? The day I almost fucked you against the kitchen counter?"

"*Yes,*" I cried. I knew what I'd done that night.

His teeth tugged through my top. "I stroked myself with one hand while holding that scrap of lace you call a bra in the other."

"Please, Mal," I moaned, but he continued his lazy licks, lingering on each nipple just long enough to make me lose my mind and then switching to the other. I didn't even know what I begged for. Anything. *More.* "I need you, Mal."

My plea must have unlocked something in him because within a heartbeat, he'd tossed me over his shoulder, giving me a perfect view of his firm behind as my hair hung long and loose down his back. Striding for the stairs, he held me secure with his hand to my arse, squeezing and caressing as he went. "Faster, Mal."

"*Jesus*, woman." He took the stairs two at a time, jostling my weight in such a commotion the dogs chased after us. He crossed the threshold to my bedroom, kicked the door closed, and dropped me to my feet so my back hit the wall. I didn't have time to feel dazed because his lips were back on mine, the world smudging at the edges as he held me steady. "This okay?" he pulled away just far enough to ask.

"Yes." He looked at me like I was fragile, treasured, but he didn't touch me that way. He kissed me harder, squeezing anywhere his hands could reach. His fingers gathered my shorts, pulling the hems up over the curves of my hips until I feared they might rip. I whimpered, clinging to him, lust a hot chasm in my belly. In the kitchen, I'd asked him to push my boundaries and he listened. When I told him I was okay, he believed me without second-guessing, trusting that I knew my own mind.

His thick length pressed into my stomach. "Do you feel how hard I am, princess? I've been this way since you walked back into my life in those tiny shorts you love so much."

My laugh was breathy. "I'm starting to think *you* love my shorts."

"Of course I do." The grip of his hands turned possessive. "There should be sonnets written about the way your arse looks in shorts."

A small cry left me. "I need you, Mal."

He maneuvered us to the bed, turning me and pressing until my elbows met the mattress. I went without question and he palmed my behind again, squeezing and lifting my cheeks in his grip.

"Hands flat. Keep them there." I complied, so turned on I could barely breathe. Then he tugged my shorts down, letting them pool around my ankles. Moonlight streamed through the window and I knew he could see everything. Normally, I'd feel vulnerable in such a position, but I arched further and he groaned in appreciation. Running his hand along my spine, his finger grazed down the center of my arse, then the crease beneath both cheeks and finally, between my legs. He offered one light caress to my clit then retreated, leaving me moaning and chasing the sensation with my hips. He tugged up my top next, bunching the material high enough for my breasts to hang free. "Yeah?"

"Yes."

His fabric-covered thighs brushed against me and I pushed back, desperate for the slightest sensation. "Thirty-three days." His hands squeezed my hips.

"What?"

"Thirty-three days you've been back on this island. That's thirty-three days I've imagined you bent over a whisky barrel, those tiny shorts around your ankles. Have you enjoyed tormenting me?" When I wasn't quick enough to answer, he thrust against me. "Tell me."

"*Yes*," I gasped. "Yes, I enjoyed it."

He made a satisfied grumbling noise and his hand dipped between my legs again, stroking with one finger. "Do you think I should torment you in return?"

My head dropped to the mattress, muffling my moans. "*Yes*." I said it over and over again—it was the only word that existed.

"Tell me if it's too much." He didn't wait for further confirmation, keeping me bent over the bed and lowering to his haunches.

The first touch to my ankle surprised me. The part of me that had been with too many selfish lovers expected him to get right to it. But when he said he planned to torment me, he'd meant it. He traced up my leg first with his tongue and roughened fingertips. He strayed no higher than my calf before repeating the process on the other. It was only when he had me crying out and squirming that he moved higher. There wasn't an inch of my skin his fingers didn't touch. My fingers, the crease of my elbow, the sensitive patch of skin behind my ear. He licked the base of my spine and caught the soft flesh over my hip between his teeth. He touched me until my legs trembled and my knees weakened. The moment they gave out, he caught my waist and stood, holding me up with one hand while unzipping his fly with the other. "Now, Mal." I might have been crying. "As hard as you can."

I felt the head of his cock brush my entrance, just the tip pressing in, teasing me how I'd teased him the night before. He learnt too damn fast. "Does my princess want a mean little fuck?"

Holy shit.

Holy shit.

I nodded frantically against the sheets. And then he was in me, thrusting so hard I didn't have time to brace myself. He kept thrusting and I scrambled for purchase, fisting the bed covers and pushing back, taking just as hard as he gave.

"You love talking, baby, let's hear it," he growled, and I cried louder, gasping his name over and over again. Begging him to take me harder, to make me *his*.

"I'm so close, Mal. So c-close."

"*Good*. Stop moving those hips. When you come, I want to deserve it." He punctuated his point by grasping my hips so tightly,

I couldn't have moved even if I wanted to. "That's it, *fuck* baby . . . that's it."

Baby.

I loved when he called me princess, but I *adored* when he called me baby, because I was only baby when he was deep inside me.

His thrusts picked up pace, our skin slapping together hotly. Trapped in his hold, the pressure built quickly, steaming toward the crescendo my body demanded but didn't want. I needed this to last forever. "Open your legs wider," he grunted. "I want to see what I'm earning."

"*Jesus* . . . Mal!" As soon as I complied, his fingers were there. All it took were two soft strokes on my clit and I broke apart. Not just coming, *shattering*. Screaming and shuddering. Back bowing. Knees buckling. Mal's shout of release was hoarse and so damn masculine. His entire body jerked, arms snapping around my waist and lifting my entire body onto my toes and flush with his chest, he thrust into me over and over again, trying to prolong our pleasure as long as possible.

"Holy crap, what the hell just happened?" I half laughed. Seemingly incapable of words, he held me tighter, his nose buried deep into my tangled curls. What felt like a lifetime later, he pulled out and flipped us around, sitting on the bed to pull my body into his lap. His trousers were around his ankles, shirt still fully buttoned. I fingered the collar, smiling lazily.

His hand touched my cheek, tipping my head back to meet my eye. "It wasn't too much?"

"It couldn't have been more perfect," I assured him, and a smile split his face in half. Then he pressed a sweet kiss to my lips and curled a hand around the nape of my neck.

"April, I want to date you." The words came in such a rush it took a moment for me to compute. He swallowed tightly, shifting beneath me, wide open and vulnerable. "What I mean to say is . . . I would like to keep spending time with you—while you're here. As much as you'll allow."

My thumb brushed one of the buttons on his shirt, just beneath the golden little hollow of his throat. "You want to be my boyfriend?" A groove deepened between his brows. He looked as though he were trying to translate a language he'd never heard before. And then, so slightly someone less attuned to his every move might have missed it, he nodded. I felt shyer than I'd ever been when I answered. "I'd really like that."

27

MAL
Perfect Places – Lorde

Expecting to find April curled up cozily beneath the bed sheets, my eyes bounced several times around her bedroom before finding her. On her hands and knees with a stack of books, she'd shed the tiny pajamas we'd made filthy and wore a long graphic T-shirt and nothing else. Bent over the way she was, I got an excellent view of the *nothing else*. "What are you doing?" I set the glass of water and ice cream I'd dug out of the freezer on the side table.

"Getting an answer once and for all." She lined several more books up on the floor until they formed a long oblong shape and took a step back to regard her handiwork. I'd never seen so many scantily clad women and rippling chests staring back at me.

When she stepped into the outline and laid down on her back, holding her hand out to me, I laughed throatily, finally getting it. "This is the door from *Titanic*?"

"Yep." She grinned cheekily and her fingers curled, beckoning me. I followed—*of course* I followed. Lying on April's childhood bedroom floor, I eagerly let her order me into any position she pleased. Her head by my feet. Face-to-face. My front to her back.

It was ridiculous and I grunted my way through every transition, nervous to reveal exactly how happy this made me. I felt like the Grinch, my heart doubling and then tripling in size until my chest contained no room for anything but this—*her*.

Click.

When she climbed astride me, dragging her lovely hands up my chest, I couldn't take anymore. "Your ice cream is going to melt," I warned.

She considered for perhaps half a second, then leapt to her feet with a *"screw Jack,"* and immediately started on the chocolate ice cream. I pulled the bed covers back, ushering her in until she settled in the very center with Boy and Dudley at her feet.

Click.

I knew what I was doing. Saving all these little moments with her like shells collected at the beach. An April album for my mind to flip over when she was gone, proof that I was happy, if only for a short time. My heart strummed so fiercely I had the strongest urge to reach up and soothe the spot. I moved to her small television instead, starting up whatever movie she had in the DVD player. *When Harry Met Sally.*

"I love this movie," she mumbled around her spoon.

"I've never seen it," I said, turning back.

"Blasphemy!" Despite her outrage, she tucked herself close when I climbed in beside her, settling my arm around her the way I had the last time I was in her bed. The movie began and we ate in silence, her bringing the spoon to my lips once for every two bites she took. I didn't see a single minute because I couldn't stop looking at her. *Is this what contentment feels like?* I wondered. Feeling excited and comfortable. Treasured and so damn safe. If *this* wasn't it, I didn't know what was.

After a short while, her eyes began flicking to me too. Then finally, after setting the ice cream aside, she asked, "Have you spoken to your brother today?"

I paused. *Why would she ask about Callum?* After all that had transpired in the past days, I knew it was me she wanted, but it didn't stop that little spike of fear. "Not since this morning . . . should I have?"

She grinned, flashing all of her square little teeth. "Just wondering if he fessed up."

"To what?"

Her fingers walked up my chest. "Pushing us together. Apparently, he and Heather have been trying to set us up for weeks."

What? I shook my head. That couldn't be right. My mind tumbled back over our every interaction with fresh eyes. "How did I not see this?"

"I didn't either, not until I went back to the tasting event last night and he basically admitted to seeing us together in the dunnage. Then Heather confirmed it today."

I shifted to my elbow, facing her fully in the bed. "Why would they go to all that effort? Why not just tell me?"

She smirked, pretty green eyes sparkling with mirth. "You've met you, right? It probably would have made you hate me more."

I flinched. Is that what she thought? Stroking her cheek, I tucked a curl behind her ear. "I'm sorry I made you feel that way. Every awful thing I ever said to you was a manifestation of my own fear, my own self-doubt." I looked directly into her eyes so my words could not be misconstrued. "I *never* hated you. I tried at first, but even believing what I did about you, it didn't work. Would I have liked everyone having an opinion on my feelings? Probably not. But it wouldn't have pushed me further away—it *couldn't*." I stroked her ear lobe with my thumb. "There wasn't a day or a moment when you finally worked your way beneath my skin, you were already there . . . every time I saw you, you buried yourself a little deeper. You were inevitable, princess. Holding back my feelings was like trying to hold back the tide."

Her entire being seemed to light from within and the next thing I knew, she was in my lap, her tiny hands taking mine. "I think those big shoulders of yours would have been up to the task."

Chuckling, I brought her hand to my mouth, nibbling on the end of her index finger. "From now on, every time you sass me, you'll lose a finger." She gasped a little when I bit down.

"You wouldn't. You've become too attached to my fingers."

Her words sent a flush of heat up my neck and she hummed at the sight, bringing our foreheads flush. "Please never stop doing that." My confusion must have been apparent because she continued, "Blushing . . . after every filthy thing that's happened between us." *Oh.* Instinct had me dropping my chin, but she caught my jaw before I made it very far, looking at me head on. "You're beautiful."

"*You're* beautiful," I returned, stroking her hair back. "So beautiful it's hard to look at you sometimes."

Her hips dipped against me. Mine punched right back. "I want you to look at me. I never want your eyes anywhere else."

Our lower bodies fell into a steady, sensual roll. We couldn't help it. When I was with her, I needed to touch her. When I touched her, I couldn't ever get enough. It took all of my strength to hold myself still. "I don't . . . I don't want you to think this is all I want from you."

"I know." Her expression softened and she kissed me, tongue flicking over my top lip and tracing along the scar cutting through my facial hair. "Can I ask about this?" she pulled back to whisper. Her face was so open, I knew I could refuse and she wouldn't resent me for it.

"Yes." My swallow felt tight. "It's never been a secret."

Her finger hesitantly replaced her tongue, stroking the raised flesh with a reverence that had me biting the inside of my cheek. "You always seem so self-conscious of it . . . you shouldn't. I meant it when I said you're beautiful. Every little part of you."

I stole her hand, pressing a kiss to the palm and then holding it between us, content to count every freckle across her knuckles as I spoke the truth. "It's not the scar I hate, it's as much a part of me as my eyes or my hair color. It's . . . it's what it represents, I guess."

"What does it represent?"

I shrugged, suddenly unsure how to explain it. "All the ways I grew up differently. My cleft palate was on the severe end of the scale, meaning the tissue all the way to the back of my mouth didn't join up while I was in the womb. Because of that, I needed multiple surgeries over several years as a child, as well as speech therapy. You know my dad's a doctor—an amazing one—but also old school."

I felt her stiffen slightly. "In what way?"

"He put all his efforts into 'fixing' me, finding the best surgeons on the mainland, the best speech therapists, even when it meant paying privately. But once the surgeries were over, he had no knowledge on how to deal with the mental aspects that developed along with it. I was continually out of school, always healing at home rather than playing outside with my siblings. When I *was* in school, I grew anxious—worried about looking different and sounding different. The few times I went to him, he essentially told me to man up, so I stopped asking for help and now . . . I don't know how to be around people. I either grow anxious and I say the wrong thing—" I broke off as my chest began to tighten.

April was already shaking her head, pressing her chest flush so I couldn't escape. "Your words are perfect."

"For *you*. Though I still don't know how, I feel like everything I say is wrong."

"Because I know your heart." Her hand flew to my chest, like she could heal the bruised organ with her caress alone. "Everyone in Kinleith knows. Why do you think the tasting event was so successful? They weren't there for me or Kier's legacy. It was *you*, Mal. People care for you and want to help."

That couldn't be right. That voice in my head immediately started to shut her words down, then I stopped, tired of that old behavior. Sure, I kept to myself, but I was an active member of the community. The distillery provided local jobs. I helped my neighbors whenever I could. I stepped up when Kier needed it. I had my siblings and April. "I guess I got so used to doubting everyone's motivations . . . even yours," I said somewhat guilty. "When you arrived, I used every excuse I could think of to try to explain away the connection between us. You were sad about Kier, or you pitied me." I cringed. "I stopped expecting anything from anyone so I wouldn't get hurt."

"You can have expectations with me. I want you to have them."

Her words were fierce, spoken directly to my lips. "When you feel anxious, what can I do? How can I help you?"

She can't be real, the thought struck again. This time, I shoved it to the furthest recesses of my mind. Bolting it behind an iron door. Because she *was* real, more real than anything I'd ever known. "*This*, princess," I husked, sinking my hands beneath her T-shirt to feel her skin, feeling every ridge up her spine. "I need you to do exactly this, be exactly who you are. Always." And then there was no more talking.

28

APRIL

Belter – Gerry Cinnamon

Hold on to the headboard." Mal's voice was a dark caress down my neck. Sunday morning had risen all too swiftly and we'd both had little sleep, but that didn't stop us reaching for each other again as soon as dawn broke. Sheets rumpled around my knees and hands clinging to the metal spokes, I felt him—

A pounding at the door made us still. "No," I cried as Mal panted. "Ignore it, they'll go away." His lips pressed hotly to the base of my neck, leaving a wet trail along my spine that made me curl like a cat. The pounding grew louder. A phone rang from somewhere in the house. "For fuck's sake!" Mal lashed wickedly. Giving my hip a squeeze, he climbed from the bed, pulling on his boxers and dress trousers from last night. "Stay exactly like that. I'll get rid of them." Then he bent, giving my arse cheek a quick, sharp nip with his teeth.

I remained right where he left me until voices murmured up from the kitchen. Someone laughed, low and masculine. It didn't belong to Mal. Curiosity peaked, I pulled on underwear and my discarded T-shirt and headed downstairs. As soon as I stepped into the kitchen, I saw the top of Callum's head on the other side of the glass pane, Mal white-knuckling the door frame to stop him entering. "What's going on?" I asked and they both turned to look at me. Mal's stare was full of fire as he looked from my bed hair to my bare legs.

"*Ah*, the lady of the house." Callum grinned boyishly from the threshold.

"Callum." I nodded back, then looked at Mal. "You're not inviting him in?"

"No," he grunted, before he was interrupted by Callum.

"No time. I came to check on Mel C and to see if I could steal Mal for a few hours—"

Mal shot me a look. "You're still feeding the bloody foxes?"

"Of course I am." I went to the cupboard where I stored the treats for the dogs and the foxes I could already hear yipping outside.

Then back at his brother, he snipped, "And I told *you* no."

"Come on! We need you, we're already a man down and we're playing Portree, they beat us last month. Don't you care?"

Mal's arms folded over his stunning chest. "Not really."

"What are you talking about?" I glanced between the two of them.

"Nothing—"

"Shinty," Callum offered. "We play every Sunday morning in the summer and my brother refuses to join the team even though he's the best player on the island."

Mal flushed, jaw ticking as he stared at the tile. I didn't want to push him, but at the same time, maybe he only needed a little encouragement. "I didn't know you played."

"I don't . . . not really."

"That sounds like fun," I said.

Mal's gaze flew to mine and Callum clapped his hands together. "*Yes!* See . . . ? I knew I liked you."

I came to stand beside Mal, twining my fingers through his until he looked at me. "I'm not telling you to play if that's not what you want. It's going to be a nice morning, maybe we could go and watch?" I silently implored Callum not to say a word. This was Mal's choice. He must've sensed it because he kept his mouth shut, letting his brother think through my words.

Finally, Mal's hand tightened around mine. "It might be fun to play."

I grinned back at him. "You feed the foxes, I'll get dressed."

"REMIND ME OF THE RULES AGAIN?" I SAID TO HEATHER, pulling my sunglasses down as I gazed at the wide green space looking over the cerulean water. Two groups of twelve men stood on a pitch that looked very similar to a field hockey pitch, handing out jerseys.

Heather snorted, chugging back her takeaway coffee. It was barely nine a.m. and she'd somehow managed to wrangle the twins down in time to see their uncles play, even if they had more interest in making daisy chains. "Are you even Scottish?"

"Excuse me for having other interests as a teenager." Though, watching Mal stride across the pitch and accept a navy jersey from Callum, I wondered why I'd ever spent time doing anything else. When he slipped off his own T-shirt, I could swear I almost whimpered. Mine weren't the only eyes on him. Looking down the perimeter of the pitch, I noticed Jasmine and several other women eyeing him. Mal noticed too, shifting from foot to foot as he switched out his own shirt and threw the team strip over his head as quickly as possible. I want to erect a tent around him, protect my gentle giant from the unwanted attention.

Heather didn't seem to notice the death grip I had on my own coffee as she launched into a rundown of the rules. "The game has two forty-five minute halves, like football. The aim is to score more goals than the other team, getting the ball in the net with their caman—"

"Caman?"

"The stick they're holding." It looked like a hockey stick with a more pronounced curve. "Players can tackle using their caman or their body, as long as it's shoulder to shoulder."

I looked at her, then back to the field, all the men spreading for a final drink before beginning. "That sounds kind of rough."

She nodded. "It can be. I haven't heard of any broken bones for a while, though."

My eyes bugged. Broken bones?

Before I could question further, I noticed Mal striding toward us. I pulled my metal water bottle from my bag and extended it to him. He took it, thanking me before drinking deeply. "Are you wearing sun cream?" he asked, handing it back. "It's hot out today." Heather *awww*ed obnoxiously. We both ignored her.

"Yes, grumps. And I have more in my bag if I need it," I assured him. I didn't want him worrying about me and not paying attention on the field. Before he could disappear again, I caught his arm. "Please be careful."

For a moment, I thought he might kiss me right there, in front of everyone, but the whistle blew and he strode back to the pitch, leaving me wondering why the hell I convinced Mal to play.

"THAT'S A FOUL!" I SCREECHED, THROWING MY HANDS IN THE air. "That's definitely a foul, right?"

Heather's face was set. "Aye, that's definitely a foul—come on, ref!" she shouted right along with me. At eighty minutes, the game was tied and a player from Portree had just come down hard on Mal's caman with his own, in an illegal move I'd learned was called hacking.

The older, balding man acting as referee blew his whistle, indicating the penalty spot. The Portree players threw up their arms. "What does that mean?"

"They've awarded Mal a penalty hit."

"That's good?"

She nodded. "That's good."

I'd been taken back by the speed of the game. The pitch was large and the men continually raced back and forth, the pace of play changing in an instant. And through all of that, I'd admired Mal most of all. I had nothing to compare to, but when Callum had spoken of his talent, he wasn't exaggerating. Mal was shockingly quick for his size, intercepting plays the shorter men couldn't. And for a sport designed around physical contact, he was considerate. Where other players leaned into tackles, hoping to trip or hurt their opponent, Mal did the opposite, avoiding contact wherever he could, always the first to help another to their feet. That seemed to enrage the opposition even more and it put a target on his back.

The Kinleith players exchanged a few hushed words, then a sweat-soaked Callum looked at Mal. Mal nodded in return, grip tightening on his caman as he approached the penalty spot. "Mal's going to take it," Heather said.

My heart drummed as I watched him. Dirty and soaked in sweat, he'd never been more beautiful. "Go, Mal!" I screamed at the top of my lungs and everyone along the sideline joined in, whooping and hollering his name. Some of the players glanced my way and I felt the stare of the man who'd tackled him. I'd already felt his eyes on me multiple times during the game and ignored it.

Mal didn't hesitate; the second the referee blew his whistle, he struck. The goalkeeper dove, trying to block with his hands, but he stood no chance. The ball flew, strong and sure into the back of the net, and we all screamed, hands flying into the air. Mal's eyes found mine, exhaustion and a lick of heat in their depths. I couldn't help winking back so he knew exactly what he'd be getting at home.

"Impressive, isn't he?" A voice came from my left and I turned to smile at Jasmine. We'd barely had a chance to talk at the tasting. I opened my mouth to thank her for coming but she got there first. "Now I'm really regretting not getting that second date." My thanks died on my lips. *A second date? With Mal?* I looked at the pitch again where they were already back in play, sticks flying with fervor as the final minutes of the game ticked away. "Perhaps he'll change his mind," she continued with a small laugh, not seeming to sense my stunned silence. She hadn't said the words maliciously. Still, a burn singed its way through me. *Mal had dated her and didn't tell me?*

I was saved from forming an answer when a scuffle broke out on the pitch. Mal and the man who'd fouled him were chest to chest, only this time, Mal appeared to be the instigator. He held the man by the scruff of his shirt, growling into his face as other players scrambled to break it up. Mal jerked from their grip, snatching up his caman and stalking to the other end of the pitch.

"What's going on?" I asked Heather.

"No idea, he said something to Mal, and Mal just lost it." She worried her lip with her teeth. "It's not like him."

The remaining minutes were tense. Kinleith scored a final goal, though the cheers were less enthusiastic. The final whistle blew and the players streamed off the pitch. Mal came straight for me, not even stopping to celebrate with his teammates or speak to his siblings, his entire body strung tight. "Ready to get out of here?"

I nodded, lost for words. I could feel Jasmine's eyes on us and I didn't know what to think about it, but I gave her and Heather a wave before he grabbed my hand, dragging me to his Land Rover without looking back.

HE WAS QUIET ALL THE WAY HOME. NOT HIS USUAL QUIET. THIS was intense. Brimming with energy even though he'd spent the last ninety minutes running around. I unlocked the kitchen door with trembling hands, dropping the keys when I felt the press of him against my lower back. He snagged them, opening the door and holding it wide for me.

The dogs barked, jumping from the sofa and racing to us. We both bent to greet them, still neither of us speaking a word. I knew something was about to start, but I wasn't sure what. Could he be mad at me? Was I too obvious at the game? He'd said he wanted to date me, but we hadn't discussed what he was comfortable expressing in public and I—my job was very public. I wanted to ask him about the fight. I wanted to ask him about Jasmine. I didn't know how.

Unsure what to do, I rounded the island, my hands shaking as I flicked on the kettle to make tea. *Tea was always the answer.* Before I could even pull mugs from the cupboard, Mal gripped me around the waist, hauling my body up like it weighed no more than a sack of barley and depositing me on the island. I squealed in delight and he dropped his sweaty face to my neck, then withdrew just as quickly. "Sorry—I should shower."

"No. I like you this way." I caught him, tightening my legs around his waist. "What did that guy say to you?" He didn't look at me, thumb stroking over the tie holding my summer dress together. "Something about me?" I guessed. The tightening of his jaw confirmed it. "Was it my tits or my arse? Or things he'd like to do to my tits and arse?"

His eyes were pools of liquid steel. His voice razor sharp. "He suggested things he had no right suggesting."

"Mal . . . are you jealous?" I attempted a joke, the notion beyond ridiculous. This man had every part of me in the palm of his hand.

"I'm not jealous . . . I'm *pissed*," he snarled, tugging on the tie around my waist. My dress gaped over my bare shoulder, revealing the hurry with which I'd dressed. "I should have cut out his tongue."

I was panting and he hadn't even touched me yet. "You could have, but then you wouldn't be here with me." I licked at my dry lips. "It's gross, but I'm used to it. That guy is a lowlife who's gone home to nothing but a shower and his right hand. Who's really winning here?"

"You shouldn't have to get used to it." He parted the material over my chest. I freed my arms, letting it pool around my hips. His eyes flared, catching on my bare breasts, but he didn't touch me. Instead, his hands dipped beneath my skirt, pausing at the band on my underwear and meeting my eyes. I lifted my hips and he drew them down my legs, stuffing the lacy pink fabric into his back pocket.

"Dirty." I grinned. He smirked back, pulling out one of the stools at the island and sitting. Lifting my right foot, he slid the sandal off and set it atop his thigh. One then the other, spreading me open until my center was only partially hidden by the skirt of my dress.

His eyes found mine, the silent question there. *Is this okay?* I nodded.

He descended, pressing a kiss to the inside of both my knees that I felt all the way to my toes. Just when I thought he was about to go further and make my morning, he settled back in the chair. "Have I told you how beautiful you are?" he said.

"Not today."

"That's careless of me." His hand curled around my calf, thumb rubbing. I gasped. "You are so beautiful." He leaned in again, pressing a kiss to my bare stomach then laying his forehead against my skin. "When I first saw you that night in the manor . . . you took my breath away."

"You took my breath away too." For the first time, I think he believed me because he sat back in his chair, expectant. It took me a full thirty seconds to realize what he wanted. The tips of his ears flushed and I knew he was too nervous to ask for it.

"You want to watch me?" I asked, my hands tracing up my thighs. "Like this?"

"Yes." The single syllable was guttural.

With a riot of butterflies in my stomach, I fell back on the island, flipping my skirt to my lap so he could see when I dipped my fingers between my thighs. Our groans came in tandem. "You're so pretty like this, princess." I opened my eyes to find his stare not between my legs or the bounce of my breasts, but on my face.

With anyone else, this would feel strange—wrong. But with him, I wanted to give a piece of me that no one else would ever have. A piece that would forever live and breathe in this moment. When I gasped out, "I want to see you too," he didn't even hesitate to free himself from his shorts, groaning my name as he brought himself pleasure. It took only minutes to come apart, our gazes twisting and tangling into an impossible knot I never wanted to untie.

MAL LOUNGED ON MY BED, STILL DRESSED IN ONLY A BATH towel when I entered the bedroom. Wrapped in only my dressing gown and scrunching the moisture from my curls with a microfiber towel, I eyed him with conspicuous little looks, wondering if I'd ever grow sick of the sight. I didn't think so.

After the . . . *events* . . . in the kitchen, Mal had been keen to shower together. I'd rebuffed the idea out of real concern for our personal safety. If we'd squeezed in that tiny shower stall together, we probably would have drowned. I also needed a little bit of distance to think over the Jasmine situation—not that it felt like a *situation*, but it had the potential to become one. It wasn't jealousy; I trusted Mal wanted me and only me. Okay . . . perhaps I was a little jealous. Jasmine was stunning and curvy with legs for days you'd have to be blind not to notice. My worry came from the fact he hadn't told me, and I detested being blindsided.

Hooking my hair towel over the end of the bed, I curled my fingers around the metal frame. "Can I ask you something?"

His warm eyes were already on me, taking in my dripping silhouette as though memorizing me. "Of course."

I tried to school my features. "Jasmine," I started.

"What about her?" A groove appeared between his dark brows.

"You went on a date with her. Why didn't you tell me?"

His hand froze in motion, damp hair half slicked back. "Who told you that?"

It wasn't exactly the response I'd been hoping for. "She did."

He drew up. His mouth opened and closed once. "But . . . it was barely a date. Why would I tell you that?"

My expression suggested he couldn't truly be that clueless. "Because I've been chatting to her in the pet shop nonstop. She joined June and me for lunch last week." I flung a hand at him. "If it were me and another man, wouldn't you want to know?"

His voice flattened, his entire face along with it. "Not really."

"Did you sleep together?"

"No!" He was on his feet. "Come here." In a single heartbeat, he caught me around the waist, lifting me in one smooth motion until he was back on the bed with me splayed over his lap. My gown gaped to my navel but neither of us even blinked.

"This isn't talking," I pointed out.

"Yes it is, I'm getting to it." His fingers brushed through my wet hair. "I need you to touch me—I think best when you touch me."

I moaned, thunking my head off his muscled chest. "Be fair! How can I possibly be annoyed when you say stuff like that?"

He didn't laugh like I expected, instead he said, "I don't have a lot of experience here, princess. I'm going to need you to talk me through what you're feeling."

I blew out a breath. "All right. I'm worried that you didn't tell me."

"I didn't *not* tell you as a way to keep it a secret. I didn't say anything because it didn't even enter my mind as something that required discussing. It wasn't a date, not on my end at least. My Land Rover broke down in the village and she offered me a ride home. When she dropped me off at the cottage, I invited her in for a drink to say thank you. To be polite. I never expected her to proposition me."

"She propositioned you! What did she say?"

He laughed then, the corners of his eyes crinkling. "I don't re-member the gory details. She made me aware she'd like to sleep with me and I said no."

"You must have been tempted." I scoffed, folding my arms across my chest.

"Yes." When I opened my mouth, he winced and sealed his palm over my lips. "Just let me finish . . . there's a cosmic differ-ence between being tempted by sex to scratch an itch and what we have. I literally couldn't stay away from you, April, even in my sleep I couldn't stay away. You've possessed my every thought for weeks."

That didn't sound good. I tugged his hand away. "You can't stay away, or you don't want to?"

"Both. *Jesus*, both. It's always been both." He held me tighter, his grip both worshipful and greedy. "You are the only person to ever make me want to step outside my comfort zone. For you, I want to run from it."

My arms circled his neck. "That sounds . . . not awful."

"Not awful?" His fingers dipped into the sensitive skin at my ribs, making me squirm. "I think my oral skills are improving. We should test it out."

He flipped me onto my back, fingers loosening the knot holding my gown closed. I fell back against the mattress as he stretched my thighs open with his shoulders, a groan already working its way up his throat as he got a good look at me. He licked his lips. "So fucking pretty."

I swallowed in anticipation, but halted him. It was important I got this out. "We need to be open with each other," I said, knowing it meant I needed to come clean about Kier.

His gaze flicked up my body, pausing a moment before he said, "Done, princess. Whatever you need, it's yours."

"I HEARD ABOUT THE FIGHT YESTERDAY MORNING." JUNE smirked from behind her coffee cup.

"What fight?" We sat at a small table in the corner of Brown's. The village was busy today, tourists decked out with backpacks and hiking boots dropping in for last-minute refreshments.

"Mal and David McLeary."

Oh. I accepted a pot of tea from Jess with a smile. "Thanks, Jess." She didn't have a single hair out of place, despite the queue of customers half out the door.

"Nae problem, hen." She wrung her hands on her apron. "I heard about the fight too, that McLeary boy was always good for nothing, even as a wee lad. It was nice o' Malcolm to come to yer defense and state his intentions."

"I don't think that's what he was doing," I protested, and they both stared back at me.

"Please." June snorted. "I've seen Malcolm Macabe full-on ghost people that owe him money rather than deal with the confrontation. He's come rushing to your defense twice now, that's basically a proposal." Her words triggered the unsolicited image of Mal on his knees, a ring in his hand. An image I enjoyed far too much.

After the game, we spent the remainder of the day and night in bed, only pausing for a quick dinner and to walk the restless pups along the beach. He'd said he wanted to date me, but we hadn't spoken any further on what that actually meant. Until then, I would keep my mouth shut.

"I think he was just being nice." I shoved half the buttered tea cake in my mouth, hoping for a change of subject. It came in the form of the bell above the door sounding again, one group of customers leaving to be exchanged for another. Jess rushed back to the counter with a bright *hello*, and I seized my chance. "What about you?" I said to June.

"What about me?" A perfect black brow arched.

"You left the tasting early the other night." *Very early*, in fact.

"I didn't feel well."

"So it had nothing to do with whatever Callum said that had you scowling."

A mirror scowl twisted her features. "No, I did not run away because of Callum bloody Macabe! He just infuriates me. He's always *there*, making snide remarks and teasing me. He and Alastair are so close it's like he's laughing at me, reminding me I wasn't good enough for his precious brother."

I kept my voice soft. "I don't think that's what he's doing." Callum might be a player and flirt, but he didn't strike me as cruel.

"It feels that way." Her fingers tightened on the tabletop. "I want *nothing* to do with him." I was about to suggest that if she felt so strongly she could try explaining that to him, but the door went again and June whistled through her teeth. I turned, surprised to find Mal standing in the entrance, his unsteady gaze flicking around the tables until he spotted me. A small smile curled his lips when he did. My breath caught.

Rather than coming over like I hoped, he strode straight for the counter. Jess handed him a wrapped sandwich and a bottled juice and I let that breath out slowly, feeling disappointment lick up my spine. *I was right to keep my mouth shut, he isn't ready for anything else yet.*

I turned back to June, keeping my expression as neutral as possible, like something massive hadn't just occurred with something as simple as a takeaway lunch.

A shadow fell over the table. "Can I sit here, princess?" Mal's words washed over me. June's eyebrows lifted and her lips silently shaped the nickname.

He was nervous. Cheeks flushed, weight shifting from foot to foot. "Of . . . of course." My voice wavered. It felt like high school all over again. I sensed every pair of eyes in the room on us as he took the seat beside me, arm wrapping around the back of my chair until his fingers laid flush with my shoulder. June must have read his tension, because she greeted him quickly, then fell easily into a description of the bathroom remodeling she was going ahead with at the guest house (without her mother's permission). Mal fidgeted the entire time, fingers tapping against my shoulder while he silently sipped a bottle of orange juice. I laid a hand on his thigh and it seemed to help, the tension easing from him in slow increments.

As soon as we finished our drinks, we said goodbye to June on the high street. She threw Mal a wink before stalking away, so it was safe to say *this* Macabe brother had her approval at least.

"You're in the car park?" Mal asked once we were alone. I nodded and he took my hand. "I'll walk with you." A few locals paused to acknowledge us along the way, glancing at our joined hands and whispering as they hurried away.

I held our hands aloft. "The entire village will be gossiping by sundown."

He pulled me even closer, arm slipping around my shoulders as he nipped at my earlobe. "Good."

My laugh held delight, but it quickly sobered. "Soon it won't only be the locals," I warned, needing him to be aware of all the facts. It would only be a matter of time before pictures of us spread online, untrue stories in the paper. That was just how it went.

He nodded, gaze unwavering. "I know, I understand."

I wasn't certain he did, but I couldn't bring myself to spoil the moment, so I said instead, "Dinner tonight?"

"Definitely. It's my turn to cook."

"Hmm." I turned to him playfully, biting my lip as I backed against my car, slowly dragging my hands up his chest. "Dinner and then a bath, I think."

"*Christ.*" He dropped a hot kiss on my lips, molding my back to the metal. "Get out of here, princess. I'll see you at home."

Home. The word wrapped around me like a warm blanket. "See you at home," I echoed.

29

MAL
Daylight – Taylor Swift

Everyone's talking about your performance in the café the other morning," were the first words out of my sister's mouth as she climbed from her car.

On my knees, I didn't look up from my task of replacing the hinge on the dunnage door. "It wasn't a performance," I said. It wasn't. *Hell*, maybe it was. In Brown's, I'd been seconds away from doing my usual: grab my takeout and run before I made eye contact with anyone. Then I heard April's laugh and I wanted to sit beside her— I wanted people to know that *I* was the one who got to sit with her, no matter how temporary my place may be. Then I'd pressed her up against the door of her car and kissed her until we were about ready to climb each other. It was some real alpha-male shit.

"*I know that.* But people are talking like you had sex on top of the sandwich selection."

I tossed my screwdriver into the dry earth. "*Damn* village. Maybe if they put this much energy into their own lives, they wouldn't be unhappy enough to spread gossip."

Heather leaned her hip off the door, keys still jangling between her fingers. "I agree, I'm just glad to be free of their wagging tongues for a few weeks."

I frowned. I didn't realize Heather had been the subject of gossip. Not much happened around these parts, and while small communities could be an irreplaceable support system, they also lived by traditional values. *Of course* anyone who fell outside of that would be the subject of talk. "I'm sorry," I said.

"For what?"

"Not being a better brother."

Her lips parted and for the first time in her life, my baby sister didn't know what to say. She threw her arms around my neck and I stood, pulling her to me until my chin sat atop her head. "You're a wonderful brother, you know that, right? The only thing I want is for you to allow yourself to be happy."

"I'm getting there," I promised, throat tightening at the thought of the redhead who'd turned my world upside down in only a few short weeks. "I don't want April overhearing whatever crap they're spreading."

Heather pulled back and tapped my shoulder. "She's a big girl, I think she'll find it amusing."

Maybe. *Hopefully.*

And when she leaves? What will you do then? a voice niggled. The thought didn't just occur to me, it had been a constant thorn in my side from the very first instance my heart stuttered in her presence. I held no plans beyond this time with her. I wanted more of her, sure. I knew if I was selfish enough—*stupid enough*—to dream about it, I would want to keep her for the rest of my life. But I couldn't let myself. She may have agreed to date me for now, but I had no illusions I'd get to keep her at the end of it. What more could I expect? April to stay on an island she'd already fought tooth and nail to escape? To sit in my cottage every night watching movies and playing with puzzles because I was too bloody anxious to go to the local pub? I'd barely made it through lunch at Brown's without sweating.

"What are you doing here anyway?" I asked, shifting the subject from April.

She thumbed over her shoulder to the main building. "I'm helping April with the tasting." I'd forgotten about that. After the success of her whisky night, April had taken a few small bookings through the website and they'd sold out within hours. I'd licked her pretty pussy in my shower to congratulate her.

"Are you coming to lunch today? Apparently Mum has something she wants to tell everyone."

Never had I been more relieved to have an out. "Can't. We have plans, maybe next week."

"Since when do you have a better social life than me?" *Since I've been fucking April twice a day for the past two weeks.*

I didn't have much to compare it to, but I knew the level we went at each other wasn't common. I couldn't get enough. It was like we were making up for lost time. *Or trying to fit a lifetime of sex into a few weeks.* My stomach soured and I cut the thought off.

"I have to get back to this," I said more sharply than I intended. Heather being Heather knew exactly when to back off, so with a ruffle of my hair, she disappeared around the corner.

"HEATHER INVITED US TO LUNCH." APRIL'S HEAD POKED around the door to the malt room later that afternoon. I smiled, setting down a crate of empty bottles the moment I saw her.

"How did the tasting go?"

She skipped closer, arms looping around my waist as soon as she got within reach. "Oh, you know. *Amazingly.*" She kissed my chin. My hands fell to the dips in her waist like they were made for that little spot. "They didn't know anything about whisky and had a lot of questions, though. I'm glad Heather was with me because I couldn't have answered them all myself."

"The amount you've learnt in only a few weeks is incredible." As was the level of research she put in, but you never stopped learning when it came to whisky.

"*Hmm.* It helps that I have a very hot teacher." I bit her neck for that. "I was thinking, if we keep booking tasting groups regularly, we could look into hiring Heather."

"Permanently?"

She nodded. "Maybe not right now, but eventually. We could offer her good pay and steady hours, no more picking up whatever shift she can get her hands on."

This woman was too good to be true. I ravaged her mouth, deep and consuming. When I broke away, I said, "You think we can afford it?"

"Down the line, I hope. We can give it a few months to see how things play out, but there's been a lot of interest."

A few months. I had to forcibly rein my heart in before it began to soar and kissed her again. "I love that idea."

"Good. You didn't answer about lunch with your family." Her nose wrinkled and I knew it was at the prospect of seeing my dad. "We don't have to go."

"I already told Heather no," I said. "We have other plans."

"Do these plans include me sitting on your face, because I'm so down for that."

My laugh was so colossal, my entire body rippled with it. "Princess, having those sweet thighs around my ears is always on the agenda."

"What are we doing?"

"It's a surprise." She managed to look excited and pouty at the same time. "Can you be ready in thirty?"

"How can I be ready if I don't know what we're doing?"

"Wear something warm, with comfortable shoes."

One perfect brow arched. "You're a mysterious man, Mr. Macabe."

"HOW MUCH FURTHER?" APRIL PANTED, DROPPING HER HANDS to her knees. Boy took complete advantage of the situation and gave her fingers a thorough lick.

I paused a few steps ahead, pulling the canteen of water off a loop on my belt. "Not far."

"You said that *hours* ago."

I held the bottle out to her. "We've only been walking for one."

On the drive, I worried this was a terrible idea for a date. April had been saying since she returned that she wanted to climb Old Man of Storr, a large rock formation that made up part of the Trotternish Ridge on the north end of the Island. Considering how she was faring now, I was glad I'd kept her from doing it alone. Her honest enthusiasm as we pulled into the car park had eased my nerves. That enthusiasm had steadily waned as we made our ascent, and I couldn't help but find the entire thing hilarious. April out of her element was a sight to behold. She was grouchy and maddeningly adorable. We stopped often and she'd already drunk the majority of our water supply. I didn't care how long it took, April was making it to the top if I had to carry her there myself.

About a mile back, we'd veered off the tourist trail in exchange for this quiet route without a single other soul in sight. It would be worth it when we reached the top for the undisturbed views over to isles Raasay and Rona, but it meant saying goodbye to the stone staircase that made the climb considerably easier. She straightened, accepting the offered water and taking several mouthfuls. "Don't give it to me in time," she said, clearly unsatisfied with my answer, "give it to me in steps. How many more steps do I have to walk?" *Damn*. I wanted to kiss her when she was like this, though I didn't think she'd appreciate that right now.

I eyed the trail again, calculating. "Two thousand maybe?"

"Two *thousand*?" She groaned and her hair swept back like liquid fire as her head dipped between her shoulder blades, wispy curls sticking to her neck and temple. "I shouldn't have asked."

"Want me to carry you?"

"How? You're already carrying the camping equipment and Dudley."

I shifted Dudley's sling to my hip, patting the small space around my waist she could squeeze into. "Right here, princess. I won't drop you."

She considered it for half a second then shook her head manically. "Nope, not happening. Let's get this over with." She stalked ahead with harsh strides and I chuckled again, my chest the lightest it had ever been as I admired her sweet behind the entire way up the incline.

"YOU WERE RIGHT. THANK YOU SO MUCH FOR BRINGING ME here." We were the only people for miles but still she whispered in the small enclosure of our tent. The sun had begun to dip by the time we made it to the summit and she'd marveled at the views while I made a quick dinner over a camp stove, followed by poorly made s'mores. April laughed openly as chocolate and marshmallow trickled out from the layers and down her wrist, leading me to eat more chocolate from her fingers than I did my own crackers. We spoke about everything. Favorite movies. People we remembered from childhood. Books we'd both read. Romance novels I hadn't read but was suddenly desperate to. The things she loved most about acting—a wistful gleam entering her eye that made my guts twist. The only thing we didn't talk about was the future.

Snuggled deep in our sleeping bags, dogs snoozing soundly at our feet, we'd left the entrance to the tent open. As dusk began to color the sky in shades of pink and purple, we watched the sun disappear behind the rock formation, bringing with it the old man the mountain was said to resemble into profile. I'd never been able to picture him before, thinking the peak appeared more like a bird tail than a man. But with April's freckled finger tracing the outline in the air, I saw him.

"It's like looking at an ancient giant on his throne," she whispered. "Watching the world change around him and never being able to reach out and touch it. It's sad."

Like me, I thought. *Like me before you, princess.*

That was the moment I allowed myself to admit I was in love with her. *Of course* I loved her. A part of me had loved her since I was fourteen years old. I couldn't tell her, but I'd hold that perfect little ember deep inside my chest, right alongside that dark part of myself that wasted years believing I'd never get the chance to love anyone.

She barely made it an hour before she slipped inside my sleeping bag, and when we made love, it was through hushed groans and giggles. Her body was soft and achingly warm beneath mine. The squeeze in the sleeping bag was so tight, I could only just inch my trousers past my hips, unable to get a hand between us to touch her in all the ways I wanted. We didn't kiss, too busy staring at one another in the hazy twilight. Wind rattled the tent as our cries grew, coming thicker and faster as the minutes ticked on, both of us desperate to drag the connection out as long as possible. It was more intense than anything I'd ever experienced in my life, and when I came, a tear rolled down my cheek and fell to the ground, like a wish to the land that I might somehow get to keep her.

As humans, we demanded a beginning and end to make sense of the world around us. But for *this*, there would be an after, but no end. My love for her was as boundless as the mountain we lay upon. When she left me, my love would remain, burning just as fiercely as it did now.

My final thought before sleep found me—April's hair still tickling my nose—was an old Burns poem we'd recited at school,

Till a' the seas gang dry, my dear,
And the rocks melt wi' the sun;
I will love thee still, my dear,
While the sands o' life shall run.

30

APRIL
Sweet Nothing – Taylor Swift

I woke with the sun.

It rose so early during the long summer months, it must only have been a handful of hours since we'd fallen asleep, happy and sated, whispering secrets back and forth until we could whisper no more. Something had changed during our short stay on Storr; it felt like we'd been marooned on our own little island for weeks.

Mal held me cocooned against his chest, his soft breaths stirring the hairs at my temple, Boy and Dudley snoring at our feet, and I thought: *this is it.* That unattainable feeling I'd been chasing for half of my life. I could have lived in that moment for a thousand years and never tired of it.

I kept my breathing slow and even so as not to disturb him, but all too soon he began to stir, his lips going straight to the crown of my head and kissing reverently. It might have been my imagination, but I thought he held me a little bit tighter too.

After long moments of silence, I tipped my head back for his lips, ready to sink into his kiss, when he pulled back to ask, "Tea?"

"Five more minutes," I whispered.

His lips found my chilled nose, my cheeks, my eyelids. "You can have as many minutes as you want, princess."

"Maybe ten then," I said breezily, but the words I'd been holding inside myself for days threatened to slip free. *I love him.* The feeling was so big, I was scared it would come out carelessly, like spilled milk pooling across a counter. I didn't want to pressure him, especially when I had no answers for what came next. Ultimately, my life was in London—it had to be. Being in love didn't change that.

The entire journey back down the mountain and the car ride home, I was the quiet one. Mal walked steadily at my side, reminiscing on times he'd camped here with his brothers, lifting me over rocks and pointing out plants by name. The new level of ease he felt around me made the words that much harder to hold in.

Did he love me too? It felt like he might.

Was there a way I could stay here permanently?

Did I even *want* to stay here permanently?

The questions spiraled inside me. I hated feeling so uncertain. I *hated* leaving things unsaid. The "I love you" felt like a ticking time bomb in my chest—at any moment, I would just explode and shout the words in his face.

As though the universe itself had grown tired of my shit and decided to speed along my decision-making, we found the postman waiting outside the manor, waving to us as Mal's Land Rover made easy work of the dirt lane. Clyde, the stout but cheery forty-something man, flashed me his usual flirtatious grin, stating he had a letter that required my signature. Mal practically ripped the heavy envelope from the poor man's hands.

A script. I recognized its weight the moment Mal placed it in my palms. The single one I'd physically received since being here. That alone had to mean something. Angela had sent a handful over by email, but nothing caught my interest.

Heart in my throat, I raced into the kitchen, tearing open the envelope. Pausing to read the handwritten message on a pink Post-it. *Time to get back in the game?* Then I saw the name of the director and I almost blacked out. *Ainsley Clarke.*

A three-time Oscar winning director. *She only made a movie every five or six years.*

I flipped the pages with numb fingers, finding another note on the first page. *They want you for the lead. It's not a done deal, you'd still need to screen test. But you're their first choice.* First choice was underlined three times.

"What is it?" Mal asked, unlacing his boots.

I could barely form words. "It's a . . . it's a script. From an agency hoping to sign me."

His expression shuttered in a way I couldn't understand, but he stalked closer, reading over my shoulder, attention falling straight to the note. "That's blackmail," he said. "How do you know once you've signed the contract they'll even get you a screen test?"

That old fear, the worry I could trust no one in the industry but myself, rose and came crashing like a tidal wave. "My friend Sydney is signed with them, she rates them highly."

"The friend who barely ever calls?" His words weren't cruel but still, I flinched. He was right; my and Sydney's friendship was a little shallow and she could be selfish at times. That didn't make her a bad person, it was just the way things were.

"You don't think I should do it?" My gut twisted as I waited for him to answer, not knowing what I even wanted that answer to be.

He blew out a shaky breath, and right as I thought he was about to say, *No, don't do it princess, stay here with me*, he said, "I'm not saying that. I only want you to be careful, cover all your bases, put a clause in your contract that says you can leave at any time you want."

I froze, staring at him. It was like he knew. Like somehow he understood every foolish mistake that had led me to this moment. I waited for him to say more but he only stared at me steadily.

I crossed the space to him, letting the script thud to the ground between us, wrapping my body around his. "You're right." The words muffled against his soft sweater. "I won't decide anything right away."

I love you.

I love you.

I love you.

The declaration pulsed then sank to the pit of my stomach, still as true as it was an hour ago, only now, I wasn't sure what I wanted.

31

MAL
Roots – Grace Davies

"How are the tasting sessions coming along?" my mum asked, looking between April and me. April glanced at me while loading salad onto her plate, determining whether I wanted her to be the one to answer. I gave her the smallest nod; it was her brain child after all.

Between April and Heather, they launched into a stream of amusing stories about the tastings they'd hosted over the past few weeks. Heather, making the twins giggle with her impression of a group of young guys upon realizing their celebrity crush would be their guide for the afternoon. "Umm . . . I . . . uh"—she rubbed a trembling hand exaggeratedly across her brow—"I used to have a poster of you on my wall . . . the one in the white bikini." I did not enjoy this story.

April blushed crimson while Callum hooted with laughter at my side. "How strange, I have the exact same one at home." I shoved his face into his mashed potato and the girls laughed harder.

It was two weeks since our night at Storr. Two weeks since the

337

best night of my life. Two weeks of bliss laced with worry. In that time, we'd fallen into a routine, breakfast out on the bank (I'd even started feeding the bloody foxes) and dinner split between the manor and my cottage. Days of hard work and play-filled nights, not a single one spent apart. And through it all, I obsessed over the script. I'd read it cover to cover. Twice. It was *good*. So good that if she got the part, I'd put her on the goddamned ferry myself and strap my heart in beside her.

April assured me things moved at a snail's pace in the film industry after she'd phoned the agent who had agreed to her terms with virtually no persuasion. April had even asked me to listen in on the meeting because she valued my opinion, trusted I had her best interests at heart. And I did. If my love for this woman had taught me anything, it was the lengths I'd go to keep her happy. But it didn't stop that gnawing voice that whispered perhaps I could be selfish, just this once.

Following the phone conversation, she'd sent over some self-tapes for an initial screen test and was waiting to hear back about a possible audition. I could think of little else.

"It sounds like it's going well then?" My mother smiled and April returned it somewhat timidly, dragging me out of my musings.

"As well as we could hope at this point, we've yet to make it through a quiet winter."

"Oh?" Mum looked surprised and unwittingly pointed to the elephant in the room. "You plan to stay on the island until then?"

I paused with a fork full of food to my lips. I felt April tense where her elbow brushed mine. She grasped for an answer. "Well—"

"And what about you, Malcolm? What are you doing while the women are hard at work?" My dad's voice cut through the atmosphere like alcohol at a children's birthday party. Cutlery clattered on plates. April's hand found my thigh beneath the table.

The same old tension crept up my neck, a small sting between my shoulder blades, but I didn't look up from my plate. "Same as always, Dad," I answered, loading more salad onto my fork.

My dad tilted his glass to April. "You've turned that place around, Elsie, but then you always did have ambition, Kier admired you for that."

"*April*," I corrected him bitingly. The insinuation that I lacked ambition didn't hurt as much as it once would have. I knew the work was important to me and the community. To April. My dad being unable to see the value in it didn't change that.

I shoveled more food into my mouth, content to ignore him. April had other ideas. "The new forty-seven label—the blend we sold twenty bottles of in one night alone—was Mal's creation." Her voice was cut steel as she stared down the man who I'd loved and loathed for my entire life.

"Princess," I murmured beneath my breath. "You don't need to—"

She looked back at me, eyes bright with hurt. *Hurt for me.* "*Someone* should." She glanced at my dad again, eating his food at the head of the table like nothing happened, and her glass hit the table with a thud. "Who do you think ran the distillery while Kier was sick? Actually . . . who do you think was running that place while Kier was spiraling? Putting his own money in and never taking a real wage? Who do you think carried out repairs and managed the staff and did the bookkeeping? Who do you think kept the manor from falling down around Kier's ears?"

339

I turned to her sharply, heart squeezing exquisitely in my chest. I felt the stare of everyone in the room but I couldn't look away from April. I was about to drag her lips against mine when a loud crash made us all flinch.

"Jim," my mother cried, flying to her feet and rounding to my father at the head of the table. His glass lay shattered at his feet, red wine like spilled blood on the stone tile. He was blinking furiously, hands clenching and unclenching at his sides. "What are they doing here?" he muttered. "It's only Wednesday, you shouldn't be here." His voice sounded so small all of a sudden, nothing like the man who'd raised me.

We all looked at one another, the twins giggling as Ava corrected, "It's Saturday, Grandpa." I only found grim understanding on my siblings' faces.

Dad shook his head furiously while my mother did her best to soothe him. "It's all right, Jim, perhaps you should have a lie down."

He looked at my sister. "What did you do to your hair, Iris?"

She paled. "It's me, Dad . . . Heather."

My dad made an awful retching sound and it took me a moment to realize it was the sound of him crying. We all sat frozen to the spot, stunned. I'd never heard my dad cry before. Callum was the first to react, face completely serious for once as he slung my father's arm over his shoulder and led him down the hall to his bedroom.

"WHY DIDN'T YOU TELL ME?" I SNARLED THE MOMENT CALLUM stepped into sight. I'd retreated almost immediately to my old hiding spot, out of view from the house behind my father's bursting greenhouse. I barely felt the cold sting of the wind as it tore at my clothes and hair. April tried to follow me once the chaos in the kitchen died down but I was fit to explode and I couldn't have her here for that.

My brother froze on the stone path, hands sinking into his pockets. "We planned to, but we didn't know how."

"You come out and say, 'Hey Malcolm, our dad has Alzheimer's.'" I pushed to my feet. "How long have you known?"

"Six months. Heather found out a few weeks ago. Mum kept it to herself for as long as she could, but he's starting to need more and more help."

"Six months!" I thrust an accusing finger at his chest. "Have you told Alastair?"

Callum tensed. "Yes . . . he says he's coming home as soon as he can." He didn't sound like he believed him, but I didn't care about Alastair right now.

"Six months is more than enough time to figure out a way to tell me."

"You're never around, maybe we didn't think you'd care—" He was cringing before the words even fully left his lips. He held up a placating hand. "I didn't mean that, all I meant was . . . you two have a complicated relationship, it isn't always easy to navigate that."

I snorted at the description. "Is that what thirty years of hurt boils down to? *Complicated*? That isn't fair and you know it."

"Do you think you're the only one he was hard on growing up?" He threw his hands out. "Do you think you're the only one that dreads coming to see him every weekend? But I'm the oldest son, so I don't get a free pass."

I didn't know what to think, how to process everything, so I clung to the only thing that felt certain. My blind rage. I stalked closer, snarling down into his face. It was the first time I realized I'd truly outgrown my big brother. "I'm sorry I can't be the perfect son you are, Callum. I'm sorry everything in my life doesn't happen exactly the way I want it to!"

Callum's laugh was so bitter, it took me back. "You think everything comes easily to me? That I get everything I want? You don't know shit about who—" He cut himself off, eyes squeezing shut. "—*what*, I want." I'd never seen my brother this way, I didn't know what to say. He didn't give me the chance to get there. All the fight drained out of him as he came closer and gripped my shoulder. "I'm sorry we didn't tell you sooner. We should have. But don't pretend we're only talking about Dad right now. I don't know what else is going on with you . . . but I can guess the source." He glanced back at the house. I could see April's hair through the window, smiling as she played a board game to keep the twins distracted. "If you want her to stay, you have to tell her. You have to fight for something eventually, Mal."

ALZHEIMER'S. THE WORD HAD LOST ALL MEANING, LOOPING around my mind again and again.

Alzheimer's.

Alzheimer's.

A progressive neurologic disorder that caused the brain to shrink and cells to die. I'd googled the definition on the drive home, already knowing well enough what the diagnosis meant. It wasn't until I felt the tug of April's hands on my coat that I realized we were in my cottage. The space was cold and dark, the air a little stale from disuse. I let her push me to the armchair and watched in a daze as she lit a fire in the grate, hands sure and capable. She returned to me minutes later, climbing into my lap and whispering against my skin, "Is it lame to say how sorry I am?"

I slammed my eyes shut and crushed her to me. "Not when you mean it."

"I'm so sorry if I caused all that back there—"

"You didn't cause it. He's always been an odious bastard, with or without Alzheimer's. You did nothing wrong." She'd defended me is what she'd done. I never realized how much I needed someone to do that before.

We sat a few moments in silence, the crackle of logs a soundtrack to my escalating thoughts. How many weeks had my mother been trying to get us all together? How many times had I avoided all of them? Callum's words kept replaying through my head. *Do you think you're the only one he was hard on growing up?* He was right, I had thought that. Callum was Dad's oldest boy. His pride and joy. The impossible standard for which the rest of us were measured against. But Callum was seven years older than me, there was so much I wouldn't have seen. As hard as it was living in the shadow of Callum, I considered for the first time in my life what it would have been like to set that standard.

Dad had been growing meaner lately—because of his disease, I now realized—and I'd avoided him all the more. No wonder Mum had carried it alone for so long. No wonder Callum and Heather didn't tell me.

"How do you feel?" she asked eventually.

"I don't know . . . confused. Sad. Guilty."

She turned until she could see my face. "Why do you feel guilty?"

343

"Not seeing it sooner." I shrugged. "The wedge I've put between me and my entire family."

Her hands clasped my cheeks, thumbs brushing over bristle. "You know the distance between you doesn't become your fault just because he's sick, right? It doesn't make you the bad guy."

I had to swallow back tears before I said, "I feel like the bad guy."

"No, baby, *never*. And this disease doesn't mean the end of the road. If you decide you want to forgive him, there's still time for that. But you shouldn't carry that burden alone. You need your mum and Heather and Callum. You need your family around you."

I need you, I don't know how I'll do this without you, I wanted to say—I *would* have said, but her phone flashed faceup on the arm of the chair and we both turned on instinct. She flipped the phone over, not before I saw a text flash on the screen. "What is it?"

"Probably nothing. Now isn't the time."

"Now is definitely the time, I could use the distraction."

She lifted her phone, unlocking the screen to read the message. She paused, her eyes lifting to search mine. "I got the part."

"But you—" The words cut short. I felt like I was drowning. "You didn't audition yet."

"According to Angela, Ainsley Clarke was already pretty certain before receiving my tapes."

I couldn't answer, so I held my hand out for the phone instead, needing to see it in black and white. The words blurred on the screen, jargon I couldn't even begin to decipher as the room swayed around me. Only two things stood out. *London. Two days from now.*

"You're going to London." It wasn't a question but she answered anyway.

"Yes."

My breathing became rapid. Hands sweating as they began to tingle. Then a notification containing a single word flashed across the top of the screen, confusing enough to settle me.

Slut.

I clicked it without thinking, a little surprised to see a picture of myself on the screen. I recognized it as the day I walked April to her car a few weeks back. I stood in profile, my features barely visible, my body curled protectively over April's smaller one. We were locked together, my hands pinning her to the car as we kissed wildly. We look good together. *Right.*

Then I noticed the comment again, *slut*, her name tagged beside the word. Before I could stop myself I clicked on the responses and scrolled through comment after comment, insult after insult. Not a single one aimed at me. My body must have revealed my fury because April peered over the top of the screen. "What is it?"

"These comments, who are all these people?" My voice was a white-hot poker.

The change in her was instantaneous. Her shoulders curved in on themselves, the light in her eyes dimming as she tugged the phone back and locked the screen without looking at it. "Ignore them . . . it's just random trolls online."

How could she expect me to ignore that? The things they were saying, what they'd called her. She didn't even look surprised.

"We have to report it."

"Who would I report it to? Social media companies don't care. For every one hundred comments I report, maybe one gets removed, if I'm lucky. It's better not to read them."

This is the reality of her life, I realized. Her sorrow that drunken night on the bank coming back to me, the memory as fresh as she was before me now. "I don't get it." I tried to rein my anger in but the words sounded harsh even to my own ears. "Why would you want this? Why keep putting yourself out there for these bastards to hurt you?"

She looked indignant. Seconds ago we'd been closer than two people could ever be and now, while she might physically still be *here*, I could feel her slipping away. "Because it's my job."

"Just weeks ago I held you while you wept because of the shit this industry put you through, princess. I don't—"

"What?" She drew back. Her freckles stood out against her pale skin. "What are you talking about? When did I cry?"

"The night . . . the night I brought you home from the pub." Her mouth set, eyes flicking as she tried to recall those missing moments. "I didn't bring it up before because I couldn't be sure it was information you meant to share with me. I wanted you to trust me enough to talk to me yourself, not whisper confessions when you were drunk and sad."

"I told you . . . about Aaron?"

Aaron. His name slotted into place, hitting number one on my shit-list.

"You didn't tell me his name, only that you signed a contract you shouldn't have."

She must have sensed my despondence, because she said quickly, "The reason I didn't tell you isn't because I don't trust you, it's because I'm angry at myself as well as him. I want to forget it ever happened."

My hands curled over hers. "I would never judge you."

She pulled her lower lip between her teeth, biting down as it began to tremble. "You might once you know."

"*Never.*"

I waited as her fingers burrowed into my shirt and her chin dipped. "I first signed with Aaron when I was nineteen years old, he was my manager and a good one, for the most part. He got me auditions with directors I'd dreamed of working with and in exchange, when he told me to change my physical appearance, I agreed. When he suggested a rigorous diet, I did it without question. I told myself he knew what he was doing. People called him a bastard and I ignored them. He could be a hard-arse, but one you wanted in your corner." It took all my effort to keep the slow rhythm of my hands on her bare arms and not imagine them wrapped around the slick bastard's neck. "Then, a few years ago, I ended a relationship with a long-term boyfriend. Aaron offered to take me out to dinner to cheer me up, and I didn't realize until midway through the main course it was a date. I felt uncomfortable but I . . . I didn't know how to tell him, I didn't want to hurt his feelings. So when he kissed me at the end of the night . . . I let him." My hands paused on her shoulders. "I convinced myself that maybe it was a good idea to date him, we had a great working relationship and he was attractive enough." She blew out a shaky breath. "I bet you think I'm really stupid, don't you?"

"No, princess, I don't think you're stupid." Him . . . ? Yeah, I had a lot to say about him.

"Things were fine for a few weeks, he was attentive and kind, always buying me gifts. And then it all became way too much, he grew really insecure and wanted to spend every moment together. He asked me to move in with him after a month of dating and started pressuring me into having sex with him." She seemed to grow smaller as she spoke. Her voice shrinking to a whisper. "It's called 'love bombing,' a term I wasn't aware of at the time. It wasn't until I finally told him I couldn't do it anymore that I realized what an idiot I'd been, because he held my entire career in his hands. Every job that came through from my agent he blocked, every interview, every audition."

I could kill him.

"You couldn't go to your agency?" I grit out.

"He had . . . he had access to all my social media, he said he would log in and write things I would never, ever say. He told me he had . . . photos . . . of me on his phone. Though, that turned out to be a lie. He threatened to ruin me and I believed him."

I watched tears drip from her chin and fury like I'd never felt rocketed through me. I wanted to tear the world apart until I held that spineless man in my grip. Punish him for every ounce of pain he'd ever caused my woman—*any* woman, because predators never acted singularly. "I took whatever job he would allow, the stupid reality shows, the dancing and the social media, anything I could do to get by."

"And now?"

"A few of his other clients came forward with complaints and I felt safe enough to voice my own." Her lower lip trembled some more. "I was a coward not to do it straight away."

I shook my head sharply. "That's not true, you had no way of knowing he wouldn't follow through with his threats."

She wiped at her cheeks. "He didn't face any criminal charges, but he was fired and blacklisted, so I suppose that's some kind of justice."

"I wish there was a way I could change it all, to stop you from experiencing a single moment of that." Brushing her hair back, I gazed into the face that had become more vital to me than the air in my lungs. "I still don't understand why you would willingly go back to that life? Is it the paycheck? Because the distillery is making money now, you don't need it. You can just be . . . happy." *With me.*

She swiped another tear from her eye. "The distillery isn't making money."

"What?"

"It's making money, but it isn't enough."

32

APRIL

Something in the Orange – Zach Bryan

I t's making money, but it isn't enough." The words expelled from me like a great weight lifting from my shoulders. I watched his face change from pleading to confused, heavy lines creasing his usually smooth brow.

"I'm not following, princess."

The truth will set you free. In this instance, the truth felt more like a hidden blade. "The distillery and the manor . . . they were never willed to me, Mal. I already owned them."

I watched him process the information, like watching a grand clock tick away the time. "You mentioned Kier spiraling at my parents' house. What did you mean by that?"

"Kier was in debt, *a lot* of debt. When things started going well for me, I would send him money here and there. The distillery wasn't as busy as it used to be and he didn't want to lay off staff. Then one day he phoned out of the blue, a complete mess as he confessed to a gambling problem. I had my then-accountant look over the finances. He owed so much the bank was on the verge of taking everything."

"You bailed him out," he guessed.

I nodded. "I paid off most of his debt and purchased the properties, but the distillery still needed a lot of investment just to keep it running, then Aaron happened . . . and I took every job I could get to keep our heads above water."

"Why didn't you tell me?" he demanded. "I could have helped."

"I was going to that very first day, but then you told me you'd been purchasing the distillery in installments. Kier was taking money from your paycheck with no intention of ever selling, because he couldn't. He was manipulating you, Mal, how could I forever change the man he was in your eyes? I thought if we could make a steady flow of income, it would all be okay and it could be yours someday without ever having to know the truth. This movie is the only way I can assure that." That fierce look in his eyes transformed to pain and I saw the exact moment something inside him crumpled. I clutched him to me. "I'm sorry . . . I'm so so sorry." He held me back and I felt him shaking, but it turned out to be me.

"Kier had flaws, like anyone else," he eventually said against my cheek. "I always knew who he was. I felt his love for me, just as I felt his love for you. This doesn't change that."

"How can you forgive him so easily?" How, when I feared a part of me never would?

"Because I'm doing it for me. I refuse to let every moment with him become a lie. Too many people in our lives have let us down, don't let him become another one, April." He was right. I'd made my peace with my mother because I'd stopped expecting things from her. I couldn't do the same with Kier because he had always, always been there for me.

I leant back in his lap, letting his thick hair slide through my fingers. He bustled into my touch. "Are you going to apply this logic to your dad?"

"I'm going to try." We held each other in silence for a moment until he finally said, "You need to do this movie." He sounded weary. Defeated.

"I need to do this movie," I agreed.

I expected him to say more, but he only swept an arm beneath my knees, pulling me into his chest. "Let's go to bed." He stood and crossed the room, laying me atop his mattress. He undressed me slowly, eyes holding mine as he slipped my sandals from my feet, then unzipped my dress, folding it neatly away in his drawer. My underwear followed and only when he had me fully naked did he scoop my hair into fists and kiss me, worshipping my mouth. It was a kiss that said what our words couldn't. *He loves me.* He kissed the declaration on my lips, my eyelids, the skin over my heart. My lips on him said the same. On my knees, I watched him tumble into ecstasy, humming the words around his hot flesh as he cried out.

When he pushed inside me, I whimpered softly and he stilled. "What's wrong?"

"I'm sore . . . so much sex."

He started to pull out but I held him tight with my thighs, sweeping away the hair that had fallen into his eyes. "Don't stop, I need you too badly, Mal. *My Mal.*"

"Yes, yours, princess. *Always.*" He switched our positions, making love to me slowly from behind, one hand petting me softly between my legs, the other clutching my breast, right where my heart raced. "Only ever yours."

We never said the words aloud, and for the remainder of the night not a single word was spoken. Because we both knew; I needed to do this movie and I couldn't leave him.

33

MAL
Feels Like – Gracie Abrams

Her hair was a blaze of fire across the pillow, breathing steady and even, though her sleep had been anything but. She'd tossed and turned for hours, burrowing closer in the circle of my arms only to draw away again. And with every shift, I resisted the urge to trap her to me, to hold her as tightly as I could, while I still could. Every soft exhale was like sand slipping through an hourglass. Every twitch of her eyelids a knife in my gut.

I was a riot of anxiety, my brain riddled with intrusive thoughts that had become impossible to slow as the hours ticked away. My father. Callum. Kier. April. It was all too much. I tried to even my breathing, isolate every emotion and trace it back to the source. What stood out the most was the guilt. My chest burned with it. I'd failed everyone who'd ever needed me. April most of all.

All this time, she hadn't only been carrying the weight of her own worries on her shoulders, but the weight of Kier's, and inadvertently mine. All night, our early interactions had projected through my mind like a movie on repeat. Every moment of cruelty and accusation. I'd basically called her a gold digger, and she'd absorbed every blow, carrying the burden so I didn't have to.

She shifted again, sheet slipping enticingly over the curve of her shoulder as she reached for me, a silky leg sliding between my bigger ones. How had there ever been a time I didn't love this woman? That man felt so far away from me now, I knew I would never be him again. *Good.* The only thing that mattered now was making her happy.

I wanted to beg her on my knees to stay. But what she'd revealed about Kier and his debt, it felt too big. I didn't know how to begin to solve it. I wished for an evil to vanquish. A dragon to slay. A physical challenge I needed to overcome to save the day like a hero in a movie. All I had was *me.*

I couldn't stand to gaze at a future I couldn't have for a minute longer, so I kissed her temple, traced the silky spiral of a single curl, and slipped from the bed. Dudley remained tucked into the crook of April's lap, but Boy lifted his head as soon as I shoved my feet into my boots, faithfully following me into the morning sun.

We walked up the bank, sea and salt and heather and that indescribable feeling of home drifting over me. *Would it ever feel this way again once she left?* I knew it wouldn't. I was like one of my bloody puzzles. April had disassembled my entire life in a matter of weeks and pieced me back together in a way that the old me no longer fit. I'd been irrevocably changed, but maybe, just maybe, a part of her had changed along the way too. "You have to fight for something eventually, Mal," I whispered, rocking back onto my heels. Boy gave a solid bark of agreement.

And it was there, staring out at the sunrise that reminded me of that god-awful dressing gown she loved so much, I made the decision. Perhaps I couldn't give her a reason to stay, but you could be damn sure I'd offer her a home to come back to.

34

APRIL

I GUESS I'M IN LOVE – Clinton Kane

Where have they disappeared to?" I asked Dudley, who at some point had wormed his way beneath the bed sheets and stolen Mal's pillow. My dog yawned, his entire body trembling as he stretched all three paws, performing a deep backbend that would make even the most talented of yogis weep with envy. Then he looked at me as if to say, *I don't know, woman, I was sleeping, same as you.*

"Luckily I didn't adopt you for protection," I muttered, lifting him down from the bed because his paws weren't yet steady on the cottage's hardwood flooring. I pulled on one of Mal's shirts and a pair of his thick socks I'd essentially adopted as my own and slipped out the front door to find them.

I heard Mal before I saw him.

"*Motherfucking useless arsehole!*" he roared. "Why won't you bloody work?" I spied him bent over something on the bank, about a foot back from the cliff edge. Boy hopped about at his side, his every bark magnified by the whipping wind.

"Mal?" I said, drawing nearer. The grass was damp, soaking

through my socks and turning my feet numb. "What are you doing?" He still wore his navy pajama bottoms, the hems stuffed into black boots. I could tell by the brutal red of his hands and cheeks he'd been out here a while.

He leapt to his feet, whirling and throwing his hands out wide as if to block the semi-constructed wood form behind him. "You weren't supposed to see this yet," he said, but I was too busy staring at the trail of blood trickling down his wrist.

"You've hurt yourself."

He swallowed, tucking his hand behind him. "I was trying to do something for you, but apparently I'm not even capable of basic woodwork."

"I don't care about that. Let me clean your hand." I reached for him and he backed up a step; holding me off. His entire body shook.

"Wait . . . just, let me say what I need to say."

The wind was cold, molding his shirt to my body, drawing goose bumps all along my skin. But it was fear, not the cold, that had me shivering.

"Okay." I nodded, arms tightening around myself. He was so agitated I wanted to run to him. I forced myself to do as he asked and held myself still.

A trembling hand passed over his face. "I've been awake all night trying to figure this out and . . . I have nothing, princess, absolutely nothing to offer you, except this—" He stepped aside, revealing what I assumed was supposed to be a bench. One leg was shorter than the other three and it looked like one stiff breeze might tear it apart. Tears gathered in my eyes. "It's terrible. A monstrosity! It turns out I can't make a bench to save my bloody life and I love you!" He practically shouted it at me.

I held myself tighter. I could tell his jaw was tight beneath the scruff of hair, like the words had slipped free before he could stop them. "You love me, or you're in love with me?"

"The bench—"

I shook my head. "Mal, I don't care about the bench. Are you in love with me?"

All his breath exhaled in a single puff and he drew closer until all I could see was him. "Desperately." He looked defeated. "I'm not Tom Hanks, I don't have the words you deserve. I can't meet you at the top of the Empire State Building." He started to run his hand through his hair, realized it still bled, and dropped it to his side. "You *need* to leave and I won't ever try to hold you back. But how about this . . . when you go, what if I just keep on loving you. For the rest of my life. Would that be okay?" I had no words. His declaration had carved its way inside my chest and stolen everything I'd been dying to tell him all these weeks. "I get that this isn't the most healthy declaration of love," he continued, "but you literally brought me back to life and made me believe in myself like no one else ever has. I wanted to give you something in return. I wanted you to know you'll always have a place in the world where someone adores you, a place where someone is wondering where you are and if you're okay. A place where you'll be safe if you ever feel like coming back. A *home*."

"Mal—" His name came out as dry as desert sand. "I don't just need to do this movie, I want to do it."

"I know." He gave me one sharp nod and I watched him try to

force the pieces of himself back together. "I shouldn't have put all that on you . . . I'm sorry."

"But how about this," I repeated his words back to him, letting all the warmth inside my chest leak into my voice. "I leave sometimes . . . only when I have to. But I always, *always* come back to you."

His dull eyes sparked. Wariness and uncontrolled hope collided until they rolled as thunderously as the waves below him. "You were leaving," he said finally, not accusingly.

"Yes . . . you read the email. I'm needed in London for three days, just enough time to do some chemistry reads. Then I'm coming straight back to you. Acting is my job, but this is my home, Mal, like you said. This place, but more importantly you. I've never felt so at peace, so *myself*, as I do here with you. I love my job, but I'm never going to let it consume my entire life again."

He looked stunned, his fingers flexing by his sides. "You were always coming back?"

"Of course. I love you too," I cried. "We lost so much time, Mal, I never want to be apart again."

Within a heartbeat I was in his arms, my feet leaving the ground and curling around his waist. He held me to him, both of us crying unabashedly as he looked at me with a tenderness I never would have imagined him capable of weeks before. "Everything is going to be all right, princess. We can sell the distillery, I'll get two jobs, I'll do whatever it takes."

I pressed my forehead to his, letting the blue-gray of his eyes eclipse everything else. "You might not need to. If this movie goes as planned, it will be enough to clear the rest of the debt and more." As I spoke the words, he was already moving, maneuvering us into his cottage with muscle memory alone and heading straight for the bathroom. We shed our clothes in record time, not even waiting for the water to heat before stepping into the shower. But when we joined together, it was with one lingering taste at a time, because we had all the time in the world.

And just as he pushed me against the fogged glass, trailing those calloused fingers around my thighs to spread me wider, I whispered, "Mal, does this mean I can have my underwear back?"

His laugh was soft. Husky. *Happy.* "Oh, princess, that's never going to happen."

EPILOGUE

APRIL

Calm – Vistas

I stomped my feet on the porch step of the cottage, shaking snow from my boots while my key twisted silently in the lock. The warm blast of air inside was like a pair of welcoming hands. Soft light soaked around me from the small but heavily decorated Christmas tree tucked into the corner between the armchair and fireplace.

Unsurprisingly, Mal turned out to be a Grinch that refused to decorate for Christmas and I was determined to wear him down over multiple video calls from my too-hot film set in Algarve. I'd put up a portable little tree along with some inexpensive decoration in my trailer late-November, but it didn't quite have the desired effect.

In the end, I didn't even have to ask. Mal had video-called on what he knew had been a very grueling day of filming, his brand-new iPhone propped up on a stack of my romance novels he'd cleared space for on his already overflowing shelves. He told me to watch as he packed a rather sad little tree full of multicolored lights and hideously ugly baubles until the branches began to buckle under the weight. He'd even played a Christmas playlist. I'd wept, of course. I'd been gone five weeks by then and missed all three of my boys terribly.

Setting my bag down by the door, I unwound my scarf and slipped off my boots with hushed movements, desperate not to wake him as I slunk closer to the bed. Mal lay fast asleep in the tangle of navy sheets, his soft breaths mixing with the heavier snores of the dogs. Even in sleep he looked exhausted. Once it had become widely known I was the owner, or part-owner as was now the case, the distillery had started to grow steadily in business. We'd even signed a few wholesale contracts. By the summer, Kinleith Whisky would be in supermarkets around the country.

It felt a little wrong at first, using my celebrity status to gain free publicity. But as our new manager, Heather, very wisely pointed out, as long as I lived in the public eye, my life would be up for discussion, so we might as well get something good out of it.

Boy was the first to spot me, head jolting from the foot of the bed, tail beating furiously. I moved quickly, sinking my fingers into the mound of golden fur at the base of his neck before he could bark. "Hey, handsome. Have you been taking good care of our boys?" He licked my wrist in confirmation and I ruffled his ears, already beginning to sniffle when I spotted Dudley's tiny body tucked beneath Malcolm's chin.

I stood arrested, taking in the sight, my heart thundering *home, home, home* inside my chest until I couldn't hold back any longer. I climbed onto the bed, giving Dudley a soft stroke while my lips trailed across Mal's forehead. He stirred sleepily, a hand curling around my waist and up my spine like it was second nature.

His hand made it all the way to my shoulder before it paused, stunned. "Princess?"

"Merry Christmas," I whispered. Christmas was technically still three days away, but it hardly mattered.

In the shadow, I could make out his furious blinking, as though trying to be certain he wasn't dreaming. Then he shot to sitting and yanked me into his lap. Dudley gave an undignified yowl and slunk to the foot of the bed. "What are you doing here? I'm supposed to pick you up from Glasgow Airport tomorrow." Calloused hands clasped my cheeks, my shoulders, the ends of my curls.

"We wrapped early for the holiday. I couldn't wait another day." I wrapped my legs around his waist.

"You should have told me, I would have met you."

"That would have ruined the surprise," I said, and just like that, all the fight fled him and he dragged my lips to his. Kissing me urgently but softly. Full of love and longing.

"I missed you, princess," he husked against my lips. "I missed you so fucking much."

"I missed you too." I tore at his long thermal top while he tugged down the band of my leggings, already positioning me over him.

"Need you on top," he was saying, lifting his hips to drag his own bottoms down. "Always on top, baby." He was in me in a heartbeat. Holding my hips, he sank back against the pillows, watching through low-lidded eyes as I rode him hard and fast, moaning his name over and over until it became intangible to my ears. "Just look at you . . . I can't believe I get to see you this way.

You look like a goddess." When I came and he cried out along with me, every muscle in his beautiful body trembling from the sheer force of it, I *felt* like a goddess.

I collapsed over his chest, smattering kisses on every patch of skin I could reach as we fought to catch our breath. "How are the foxes?"

He shifted to look at me. "That's really your first question?"

"They're an important part of this family."

He grunted my favorite of all of his grunts. It was his trying-to-act-annoyed-and-failing-miserably grunt. "A pain in my arse."

"Liar, you love them."

"I love them," he agreed, eyes shining, and the words just burst out of me.

"Marry me." I'd planned to ask a little more romantically, out beside our bench on Christmas morning, but there was no taking it back now.

"What?" His hands tightened on me, as though I might fly away.

I pushed up, staring into his eyes that held mine just as steadily. "Marry me."

"Did you look in my sock drawer?"

I bit my lip. "Yes. I'm sorry, it was an accident, and I got sick of waiting." I'd seen the ring months ago.

Mal groaned, squeezing his eyes shut. "I didn't want to rush you."

"It's a good thing I'm happy to rush you, then. I think we should get married tomorrow."

His eyes flew back open. Full of wonder and disbelief. "To-morrow?"

"I want to get married before I leave again." I had three weeks off over Christmas and then a final eight weeks of filming in Portugal, though Mal was coming to stay with me for two of them. He'd been attending therapy twice a week since the summer and felt certain he was ready for his first plane ride. "Plus, Alastair can be there and your dad is still well enough to attend. We don't know if that will be the case in a few months." It was a hard transition for Mal and Jim over the last six months. Mal was trying to be there for his family and Jim, aware of his condition, wanted his son around. That was easier said than done when Jim wasn't entirely capable of making up for the sins of the past. I doubted he would ever truly know the lasting effect his outdated views on mental health had had on his youngest son. And in order to make peace with his father, Mal felt he had little choice but to let it go. Again, easier said than done. He didn't always tell me what was discussed in his therapy sessions; sometimes he returned home weary with purple shadows beneath his eyes and I would hold him or talk to him on video-call until that spark reignited. Other times, he would appear a million times lighter than when he left. He said they were helping, and in the long run, that was all that mattered.

"I don't care about Alastair and my dad. I care about you, the wedding you want. We don't need to rush it."

"I want to marry you out on the bank beside that hideous bench you built for me. Tomorrow or in a week or two years from now." I leant down to kiss him, licking softly at his lower lip. "But I'd prefer tomorrow."

Mal swore, flipping our positions until I was beneath him. "You drive a hard bargain, April Sinclair."

I giggled. "What can I say? *Us actors* are used to getting what we want."

Just as I expected, his cheeks reddened as he smiled. "And did you? Get what you want?"

Outside, snow began to fall again, a frosty blanket of white. Tucked cosily in our warm bed where it couldn't touch us, I smiled. "Don't ask stupid questions, Macabe."

Acknowledgments

Writing might feel like a solitary affair, but to get a book published, it truly takes an army.

Firstly, my incredible husband. If I don't say it enough every day, thank you! Thank you for your endless support. Thank you for believing in me on the days I didn't. Thank you showing this romance author that true love does exist.

My family, for their unending support and agreeing not to discuss the spicier scenes. I think my mum has sold more copies of my book than I have.

My incredible agent, Katie, for seeing the potential in the book and giving it wings. Without her hard work and support, this book would not be in your hands.

The entire team at HarperCollins and Avon for taking a chance on my story: Lynne, Tessa, Lucy, Morgan, Madelyn. (Sorry if I'm forgetting anyone!)

Britt. Thank you for your knowledge and kindness. Thank you for loving and believing in this book and these characters.

Sam (Inkandlaurel), queen of book covers. Thank you for bringing April and Mal to life with this dreamy cover.

My incredible beta readers. Thank you for taking the time to make this book better and thank you for shouting in my DMs about these characters.

I adore you all.

The bookstagram community. Thank you for being as obsessed with tropes and impossibly perfect book boyfriends. Thank you for taking a chance on unknown authors and for making it possible for indie authors to achieve their dreams.

Lastly, thank you to every person who picked this book up and spent a little of their time in Kinleith. Mal is my soul character, my worries and my fears. His anxiety an extension of my own. Every time I see someone take him into their heart, it heals a little part of mine.

About the Author

Elliot Fletcher is a British romance writer who's currently residing in Edinburgh, Scotland. She lives near the beach with her husband, cat, and dog (the animals get along most of the time).

When she's not writing, she's reading any genre so long as there's a romantic subplot. Finding parts of Edinburgh she's never visited before or dreaming of a life in the Highlands.

She loves creating emotional connections between messy characters, backdropped by some of the most beautiful places in the world. Maybe one day she'll be brave enough to try her hand at a fantasy novel.